THE COWBOY AND THE DEALER

ALSO BY JACKIE NORTH

The Farthingdale Ranch Series

The Foreman and the Drifter

The Blacksmith and the Ex-Con

The Ranch Hand and the Single Dad

The Wrangler and the Orphan

The Cook and the Gangster

The Trail Boss and the Brat

The Farthingdale Valley Series

The Cowboy and the Rascal

The Cowboy and the Hoodlum

The Cowboy and the Outcast

The Cowboy and the Dealer

The Cowboy and the Hacker

The Cowboy and the Wheelman

The Love Across Time Series

Heroes for Ghosts

Honey From the Lion

Wild as the West Texas Wind

Ride the Whirlwind

Hemingway's Notebook

For the Love of a Ghost

Love Across Time Sequels

Heroes Across Time - Sequel to Heroes for Ghosts

THE COWBOY AND THE DEALER

JACKIE NORTH

To Jess, All the best & happy reading! Love Jackie North xo

Jackie North

MM Romance Author

The Cowboy and the Dealer
Copyright ©2024 Jackie North
Published July 31, 2024

This is a work of fiction. Names, characters, places, and incidents are a product of the author's imagination or are used fictitiously. Any resemblance to people, places, or things is completely coincidental.

Cover Design by Cate Ashwood

The Cowboy and the Dealer/Jackie North

ISBN Number:

Print - 978-1-942809-82-1

Library of Congress Control Number: 2024912216

This book is dedicated to...

Those who know that there are all kinds of love in the world, and that there is nothing more beautiful than the giving and receiving of it...

...and to those who look to the stars.

"O, thou art fairer than the evening air clad in the beauty of a thousand stars."
— Christopher Marlowe
The Tragical History of Doctor Faustus

CONTENTS

CHAPTER 1
BEDE

As the white prison van trundled along the dirt road that rolled itself out like a ribbon of dust, Bede thought, not for the first time, that the driver had taken a wrong turn. But he didn't say anything, because in his line of work, the one he'd been arrested for, the less you said, the better.

Besides, saying something to irritate the driver, who was already tight around the neck, a vein jumping in his temple, was a guarantee that you'd get hauled up and smacked back down.

Bede could withstand the blow, sure. What would make his heart race would be the uncertainty of what might follow. That the driver would turn around and take them all back to Wyoming Correctional in Torrington. That he would be thrown back in the slammer.

Bede put his concern down to the fact that five years before, when he'd been a very cocky young man of twenty-eight years, he was his own driver, with his hands on the wheel of a very nice, spicy fast, two-seater BMW convertible. Blue with sparkles in the paint job.

He'd been his own man then, only now his life was at risk because of the driver who, barreling through the countryside, barren, blue-skied, dusty and windy, didn't appear to be taking safety into consideration.

Bede was on the verge of having a headache. And he never got headaches.

As for his van-mates, Toby and Owen, they were wide eyed and looking to him for direction.

Toby, with dirty dishwater hair and skinny shoulders, was the younger, the low man in a two-man pair.

In contrast, Owen, dark-haired and flash-eyed, seemed to have more swagger. Maybe he was older than Bede's thirty-two years, or maybe it was prison or a decades-long smoking habit that had scored lines into his forehead, deep curves on either side of his mouth.

Bede didn't want to be responsible for the two low-life, dumb-as-rocks housebreakers, but yet he was, because who knew what would happen to them if the driver turned around.

"I think this road curves south and turns into pavement," Bede said, keeping his voice low and slow.

"What?" asked the driver with a snap, his eyes seeking Bede's in the rearview mirror. "What'd you say?"

In the back of Bede's mind, he knew he did not control the universe, barely had control of his little corner of it. But it was a mild conceit that he could manage the outcome of this little drive that he'd never wanted to be on in the first place.

Bede stood on top of a cliff, about to dive into freefall. It could go either way. The driver either would turn the van around or keep going, depending on Bede's answer.

"Ah," Bede said, again low and slow. "Got curious. Looked at a map. I'm pretty sure you're going in exactly the right direction."

Whether or not the driver—Lenny? Bernard?—believed him, Bede felt the tension in the van go down a notch. And he wasn't lying. Curious as to his final destination, he'd checked out twenty minutes on the slow-cranking computer in the prison library and pulled up Google maps.

Highway 211 was the only way to get to Farthing and, from there, to Farthingdale Valley. But rather than go all the way down I-25 to Cheyenne, the driver had gone over to Chugwater and taken the back-road from there. Maybe to make up for lost time, since they had been an hour behind schedule when the drive began. Maybe to get the drive over with and go back to the break room and his pals at the prison.

Bede had no idea what was going on in the driver's head. All he knew was that the driver was going too fast around corners, barreling down the corduroy road with enough force to raise tornados of dust in the van's wake.

Yet, Bede's attempt to calm him, the driver—Lenny!—seemed to make Lenny slow down, and he appeared to start taking in the conditions of the road, and the fact that he had three ex-cons buckled into the bench seat behind him. That if he got into an accident and killed everyone in the van, including himself, it would be his own damn fault.

Then, lo and behold, around a sharp corner, a red-roofed farmhouse hove into view, and the dirt road turned into blacktop.

Letting out a slow breath, Bede settled back into the seat, his hand gripped the buckle of the seatbelt. Beside him, Toby and Owen did the same, looking at each other like they had found the only bulwark in a storm.

Bede knew full and well what it was like to have a bulwark. He could remember that feeling of solidness around him, though Winston was long gone from his life.

In Winston's place had come various cellmates—cellies, they were called inside of Wyoming Correctional, including Ellis, who was now with his forever partner somewhere in the Farthing area, and Kell.

It was Kell who, through charm and pure love, had talked Bede into applying for the Farthingdale Valley Fresh Start Program.

He still wasn't sure why he'd been accepted into the program.

Of the parole board, only Mr. Webber had been supportive of the idea. The other two board members had judged Bede as soon as they'd looked at him, and expressed their concerns over his exodus from prison. *You're not suitable for the environment,* they had said, almost together, heads nodding.

Bede might have agreed with them. The wilds of Wyoming were most certainly *not* the environment he was suited for.

He was a city boy since birth, having grown up with paved streets and scraggly city trees and the constant grind and hum of cars and trucks. The smell of exhaust, and odors from the dog food plant when the wind came from the east, that had been his world.

He couldn't imagine staying in a windy, rugged place where the sun glared down and wild animals roamed. Where the air smelled of things he could not identify.

Sure, he'd spent five years in Wyoming, but that had been behind bars, in a controlled environment. Now he was being driven into the wilds of nowheresville.

He wasn't sure whether it would end up being a dream or a nightmare, but his alternative would be to head back to Denver. There, he could pick up the threads of his old life, which were selling and buying and dealing cocaine.

He could also go back to the tattoo parlor on the east end of Colfax and have his Maori-styled tattoos of circles and half-triangles freshened. Maybe get a new one, a band of barbed wire on his upper left arm to mark the memory of his time in Wyoming Correctional.

He should have done his nickel stint in Denver County Jail, but the overcrowding, and the fact that the other gang in the disastrous drug deal gone wrong were also incarcerated in the Denver County Jail and had already squeezed out the message that Bede was a dead man at their very first opportunity—all of this meant he'd been outsourced to Wyoming Correctional almost as soon as he'd been judged guilty.

He could barely remember the bus ride from Denver County Jail to Wyoming Correctional, still bleeding on the inside from the shock of the shootout that not only had cut short his amazing criminal career, but had taken his beloved Winston from him.

Winston had been more than the love of his life. Winston had been the core of him. He'd burrowed his way into Bede's heart and stayed there, loving Bede, making him feel strong. Ten feet tall. Powerful as a king.

There was no getting over something like his relationship with Winston. He might never get over it, and during his time in prison, the clawing feeling snuck up on him often, dragging him into the undertow.

Bede mentally shook his head. There was no time for that now. He needed to pay attention to his surroundings, the blindingly bright midsummer day, the spill of mountains to the west, tumbling laths of granite rock and dark green evergreens. The shimmer of river among flat panels of grasses waving in the warm breeze.

"Fuck, there's nothing out here," muttered Toby as he glared out the windows.

One of Bede's mad skills was the ability to quickly get a read on people, even those he'd only just met, which had come in handy when making drug deals.

He had met Toby a few times at Wyoming correction, both in the dining hall and in the yard. However, he'd never seen Toby in the library or computer room, because Toby was one of those guys who sneered at books and walked around with his fists clenched, ready for a fight.

Owen, the smarter of the two men, had been the guy keeping Toby out of unnecessary fights.

At any rate, what Toby seemed to want was someone to look out those windows with him and agree that there was nothing to see there.

Bede looked where Toby was looking, just to be a go-along-to-get-along kind of guy, at least for a minute or two.

Behind bars, he'd been unable to imagine staying in Wyoming a second longer than he had to. But now, in a sudden dash of reality right in his face, he could not disagree with Toby more.

There was a *ton* to look at. Miles of blue sky with small puffy clouds, their tails wisping in the breeze. Rolls of brown and green hills, stark outjuts of granite rock and, from time to time, a long dirt driveway leading to some unseen farmstead or ranch house. A small herd of what might be deer or antelope.

Two broad-winged birds circled in the warm air overhead. Might be falcons. Could be eagles. The idea of being able to find out—to know—what kind of birds those were, stirred something inside of him.

None of this mattered to Toby. Toby just wanted to be pissed about something.

For the sake of keeping things quiet, Bede frowned and looked out the windows and shook his head.

"A whole lot of nothin'," he said, because he could say it even if he couldn't believe that any longer.

"We can always leave, kid," said Owen. "Just light out and do our parole elsewhere."

From the way he said it, Bede imagined that Owen already had a plan in mind.

Toby grunted like he didn't care. He probably didn't. Didn't care about anything, even about the consequences of being one half of a housebreaking duo with Owen.

Bede back settled in his seat, looked at the passing landscape, and contemplated the consequences of his choices. That of filling out the paperwork for the Farthingdale Valley Fresh Start Program, and of being on a Zoom call with a guy called Leland Tate, who ran the program and, according to the prison grapevine, a whole lot else besides.

All three members of the parole board spoke in glowing terms about Tate, how much good he'd done in the area. Underneath that it was easy to see that Tate was a man of power. Nobody you'd want to fuck with.

Bede didn't plan to. Though how he was going to manage in Farthingale Valley was beyond him.

The reason he'd applied for the valley program, the *only* reason, was Kell, his ex-cellie.

Kell Dodson was a slip of a kid who'd been thrown into the slammer for ninety days on account of he'd dared to trespass across land owned by the BNSF rail company. With a bundle of stolen food, no less.

That Kell had good reason to be hopping trains, being on the run, stealing food from garbage bins and, when he could or had to, from convenience store shelves, hadn't mattered at all to the cops. They could have let him go with a warning, but instead had cuffed him, fingerprinted him, and thrown him in jail.

Bede had seen Kell in the prison yard, the first day he'd been let out from mandatory three-day solitary. And then looked away.

It wasn't his business to interfere with other people's lives. It wasn't his business that Kell was chatting with Ryan like they were old friends, as if Kell was unaware that Ryan was a full-on, foam-mouthed skinhead. Trouble. Something to stay away from, like a rattlesnake in the grass.

Except the next second, Bede had seen Kell walk away, which meant that he was smart, for all he was so young.

That hadn't kept Kell out of the stench of trouble that Ryan dragged around with him everywhere he went.

Quite soon, in the yard once more, Ryan and his buddies were all over Kell. Ryan had that *I want you* look in his eyes, and he wasn't the kind of guy to take no for an answer.

Kell had been doing his best to stand up to the onslaught. It had been about to turn ugly, with older cons taking small bets whether Kell would say yes or no to being Ryan's sex slave. Or whether he even realized what Ryan was truly offering him.

Which was nothing good. But did Kell know that?

It had gotten as far as Ryan hauling Kell up out of the mud after having slapped him.

Bede had stepped in. Did the prison yard power dance to show Ryan that he was not boss.

Then Griff, a cornerstone man with a life sentence for ending a brawl in a Cheyenne truck yard using a piece of metal to cave in at least half a dozen skulls, had stepped in and called the shots.

Griff had made Kell decide between Ryan and Bede so that Griff could more peacefully sun himself in the prison yard without a fight going on. Griff was old. Had done his crime and was doing his time, and he practically ran the yard.

Up close, in those green eyes of Kell's, Bede had seen an old soul.

And an expression a little like Winston's, which showed Bede that Kell had seen some shit.

That shit could have made him bitter. But instead, beneath the surface, and not very far, lay a warm sweetness that needed only a bit of kindness to come out. A small brightness against the gray backdrop of prison walls.

There was a scarcity of kindness in prison, but that was self-evident, simply because of the high-tension environment.

There wasn't much kindness in Bede's old life, either, though he had fond memories of the party to celebrate his first real drug deal, standing in an abandoned house north of Five Points in Denver, holding out a plastic-wrapped burrito of white powder in exchange for a bundle of cash.

In the prison yard, the crowd that had gathered around Kell and Ryan waiting for blood, or something juicy to watch, had not seen Kell's expression, as Bede had. Nor would they ever know of the twinge in Bede's chest at that expression. Wise and frightened and brave, all at the same time.

When Griff had told Kell to choose between Ryan and Bede, Bede had thought for sure Kell would be taken in by Ryan's sudden sweetness. And that Kell would be put off by Bede, muscled, tattooed, grim.

To Bede's almost-surprise, Kell had chosen Bede. Kell wasn't a fool and had seen beyond Ryan's facade.

In their cell that night, Kell, subdued, shoulders slumped, had offered a blow job in payment for Bede's protection services. Bede had turned Kell down, of course. Kell was way young, and, as Bede found out, a virgin.

The tumble of Kell's offered innocence struck Bede to his core. Unsettled him. Made him want to rage at everything in his life that had brought Kell to that point.

But he didn't say it. Rather than telling Kell how much he reminded Bede of Winston, Bede dismissed Kell's offer, and casually allowed that it might be better if Kell was not so forthcoming about his virginity.

From that point forward, Bede protected Kell without telling him why. He shared his books. Gave him pointers. Went with him to the showers.

He even had a bit of fun pretending they were lovers, just to show Ryan what a loser he was. To which Kell responded like an old hand at improv. Looking up at Bede adoringly. Fluttering his eyelashes. Flirting in the food line.

And, in return, Bede had a shadow that almost never left his side.

Bede's situation could have been worse. He could have ended up with dull, rage-filled Toby as a cellie, or the snarl-mouthed Owen, rather than the bright-faced, quick-learning Kell.

This blessing turned into a curse, for just about as soon as Kell had applied for and been accepted into the Fresh Start Program, he started bugging Bede to also apply.

Frequent phone calls during Bede's phone time brought Kell's voice into his ear, describing the delights of the valley where he now lived and worked. How much fun it would be if Bede was also there.

There was also chatter about some guy named Marston, who, according to Kell, was so amazing. So handsome. Such a great kisser.

Bede did not care that Kell had found someone to be with, someone who took his virginity with what sounded like the utmost gentleness.

He was not jealous, not of Kell's happiness. Not of Marston. Though, if Marston harmed a single hair on Kell's dark head, Bede discovered he'd willingly do another stint in jail, just for the pleasure of skinning Marston alive. Nobody, but *nobody*, was going to take the shine out of those old-soul eyes.

CHAPTER 2
GALEN

As Galen waited for the prison van to show up on a fine Monday afternoon, he thought, not for the first time, how very different Farthingdale Valley was from Farthingdale Guest Ranch.

On the guest ranch, you could see for miles. If you stood in the right place, you could see all the way to Montana. It was gorgeous. The people were friendly, the customers, all rich, were fairly down-to-earth. The work was straightforward.

The valley, on the other hand, rather than being at the top of a hill that sloped down into a glassy river, was tucked in a scoop of land, thick with trees. It was currently populated with four team leads and a bunch of ex-cons who were obviously taking the easy way out by doing their parole in a situation which wouldn't ask very much of them. They'd skate by, living off handouts. Lazy freeloaders.

When Galen had left his father's farm two years prior, he'd made a home for himself at the guest ranch, working through two summer seasons. In the winters, he'd gone home to help his dad with the bees and the goats and the fields and, come spring, mulching and tending in preparation for going back to the ranch. All in all, a good life.

But, the summer before, in the middle of a typical week tending horses, hauling hay, helping guests, Galen's dad, Earl Parnell, had passed away.

For Earl, it had been a gentle going in a hospice facility in Cheyenne. There, due to complications from a summer pneumonia, brought on by who knew what—working in the rain or a kid with a cold at the local McDonalds, or some germ—he'd passed away.

Galen had held his dad's hand all the while. He'd signed papers, then signed *more* papers. He drank bitter cups of coffee from the machine at the hospice until a kindly attendant showed him how to work the machine.

That coffee had been milky and sweet, like a kiss from an angel. Which didn't stem Galen's tears, nor his grief.

At least his dad had not been in pain. Instead, he'd been tended to night and day by the hospice workers, angels in soft blue and pink uniforms, cheerful sweaters. Galen would be forever grateful to them.

He'd be forever grateful to Leland Tate, as well, who ran Farthingdale Ranch, a hideaway-getaway for rich folks who wanted to play at being cowboys.

Galen was a mere ranch hand, but Leland had given Galen two full weeks off *with* pay, and held his job for him until his return. The offer of funds, a no-interest loan, if Galen wanted it. Time and patience and understanding. More time off if he needed it.

Which would have been nice, but once his father was buried in Iron Mountain Cemetery, there wasn't anything Galen wanted more than to be distracted by work.

Even with his job at the ranch, he struggled with the mountain of medical debt and the small stack of regular farm bills that needed to be paid.

He sold the goats, a small herd of soft eared does and one billy. Then he used that money to hire a guy to harvest the lavender, then the money from lavender sales to put out ads for someone to rent the farm the following summer.

He even made a deal with a Colorado-based beekeeper, Jared Keating, to come and harvest the honey. They split the proceeds from that, fifty-fifty, and made an agreement for the following fall.

Over the winter, Galen had spent most of his time at the old farm table, elbows on the red-and-white checked oil tablecloth, chin in his hands, watching the snow fall as he looked out the large windows at the white landscape. Swamped in grief and memories, he felt like an old man, rather than a twenty-eight year old with his whole life ahead of him.

His dad's passing had left a jagged hole in his life, his soul. With his head tangled with all he needed to do, the fear that he wouldn't ever live up to being as good a man as his dad had been grew into an almost insurmountable pain that stabbed at his heart.

He'd looked at his finances. Then looked at them again.

He needed new tires for his truck. The medical debt from his father's treatment and passing needed paying off. He wasn't sure about the taxes that needed paying, as his dad had always taken care of that, but Galen was sure the bill would come due at some point.

All the while, he wondered if he should take up his father's life, that of running the farm. Which was certainly too much for one person, though the thought of leaving it behind stabbed at him until his heart was bleeding.

He found a young couple to rent the place for the summer. When they showed up with their two-year-old in the spring, they had cheerful smiles and hundred-dollar apron smocks. They talked of making bread by hand and how they were going to take photos and videos for their Instagram account, and how wonderful everything was.

With handshakes and a verbal agreement about what needed paying attention to—the gate, the irrigation system, the shed door, the screen door—Galen headed back to the guest ranch, expecting to get back to his regularly scheduled summer life. Horses and guests and hay. Eating in the large but inviting dining hall. Watching the sunsets over Iron Mountain, which loomed in the west, ever present, always watching.

The snag came when Leland Tate, foreman of Farthingdale Guest Ranch, wanted Galen to be a team lead in his newly launched Fresh Start Program.

The program used ex-cons as labor to develop the valley into a first class, high-dollar retreat. The ex-cons, in return, were able to do their parole and learn life skills along the way.

Galen knew about the program, which had been an experiment the summer before. Leland had assigned Jasper, the guest ranch's blacksmith, the task of taking charge of an ex-con by the name of Ellis. Jasper had, in essence, become Ellis' parole officer, with the goal of teaching Ellis how to be a blacksmith.

As to how successful that had been, the proof was in the valley program, already underway. But, in spite of Galen's personal opinion that the whole thing was a bad and enabling setup, the grapevine had it that the valley program was bringing in more tax dollars for the valley and the ranch than even Leland had foretold.

The valley was to the south of the ranch, a long green swath of land with a deep blue lake at the bottom of it. The only way you could get there was to climb to the top of the wind-swept hill above the ranch, and then go down a very steep road that was all switchbacks.

Galen had never been to the valley, but he'd gone along the road that was parallel to the valley, on his way to the hospital, and then hospice, in Cheyenne.

From the road, the valley playfully lurked behind a curtain of green pine trees, through which could sometimes be seen Half Moon Lake, or Guipago Ridge, or even Horse Creek River, glistening, like a secret string of blue diamonds among the trees.

"Work with ex-cons?" Galen had asked rather bluntly as he'd sat in Leland's office, taking the bottle of home-brewed root beer but not drinking it. "Me?"

"You'd be great at it." Leland leaned forward, his own bottle of root beer between his two strong hands, elbows on his knees, as if that would, in any way, diminish his height or his control of the conversation. "I need you there."

"Can I be honest?" asked Galen.

"I'd appreciate it," said Leland.

Galen echoed Leland's pose, elbows on his knees as he held his bottle of root beer in exactly the same way.

"I am not interested in working with ex-cons." Galen's voice came out a bit more stridently than he'd expected, so he softened it. "They were stupid enough to commit crimes, and now they're getting a free ride? Training? Food and lodging? They have it easy."

"These aren't violent criminals," said Leland, as if that were the issue. "And they've all done their time."

"I don't care if they were arrested for shoplifting gum." Galen sat up, putting the bottle of root beer on Leland's wooden desk with a loud clonk. "I've worked hard all my life and no matter what dire straits I was in, I would never commit a crime. I'm not interested."

"There's a five thousand dollar bonus at the end of summer." Leland took a swig of his root beer and then placed his bottle next to Galen's on the desk, an echo. "You could pay off the rest of your medical debt and still have money for tires for your truck."

"I said no." Galen stood up, ready to leave.

He'd worked hard all his life. So had his dad. They'd made a life that did not involve stealing from other people. There was nothing Galen would ever commit a crime for and he wasn't about to participate in any program that gave criminals an easy time of it.

"It's important to me," said Leland. "I need you in this program." He paused and looked right into Galen's soul. "Please?"

Galen knew he owed Leland for more than the time off when his dad had passed. The comfort and support Leland had offered was an invisible debt that could never be repaid. More, Leland's quiet *please* struck him to his heart.

Looking through the open doorway of Leland's office into the lofty space of the main barn, where ranch hands hustled, and the smell of warm hay filled his lungs, he thought of what his dad, Earl, might say at that moment.

Earl hadn't been as dismissive of an ex-con living and working at the guest ranch as Galen had been. Earl was of the mind that you just never knew. That you made your own luck and trusted in the future. Feelings and opinions that Galen would have been happy to share had Earl lived.

Now, the bitterness surged up, almost swamping him, but through it all he could almost hear his dad's quiet, slightly rumbly voice. *Say yes, son. It'll give you time to figure out what to do about the farm. It's yours now. You get to decide.*

"Yes," said Galen. He breathed out a long, slow breath. "Okay, I'll do it."

"Great." Leland rubbed his hands together, though he was the farthest thing from an evil overlord gloating about his plans for world domination coming together. Well, almost.

Leland usually got his way. While he didn't own the guest ranch, he managed it. He *did* have partial ownership in the valley; it was his baby, his pet project. He wanted it to succeed, and when Leland wanted something to happen, it usually did.

"You can keep working to help set up for the season at the ranch, then I'll send you to a two-week training course in Torrington."

They shook on it, then Leland said, "Thank you. I think you're going to be a real asset to the program."

Wondering if he'd made a huge mistake, Galen went back to work at the ranch, doing his best to normalize, to get back to the life he remembered before his dad passed.

Or at least he tried to normalize. But he'd been lonely.

One mistake he'd made after his dad's funeral service was to blindly reach out for companionship. His attention had landed on one of the ranch's star hands, Zeke Malloy.

Zeke was an ex-bull rider who'd busted his leg reaching for eight seconds and couldn't do the rodeo circuit anymore.

Zeke had told Galen that he'd tried trucking, and working in a granary, feedlot, slaughterhouse. And had landed at Farthingdale Ranch the summer before.

He was lanky and lean, with an insouciant walk, and a slow drawl that crawled up Galen's spine, making him feel things he thought he'd forgotten how to feel.

Flirting with Zeke took Galen's mind off everything. Everything.

Zeke had a dry laugh in response to Galen's small wit, his eyes crinkling at the corners, their green sparkling like emeralds in rich earth, blazing against his dark tan.

Encouraged, Galen had tried harder, only to learn to his dismay that Zeke was as straight as an arrow.

"You're a good man, Galen," said Zeke, arms folded across his muscled chest, every inch of those muscles hard-won, honestly won, through long hours of work. "But I am straight. Why, I dated Betty Sue for three years before I busted my leg. She only wanted a buckle-winning kind of man. Not a broken one. Hence, I am on the shelf, on the lookout for a nice woman to settle down with."

Galen had admitted defeat. Outwardly, he'd behaved in a gentlemanly manner. Only to feel, on the inside, like a loathsome worm for bothering Zeke that way. Practically throwing himself at a man who was straight? The worst manners. The *worst*.

So, perhaps, packing up to go to training for team leads in Torrington, and then moving into a green canvas tent in the valley wouldn't be such a bad idea. The change of pace might also do him good.

Absenting himself from anywhere he might run into Zeke was also a smart move. He could still remember the hard flush on his cheeks, the way the heat crawled down his chest when Zeke had turned him down. The maze of embarrassment that took him ages to work his way out of.

His training in Torrington included a whole lot of close-up examples that only supported his distaste for Leland's valley program.

On his first day, one of the guards had taken him and a few other special guests on a small tour of Wyoming Correctional.

During the tour, one woman had remarked how polite and well-mannered all the prisoners seemed.

It was something that Galen had been thinking as well and he wasn't altogether surprised when the guard said, "Many of them are at their most docile behind bars."

After the fast-paced blur of his training at Wyoming Correctional, he had a notebook from his training, and the files on the members of his small team. He had read those files and shaken his head at the stupidity of any man who thought that the way to go about things was to simply take what they wanted.

Two of the men on his little team, Toby and Owen, were small-time crooks, arrested for a short string of breaking and entering.

From their descriptions, they seemed almost harmless. The kind that might be secondary characters in a cop show, low-level men to heighten the effect of another criminal, higher up in the food chain.

They were still stupid, even if their files didn't describe either of them as particularly violent. He probably wouldn't have any trouble with them.

The doubt in his brain sped up when he'd reviewed Obadiah Deacon's file. If the darkly scowling mug shot of Deacon didn't spell danger, then reading his file certainly set off all kinds of alarm bells in Galen's head.

The image in the mug shot was rude, crude, and tattooed. Deacon was an oily haired thug in all the ways that mattered.

There were also surveillance pictures that showed Deacon in a three-piece suit, tipping a valet as he handed over the keys to a very nice sports car. Deacon slipping past a velvet gate that someone had lifted for him. Images in motion, images of a man of power.

Deacon's file included not just information about his five-year stint in Wyoming Correctional, but also the fights he'd gotten into, his several sessions in solitary.

There was a long passage about his odd and unwholesome relationship with Kelliher Dodson, a parolee who'd entered the valley program a few weeks prior, and also the long list of crimes Deacon had committed before he'd gotten arrested. Drug-related crimes. Making, marketing, *and* selling.

And though the crimes didn't include selling meth and cocaine directly to children while lurking at the edge of a schoolyard, the potential connection made Galen's skin crawl just the same. Those drugs had probably been used by kids, because if parents were buying, their kids might have access.

If Galen might have some sympathy for Deacon, it was when he read about the shootout that had disrupted some tawdry drug deal. In that back alley, several drug dealers on both sides of the line had lost their lives due to the spray of bullets coming from all directions.

One member of Deacon's gang had died, and three on the other side. Two cops had gotten injured. Blood had drained into the gutter in red ribbons before drying to brown. It had taken at least a week to clean up the mess, though Galen imagined the ramifications were still continuing.

Deacon had not been the only drug dealer arrested that day, though, due to overcrowding in the local jail system, he'd been moved up to Wyoming Correctional.

A hand-scribbled note indicated that the transfer had also removed Deacon from contact with the jailed members of the other gang. To keep the peace, as ironic as that was.

Galen had been hearing about the valley program for weeks before he'd moved into the valley. As far as he knew, Deacon was one of the most violent criminals, one of the most depraved, that the valley had ever taken on.

It might be the valley had other violent criminals, like Kurt, who'd tried to kill another ex-con, but for the most part, all the parolees seemed to be more like Toby and Owen. Low level crooks just looking for a handout. An easy way to do their parole.

Which begged the question: how the hell had Deacon slipped through the cracks? Just who the fuck thought it would be a good idea to let that guy walk free? Let alone breathe free air in the valley? Get handouts? Opportunity and training? It was all bullshit.

Well, his was not to judge, but rather to just do his job.

He was not like them. He would work for his pay and earn the bonus and the trust Leland Tate had invested in him. He could do that much. Then, at the end of summer, he'd just have to see which direction his life would take.

CHAPTER 3
BEDE

I t wasn't a sure thing that Lenny had not taken a wrong turn because the white van was now going down a set of switchbacks that had what must have been at least a six percent grade.

In spite of this, Bede was distracted by the thickness of the green pine trees and the way the temperature dropped as they went down into the valley. He could see the there was a blue lake, and an enormous, gray ridge to the west that flickered in and out of sight.

Bede wanted to ask Lenny to roll down the window so he could smell the fresh air, but then that would mean Lenny's hands would not be on the wheel, and they very much needed to be, just then.

Steadily, the van trundled down the switchbacks before pulling into an opening in the trees and stopping at a round, gravel parking lot.

Two silver trucks were parked along one side of the gravel. Beyond that, between the thick forest of trees, Bede glimpsed what looked like a long sage-green tent, and a few small white-painted buildings. Beyond that were even more trees and maybe even a few more tents.

It looked pretty sparsely built up for a place that would, come the following summer, be charging four hundred dollars a night. Who would want to pay that much to sleep in a tent was beyond Bede, though Kell had assured him that the food was amazing, the showers swank as hell, the beds soft as clouds.

All of this was beautiful in theory, but it was just another landscape for him to traverse. Besides, the work he was going to be required to do would be, he was quite sure, backbreaking and never-ending under a blazing Wyoming sun.

Never mind. He could always leave. In fact, he planned on leaving just as soon as he could get himself situated and figure out where he wanted to head next. Except—did he want to go back to Denver to pick up his old life? Or maybe he would head out to the coast and the ocean. Or to Vegas and the never-ending party there?

Lenny parked the van, jumped out, and pulled open the sliding door. All of them, Bede, Toby, and Owen, blinked at the sun amidst the trees.

Bede shivered as he got out, not yet used to seeing the blue, tree-shaded sky that wasn't framed by a scrim of razor-edged barbed wire. After five years behind bars, he didn't know how long it would take him to accept freedom as a reality.

He didn't have two seconds to take a breath before a slender body barreled into him, wiry arms wrapping around him without even so much as a how-do-you-do.

Laughter rang in his ears, accompanied by a hug of such intensity that he was on the verge of shoving back, of using his brawn to fell his assailant to the ground.

But it was Kell who hugged him, dark hair spilling across his face, those old-soul eyes full of laughter. Up close. Holding onto Bede like there was no tomorrow. As though Bede was the one person in the world that Kell had most wanted to see. Had waited for. Would have waited for a good long time.

Bede didn't deserve such a warm welcome. When he'd befriended Kell in prison, it had been more for himself than for Kell's benefit. Anything Kell had gotten out of it had been a bonus.

As Kell pulled back, Bede could see that Kell was rested, well-fed, well-cared for. Sleek. He'd gained weight, all of it good muscle. Those green eyes of his were bright as emeralds.

For all the doubts Bede had about the Fresh Start Program, it certainly had done well by Kell.

"You're here," said Kell, breathing the words out like a song of joy.

He took his arms from around Bede's neck, though his hand trailed on Bede's t-shirt, fingers tightening for a quick second before letting go.

"Sorry," Kell said to the gathering at large. "I know you got protocols and stuff. I just couldn't resist." But before Lenny could pick up his clipboard and have someone sign for them, Kell pointed. "That's Marston. Marston, this is Bede. I told you about Bede, how he protected me. Remember?"

Marston, the man of whom Bede had heard so much from Kell, was a blond-haired, steely-eyed, hard-jawed giant standing guard.

Marston did not come forward to shake Bede's hand, but only scowled. Like he knew all about Bede and didn't care for the kind of man Bede was.

Well, Bede didn't blame him. In spite of Kell's glowing comments about Marston, Bede had his doubts, and was now pretty sure, by the size of him, that Marston had taken advantage of Kell.

Kell reached out, like he wanted Marston and Bede to shake hands and bond right then and there. Kell even went as far as to go up to Marston and tug on the sleeve of his long-sleeved shirt, like he'd tugged on Bede's shirt.

In that moment, as Marston looked down at Kell, his face softened, just like butter in a hot pan. His eyes were half-lidded, a tender glint there, and his mouth curled into a smile along one corner.

Bede's people-reading skills kicked in. Soppy in love, that's what Marston was.

None of this completely changed Bede's mind about Marston, but it was easy to see that Marston would kill or die trying to protect Kell. Move heaven and earth. Whatever was called for. With Marston looking out for him, along with his own sensible self, Kell would be fine.

The only thing standing in the way of Kell's continued safety and happiness was, of course, Bede himself, at least according to Marston's glare, sent Bede's way. Which meant that one thing Bede needed to do was convince Marston that he was harmless.

Whether or not he could manage that Herculean feat was another question, but he had the rest of the summer to do it. It was either that or he could challenge Marston, and the two of them could get into a beat-down with the watching crowd declaring the winner. Which would be Bede, of course. All of which would upset Kell.

Bede sighed and shrugged his shoulders. A sure sign in the prison yard that while a fight was not out of the question, he personally was backing off. For now.

Maybe Marston knew prison-speak, or maybe he'd been affected by Kell's bubble of joy as he'd greeted Bede, but he seemed to back off, as well.

"Let's get this paperwork done," said Lenny, tapping his pen against the metal clip on the clipboard. "Then I can be on my way."

The mood of the group shifted, and Bede looked around as Lenny shuffled through the papers on his clipboard.

In the middle of this, as Bede waited for his new life to begin, a man came walking through the woods in the swirl of a breeze, longish hair lifting.

He was dressed much like Marston in dusty blue jeans, work boots, a snap button shirt in pale blue, which gave Bede the impression was a sort of uniform in the valley.

The man was whip-thin, lanky, and as he came up to the group, he wasn't smiling. Which made Bede want to crack a joke, because, man, what did this guy have to be unhappy about?

His gray eyes cast a wide glance, narrowing as he looked at the three of them: Bede, Toby, and Owen. Like he could spot an ex-con at a mile's distance and didn't quite care for the view. Had he been on the parole board, he would not have given any of them the green light to walk free.

All of this was in his gaze, the way he lifted his chin and looked down his aquiline nose at them.

"This my group?" the man asked, as he pushed a long lock of hair back from his face.

"You Galen Parnell?" asked Lenny, looking up from his clipboard.

"That's me."

Galen's lips barely moved as he spoke, and he looked away as though he'd seen what he needed to see and wasn't impressed. He took the clipboard from Lenny, signed it, and handed it back in utter silence.

It was hard for Bede to get a read on a man who held himself so tightly, like he was standing behind an invisible barrier so nobody could get through.

Again, Bede had the rest of the summer to figure Galen out, which was key, because it looked like the guy was now in charge of him. That is, unless Bede simply up and left the valley. Which he could do.

"See you," said Lenny. He got into the van and drove away, chugging up the switchbacks, disappearing into the pine trees with a flash of white and a sparkle of sun off the chrome bumper.

"Thanks for being part of my welcoming committee," said Galen to Marston and Kell. It was acknowledgement and dismissal at the same time. "But I better get to it."

"See you at dinner," said Marston, tipping his chin at Kell as if to say, *We're not wanted here.*

With a wave, Marston and Kell walked across the parking lot and into the woods.

From his and Kell's phone conversations, Bede knew that Marston and Kell made signs and were setting them up around the compound. Digging holes. Pouring cement.

Was that just a two-man job, or could Bede bribe someone to be put on the same team as Kell? On the other hand, Galen didn't seem like he'd be pleased to do anybody any favors.

"You're my team," said Galen, as though he didn't like the idea of it very much. As though he didn't want anything to do with ex-cons.

Bede had seen expressions like the one Galen currently had. The tight scowl, the sneer of disdain represented by a flare of his nostrils.

"I'm Galen Parnell, and you are?"

"Toby Thorne," said Toby, with his hand to his chest, like there was another Toby in the group and he wanted to make sure Galen didn't confuse him with somebody else.

"Owen Feeney," said Owen. He had a smile like a guy who would promise to redo your driveway, get you to sign on the dotted line after paying a hefty deposit, only to never show up.

"Bede Deacon," said Bede, without waiting for Galen to look at him.

"Bede?" asked Galen sharply, looking up, gray eyes snapping. "There's no Bede on my team." Then he paused, as if reconsidering. "Unless Bede is short for Obadiah."

"That's right."

Bede smiled at Galen, half on the verge of daring him to make something of it. To insist that Bede go by his full and given name, like his teachers used to do back in school. Like the prison guards would sometimes do, just to mess with him.

Galen glared at him as a bit of wind lifted his brown hair and tossed it in his eyes. He used long fingers to pull the hair away, then glared at all of them, as though they'd been causing problems all morning and he'd had just about enough.

He'd be pretty if only he'd smile a little. If only he'd relax those shoulders a little. With those eyes and that sweep of hair, Galen would have been in high demand in the prison yard.

Bede shoved those thoughts away. The last thing he needed was to be distracted by a pretty face. He'd held onto his emotions for the last five years while behind bars, even as he'd looked at the other cons or the guards.

One man had nice shoulders, like Winston had. Another one had long eyelashes, dark, spiky. Like Winston had. Whispers of the past, a love long gone. Chasing him through the hours and days and years like ghosts across the shiny, well-mopped floors of the corridors of Wyoming Correctional.

This guy, this jerk off, was nothing like Winston, who could tease a laugh out of Bede in a heartbeat.

Bede couldn't remember the last time he'd even smiled, and this guy was now in charge of him, could try all he wanted and never succeed. Not that he would try. Not that Bede wanted him to.

Galen remained unsmiling and hard to read as he looked them over once more and took a long hard breath, like they were all on his last nerve and he had no idea how he was going to make it to the end of the day.

"I'm your team lead. You work for me now." Galen paused, looking over their shoulders at the rest of the compound, like he was searching for something he'd forgotten to do or say. "I'll take you around, give you a tour. Show you your tents, where you'll be staying. Then you'll have a chunk of time to get settled, and you'll meet me in the mess tent when the dinner bell rings. Got it?"

The three of them nodded, with Toby looking to Owen as if to make sure that was the right kind of response.

Galen took them on the tour, a stiff set to his shoulders, squinting at them as the sun speared through the trees. Like he'd forgotten his hat and, only just realizing it, was blaming them.

His voice didn't reflect any anger, though, and seemed to stay level as he led them along paths through shimmering green forests, where the air was fresh and bright and breezy, smelling like pine and other good things.

Galen showed them the green canvas mess tent, which looked fairly ordinary, just a bunch of tables, some standing fans, and a small area that looked like it was trying to be a home office. There were books on the shelf that grabbed Bede's attention, but Galen didn't give them any time to pause.

Then Galen showed them the white first aid hut, and the hut where they could do their laundry.

He showed them the showers and the toilets, which were just as Kell had described them and as fancy as anything Bede had ever seen.

Then Galen took them down to a shining blue lake that just about took Bede's breath away, in spite of himself.

The thing he'd missed while being in prison was being able to submerge his entire body in water. Prison showers were unsettling affairs with half-ass water pressure and not enough time to relax.

He couldn't imagine that permission would be given to go swimming, but his skin, his soul, was already aching for it because being surrounded by cool, fresh water sounded way better than just about anything else.

"This is Half Moon Lake," said Galen, his arm stretched out, pointing, staying that way like he was posing for a statue that might be made in his likeness.

His hair lifted in the breeze, and his gaze was long, as though he wanted nothing more than to leave them behind and go for a swim, or a long walk around the lake, anywhere but where he was.

"There's a dock down that way. Sometimes we go for a swim, like in the evenings, after work is done. We might get canoes or kayaks before the summer is over."

Feeling a surge of interest, Bede almost let his jaw drop in astonishment at the idea that they could go swimming. That he could finally, *finally*, get clean all over.

There was no way he wanted anyone to know what he was feeling, so instead Bede asked, "What kind of work?"

Blinking, Galen turned to him, a furrow of a frown across his forehead, like he'd forgotten who Bede was or why he was there. With a quick sigh, he slid his hands into the back pockets of his blue jeans.

"We're mostly going to be digging up knapweed, which is a real hazard, though that may change later. Then I'll be giving you riding lessons." He paused, as if considering whether or not to share more with them. "There was talk of us building a few yurts on the other side of the river."

Yurts? Was any of this for real? Bede was not a carpenter, that was for sure. Or a cowboy. He belonged in Denver, where the city streets were as familiar to him as his own skin.

"What's a yurt?" asked Toby. Owen elbowed him. "Hey! I wanna know, is all."

While Galen explained what a yurt was, Bede watched him.

Galen seemed patient, not at all troubled that Toby was a loser who didn't know any better than to reveal his ignorance.

His face softened as he went into teacher mode, the way some of the aids in the prison library would. As if it was their dream to explain to a convicted felon how to use Microsoft Word.

Well, if Galen was one of those do-gooders who imagined they were one of God's angels, sent to help sinners repent, then Bede wanted nothing to do with him. He was a sinner, through and through.

"Come up this way," said Galen to the three of them, yanking Bede out of his reverie.

Galen took them up another path to a wooden paddock, beyond which was a long wooden shed. Beyond that was a wide space that seemed to go on forever.

"There are horses in the field, beneath those trees by the river." Galen pointed and Bede looked, though all he could see was the wide expanse of half-bitten grass and beyond that, more trees.

"We use the paddock here for lessons, to teach horsemanship," said Galen. "We'll get horses in that are being traded and sold. At some point, we'll be asked to help feed and groom and water, as needed, so be ready."

They started walking again, going back in the direction of the main camp, along a path in the high grasses and past a row of tents. These tents were of the same green canvas as the mess tents, but they were smaller, more compact. They were almost hidden in the trees.

"I'm the fourth tent along," said Galen, pointing but not stopping, taking long strides, always moving. "If you need me, I'm always around, but you can stop by my tent if you have to."

Galen plowed back into the thickness of the trees, with the three of them trailing behind.

Bede knew he'd figure out his way around, eventually, but currently he felt as though he was trapped inside woods thick enough for Hansel and Gretel to get lost in. The smell of warm pine was almost overwhelming, but it was spicy and alluring, and Bede found he actually liked it.

"This is you, Toby and Owen," said Galen as he stopped and pointed up a small path, shadowed pine branches.

"In there?" asked Owen, peering at the tent in the middle of a copse of trees.

"Yeah, this is your tent. Tent number twelve."

With a hard sigh, Galen led them to the wooden platform and up the stairs to the tent. The opening flaps were tied back, a yellow canvas rain fly stretched over the top of the tent.

All of them clomped onto the platform, crowding it, then Toby and Owen slid inside the green-tinted semi-gloom.

Bede stuck his head in to look, the smell of sun-warmed canvas all around him.

"Those boxes hold your gear," said Galen, pointing again. "You need to unpack and check the list that's included to see if anything's missing. You'll get cowboy boots and a hat later this week. After two weeks, you get a cell phone, with six months of data on it."

Standing perhaps too close behind Galen, Bede looked over his shoulder and watched as Toby and Owen opened their assembly of cardboard boxes and started going through them like two kids on Christmas morning. Socks flew, underwear too, and snap-button shirts that landed at ragged angles on the two cots like murdered bodies.

Galen turned to Bede, then jerked back as if startled at Bede's closeness. Bede just smiled at him, always a good power move in a prison yard.

"I'll show you your tent," Galen said, brushing past Bede in haste.

"Am I on my own?" Bede asked, just realizing this as he followed Galen through the woods.

"Yeah," said Galen, not turning around as sunlight sparkled off the gold in his hair.

Bede could hardly believe it. He'd lived with Winston forever, and then had shared cells with different men in Wyoming Correctional. He'd not been alone, on his own, for years and years.

It would be all kinds of weird to sleep alone in the middle of the woods, but it might be cool, too. If he didn't get eaten by bears.

But rather than express any of this to Galen, who probably wouldn't give a fuck, Bede followed silently, a cool breeze all around him, cooling him even as they went in and out of patches of hot sunlight.

They were well and truly in the middle of the woods by the time Galen slowed down and showed Bede his tent. Which was the same size as Toby and Owen's tent, but wasn't so buried in a clutch of evergreens. A little bit of it poked out from between the branches, like it wanted to be found.

"This is you, tent number eleven," said Galen. "You might get a tent mate in the coming weeks, or you might not."

Galen sounded like he very much didn't care. Like the prospect of babysitting three ex-cons for the rest of the summer while they did their parole was some kind of punishment he very much felt he did not deserve.

"Will I get eaten by bears?" Bede asked, meaning it as a joke, even though the last thing he wanted to do was create any kind of rapport with this guy, who obviously hated all ex-cons, on sight.

A snort, half-derision, half-amusement, escaped Galen, and he put the back of his hand to his mouth, like he'd not meant to respond to the joke Bede had not meant to tell.

"You likely won't," said Galen, as if doing his best to be stern and gruff, rather than amused. "But who's to say? Anyway." Galen stepped back and waved Bede into his tent. "Unpack. Shower. Change out of those prison clothes. When the dinner bell rings, come to the mess tent. Do you remember where that is?"

"Sure thing," said Bede, casual, dismissive, erasing any joy in the moment. "See you there."

As Galen walked off, Bede stepped up on the wooden platform, pausing before stepping into his very own tent.

What an astonishing thing to find in the middle of the woods. A secret hideaway. The following summer, as Galen had explained, rich city folks would be paying at least four hundred dollars a night, so he might as well live it up while he could.

There was no security on the tent, which anywhere else would invite thieves. But the lack of it indicated the lack of *need* for it. Like everybody was trustworthy or some shit. They probably were.

CHAPTER 4
BEDE

As Bede stepped from the wooden platform into his tent, he moved from bright sunshine into a cool, green-tinted cave.

There were two cots made up with clean sheets, clean blankets, and fluffy pillows. The smell of pine trees wafted on sun-warmed air through the open flap at the far end of the tent.

From somewhere came the sound of birdsong and all of it was such a far cry from prison accommodations that he stood there for a long, hard minute, just soaking it in.

On top of one of the cots was a series of boxes that Bede already knew contained blue jeans and snap button shirts and plastic wrapped packages of underwear and socks, soap, brand-name shampoo—anything he might need. All of which was a bribe for good behavior.

He should unpack rather than stare like some sort of newbie who had no idea what was going on, because he did, he sure did. He was being given the carrot before the stick.

Sure, he'd have new everything, and then the shit would come down. That would be the price he would pay for being a drug dealer amidst this paradise. He would be given hard work. The *hardest*—

He caught himself short from his mental tirade when he saw a large box which, by the flat, long shape, could only contain a pair of boots.

Sitting down on one cot, he reached for the box and opened it as he pulled it onto his lap. Yes, the box contained new work boots, just like the kind Marston and Kell and Galen had been wearing.

Bede ran his fingers over the laces, almost shivering at the tough softness of the yellow suede.

These boots would have come in handy, so handy, in prison. They would have been useful for a kick to the head or groin, useful for stomping fingers.

But then, had he owned a pair such as this, he would have been shanked within twenty-four hours of getting them, and the boots taken from him. Better that the boots had waited for him for five years, so he could enjoy them now.

A rustle outside the tent made him look up to see Kell come onto the platform. Behind him was another guy, slightly older, paunchy, red-faced, and scowling.

"You're not unpacked," said Kell, his cheery voice making it a greeting rather than a criticism. "Dinner's soon, and you don't want to miss it."

It took him a moment to realize that he'd been sitting there mooning over new boots for a good long while. Galen had given him a list of things to do, one of which had been a shower, only now it was too late.

Bede could have explained to Kell that he was a bit overwhelmed, but the experience of his criminal life and his years behind bars had taught him the folly of that. Never give yourself away. Never admit vulnerability.

"Sure thing," he said, putting the boots to the side, like they didn't matter to him at all. Like he wasn't already in love with them.

"This is Wayne," said Kell, waving to the angry-looking guy standing next to him. "He's my tent mate."

"Hi," said Bede, not waving back. Not getting up.

"How come you got your own tent?" Wayne asked, strident, loud, like Bede was miles away and needed to be shouted at. "How come?"

"Just got assigned it."

Bede didn't raise his voice to match Wayne's. No point. In the prison yard, every head would have turned to Wayne, assessing him, with Wayne coming up short. Looking away again, calculating how long till lights out, when Wayne could get his comeuppance.

"Well, it's not fair. I want my own tent." Wayne's eyes were narrow, his mouth in a scowl. Any minute and he was going to start shouting even louder. "How come I always got to share?"

Bede looked at Kell. Saw the small shrug, like the whole thing was out of control and there was nothing Kell could do about it. Wayne was a whiner, pure and simple.

How Kell had managed to live with him was a mystery. Well, Kell was adaptable. He'd managed thus far. Didn't mean he had to keep on putting up with it.

"I'll switch with you." Bede dipped his head, scratching behind his ear to show just how much it didn't matter to him. He could have gotten into a tussle with Wayne, just to blow off some steam, but perhaps it was too soon, and besides, this was the smarter move. "You can move your stuff in here now. Before dinner."

"I don't want to be so far out in the woods." Wayne pouted like he was a seven-year-old boy, rather than a fully grown man. "Kell can move in here with you."

The idea appealed to Bede. Moving into a tent where someone like Wayne had lived, shuffling around in his leavings, was an unhappy prospect. Having Kell join him in a bright, new, never-lived-in tent, had a brand new feeling to it.

"Sure." Bede stood up, pretending he didn't hear Kell's gasp of delight. "Let's make it happen."

Another gasp came, this time from Wayne, who blinked at Bede, like he couldn't believe what had just happened. Like he'd never experienced a single bit of kindness in his whole lumpy life. And like maybe Bede was playing a trick on him.

"I mean it," said Bede. "Kell was my cellie before, so he can be again."

Wayne actually grabbed Bede's arm and tugged, like some impudent greenhorn who was newly arrived and didn't know the protocols of prison. Never touch another man without his permission. Didn't matter. Wayne had probably been a lightweight in prison. A second rung man.

Bede's kindness to Wayne could probably be leveraged. In the meantime, he shooed them both out of the tent, and together the three of them went to what Wayne proudly announced was tent number one.

As they entered, the tent had a musty smell, a sense of clutter. Bede could feel his mouth curling in distaste.

They grabbed Kell's stuff in armfuls and made several trips to tent number eleven, where they plopped everything on the empty cot, empty except for Bede's new boots, which Kell showed him how to store beneath his own cot.

As Wayne raced happily away, back to his own fortress of green canvas, Kell plopped down onto the cot with his pile of things, and smiled up at Bede.

"My summer just got a fuckton better," said Kell, grinning, his dark hair slipping across his forehead. A satisfied sigh escaped him, those green eyes, that old soul, happy at last.

"Was it bad?" asked Bede, even though he already knew the answer.

"Oh, he's just—" Kell made a waving motion in front of his face. "He's just sort of all over the place. Like his half of the tent was his, and then my half of the tent was also his. You know?"

Bede did know. In a prison cell, you had to draw strong lines about territory, otherwise you'd get walked all over. Kell had probably been doing his best to keep the peace. Only now, he wouldn't have to.

"Guess that cot's yours. That work for you?" For anyone else, Bede would have made the determination, rather than asking, and the other guy could like it or lump it. But for Kell, it was going to be fifty-fifty.

"Sure does." Kell made a little bounce on the cot, which hardly moved nor made a single sound, which showed how sturdy and well-made it was.

While they shared the silence while quickly unpacking, Bede kept a weather eye out in case Galen came by to put the kibosh on the move, and realized how much he'd missed Kell's presence. The quiet companionship of a reasonable man.

He wouldn't say anything about it, because while his friendship with Kell seemed solid, there was no point digging in deeper when it would all come to an end at the end of summer. Or if Bede decided, which he might still do, to take off and do his parole another way.

Finally, when the tent was mostly squared away, a bell rang, the sound echoing through the thick trees.

"That's dinner," said Kell. "C'mon, you won't believe how good the food is."

Kell led Bede through the woods along the path strewn with pine needles. The mess tent hove into view, a long, green-canvas structure with wooden steps leading up to it.

Bede was just about to follow Kell up the stairs, toward the good smell of salt, hot bread, something sweet with sugar, when someone grabbed his elbow from behind. Another idiot who didn't know the rule about not touching—

Bede whirled around, grabbing, and found himself just about nose-to-nose with a very angry Marston. Who didn't seem to care that Bede was a hardened criminal who'd done five years for making and selling and dealing very hard drugs. He was just plain mad, though about what, Bede had no idea.

"Hey, fuck off," he said, prying at Marston's very strong fingers.

"What the hell is going on?" Marston's teeth were bared, and his eyes glittered as he towered over Bede.

"What the fuck do I know?" Bede finally got free of Marston's grasp, and stood above him on the stair, though they were still the same height, since Marston was so tall. "What's your problem?"

"I went to get Kell for dinner, and his stuff was gone."

"Yeah, he moved in with me. So?"

But that, it seemed, was the problem. Marston had a setup just like he liked it, and Bede had come in and shuffled his world around.

"So? I'll tell you so," snapped Marston. "You're the *last* person he needs to be hanging around with."

Marston raised himself even taller, puffing out his chest, a move that was completely unnecessary, as he had enough height already.

He obviously felt Bede was a threat to him. Bede and his friendship with Kell.

Marston was fighting over territory that he didn't need to defend, but in spite of that, Bede wasn't about to back down, not to some lunkhead with delusions of power.

"You want to throw your weight around, buddy?" Bede made a wide gesture. "Come at me."

He couldn't give a shit how much damage a fight would cause the other guy, though he did sense Kell at his side, urgently tugging on his t-shirt. But Bede wasn't about to be pushed around by some guy who'd obviously never had a hard day in his life—

"Hey now."

Inside of a heartbeat, Galen was between them, his back to Marston, the lesser threat, his hands on Bede's chest.

Bede was about to grab Galen and use his weight to send both of them tumbling to the ground, their asses in the dirt, when he saw Galen's expression. He was dead serious, his mouth in a thin, grim line.

"That's enough," said Galen, quite low, as though utterly confident how much weight his words had. Which they did, more weight than either Bede or Marston's muscles and anger. "Quite enough. We don't act like that here. Now what's the problem?"

All of this washed over Bede as he teetered on the edge of a fight where he could let off steam.

Utterly astonished at Galen's lack of fear, and somewhat mesmerized by the pink flush in those cheeks, the sweetness, the prettiness, contrasting with the sternness in those serious gray eyes, Bede let himself be stilled.

"He went and moved Kell into his own tent," said Marston, mouth barely moving, eyes still drilling into Bede's. "Like he has a right to make those kinds of decisions. Plus, if you'd read Kell's file, you'd know what a bad idea that is."

"What difference does it make?" Bede jerked his chin in Marston's direction, dismissal and threat all at once.

Marston lunged at him, pressing Galen between them. Galen, on a step lower than the top of the wooden platform, was smashed against Bede's chest, his hands clawing at Bede's t-shirt to regain his balance.

Bede felt a huff of warm breath, the whisper of a curse, and looked down to see the disbelief in Galen's eyes. The anger and resolution.

"Up you get," said Bede, grabbing Galen's upper arms to tug him to one side so he could get back at Marston.

But Galen held his ground and reached to push them both back at the same time.

"I said that is *enough.*" He glared at both of them. "Bede, you should have asked Gabe. He's the one who decides what tent each parolee is in. Besides—" Galen paused to take a breath. "Wayne's always wanted his own tent, and Bede and Kell are used to being roommates. Maybe this is a good idea. What do you think?"

There was a very long pause as Marston thought about this, then he looked at Kell, who smiled and said, "I think it's a good idea. I'm happy to be rooming with Bede."

"Okay?" asked Galen.

"Okay," said Marston, though he still looked like he was on the edge of being riled up about it.

"Now. Everybody, it's dinnertime, and I, for one, am starving."

Out from the woods came a group of men who looked as though they'd just washed up, were expecting their suppers, and who wouldn't stand for anyone getting in their way. Half of them looked like they'd done hard time, and the other half looked like butter wouldn't melt in their mouths.

Bede had not thought about the other parolees in the valley, other team leads, but of course there would be.

They came up to the wooden platform of the mess tent as if they wanted to mount the steps. Only Marston, Galen, and Bede were still there, in the way, fists clenched, jaws jutted.

"Is there a problem?" asked the man in front, quite calmly. He looked blocky and strong, and didn't seem at all worried about what was going on, confident that he could stop it.

Bede didn't want another argument. He only wanted a hot meal and a time to lie on his cot and stare at the canvas ceiling of his tent before figuring out his next move.

Marston froze too, and the two of them looked each other in the eye. Marston shook his head. Bede nodded. A truce then. At least for now.

"Just an issue about who's bunking with whom, Gabe," said Galen. "We moved Bede and Kell together, leaving Wayne on his own, the way he's always wanted. It's under control now."

"Good," said Gabe. "Now maybe we can put that aside while we have our dinners."

Maybe Bede should have asked for permission to move Kell into his tent. But he hadn't, and it was too late now and Galen hadn't objected. He'd even approved of the change. Which was crazy. Guards in prison would come down hard if they felt their authority had been challenged in any way. But not Galen.

Bede's body shuddered into stillness as he and Marston stepped apart and let the group of men climb the steps into the mess tent. It might have been nice to have that fight and let off steam. On the other hand, whatever was cooking smelled amazing, and there would always be other chances to go toe to toe with Marston, if he had to.

CHAPTER 5

BEDE

B ede moved up the steps to the wooden platform. Galen was
right behind him, silently directing him as to where the line
for the buffet dinner began.

The sizzle beneath his skin, the urge to fight, seemed to dissipate
within Galen's nearness. Normally Bede would have turned that
closeness into a shoving match, because having someone so close that
he could feel their breath on his neck was worthy of retaliation.

But somehow, this time, when Galen took a breath, Bede took a
breath. He felt a flicker drawing him closer, as if there was more to
discover there, but Bede shook this off. It wouldn't do to count on it,
and besides, he was at the buffet line.

The food laid out on a steam table was an array of temptation, so
unlike prison food that for a moment Bede found himself dizzy. To
begin with, there were BBQ ribs with crisp edges, juicy meat. Nothing
dry or gray, like in Wyoming Correctional, where food was
punishment.

Here, the mac and cheese had a crispy crust, rather than consisting
of noodles lying in a soup made of fake cheese. There was warm cornbread, still hot from the oven. Fresh butter in little tiny paper tubs.

Baked beans that looked heavenly. Coleslaw that actually looked appetizing, rather than a gray soup of old cabbage and Miracle Whip.

Bede took too much of everything onto his plate, just about smiling when he sat across from Kell and Marston at one of the long tables. There was probably some sort of pecking order for seating arrangements, but he was too hungry to pay it any mind. He'd figure it out in time. Screw Marston and his scowl. Not worth Bede's time. Not with food in front of him.

In the meanwhile, not paying much attention to the general chatter around him—though he should, he really should, as it was important to get a bead on who everyone was, how important or dangerous they were—he ate. And ate some more until his stomach was pleasantly groaning.

In prison, he'd made himself eat everything on his tray to keep his strength up, no matter how bitter or made of gristle. Here, it was easy. His foodie nature could have a good time, and he'd work off the extra pounds doing whatever stupid shit they asked of him.

"Save room for chocolate cake," said Kell, his voice cutting through the fog of Bede's gluttony. "You don't want to miss out."

"Is every meal like this?" asked Bede, scrubbing his mouth with the back of his hand. He ignored the fact that Marston was still glaring at him.

"Every meal," said Kell. He pointed to the quart bottle of milk in front of him. "You can have some of this if you want."

"No thanks. Iced tea is what I like."

He took a sip, relishing the crisp clear taste of unsweetened tea as he looked around the mess tent, more cozy than spartan, as he scoped out the place. Taking in the placement of the tables, who was sitting with whom, as he had pretty much every day of his life.

Every man was focused on his meal, and a low chatter swirled in the air amidst the clank of a fork on a plate, the clink of ice in a glass. He was going to get spoiled and quickly, too.

The chocolate cake was amazing, as promised, and the general din faded as the chocolate kicked in. Out of the corner of his eye, he noticed someone had gotten up to clear their place.

When that man moved out of the way, Bede could now see that Galen was sitting by himself at the end of the next table over, half-slumped over his slice of cake. He ate slowly, eyes closed, as if he were experiencing a rush of pleasure, a sugar buzz, and it was all too much.

When he opened his eyes, cake finished, he cast a half-sleepy look Bede's way. It was almost a come-hither expression Galen probably didn't know he was making. It was on the verge of being flirty, and Bede looked away. That expression was not on purpose, of course not.

"You coming to the campfire this evening?" Kell asked. "It's totally cool."

Bede looked at Kell, and at Marston on the other side of him, a silent watchdog.

"Sure," he said. Over the prison phone, Kell had told him in detail what the campfire entailed. How much fun it was. All of this had seemed rather lame to Bede, but considering how high-end and lush everything else in the valley was, it probably wouldn't be so bad.

"You might need a jacket," said Kell. "It gets cool when the sun goes down."

"You might need to wash up," said Marston, looking pointedly at Bede's front. "The program provides clean clothes, you know."

Bede looked down. A small smear of bbq sauce was emblazoned right in the middle of his t-shirt. Then he looked up.

Everyone else was wearing crisp, clean snap-button shirts of various colors, cool blue, cool white. He alone was still in his prison-issued, once-white t-shirt.

He alone hadn't showered and shaved because he'd been busy helping Kell move into tent number eleven and there'd not been time.

Before he'd gone into prison, he'd worn high-end clothes and taken pride in his appearance. Now, he stood out, like some newbie who was just asking to get jumped at the first opportunity. But he couldn't show he was embarrassed, no way.

"And you might back the fuck off." Bede looked around. Nobody but Marston had heard him. "Just back the fuck off."

Marston stood up, pushing his chair back with a loud scrape. Bede stood up as well. He wasn't intimidated, even if Marston was half a foot taller, and brawny by anyone's standards.

Every head in the mess tent was turned toward the little tête-à-tête between him and Marston.

"Oh, not again," he heard someone say. Probably Galen, who was up and coming over to them, wading into the melee without any fear whatsoever.

"Get it through your fucking head, Marston," said Bede quite clearly and loudly. There was no point pretending they weren't on the verge of coming to blows. He wanted to say more, but held back from exposing even more about himself in front of a crowd of near-strangers.

"That's enough," said Galen.

He came right around the table to where Bede was. Unafraid.

He looked up at Bede, chin out, eyes glittering. There was a lovely flush to his cheeks, and in his anger he was even prettier than before, pulling Bede's attention to him like the call of a bright blue sky.

"What did I tell you before?" asked Galen, stern. "Marston. Bede. I want you outside. Now."

"Can I come?" asked Kell.

"No," said Bede and Galen at the same time. Marston shook his head.

"We'll see you at the campfire," said Marston.

Following Galen, Bede came out of the mess tent into the slanting shadows of evening. Long shadows of trees cut along the ground in rows, like bars in a cage.

Galen took them all the way to the gravel parking lot, then stopped and looked at both of them.

"We don't get into fights here," said Galen. "What is the problem? Marston? Bede?"

Neither of them said anything, but only glared at each other. Bede realized he was breathing a bit hard and took a deep breath.

A fight with Marston seemed the obvious next step, but Bede didn't like feeling so out of control. Not to mention, he was distracted and intrigued by Galen. By his lack of fear. The way he stood between

44

the two of them, quite calm, as if he felt his very presence was enough to make them stop.

"Are you fighting over Kell?" Galen asked now.

Bede knew it was a question of dominance *about* Kell. About who was his friend and who wasn't. In prison, you always had to fight your way to the top of the pecking order. For some reason, Marston was acting as if that was what he was doing, too. As if he had to fight Bede to keep Kell safe.

Bede could sense Kell watching them through the trees.

That stopped him. He was in a new world with new rules and he'd not even paused to figure them out.

If he was going to give himself time and space to decide what to do next, he needed to stay out of trouble. And that included not giving Marston the slap-down he so obviously needed. Kell deserved a stable world, not two guys fighting over him.

"We're not," said Bede, short. "But Marston here's got it in his head that I'm a danger to the kid. I'm not, you know." He settled himself, made himself breathe slower, stop glaring. Uncurl his fists. "Kell is like a brother to me. You read his file, I'm sure. I'm always looking out for him. Always."

Marston's eyes lifted. Then he paused. Bede looked over his shoulder to see what he was looking at.

Yes, Marston had seen Kell, and once again, his expression softened like butter in the sun. The guy was crazy in love with Kell. Part of that crazy had taken Bede as a threat, even though he probably knew better.

"Hey," said Bede, more softly, drawing Marston's attention to him. "I'm just his friend. That's all. I could see that Wayne has been a problem about sharing. Kell and I know how to room together. Wayne's got his own tent. He's a happy camper now. Literally."

Bede heard Galen's half-smothered snort of a laugh. He found himself returning that laugh, a half-smile, then he had to put the brakes on that to deal with the situation at hand.

"I'm not here to get in anyone's way, least of all *Kell's*." He said with a small shrug. He emphasized Kell's name to draw Marston's focus to the most important part of all this. To help Galen by defusing the situation. "He's going to be upset if we keep going at each other like this. You know?"

"Okay," said Marston. His shoulders relaxed a little, and he too took a deep breath.

Bede could almost see the thoughts behind Marston's hard eyes. Love for Kell battled with his animosity toward Bede. Obviously love had won this round, but Bede would make a special point to stay out of Marston's way, just the same.

"Okay," said Bede. He held out his hand for Marston to shake and Marston did, though his lip curled in derision.

"Okay," said Galen, with a hearty sigh. "This was not in my job description. Well—" He shook his head. "Actually it is. So. Marston. Go look after your guy. And Bede? Maybe a shower is a good idea."

"Got it."

It was almost as bad as prison, being told what to do. How to act. But if he was going to get through this, he needed to buckle down and learn what the rules were. Abide by them. Then figure out what came next.

For a moment, the smile that brightened Galen's eyes made him seem like a regular guy, rather than someone set on making Bede's life difficult.

So far in the valley, it hadn't been anywhere near hellish as prison. Far from it, in fact. Not to mention that the idea of a hot shower, especially the way Kell had described it to him, and the fact that Bede had seen the high-end luxury of those showers first-hand, made a very fine prospect.

"Maybe I will take that shower," he said. After all, he owed this chance, this rustic interlude, to Kell and, for that reason, Bede was going to do his best not to cause another ruckus.

"Good idea," said Marston.

"Hey!"

Marston's lip curled and maybe he was laughing at Bede a little bit. "Just joking," Marston said. "But as Kell would say, the showers are heavenly."

A hand of peace, maybe? Well, Bede would take it.

"See you all at the fire pit," said Galen, as if the quick talk was enough to settle the matter. And, unlike prison, it obviously was enough. There was no penalty, no threats of time in solitary, no black mark on his record.

A little dumbfounded, Bede, on his own, trundled through the woods, following the path that led to his tent.

Once there, he sat on his cot and pulled off the bbq-stained t-shirt. It was the same shirt he'd worn while in prison, part of his uniform there, along with the thin canvas slacks. Those damn slip-on sneakers.

Clutching the t-shirt, he held it to his nose. It smelled like sweat, the dank, cloying smell of prison soap, old onions. A prison smell. Not a valley smell. No wonder Marston had been up in arms about him. He smelled like bad news.

Well, he was bad news. A criminal with a hard background and the tattoos to prove it. A history of drug dealing. A rap sheet a mile long.

Compared to him, Kell must seem like a fawn in the grass, hiding for its life. Bede, the sharp-toothed wolf.

In prison, their relationship had served a purpose, but suppose he really meant it that Kell was like a brother to him? Well, maybe Kell was like a brother to him, even if only for a summer.

What would it hurt? Would anyone care if he started acting like a nice guy?

Probably not. Least of all Galen, who seemed to enjoy laughing at Bede's very small jokes, and who seemed smart enough to see right through to the real Bede. Like he'd be easy to be with. Easy to trust.

It was too bad that Bede had to keep Galen at arm's length because he had a great laugh, half snigger, half belly laugh. Like he blissed out when things got funny.

And the blush Galen had, pink as a rose. Soft as a petal, that skin of his. It must be. As if Galen had barely started shaving, though he was obviously old enough to be a team lead for a trio of ex-cons.

Bede needed to set his sights elsewhere, and pronto. Five years was long enough to go without affection, without sex, so maybe now that he was out from behind bars, was it time to pick up the slack? Sure, but with who?

Never mind. He'd figure it out eventually and, all the while, tell himself that it wasn't scary as shit to take a risk with someone new.

First, a shower.

He gathered his shower things and managed to stumble through the woods like he had no sense of direction until he found the facilities.

Everything in the showers had looked rustic when Galen had taken them on a tour around the place, but Bede had been in enough five star hotels to know high quality when he saw it. The faucet handles at the sink gleamed low with expensive brushed nickel.

The shower heads in the stalls were quality too, and when he turned the shower on, it dispensed hot water right away. Steam roiled up, and he got undressed as fast as he could and stepped beneath the stream, almost rising on his bare toes to get that clean, hot water all over him.

Other than Winston, of all the things he'd missed while in prison, amidst the lack of privacy, the shitty food, the constant sounds all around, a good, hot shower had been at the top of the list.

This was his second moment alone in five years. The second time he'd experienced the lack of clatter in his ears, with only the soft sounds of the water swirling around him.

As he lathered himself all over, reveling in the clean smell of soap, a faint pine scented breeze came through the screened-in transom high up in the shower stall. It rocked him on his feet and he had to place his palm against the wall of the shower stall to hold himself steady.

On the evening before the disastrous drug deal gone wrong, Winston and he had taken a shower together, as they often did before sex, after sex, and during.

That time, though, it had just been a shower, the closeness of their bodies, chests touching, thighs brushing, creating a swirl of intimacy around them. They bonded anew amidst bubbles of soap, the scent of lavender, the brush of a kiss on Bede's shoulder meant to comfort and connect rather than arouse.

That was one of the things Bede had loved about Winston, among a thousand other things, his ability to create a life that was more than just the thrust and grind, getting off, getting high. The facade of a drug dealer's life paled in comparison to one simple touch of Winston's hand. The stroke of fingers on Bede's cheek. A sleepy smile over early morning coffee.

Bede had disguised his joy in all of this beneath bluster and a sleek three-piece suit. But Winston knew better. He'd always known better and had told Bede as much with a single glance.

The pain of the memory of that day, the day he'd lost Winston, shocked him now, even as the water streamed down in a cloud around him.

In prison, he had not let himself feel any of this. It was as if the valley, its gentleness, was slicing through that bluster, right through the stone walls Bede had erected. Cutting to the bone of him, making him feel it for the very first time. The grief. The loss of love.

He scrubbed at his face, and shook himself all over, pretending that he had soap in his eyes and that was why they were watering.

The irony of it. After five years of concrete walls and razor wire and bad food and the cruelty of guards—none of this had broken him. But give him one hot shower, and he was crumbling into pieces.

He needed to get hold of himself. The lushness of the valley, the slow pace, the good food, the clean sheets that awaited him come nightfall—surely all of this was a fluke and not meant to last?

CHAPTER 6
GALEN

Right after the arrival of his little team, Galen took them on a tour of the valley. He started with the mess tent, then the first aid hut, then the showers, and was sure he'd never met a more disinterested bunch.

According to their files, Toby and Owen had been friends in prison.

Owen was the sharp-eyed one with a sneaky smile that came and went without any reason that Galen could figure out. Toby was a little younger, with dirty-dishwater hair and sharp shoulders and ribs that showed when even the slightest breeze flattened his shirt to his torso.

As Galen led them along the newly widened path to the wooden paddock, painted cedar red, and small storage barn, they stuck close together and dragged their feet, like they were bored school children on a field trip.

When shown the pastures beyond which was a small band of horses grazed in the distance, they didn't seem to care.

They weren't even impressed when he took them to the dock that jutted out into Half-Moon Lake, which, in Galen's mind, was the prettiest bit of water he ever had seen.

The blue water of the lake lapped at the pylons of the dock. Halfway out, the dock became a floating one, as the lake sank to cold depths quite quickly. At the far edges of the lake, pine trees stood, green-topped sentinels, and beyond that loomed the long, gray edge of Guipago Ridge.

Teams in the past, he'd heard, had swimming parties, but it was his secret wish to take himself down there on a moonless night and go for a silent, solitary swim in the dark. By himself. Just like he used to do in the pond back on his dad's farm.

Not that he'd ask them, but not one of his team would want to go with him. Especially not Obadiah "Bede" Deacon.

Bede stuck out. He acted differently than Toby and Owen. As he followed behind the other two, he watched with silent, dark blue eyes. Like he was taking mental notes, but didn't want to look like he was interested.

When they got to Half Moon Lake, Bede stood on the shoreline, holding his hands at his sides. He was looking over the mostly calm surface of the lake as if watching for the thing that might kill him if he wasn't on the alert.

Tension radiated off shoulders that flexed beneath the prison-issued t-shirt, his whole body stiff, eyes searching, casting back and forth.

Which must be what five years behind bars did to a man, not to mention the many years spent dealing in drugs and spending ill-gotten gains. Still, Bede was just about the last person Galen would invite to go swimming with him.

"We are going to get some kayaks soon," Galen told them. "Or maybe it's canoes."

Nobody answered him.

At the end of the tour, Galen took his team members to their respective tents.

Toby and Owen were in tent number twelve, and Bede was by himself in tent number eleven.

All of them seemed a little dubious about being dropped off without supervision beneath the sweetly spreading arms of pine trees, but it was a clean break Galen was willing to make. They needed to learn sometime, and it would help them grow into independence and responsibility.

Galen had only heard of two parolees who'd left the program. One of them was Kurt, who'd tried to kill another parolee by shoving him into a woodchopper. The other, Tom, had a fiancée and a future father-in-law, not to mention, by all versions of the story, the cutest baby in the world.

As for now, Galen was stuck with who he'd been assigned and they with him, and either he would succeed at being a team lead or he would fail. In the meantime, he hoped the members of his team would all shower and change before dinner because they smelled like he remembered Wyoming Correctional smelling, when he'd taken his training.

After he'd dropped his team off at their tents, he went back to his own tent. Sitting on his cot, then scooting back to lean against the metal headboard, he went over the files on each member of his team one more time.

The files didn't show him anything he didn't already know. That Toby and Owen were probably not very smart, having decided a life of breaking into other people's houses was a good idea. And that Bede was too smart to have chosen a life of crime, yet he had.

Bede's file mentioned a woman named Lorraine Sheffield, who was his aunt, and a Winston Ludlow, though Galen couldn't figure out who he was. Still, it was soothing to sit and read everything, as though none of it had any connection to him at all.

However, the little bit of stillness he'd gathered to himself was completely undone because by the time dinner rolled around and he came up to the mess tent, a fight between Bede and Marston was just about to explode.

The two men were poised on the wooden platform in front of the mess tent, chest to chest, fists curled, invisible sparks jumping between them. They were on the verge of coming to blows as though they'd known each other for years and their mutual dislike was finally exposed in a cloud of rage.

Without thinking, Galen stepped between them, pushing Marston away, pressing his palms on Bede's chest.

Encountering solid muscle beneath that white t-shirt as he looked up at Bede, his own breath started coming fast and his heart was beating so hard, he barely remembered saying, *That is enough* and *What is the problem?*

Everything was on the verge of becoming a royal shitshow and every minute he expected that Gabe was going to step in and stop things.

But while several parolees were there, they only watched. As if they fully expected that Galen was man enough to handle it. That, as a team lead, it was his *duty* to handle it.

When he finally was able to find out that Marston was mad because Bede had taken it upon himself to rearrange who slept where, Marston was incensed, and as Galen looked up into that angry face, he could see the passion there, the love Marston had for Kell.

As for Bede, it was like shoving against a brick wall. Up close like that, smashed between the two men, he thought he was going to get smothered.

Yet, even as he shoved to get free, traces of Bede's scent stayed with him, traces of energy and anger and distrust that seemed to press into his skin.

Gabe's intervention had come late in the battle, but Galen was glad of his steady presence, though by the time Galen had calmed both men down, and a blanket of stillness settled around him, Galen thought his heart would have slowed down.

It was still thumping when he sat down with his tray of good BBQ and fixings, digging into his meal, exchanging pleasant everyday chat with Royce, even as he watched his small team out of the corner of his eye.

Feeling his sweat drying around the back of his neck and beneath his arms, he considered the fact that maybe he wasn't cut out for being a team lead. He certainly couldn't deal with fights breaking out every day. That wasn't what he wanted his summer to be like.

He had to break up another fight after dinner, though the short, terse conversation among the three of them, Marston, Bede, and him, seemed to clear the air a bit more.

He could even say it was interesting watching the way Bede's mind seemed to work, especially when Marston told him to take a shower. There was lightning in Bede's eyes, dark eyes like hammered blue stone, as he seemed to make corner-sharp decisions about how he was going to keep the peace between him and Marston.

Both men seemed to care for Kell a great deal. Marston was in love with Kell, obviously. Who knew how Bede really felt, though he seemed to be struggling between pretending he didn't care and admitting that he did care. A lot. *He's like a brother to me.*

Well, Galen could go along with that, and maybe this was the hump he had to get over before settling into the job he'd signed up for. He just had to remind himself that just like on the farm, everything in the valley would have its own season, and that time and water could wear away stone. All he had to do was be observant enough to see how the dynamics on his team unfolded.

In the meantime, he went back to his tent after dinner, his little green canvas sanctuary, unlaced his boots, took them off, and put his feet up, head on the pillow, stretched out on his cot, while he went over the files one more time.

Nothing new popped out except that Winston Ludlow was the only member of Bede's gang to get shot and die.

Too bad for Bede. Too bad for Winston. People who attended drug deals in unsavory back alleys kind of deserved what they got. Didn't they?

He must have dozed off, the open folders slipping from his chest to the wood platform beneath his cot. When his eyes flew open, he realized how dark it was getting, and that he might be late for the evening's campfire, surely one of the sweetest points of the day, at least to hear Gabe, Royce, and Marston tell it.

Hustling, he stashed the papers in his little storage shelf, then put on and laced up his work boots. Grabbing his jean jacket on his way out of his tent, he made his way through the shadowed woods to the fire pit.

There was no telling whether the night would be warm or whether the darkness would cool it down. He put the jacket down on a bale of hay and gathered up dry sticks and twigs before going to the fire pit.

There was someone already there, skillfully stacking logs. Galen recognized him as Blaze, a member of Gabe's team.

In spite of briefly having met the other parolees in the valley on Sunday, Galen hadn't worked much with any of them, and was surprised to see Blaze working away like an ordinary citizen. Someone who might be a decent guy. Gabe seemed to like him, and Blaze was a whiz at finding just the right shape and size of sticks for roasting marshmallows for s'mores.

"Here and here," said Galen as he handed Blaze his hastily gathered sticks.

"This one and this, yes. But not that one." Blaze tossed a few sticks onto the pile of logs that Gabe was just kneeling to light. "You did good, though."

Blaze laughed, his smile wide, like he'd not just gotten let out of prison after two years behind bars. So nonchalant. So *whatever* about it all.

This was not an attitude Galen had ever felt comfortable with, but maybe he could understand how prison might cause Blaze to think that way. To make all ex-cons think that way.

However, he couldn't change any of them, and it probably wasn't smart to spend so much time focusing on something he couldn't change.

It was only for the rest of the summer, anyway. He'd do the job he'd signed up to do and move on. But to where? Back to the farm?

To combat wasting any more energy on the overwhelming choices that loomed in front of him, Galen stood by the fire pit and focused on the small flames licking at the small teepee of kindling that Blaze had arranged and set alight.

The air was bright and warm by the fire, the gold and orange and blue flames making the night seem darker all of a sudden.

Galen shivered. Maybe he'd need his jean jacket after all.

CHAPTER 7
GALEN

Going back to the hay bale, Galen reached for his jacket, almost bumping into Bede, who gave Galen a quick glance, then laid his own jean jacket next to Galen's on the hay bale.

"I can't tell whether I'm hot or cold," Bede said, as he sat down on a hay bale one over from the jackets.

Galen sat on a hay bale on the other side of the jackets. He was close enough to the fire to feel its warmth but far enough away to feel like he was in the shadows, so he could watch without being seen.

Bede showered and shaved and changed out of his prison garb and into the uniform of the valley: blue jeans and blue chambray shirt.

Firelight flickered off the curves and angles of the circle and triangle tattoos on one side of his neck. Galen had noticed them before in the photos in Bede's file, but now they were up close. Quite fresh looking and visible.

With dark hair sleek against his head, and a freshly shaven jaw, Bede looked just about as dapper as a man could. As if he'd not just spent the last five years in prison for making and selling drugs.

Maybe Bede didn't realize Galen was studying him, didn't know that Galen could see, quite clearly, an odd vulnerability in Bede's expression as he cast his gaze over the fire pit.

It was an ordinary setting of a newly built campfire, a few men hovering over the growing flames as if trying to be helpful when only one man was needed to tend the fire and another man to lay out the supplies for making s'mores.

To Bede, after five years in prison, it must have seemed like he'd landed on the moon or found himself in some faraway, unknown country.

Galen watched Bede settle forward, elbows on his knees like a man who has arrived early for a meeting and doesn't quite know what the meeting was about. The cloth of his shirt along his arms pulled across muscle.

Galen tried to look away. It wasn't right to stare, even if he couldn't be seen staring, but Bede, in the glow of the firelight, seemed transformed. From the top of his short-cropped dark hair gleaming in the firelight to the new boots on his feet, he was a new man.

Slowly, he sat up and rolled up the sleeves of his blue chambray snap-button shirt. An ordinary garment, pale blue against the tan of his forearm, veins leaving long thin shadows that trapped Galen's eyes.

Zeke had forearms like that, long, densely muscled. Casually indifferent to his own prowess, it seemed, when he'd cross his arms over his chest, and now Bede was doing the same thing. A shift of his head, dark eyelashes catching the light, a sheen of moisture on his lips. A flash of teeth as Bede took a breath.

Galen looked away. Hard. He'd just about succeeded in keeping his gaze pointed in the other direction when he heard Bede laugh under his breath. And had to look again.

Blaze was passing out roasting sticks and holding a bag of marshmallows, and Gabe was passing out chocolate bars and graham crackers.

Bede was taking the items like he couldn't believe what he was seeing. Then he looked right at Gabe and said, "What am I, a ten-year-old kid?"

It wasn't funny, but it was. The way he said it, low, his voice burry soft. Self-deprecating in a way that surprised him made Galen feel he could just about picture how Bede might have looked as a young boy. Gangly legs. Wearing a striped shirt, for some reason. Just about as cute as a cut button and ready to laugh. Smiling because he was going to make Galen laugh, too.

Galen snorted in spite of himself, surprised at how easily Bede made him laugh when, in reality, he wasn't even trying. And then thought about the last time he himself had roasted a marshmallow for a s'more. Ages ago. In another life. At summer camp. Once. Long ago.

"It'll be too sweet now," said Galen, unable to stop himself from responding, though he did have an unexpected impulse to share memories of summer camp.

"No, it won't."

He wasn't expecting a reply, but Bede sounded so sure, like he knew he didn't have to convince Galen at all, because it wouldn't be too sweet. It would be perfect.

Filled with a warmth that he couldn't tie down or dismiss, Galen pushed the marshmallow onto the stick and leaned forward to roast it.

The flames were dancing about, too high in places, too low in others. The coals were too young. Not quite right for roasting yet, quickly sending the marshmallow to brown in some spots, leaving it white and raw in others.

Gabe must have been watching because he came around the fire and poked it. Made the flames behave.

Galen tried once more, shifting on his hay bale, focusing on this task like it was his job. Ignoring Bede doing exactly the same. In echo.

Around the campfire, the other ex-cons did the same. And now they were a tighter circle, on hay bales, in Adirondack chairs, leaning forward, joined by the glow on faces, firelight flicking, keeping the shadows at bay. Just about, but not quite, transforming them from parolees into men settling in for an old-fashioned campfire after a long, hard day's work.

Galen had forgotten how this felt, but then, his summer camp days were years in the past.

Was the bonding by firelight on purpose? Some plan of Gabe's? Or was it just happening because that was the nature of fire, with memories of times gone by when evenings by the fire created a connection between those who gathered around it.

In the corner of Galen's vision, Bede was limned by the firelight. Focused on his s'more. Assembling the melted chocolate, taking the golden-seared marshmallow between his fingers. Making that sandwich.

Then Bede bit into it, eyes half closed, long shadows from his eyelashes dark on his cheeks.

His face was flushed from the warmth of the fire, the rush of sugar. Shoulders bunching beneath the pale blue shirt as he leaned forward, he was half crouched like he was preparing to spring up and dance around the fire.

Galen made himself look away. It was as if the campfire had cast a spell, and now he was inside of that spell, having thoughts that raced around inside of him, tightening his belly, his thighs.

"Your marshmallow is on fire," said Bede in a smoky, soft voice.

Unsettled by Bede's closeness and the gentle interaction between them, Galen quickly blew out the circle of gold light around the end of his stick. His marshmallow was practically melted, but it was perfect.

He assembled his s'more and chomped into it, all the while studiously ignoring that Bede was watching. He had to lick his lips free of melted chocolate and followed that by placing the backs of his fingers to his mouth to catch strings of fast cooling marshmallow.

"Do you want another?" Gabe called out, still industriously handing out supplies.

"No thanks."

One s'more was enough. Sitting so near to Bede was enough. Watching the muscles flex in Bede's powerful forearms was quite enough. Watching Bede lick his lips was *more* than enough.

His whole body went still as his mind attempted to process the signals being sent out from somewhere inside of him. Interest. A bit of desire. The idea that his loneliness might be met with companionship.

All of which was ridiculous. He was a team lead to the men placed in his charge. He could not afford to mess that up by having feelings—or whatever this was—about Bede, of all people.

Confusion warred with a sudden spurt of decisiveness.

He could leave, though it would look strange if he leaped up and stormed out of the circle of warmth to go sit in his tent by himself.

He could quit the program, but then where would he go? There was no job for him up at the guest ranch, though he supposed he could beg Leland to find him something.

There were also the renters ensconced at the farm, so he couldn't go back there. It would be hellishly cruel to evict them, besides, and he couldn't afford to return their deposit, anyway.

There was nothing for him to do but to stick it out till the end of summer. Earn his pay by being professional about every aspect of every single day. Galen just needed to get a grip.

Kell came up to Bede, smiling, a smear of chocolate on his cheek that he wiped away with the cuff of his snap-button shirt. Kell settled on the hay bale next to Bede, and then Marston came up to Galen and gestured that he wanted to talk to him.

Curious, Galen followed Marston a little way into the trees, which were lit by firelight, but embraced with a thin cloak of cool darkness.

"What's up?" asked Galen. Maybe they needed him to go to the mess tent for more supplies, which would give him a chance to walk it off. Straighten himself out.

"I just wanted to say—" Marston stopped, and seemed to shake himself. "I wanted to apologize for earlier. It was uncalled for. I talked with Kell, really talked with him, and he explained everything. About him and Bede. It won't happen again."

Galen wasn't really surprised that Marston was man enough to apologize. He'd met Marston the summer before, worked with him a few times. Marston was a bit of a dark horse, but a decent man.

"You love him," said Galen, the words slipping out. "You want the best for him. You're looking out for him."

"I do and I am." Marston looked at his feet for a moment, the long shadows cast by the flames shifting around him. Then he looked at Galen, straight on. "I might be a little bit of an asshole sometimes, but I didn't mean to cause trouble."

"It's all right," said Galen. "Thank you for the apology."

Together, they looked back at the campfire where Bede and Kell were sharing space on the hay bale. Kell was talking, his face animated, hands moving.

Galen could barely hear what he was saying, the silence in the forest all around was so deep. In response, Bede had his shoulders lowered, head dipped down, eyes focused on Kell. *He's like a brother to me.*

Then Kell jumped up, gesturing with his hands. About what, Galen didn't know, but Kell just about tumbled into the fire. Bede's arm reached out, steadying Kell with a gentle hand. Protective.

Marston believed what Kell had told him about Bede. Kell, who was a sweet, smart kid, was laughing with Bede like they were best friends. Bede's low laugh eased over to Galen, and for a moment, everything seemed normal, like Bede was a regular guy, and Galen wasn't surrounded by parolees.

There might be something good in Bede, then. Unseen. Below the surface. Or was this another example of a criminal being made docile in certain conditions?

But that couldn't be it. Bede, as well as the others, could leave anytime they wanted. They chose to stay. Chose to participate in the ancient ritual of gathering around a blazing fire. Chose to participate in roasting marshmallows and making s'mores and eating with the joy of little kids.

All of this was part of what Gabe and the others had told him on Sunday. About having a little empathy and giving it a chance.

Still, they hadn't mentioned that Galen would see Bede in the fire-light, skin glowing, sparks of joy in his eyes as he talked with Kell.

Well, listened mostly. Sparks that he might have wanted to hide had he known how obvious they were.

Galen pulled his attention away.

It would be better to focus on the job at hand, on the work that needed to get done that summer, and to pull himself away from the connection between him and Bede that would be so easy to form.

In another life, they could have been friends. In a different summer, when he wasn't responsible for his team, and Bede's presence didn't make him want to respond in inappropriate ways.

Which meant that he needed to do his best to act naturally.

"I think I'll have another s'more," said Galen, mentally hitching up his overalls. Not that he needed more sugar, certainly. But it was warm by the fire, and it was nice to be sitting still, watching deep gold, dark blue flames leaping about. Amidst a circle of men, connected by something so simple, so ancient, as a fire.

Kell returned to Marston's side on a hay bale a little way back from the fire pit. As for Bede, he was staring into the flames like he was looking for a secret wish he'd long ago lost track of.

Galen distracted himself by creating a list of what needed doing. What Gabe had asked the team to take care of.

The issue of knapweed was at the top of the list. The weed was creeping into the compound from the east, and a little bit from the west, where the wind had carried the seeds.

BLM and the forestry service used chemicals to get rid of the weed, but Leland didn't want that in the valley. Everything had to be non-toxic—

Galen looked up, his gaze caught by movement.

Bede had left the light of the fire and was walking into the woods, alone along the path that led to the tents, hands at his sides, sleeves still rolled up.

"Is he going without a flashlight?" asked Galen aloud. "And he forgot his jacket."

"I'll make sure he's okay," said Kell, jumping up to grab the forgotten jacket. Behind him, Marston gave Galen a nod, and lifted his hand to show that he was prepared to follow Kell.

"Thanks," said Galen. "Make sure he brings his flashlight next time."

As the silence settled, Galen turned it over in his mind. That he'd been worried, sure, that made sense. Bede was one of his team, after all, and it was his duty to look after each one of them.

Across the fire pit, Toby and Owen were chucking back s'mores like two men who had no concerns about tomorrow. They both had flashlights tucked next to them on their shared hay bale.

Maybe once Kell told Bede he'd need a flashlight, he'd be back to join the campfire. But he never came back, even though everyone sat around the fire for another hour until it got truly dark.

CHAPTER 8

BEDE

Sitting around a campfire on a warm summer's evening was just about the last thing that Bede expected to be doing. At least not on the very day he'd been released from prison.

During those five years behind cement walls and razor-wire topped fencing, he'd kept himself distracted by imagining this very day, the day he'd be paroled. It would be a Monday. Midsummer. He'd be putting on a new suit. Taking one last look in the polished metal prison mirror in his cell.

Then he'd be stepping outside the gate. Returning to Denver. Registering his address. Showing proof of employment that did not involve drugs in any way.

One of his employment options was to have been taking over running a liquor store that his cousin owned on Colfax in Denver. It was a fairly grotty liquor store, but it had high foot traffic, and a high probability of him having to carry a gun on his person on account of the high likelihood of the store getting robbed on a regular basis. His parole team would never allow the gun.

What was the name of the place again? Blackjacks or something.

His plan had been to take a Greyhound to Denver and pick up work like nothing had happened. Swear to his parole officer that, of course, he was not carrying a gun, because that was prohibited in his conditions of release.

Well, he wouldn't have to worry about that now, would he. All he was going to have to worry about was not getting lost as he made his way through the woods sans flashlight and without a very good map in his head as to where his tent was.

Which wasn't like him. He usually had a very good memory for keeping track of his position in the world, but then, most of his life had been lived on the same streets, in the same neighborhoods, since the day of his birth.

Here, in Wyoming, everything was strange and new, and the darkness seemed to ooze through the trees like something was pressing on it from the other side.

It wasn't like him to be itchy and fidgety, ever, sitting at the campfire with nothing to do. He could feel his body attempting to digest all the sugar he'd eaten, and it had just about driven him crazy. Even Kell's bright presence, and the flickering fire, hadn't been enough. And certainly Galen's covert, slightly intense glances his way didn't help.

He needed to get up and move. So that's what he did, catching Galen's startled glance at him as he strode into the woods.

Like he knew where he was going. Like he had any idea what would happen next.

In the past, he knew what any moment was likely to bring. Cut some cocaine and hire a guy to deliver it. Show up at a glitzy gala event wearing a freshly pressed tuxedo, one of several that he owned, and while the wives and girlfriends downed champagne, make several handshake deals for the coming year. Arrange for more cocaine to be delivered. Check out the meth trade and back away slowly.

Money had rolled across his palms. He'd stashed most of it into several bank accounts. Some, he'd tucked away, filling old coffee cans with gold and silver coins. Those, along with a black plastic bag of unmarked tens and twenties, he'd tucked in the shed in the backyard of his Aunt Lorraine's house out in Aurora.

He'd even leased a lovely blue BMW convertible, getting a new one each year.

All that was gone, now. Seized. Impounded. Except for the coffee cans and black plastic bags of money, which he hadn't told anyone about.

After he'd been arrested, he'd never had the chance to retrieve that money. Now that he was released, he could have gotten a quick bus to Denver and dug them up, but that would have drawn attention to Aunt Lorraine, which she would not appreciate, and probably get handcuffs slapped on him again for holding back from the cops.

As for now, his pockets empty, he shuffled through the woods, finally finding his tent, undoing the zipper, thinking it wouldn't keep anyone out, bear or man, and fumbled for the overhead light.

A pair of moths danced crazily around the bulb like they were waiting for him to join them. But he had no energy now and sat on his cot and looked down at the new work boots on his feet and thought about what he might have told Winston, had he been there.

Winston Ludlow had danced into Bede's life right after high school, danced out again, and then danced in again, like a tan, bright-eyed will-o'-the-wisp with a sharp toothed smile and a penchant for romance.

The last time Winston had danced in, he'd stayed, always at Bede's side, loyal, funny. Sweet.

He was a crack shot, and didn't mind getting his hands dirty, though he always made sure his hands were groomed and clean afterwards.

In bed, Winston was confident and slow, never rushing pleasure, naked on top of the bedclothes. Afterwards, they'd smoke a clove cigarette, or maybe a little weed, the breeze drifting across them both as the sweat dried on their skin.

Sometimes Bede missed Winston so much, it blunted everything else, all feeling, all sensation, all joy.

He lost Winston in that shootout in that alley in Denver. He'd never been able to find out where the bullet that killed Winston had come from. He'd never wanted to ask, either, so as not to draw attention to himself, or give away his very earnest desire to stab the one whose hand had been on the trigger.

Winston had died alone, beneath the hands of some dumb fucking cop fucking up CPR, making Winston choke on his own blood. Bede, in handcuffs, couldn't get close enough to help. He remembered screaming, throat raw with rage, as they'd shoved him in a cop car and trundled him away.

The circle of blood around Winston's head as he lay in that alley had been a near perfect halo. Winston had been no saint in life, and in death, he surely hadn't been good enough to end up in heaven. But Bede had loved him, heart and soul, and missed him with every other breath, even when it was hard to breathe.

His heart had turned off, and with nowhere for his anger to go, mostly he just sucked it down and absorbed it. Ate it, jagged bites that cut into his soul.

And now, he was all alone, for the first time in his entire life.

Before prison, back home, there'd always been something going on, mostly drug-related. Everyone in the neighborhood knowing everyone's business.

In prison, the guards were always at you. Yelling. Shoving. Making you do stupid shit like jumping jacks in the hallway outside the cafeteria, just to show you that they were the boss of you.

But here? The tent was a small cocoon in a vast forest of darkness, and not a single soul was there to witness if he cried over Winston. He never had. And now, maybe his body had forgotten how, because he could only slump on the cot and grow more aware of the sounds beyond the canvas tent.

There was a weird scree-scree sound that he imagined might be the branches of trees, high up where the wind tossed them, brushing against each other. The sound of water from somewhere. A high, thin wailing sound that he had no idea what it was.

Then there was the smell of warm canvas cooling, oddly comforting and calming.

Slowly, he undid the laces on his boots, and then, on impulse, pulled off the new socks he'd been given.

Then, in a daze, he went out of the tent, and down the wooden steps, till his bare feet touched the earth.

The solid feel of the earth, the tickle of grass, the scrape of a leaf along the side of his foot, all of these sensations compiled together, completely different from how he'd imagined it might be while in prison.

Behind bars, in the yard, in the dining hall, you never went bare-foot. He'd even had special flip-flops to wear in the shower, though it was anybody's guess where those were now.

He'd left everything behind when he'd gotten paroled. Just before he'd been escorted to the release door, he'd handed out books and socks and cigarettes and packets of Ramen with princely largess. Like it mattered at all that he should continue keeping up appearances, maintaining connections.

He'd not had very many of those connections while in prison. One of his strongest connections had been with an erstwhile cellie named Ellis. He'd gone and got himself thrown into solitary, and Bede had never seen him after that.

Bede had heard that Ellis had gone to a guest ranch to do his parole. Which, now that he thought about it, could be the guest ranch on the other side of the hill from where Bede was. But did Bede really want to open up that particular door?

His other connection had been Kell who, though still so young, had managed to pull strings in Bede's heart. He'd probably smiled his sweet smile at the parole board, flashing it around like silver, and had not only gotten Bede out of prison, but had also landed him in such a place, doing his parole. Standing barefooted in the darkness, staring up at the sky, the coolness of stars bathing him from head to toe.

What would Galen think if he saw Bede now?

Galen seemed a little uptight, maybe high strung.

He was the kind of guy who would stop at a four-way intersection at midnight, even if there was no one around. He was the kind of guy that Bede would normally have looked down his nose at, just the way Galen had looked down his nose at Bede.

And yet.

And yet they'd had a moment around the campfire when Bede had said out loud what he'd been thinking. That eating a s'more made him feel like a ten-year-old boy when the world was new and the drug world was just a flicker on the periphery of his vision.

In turn, Galen's eyes had brightened, sweetening his expression. Something shifted across his face, like he understood exactly what Bede meant beneath the words he'd actually said. And that Galen, too, had the same feeling of being a ten-year-old boy.

He'd seemed on the verge of saying something about it, but had stopped himself.

And Bede, who had been leaning in to hear what Galen had to say, had to snap himself to attention. A moment shared over a sticky summertime treat for kids did not a friendship make. Did not a connection make, even.

Except for the fact that Galen had been very brave to step between Bede and Marston and stop a fight, there was nothing between himself and a guy who walked around with an invisible stick up his ass.

Bede needed to pull himself together and keep his eyes on the prize, which was a certificate of completion at the end of summer. And however flimsy that might seem, the promise of that certificate felt like the only thing keeping him from returning to Denver and the drug trade.

Out of the woods stepped two figures. One was Kell. Bede could tell that by the chatter.

The other, by the looming height, was Marston walking Kell home, like the utterly hopelessly in love romantic that he was.

"What are you doing, Bede?" Kell called out, hurrying up to Bede, his face lit from the single bulb inside the tent. "Are you barefoot?"

Marston stopped just a half foot behind Kell, his eyes appraising Bede, though he didn't say anything.

"You can't be barefoot in prison, you know," said Bede, giving the most obvious answer, to hide everything else that he'd been feeling. "It's just something I wanted to do." If he made light of it, they would never know how much it mattered.

"Galen was asking after you," said Kell, handing Bede his jacket.

"He said to bring a flashlight next time. It can get awfully dark in these woods."

"So I've learned," said Bede. His world tilted a little at the thought of Galen being worried about him, though probably he was only doing it because it was his job as team lead.

Even if there had been more to it, Bede wasn't about to go down that road. Making any kind of connection to someone who could make a single phone call and have Bede back behind bars inside of a heartbeat seemed dangerous, even if Galen did have a nice smile. Even when his cheeks flushed when he got all riled up.

With all that, there was no point in acting like he cared, and his impulse to make Galen laugh needed to be curtailed. But before he could pull on a mask to demonstrate how little he cared, Marston leaned in to kiss Kell on the cheek.

"See you in the morning," he said. And then strode off into the woods.

"Let me get a flashlight," said Kell. "Then we can take a shower."

This said as if nothing remarkable had just happened. And maybe to him, it hadn't been remarkable. Just his very tall and imposing lover kissing him goodnight, as if he was the brightest jewel in a sea of darkness. Which he was.

Taking Bede's jacket, Kell bounded up the stairs and into the tent, and came out with a flashlight and Bede's boots.

"Yeah, going barefoot's cool, but not in the dark," said Kell, sensibly. "You might slice your foot open."

Bede stifled the impulse to ruffle Kell's hair. He might be young, but he wasn't a kid.

"Lead the way," said Bede. He gathered stuff for a shower and, stepping into his boots, sockless, he pulled up the laces and tucked them inside the boots without tying them.

He followed Kell through the woods to the facilities, keeping an eye on the darkness beyond the bright beam of Kell's flashlight. Then he showered in the stall next to Kell's, then got dried off and dressed. While he waited for Kell to finish, he watched as the evening breeze took the mist over the transom and into the dark.

Back in their tent, the overhead light was still blazing and now about five moths were doing a nighttime dance.

"Oops," said Kell, as he put his flashlight away and started scooping up the moths in the palms of his hands, tossing them outside. "They'll drive us crazy, else," he said to Bede by way of explanation. "More will always come in, but it's good to keep it to a dull roar."

Bede stripped to his new white briefs, and Kell did the same, and as Kell reached for the overhead light, he smiled.

"Just like old times," Kell said.

"Yeah, except for no books," said Bede, thinking back to prison, when Kell had stood in front of him, offering up blow jobs like he did them every day, even though he was a virgin.

"There are books in the mess tent," said Kell, clicking off the light.

Fighting a lingering sense of strangeness, Bede crawled into his cot, laying his head back on the comfortable pillow with a sigh.

"I looked. I've read all those." He'd seen the small shelf of books in the mess tent, scanned the titles. Found nothing new.

"All of them?" Kell asked, his voice clear in the darkness that settled all around.

"Most of 'em," said Bede. "I'm really not interested in how to learn chess or reading about wild birds of America."

"Ask Galen, your team lead," said Kell. "That's always a first step if there's something you need."

Bede nodded, though Kell couldn't see, and laid his hands on his chest on top of the soft sheet and blanket.

He supposed in Kell's mind that going to Marston for something he needed made sense. Bede would have to go to Galen.

He couldn't imagine asking Galen for anything, let alone for a book to read. *I think John Grisham has a new one out. Can I get a copy? Or how about something by Pat Conroy?*

Galen might say no. Or maybe he'd say yes, and would inquire about Bede's reading tastes. Or maybe he'd just order the books Bede wanted, only he'd tell Bede to put them on the bookshelf in the mess tent to share with others.

So which would be worse? Having Galen say no and turn his back? Or having Galen say yes, and then Bede would be in Galen's debt?

If prison had taught him anything, it was never to be in anyone's debt.

And then came the question: What expression would that pretty face make when Bede asked for books?

"G'night, Bede," said Kell, his voice sleepy as he turned on his side, it sounded like.

"G'night, kid," said Bede.

He lay flat on his back, the sheet kicked off, the light blanket a bundle at his feet. He breathed slowly in and out. None of this was a dream, but it felt rather dreamlike at that moment with the night settling in around him. The scree-scree of the branches. Thin wails that Bede couldn't identify.

"Coyotes," said Kell over a yawn.

Coyotes? A shiver went over Bede's skin. He was a city boy and had no experience with any of this. But Kell, who had been fearful in prison before Bede had become his bodyguard, was falling asleep. A small snore rose up from the other side of the tent.

There was nothing to fear then. Bede made himself focus on the sounds. The pattern they made. The way the coyotes wails rose and fell.

Were they singing to the moon? No, because there was no moon. Only a carpet of stars beyond the branches of the tall trees that were standing sentinel around the green canvas tent.

CHAPTER 9
GALEN

In the morning, a tad bleary-eyed, Galen shuffled through showering and shaving, reveling in the hot water, then got dressed, and trotted to the mess tent.

There, he found himself at the end of the line for the buffet. He wasn't worried about the food running out, just about having enough time to eat before he needed to round up his team for work. Put on his boss-man hat. Be in charge.

He had the training, sure, and he could do the job. But it'd just be easier if his team would all up and decide they wanted to do their parole elsewhere. Or maybe it was too late in the game for such doubts.

Then, just as he got up to the buffet and grabbed a tray, a plate, and some cutlery, he saw Bede sitting at the end of one of the long tables.

To Bede's right was Kell, chatting like mad to a silent and watchful Marston, who was sitting on the other side of Kell. Bede and Marston were two bookends, protecting Kell, like he was in any danger at all. Which he was not.

It was as if Bede was by himself in a sea of people. A very small sea, to be sure, but he was all alone. Eating a tidy pile of pancakes, sipping on black coffee, spearing his sausage patty with a severely aimed fork.

Both Toby and Owen, trays in hand, went to the table where Bede was and sat across from him. Bede's brow lowered, as if he'd suddenly developed a severe headache.

Galen might as well get it over and join his team. And no, he wasn't saving Bede from having to converse with the less-than-dynamic duo. It wasn't about Bede at all. Galen was just doing his job, so as soon as he got his breakfast, he went and sat down across from Bede, too.

A good night's sleep had done Bede a world of good, which must be what was keeping Galen focused on him. That fact and not the sleekness of the skin along Bede's neck where it disappeared beneath the trim collar of his snap-button shirt. Or where he'd rolled up his sleeves yet again, and was just now balancing his elbow on the table as he took a sip of black coffee.

Bede looked at Galen, not smiling, eyes half lidded as if assaying Galen's presence, but he didn't want to be seen doing it.

Then, after a pause, Bede asked, "What's on the agenda today, boss?"

Boss. This was the name Galen had heard all the ex-cons called their team leads, in spite of those same team leads asking *Please, please, just call me by my name.*

Something had been ingrained in the ex-cons' heads, so they continued doing it. Galen was just going to have to put up with it or cause a severe and probably unsuccessful fuss.

"First," said Galen, after chewing and swallowing a mouthful of very good pancake. "We're going to do some recon and tag all the knapweed in the area."

"Knapweed?" asked Toby.

"Recon?" asked Owen.

"Knapweed is an invasive plant," said Galen, taking a sip of his coffee, pretending he didn't hear Bede snicker into his pancakes, because he wanted to encourage questions from his team. And, also, he didn't know what to do with the fact that Bede's snicker made him want to smile. "It's poisonous to other plants and creates barren areas where only knapweed grows."

The members of his team looked at him like he was speaking Urdu. Except for Bede, who looked mildly interested.

"Recon is short for reconnaissance," he added. "It means we're going to take a look around and see what we can see." He took a look at Toby and Owen's faces and sensed a little disappointment there.

"We'll work with the horses more, once that's done," Galen said. "Care, feeding, riding lessons, all of it."

He took a sip of his coffee and let this sink in.

"You'll need to have real cowboy boots and hats for the riding lessons, but we'll be getting those later this week," said Galen.

Toby and Owen did not seem enticed by this at all, but Bede chuckled and asked, "More boots? I'm going to need a boot rack at this rate."

Galen snorted in spite of himself at the image of fancy downtown shoes and boots in racks inside each tent. Why Bede made him laugh was still a mystery, but the last thing he needed to do was to encourage it.

"Leland wants every man to have the tools he needs," Galen said, studiously keeping his attention on his meal, desperately focusing on that and not the fact that Bede's bright smile, that flash in Bede's eyes, made him feel buoyed up, like everything was going to turn out just fine.

When breakfast was over, Galen assembled his team in front of the supply hut. It was a hot morning and looking to get hotter. There was no wind, and there were no clouds hovering over the treetops.

He took up a folded paper map and pink highlighter and then held out a laminated picture of purple-shaded knapweed. This, too, made him feel good about how it was going. From his years of helping his dad on the family farm, he knew plants, that was for sure.

"It looks like thistle, right? Well, it's not. Everywhere you see this plant, put a yellow flag in the ground. I'll be marking the map to show where the largest swathes of knapweed are."

"Why don't we just douse it with kerosene and burn it?" Toby even raised his hand while asking this, like he was in school. So rather than answer Toby like the latent arsonist he was, and ignoring Owen's snort of dismissal, Galen did his best to turn it into a teachable moment. Like his dad would have done.

"That's what some people do," Galen said. "But that leaves fumes and ash. The BLM uses chemicals sometimes, but we don't want that in the valley. We're going to dig each and every plant up."

"Every plant?" squawked Toby, then Bede asked, "What's BLM?"

"BLM is the Bureau of Land Management," said Galen. "They oversee the use of all the public lands for recreation and grazing."

Galen gave each member of his team a small canvas sack of yellow flags on thin metal stems, and watched as they slung the strap of the sack over to the opposite side of their necks. Like they'd done this before, been on some kind of job duty. Maybe picking up trash.

When he handed Bede his sack of flags, Bede took it and, as he slung the strap around his neck, he said, straight-faced, "This looks like it's going to be hard. Maybe I should have stayed in prison."

Feeling a tickle of a laugh in the back of his throat, Galen concentrated on his map.

Unfolding it, he showed his team where they'd be looking, along the lake, on the path up to the ridge, the dirt road on the other side of the team lead tents. And, if they had time, on the other side of Horse Creek.

"Beyond Horse Creek, we'll be on a trail that leads to Aungaupi Valley, but we won't be going all that way, as it's a day's ride by horseback. We'll start on this side of Half Moon Lake in a group, and then spread out. It'll take us a few days to mark all the locations. Any questions?"

Every man on his team shook his head, and then they headed out as a group, going along the dirt road beyond the team lead tents first, planting flags as they went.

At first it was easy, going along the slope of the path toward the lake, where the sun sparkled on the water. Bend and stick, bend and stick.

The knapweed was thicker along one side of the dirt road, past the team leads' tents. Galen noticed that Toby and Owen were staying in the shade, along the side of the road with less knapweed. All the while, in the broad sunshine, mere feet from Galen's side, Bede was head-down, deep into the task.

Without a breeze, they were all sweating, but Bede seemed to do it more artfully, his dark hair slick like ink, sleeves rolled up, graceful patches beneath his arms, a long line sticking his shirt to his back.

Galen didn't know when the last time he thought a man sweating in the sun was a greedy eyeful. But perhaps he shouldn't be thinking about that right now.

The heat continued to rise, and only Galen was wearing his straw cowboy hat to keep off the sun. Asking the men to do more without sun protection would have been cruel, even if he felt a little hardship might do the ex-cons some good.

But perhaps he should stop thinking that way. After all, Leland had started the program, and believed in it, so there must be some good in it.

Maybe they needed those hats sooner rather than later.

Right before lunch and after they found and marked all the knap-weed along the road, he took them to the mess tent for cool drinks.

"I had no idea how hot it would get," he said as his little team gasped as they gulped down cold soda and iced tea.

"I'm going to change it up," he said. "We'll clean up, have some lunch, then go up to the ranch for hats and boots this afternoon, rather than later in the week."

This seemed to brighten all of their spirits considerably, and while it would have been nice to have a little rain, the day was a beautiful blue-sky day, and the air was sweet. Making him think it would be a good summer, after all.

Galen grabbed a clean shirt and his shower things and headed to the showers. There, he found Toby and Owen milling about in front of the mirrors, shaving, like they were going to a dance.

And as for Bede, he was still in the shower. Steam roiled over the top of the shower curtain, and he seemed to be humming to himself.

Not thinking about Bede naked in the shower, not thinking about what tattoos would look like with bubbles of soap sliding across them,

Galen took the quickest shower in his life, got dressed and headed to the mess tent.

There, he consulted with Gabe as to the change of plans, and called Maddy on the landline that sat on the bookshelf in the corner to tell her they were on their way to the ranch's store.

Then, finally, he grabbed some chili and cornbread, two of his favorite things. A nice green salad. Cinnamon rolls for dessert. A great cup of coffee to finish it off.

Then he sat down with a sigh and began to eat amidst the friendly chatter all around him.

Sitting across from him, Kell and Bede seemed deep in conversation, with Marston looking on like he was taking notes on how to behave like a human.

"Hey," said Kell, looking up, dragging Galen from his ruminations over his coffee. "Bede doesn't want to ask you about the books."

"*Kell*," said Bede, quite sternly, the sudden almost-threat in his voice drawing the attention of every man at the table.

"But you should ask him," said Kell, raising his shoulders, palms out. He wasn't at all afraid of Bede, that was plain to see. "That's what you do when you need something. It isn't like in prison."

Bede looked at Galen, studying him, and Galen's curiosity was raised beyond his ability to resist. None of his team had asked him for anything yet, but, then, it was only Tuesday.

"What do you need?" he asked, his curiosity making his voice come out a little sharp.

"Nothing," said Bede, shoveling cornbread into his mouth.

"He needs books," said Kell.

Galen looked over at the tiny library and office area that Kell was pointing at. There was a whole shelf of books.

"We have books," he said.

"He's read them all already," said Kell brightly.

"All of them?" asked Galen. He wasn't much of a reader, at least not for pleasure. "*All*? And when? You just got here."

"In prison," said Bede with a twitch of a shrug. "I've read all those books, except for the ones on birds, but I'm not much of a bird man."

Galen wasn't much of a bird man either, so he could sympathize. Royce, one of the other team leads, was a big, *big* bird man, and had donated around twenty books to the collection. Threatened to donate more until Gabe had told him that maybe they had enough books about birds on hand.

"There's paper and pen," said Galen, jerking his chin in the direction of the shelf. "Make a list. I can order any book you want. Any number of books," he added to make it clear that the sky was pretty much the limit. Then, because he couldn't help himself, he asked, "What kind of books do you like to read?"

Bede's response was a dark-eyed gaze, as though Bede was determining whether or not Galen was the enemy. The kind of smoldering gaze that Galen imagined he'd see if he'd ever encountered Bede in a dark alley mid-way through a drug deal.

Galen wasn't Bede's enemy, even if he was having recurring yet unproductive thoughts that the ex-cons in the valley were getting off easy. Except Bede had certainly worked hard that morning, as hard as Galen had.

In addition to that, he was impressed that Bede wanted something to read.

But looking at Bede, sitting very still and watchful, made it easy to imagine what five years behind bars must have been like. What being on guard all the time must have felt like. Looking every gift horse in the mouth. Not to mention all those TV shows and movies that made being in prison like staying in Motel Rape Central.

While in prison, Bede had looked after Kell. Maybe he'd done the same for others, too. He didn't have to, but he had. And now he didn't have anything to read.

Galen felt bad for him and if that wasn't a laughable topsy-turvy idea, he didn't know what it was.

Maybe he needed to shift his mind and keep up with what was really going on. Maybe those five years in prison had affected Bede to the point where he might, just might, turn out to be a decent guy.

"I'm not much of a reader," said Galen to get the conversation going again. "My dad was. He had tons of books on farming, but I donated most of those to the local library. So if there are books you need, really. Just make a list."

"Even porn?" asked Toby from the next table.

"No, no porn," said Galen, turning to look at Toby. "Be reasonable, okay?" He shifted his attention back to Bede. "So? What kind of books do you like?"

Bede must have made up his mind to answer in spite of himself, because he took a very deep breath.

"John Grisham," he said, saying the author's name as if he'd read Grisham's entire catalog and knew each book by heart. "Alistair MacLean. Pat Conroy. Stephen King, if I'm in a mood. Barbara Kingsolver, though I've only read one or two of her books."

Galen could only blink. Bede did not look like a reading kind of guy. But maybe being stuck behind bars had made him reach out for some kind of distraction, and books had been closest to hand. And maybe reading them had changed him.

"Make your list," said Galen with a nod. "I'll order those books as soon as you let me know what you want."

Bede still seemed dubious, so Galen concentrated on finishing his lunch, and then bussing his place. Afterward, he got a paper and pen from the little office in the mess tent, and gave those to Bede. Then, as Bede bent over the small desk to write his list, Galen went to Gabe and told him about the book order, then got the password to their joint Amazon account.

"You did good, there," said Gabe, pulling him out to the wooden platform in front of the mess tent.

"I did?" Galen asked, surprised by the compliment as he folded the sticky note with the password on it and stuck it in his front jean pocket. He paused, then said, low, "You know, I didn't want to be a team lead in Leland's program."

"I know," said Gabe, serious, head down, which told Galen this was a private conversation meant only for his ears. "Look, it can be hard to imagine that an ex-con has anything good to offer the world."

Gabe paused, his eyes on Galen, as if he wanted to make sure that Galen was listening.

"And maybe *they* don't think they have anything to offer, but we're going to give them a chance. You gotta shift the way you look at things, is all. Just for a while." He patted Galen on the shoulder and added, "The keys are in the truck. Did you let Maddy know you're coming early?"

"Yes, sure did," said Galen. Feeling as though he might actually get on top of things, he gathered his team.

"Who's ready to try on hats and boots?" he asked, spreading his hands wide, gesturing to the nearest of the two silver trucks that could be seen beyond the trees.

"Shotgun!" shouted Toby.

Knowing he secretly wished that Bede had shouted shotgun, Galen resigned himself to Toby sitting in the passenger seat next to him. Owen sat behind Toby, and Bede sat in back of Galen.

CHAPTER 10
GALEN

As he drove up the switchbacks, the pine-scented breeze flowing through the open windows as the heat rose, Galen could see Bede's strong fingers gripping the edges of his headrest in the rearview mirror. Feel Bede's focused attention on the way they were headed, and where they ended up when Galen parked the truck in the small gravel parking lot in front of the ranch's store. Like Bede needed to know the way because it was going to be up to him to get everybody back home, safe, to the valley.

"We're here during a regular day," Galen said. "Which means there might be ranch guests inside the store. Which means I want you to be on your best behavior. Got it?"

They all nodded, even Toby, who was overcome enough to be perfectly silent. Suddenly well behaved as if the principal had just shown up in his first-grade classroom.

His team all got out of the truck and crowded around Galen, just as he opened the screen door and waved them inside, and just as Maddy was coming over from the main office.

"Thanks for being flexible," he said to her as she stepped into the shade of the store's porch. "It's just too hot for them to be without hats."

"It's no problem, and I agree." Maddy smiled. "We'll get these guys fixed up in no time."

"Why—?" Bede stopped. "Ma'am, can I ask a question?"

"You sure may," said Maddy.

"We all got supplies, everything we need. There's even a swimsuit in there, so why are we picking out these boots and hats?"

"Well," said Maddy, then she paused. "What's your name, son?"

Bede smiled, a faint flush to his cheeks, as if getting called son was the best compliment he'd received in a good long while.

"Bede, ma'am," he said.

"Well, Bede, we think that boots and hats are too personal just to be handed out. You're all individuals, so we wanted to give you a choice in the matter. Does that make sense?"

The kind words from Maddy made every single man on his team straighten up and throw their shoulders back. It was as if she'd instilled in them a pride they'd not had only seconds before.

"Come on in now," she said, holding the screen door open, urging them inside with a wave. "Get out of the heat."

The store was longer than it was wide. The walls were crammed with shelves, and the shelves with boxes of boots, hats on racks, candy of all kinds, and t-shirts and sweatshirts and baseball caps with the ranch logo emblazoned on them. And all the while, the old wooden floor squeaked beneath his work boots.

Galen had long ago acquired his own cowboy boots, a nice pair of Ariats with a bit of an inlay that reminded him of blue rust. They were nothing fancy, but they'd been easy to break in and let him hold his head up, whether on horseback or on the dance floor.

There were a few customers in the store milling about the glass case with the cowboy buckles. They were focused on their purchases and didn't seem to notice that Galen had three ex-convicts with him.

As for his team, they kept to the walls and looked at hats and boots with wide eyes, as though they'd suddenly landed on the moon.

According to what Galen had learned, men in prison operated on a trade and barter system, which bolstered what they could buy in the prison commissary. So yeah, going on a shopping trip with carte blanche must feel like it was suddenly Christmas and very over-whelming.

"Can we get *any* boot, boss?" asked Toby, coming up to him with very wide eyes.

"Any boot, any hat," said Galen with a firm nod. "There are some higher end prices, and those boots are included, so be reasonable. And," he added as a caution, "you're going to be using those boots for riding lessons, and maybe even dances, if we can arrange any."

As Maddy pointed Toby and Owen in the right direction, over at the end of the shelf of men's cowboy boots, Bede had picked up a pair of oxblood-colored boots, tooled by hand. The leather looked soft, so buttery that Galen knew why Bede was practically stroking the toe of the boot in his hands.

It was an expensive pair, Galen could see even at a distance, more expensive than even Toby might pick out.

Galen knew he should say something like *Get something cheaper*, but when he got closer to say that very thing, he saw that Bede's fingers were hard around the boot-heel, his jaw tight, as though he was holding back a great big yelp of pain.

"Everything okay?"

Bede's eyes flashed open like he'd just come up from a great depth beneath the water and very much needed air.

Galen had no idea what was going on and didn't quite know what to say, when Bede took a sharp breath and said, maybe to Galen, or maybe to no one at all, "These are gorgeous."

"Those are Tecovas," said Maddy, coming up to Bede, completely fearless, like she simply did not care that Bede was a hard-core drug dealer who'd done a lot of time behind bars. "One of our best wranglers on the ranch favors those. You're a twelve, right? Maybe twelve and a half with thick socks?"

Goggling after her as she went to get help reaching a pair in the right size down from the high shelf, Galen knew that Tecovas pretty much started at five hundred dollars a pair. His own pair of Ariats cost less than two hundred and fifty and he'd paid for them out of his own hard-earned money.

Before today, he might have made a comment about ex-cons getting handouts. Now, as he watched Bede put the blood-red boot down and reach for a plain, dusty brown boot with a flat heel and a square toe, a basic boot, nothing to write home about, he wanted to figure out the right thing to say to get Bede to take home the Tecovas.

"I'll just get these," said Bede as he tapped the sensible display boot.

"Here we are," said Maddy breezily. She handed Bede a fancy box that looked just about as expensive as the boots. "Sit over there and try them on, will you? I'm going to help Toby narrow down his selections."

Galen turned to look and saw that Toby had a dozen boots lined up in front of him as he sat on the small stool in front of the shelf of boots. Owen was laughing at him, and the two looked like they were having a good time.

They weren't bothering anyone and, to anyone else, they probably looked like they were normal citizens. And maybe, in that moment, they felt more normal than they had in ages.

Galen turned his attention back to Bede, who seemed frozen with indecision.

"Go ahead," said Galen when it looked like Bede wasn't going to move a muscle without instruction. "Get the ones you want."

Far be it from Galen to come between a man and a new pair of boots that were practically making Bede drool. Besides, it wasn't Galen paying the tab, and Maddy *had* brought the pair over to Bede like it was okay that he was going to select a pair of boots that cost a bazillionty dollars.

The second after Galen said *Go ahead*, Bede's dark eyes flashed something at Galen, a signal, giving him a peek behind the mask that Bede always wore. Was it gratitude? Or was it something more? And would finding out break some unwritten rule about no fraternization?

Bede bent to unlace his work boots and slid his feet into the Tecovas. They went on easily, like he'd owned the boots for years. Like they were already a part of him, which was the sign of a very well-made boot.

Bede stood up and looked at the boots in the foot mirror and himself in the wall mirror. Galen looked, too.

In the slightly dusty blue jeans he wore, Bede's legs became a mile long. His whole body pulled into alignment, shoulders going back, chin going up. He was more imposing now with his arched neck, pride tightening his jaw, the flash of dark tattoo above his shirt collar.

But before Galen could focus on what this revealed about Bede, Bede sat down and began tugging off the boots, laying first one foot across one knee, and then turning the other way.

"I don't need those boots," Bede said.

"Well, you actually do," said Galen, suddenly finding himself in the odd position of convincing Bede to keep a pair of rather expensive boots, rather than encouraging him to take the plain brown pair. Why did he care so much?

"Why?" Looking at Galen with dark eyes, Bede placed his palms on his knees and seemed to be holding himself upright.

"Everyone who comes through the Fresh Start program gets a pair," said Galen. "You need them for riding lessons and for when we go to the tavern in town. After you leave the valley, they'll be a token of your accomplishments. Something to brag about to your fellow drug dealers."

That last part slipped out. He shouldn't have said it, as it was rude and certainly not behavior befitting a team lead.

Bede looked up at him, brows lowered, like he was going to stand up and punch Galen right in the face. Then he just snorted and shook his head.

"I don't even know if I could go back to that kind of life," he said. "Don't think I want to, actually."

A lot of ex-cons, Galen had learned, went right back to their old life of crime. Recidivism was high. Very few climbed out of the trough of illegality and made it to the next level of living a regular, law-abiding life.

Galen didn't know if Bede was going to be one of the former or the latter, but he wanted to make sure Bede got the boots he so obviously wanted, but wasn't sure he could have.

"The boots suit you," Galen said. "Besides, Toby over there is getting two-toned boots. Garish blue on the bottom, glow-in-the-dark star-emblazoned white on the top. He's going to be the fanciest guy in the valley. You gonna let him show you up like that?"

Again, Bede snorted and seemed to drop his shoulders as though giving in to great wisdom. And it occurred to Galen that, even draped in burlap, Bede had more taste in his little finger than Toby ever would. Plus, Bede made him laugh, and he made Bede laugh, and that, he'd not been expecting.

"What kind of boots do you have?" asked Bede as he put the oxblood colored boots carefully back in their fancy box and then tucked the box under his arm.

It was a big box, and Bede's muscles bulged beneath the seams of his pale blue shirt. Again with the shirt sleeves rolled up.

"Those." Galen pointed to a pair of Ariat boots that were like the ones he had picked out two years ago, the action jerking him away from the realization that Bede was a handsome man. "Those are this year's model, but mine are similar."

"They're classy," said Bede. "I like the blue inlay."

Galen wondered at the compliment. Wondered why he was glad to see Bede go up to the counter with his expensive boots, rather than being pissed about it. Wondered if maybe he was getting the hang of this team lead thing.

"You're not done," he called out. "You guys need to pick out hats, too. Take a look at the straw ones, rather than felt, since it's summer."

As his team fluttered over to the selection of pale straw hats, some with leather hat bands, others with braided cord, Maddy said to him, "You should get a new one as well."

"Okay," said Galen, not one to turn down a new hat. He joined his team and looked at the patterns in the crowns and brims, some wheat-shaped, others like arrows.

After touching several hats, he found that his eye was drawn to those with a cattlemen's crown, two folds in the crown that allowed a cowboy to take his hat off and put it back on with ease. He liked the more narrow leather bands, and he liked the patterns of small arrows on either side of the crown.

One hat had a tooled leather hatband, still narrow, with small round and diamond shaped tacks as decoration. Grabbing a box that indicated the hat inside was his size, he gently placed the hat on his head, relishing the cool, balanced weight of the circle of straw.

"What do you guys think of this one?" he asked. "It's a Resistor, which is a good brand. Lasts a lifetime."

"Looks good, boss," said Bede, drawing the words out, but it was mockery without a sting. More, it felt like teasing. The way old friends might do.

"I'm going to try that hat," said Toby, lifting hats in the same style off the display and out of boxes to find his own size.

"Me too," said Owen, and then they were all elbows and shoving, and at one point, Toby pulled away from the stand with three straw hats identical to the one Galen wore on his head.

Bede reached out his hand, received his hat, and plonked it on his head. Toby and Owen did likewise, and now his team had matching hats.

They all had *matching fucking hats*.

He hadn't expected to start feeling like Father Christmas as he stood at the counter and signed the slip for the boots and hats, but he did. They wore their hats out of the store and carried their boot boxes under their arms, and not one of them wanted to let go of the boxes and store them in the truck bed for the short ride down the hill into the valley.

On impulse, he stopped to show them how to handle their hats, how to tilt them. Then, rather than going straight back to the valley, he drove them up into the main part of the guest ranch, pointing out the main features, such as the barn and the dining hall, where dances were held on Tuesday nights.

As he drove the truck down the steep switchbacks, a sweet wind blew through the open windows. Toby whistled through his teeth as his dishwater blond hair whipped around and, meanwhile, Owen, looking like he'd like a toothpick to worry, sighed and relaxed in his seat. Next to Galen, in the passenger seat, Bede, who had elbowed Toby out of the way, winked at him.

Galen didn't wink back, but he smiled. He couldn't help it. This was the best he'd felt since his dad had passed away, and Bede was part of that. And if that didn't surprise the hell out of him, he didn't know what would.

Maybe he'd take a swim all on his own later, when it got dark so that, all on his own, he could figure out what was going on with him.

He waited all through dinner, and the evening's campfire, keeping to himself, waiting until he could slip back to his tent. There, he looked for the red swim trunks that Maddy had so thoughtfully ordered for everyone, but couldn't find them, so he stripped to his briefs, threw on his shirt and boots, grab a towel and a flashlight and hoofed it through the woods to the lake.

Nobody was there as he stood on the end of the dock, which swayed softly up and down in a slight, self-produced wave. When he clicked off the flashlight, and his eyes adjusted, it became pure dark and then slowly, bit by bit, the ambient light of the stars overhead made the lake a pool of still, black ink.

He put the flashlight and towel down, stripped off everything and, bare to the skin, stood in the faint, pine-scented breeze, a little damp from the lake water, a lazy swirl of air that touched him everywhere. It was perfect, and he dove in, spearing into the dark waters that swallowed him and soothed him all over. Making his troubled thoughts from before vanish.

When he surfaced, the lake was calm, except for the black rings of water that spread out from where he was treading water.

"I can do this," he said out loud, the words barely a whisper over the surface of the water. He could lead men and make good decisions and soon his heart would heal from the heartbreak over losing his dad, and over the turmoil of maybe having to sell the farm.

In the daylight, selling or leasing the farm was a solidly thought out plan. But at night? He was consumed by loss.

Having a moment alone helped. Being in the water helped because the water always washed him clean. Made his heart feel strong. Steadied his mind.

He swam for a bit, smooth silent strokes that cut through the black water, which curled around him as though in a loving caress. When he swam back to the dock and pulled himself up, the dock swayed beneath him, his legs rising and falling in the water as water rolled off his back and dried, and dripped in his face from his hair.

With his fingers curled around the edge of the dock, he took a deep breath.

"I should do this more often," he told the nighttime sky. "I really should."

What he should also do was get back to his tent and get a good night's sleep. It would be his third day leading his small team, and he wanted to be well-rested.

As for the strange way Bede Deacon seemed the most interesting man that Galen had met in a good long while, a man who could make him laugh inside of a heartbeat, well. That was a problem for future Galen, because present Galen had no answers for him.

CHAPTER 11
BEDE

Holding the new boots in the small space of time between hard work in the hot sunshine and a rustic meal fit for a king in hiding brought back all the memories Bede had been holding at bay for five years.

Winston would have bought him a pair of boots like the ones he held, dark blood red and soft as butter. Sophisticated. In keeping with a drug dealer image. They were boots that could have been worn in a five-star restaurant. Winston had good taste like that.

It was as if the soft yellow work boots had cracked his armor, making him swoon with delight. Making him feel pleasure at the thought of wearing them. Now, the blood red boots were the battering ram, pushing through the final breech into his locked-up heart.

He'd have to hold those memories back a while longer because Kell came tromping up the steps, alone, for once, a big smile on his face.

"I heard boot and hat day got moved up for you guys, and I came to see."

Kell plopped down next to Bede on the cot, picking up the new straw hat and trying it on for size. It was too big, so, with a smile, he put it back down again and reached for the boots.

There was only one person living on the planet who could have done what Kell had just done, shoving his way into Bede's space without Bede minding.

All of his feelings about Winston and the love they'd shared, now gone forever—all of this rippled through him. But he swallowed it all down as he handed the boots over to Kell. He remained focused on Kell so that he would never suspect how close Bede was to the edge that threatened him with a tumble into a dark abyss from which there was no return.

"These are nice," said Kell, turning the leather boots this way and that in his hands. "Marston and I have matching boots." With a laugh, he added, "Not on purpose. I just happened to pick out the same boots he had." He arched his neck. "We're very cute when we both wear our matching boots."

"You're cute anyway," said Bede, taking the boots back, rubbing the leather with his fingers, tracing the seam where leather met sole. "My team all got matching straw hats."

"Oh, yeah?"

A bubble of amusement, a glowing glittery thing, swirled inside of Bede at the memory of the visit to the ranch's store, where Toby and Owen had acted more well-behaved than he'd ever seen. Where Maddy, a no-nonsense woman if ever he saw one, had treated all the parolees like they were regular guys. And where, of all things, Galen seemed to have pulled the stick out of his ass and relaxed for once.

More than that was his pleasure at the memory of all three of them picking out straw hats to match Galen's straw hat, and the disbelief on Galen's face, that secret flush to his cheeks as he tried to hide his pleasure.

And how fun it would be to tease Galen about the matching hats in the days to come. To see the laughter in those gray eyes.

All of this, the joy, the bubble, the anticipatory pleasure, faded as Marston appeared on the wooden platform outside the tent, taking Kell's attention entirely.

"Dinner bell's just about to ring," Marston said, then, looking at Bede, asked, "You coming?"

That was Marston being polite. Which seemed to be the way things would go, now that Marston was over his jealousy of Bede.

Which didn't make him any less protective for, hand in the small of Kell's back, he led Kell away to the mess tent.

At the mess tent would be the most amazing food, and that wasn't just five years of horrible prison muck served on plastic trays masquerading as food, talking, no. It was, quite simply, good and hearty and filling food, in all the best ways.

Bede should go to dinner. Pull himself away from the buttery boots and thoughts of home, a home with Winston that simply didn't exist anymore.

Those suit you, he heard Winston's voice say. *You should wear them to dinner.*

That voice. Quick, with rippling hints of the east coast whence Winston hailed. A city boy, finding a life in the grown up cattle town of Denver.

Bede's eyes grew hot, and he scrubbed at them, pushing the boots away as he stood up.

To distract himself, he picked up the straw hat, and turned it around, fingers gentle on the brim. It was a very simple hat with a tooled leather band and matching arrows cut out on each side.

The crown was folded in a way he'd been told was a cattleman's fold. Which made it easy to pick up the hat between his fingers and put it on his head.

The image of Galen laughing in surprise when he'd selected a hat for himself only to find out that all three ex-cons on his team had picked out the exact same hat made Bede feel more like smiling. Like laughing again.

He'd almost heard Galen asking himself whether it might be a good team-building move to break down and say yes to the hat. When he had, placing the hat on the counter with the others, a little cheer had gone up, Toby and Owen crowing and fist pumping as if Galen had just come over to the dark side.

Standing by the silver truck as he demonstrated how to properly wear a straw cowboy hat, Galen's guard had gone down even further, like he was with his good buddies and showing them all how to be that much cooler, and looking pretty adorable himself.

Then he'd looked up and probably realized what he was doing, acting all nice instead of like some guy with a pole shoved up his ass, and got serious, clicking on his key fob in his pocket and waving them to get in the truck.

Bede had grabbed shotgun just to see what it would feel like to be up front in a moving vehicle, and a pretty nice vehicle at that.

Galen had driven up the road to the ranch, rather than going straight back to the valley. Galen had said, for reasons of his own, *I'll give you a quick tour of the guest ranch. Might as well, long as we're up here.* Casually, like they were all friends on an outing, rather than one team lead and three parolees, one of whom was a dangerous drug lord.

Up close, in the confines of the truck's cab, Galen smelled amazing, his scent pulling Bede in, though he stopped himself, and asked if they could roll the windows down. Galen agreed, and the bright breeze flew into the cab.

The dirt road went in and out of clumps of green-leafed trees, over a stone bridge, and finally along the middle of the main compound. With a dining hall on the left, cabins on the right, and a barn and paddock up ahead, Bede could see it was a posh place, even more lush than the valley.

Most notable was the wide, glassy river that separated the ranch from the empty green prairie that seemed to go on forever. Not that Bede could see all of this at once, the place was huge. Spread out. Verdant, with plenty of shade and places to sit between activities.

As they drove back down the road, there were ranch hands out in front of the large wooden lodge, stringing up lights. Other ranch hands were rolling out what looked like oak barrels full of ice.

"What's that for?" asked Toby, pointing, his arm jutting out from the rolled-down window in the back of the pickup cab.

"It's for the Tuesday night dance," said Galen. He slowed down so they could all get a good look.

Bede figured that if you were a guest at the ranch, you got to go to the dance. But if you were a parolee, even if you had new boots, you wouldn't be allowed anywhere near any good law-abiding guests, regardless of your ability to do the two-step.

Swallowing the sour taste in his mouth, Bede stayed quiet all the way back to the valley.

Before prison, he and Winston had talked about taking country line dance lessons together. They would have learned the two-step, and Bede could have gone to one of those Tuesday night dances. The crowd would probably be small and friendly, and those lights he'd seen being strung up would be at just the right warmth and brightness.

He'd never been one for going to popular clubs. There were just too many people he didn't know. Too many chances to bump into the kind of people he never wanted to bump into. Other drug dealers, for example.

He didn't imagine that parolees would be invited to that dance, but now, sitting on his cot, his boots in his hands, he changed his mind. He might not be able to go to the dance, but he'd sure as hell wear the boots.

Quickly unlacing his work boots, he slid the new cowboy boots onto his feet. Standing, the boots felt sturdy and new, and in them he was ten feet tall. Then he put on a clean shirt, snapping the buttons closed slowly, one by one.

Had Winston been there, he would have whistled at Bede, and, with his eyes, told Bede how good he looked, and that Winston might actually prefer it if they didn't leave the tent. That they go back to bed and rumple the bedclothes.

But Winston wasn't there, so Bede walked to the mess tent by himself, his new boots leaving tiny triangular toe prints in the pine cones and dust.

Along the way, he swallowed hard and then swallowed again, sweeping his hair back from his face, straightening his back. Hardening his heart against memories of Winston and the future that they would never have.

He couldn't let anyone know, not Kell, not Galen, not anyone, how he felt as though he was being torn through by rotating blades. It was a new world, and he needed to either shrink into a ball of nothing-ness, or march right on into it.

In the buffet line in the mess tent, he barely knew what he grabbed from the steamers, and when he sat down at one of the long tables with his tray of food and began eating, he could barely taste it.

And when Galen spread his hands wide, Bede could only blink at him, confused by what he wanted.

"Where's your list?" Galen asked. And then added, "Of books."

"It's in his pocket," said Kell, giving Bede a soft elbow. "I saw him put it there."

Bede took a moment to silently pull out his list, folded and double folded, a little jagged around the edges where it'd been torn from the tablet. He gave the piece of paper to Galen without looking up.

It didn't really matter what books were ordered for the library, but it was important to make sure nobody knew how shook he was inside. How he'd kept up a barrier for five years and now it was crumbling. All because of a stupid pair of boots that Winston would have loved to see him wearing.

Maybe he'd throw those boots in the lake and say he lost them.

CHAPTER 12
BEDE

After dinner was another campfire and, wondering if anybody ever got tired of them, Bede made himself sit through it, creating and eating a s'more, engaging in small talk he couldn't remember a second later. Barely aware of the perfect summer night all around.

When darkness had truly fallen and he was back in his tent, Kell, high on chocolate and sugar, talking a mile a minute, got ready for bed. When he was tucked in his cot, Bede said that he needed to take a trip to the facilities.

He made it sound boring because he didn't want Kell coming with him. He just wanted a moment alone, a moment in a lifetime of being alone.

He shoved his bare feet into unlaced work boots, jammed the laces down around his ankles, grabbed his flashlight, and headed along the path to the fire pit. It was empty now, quiet, still smelling faintly like ash and chocolate and the cool sand that had been poured over the coals.

Beyond the fire pit loomed the lake, flat and still in the darkness. Beyond that, the layer upon layer of pine trees surged upward along the hills to the barren rocks of Guipago Ridge.

Going a little way along the path by the edge of the lake, he didn't quite know where he was, only that the faint breeze across the still lake was cool on his skin, and that his boots were rocketing around his ankles. So he stopped and took them off and stood barefoot in the uneven grasses, feeling them along the sides of his feet, his toes, a nighttime caress, absentminded. Soft.

It was that softness that broke him. Dropping his flashlight, he crouched down on his heels, face in his hands, and sobbed.

Winston was never coming back to him.

During Bede's five years in prison, he had played a continual game of make-believe. That he never heard from Winston because Winston was in hiding. That Winston never called Bede in prison because those calls could be traced back to him. That Winston never wrote an old-fashioned letter, because the postmark might lead the cops right to Winston's door.

And last, the most painful hope of all was, upon his release from Wyoming Correctional, that Bede would find Winston outside the prison, keys to a 440 Dodge Monaco in his hand. Saying, *Lookit what I got. Cop car. Cop tires, cop suspension, cop shocks.* Laughing, mouth open, head tossed back at the joke.

But instead of being met by Winston, Bede had walked out of prison empty-handed, and only a white van, the driver, and two fellow ex-cons were waiting for him. All of which was geared to blast Bede toward a Winston-less future, with uncertain horizons and along the bumpiest, most flint-flecked road he'd ever had to go down.

In prison, Bede had never cried, so he'd never needed to hide, either from his cellmates or the guards. He'd held back the tears and the pain in his gut every time they spiraled upward, tearing at him, razor-toothed. Relentless. He'd locked it all down, bolted it tight and never looked back.

Now, it all came pouring out, floodgates unleashed. A torrent of black-ripped grief that left him shaking, crouched down in the grass. Hiding, his palms pressed to his eyes as if to hold back the tears.

But they would not be held. Having waited five years, their turn had come, and there was nothing he could do to stop it.

Maybe this was good. He'd get it all out and then bolt everything back down again. Continue on with only the memories of Winston and their time together, the rough drug life contrasting with the silk-soft cotton sheets, the open window carrying the soft breeze and the sounds of the city.

He could carry with him the memory of traces of love on his skin, Winston's low laugh in his ear as he reached across Bede's body to the nightstand and the half-smoked joint that he obviously intended to finish off before the sun came up. Make Bede share it with him so their bodies could curl around each other, relaxed supple warmth pulling them into deep sleep.

"Bede?" asked a voice that cut through his grief so sharply it was like a blow. "What are you doing out here?"

Bede leaped to his feet, face damp, his eyesight blurred with tears, the rustle of the woods all around him fanning coolness across his hot skin.

"Bede?" asked the voice again. The beam of a flashlight swept across him. "Are you okay?"

Wiping his vision clear, Bede blinked at the figure in front of him.

It was Galen, the flashlight beam drawn to his side as he held it away from glaring into Bede's eyes.

Bede could see that Galen wore cowboy boots. Clamped to his chest was a bundle that might be folded clothes and certainly was, for Galen was naked except for a snap-button shirt, currently unsnapped, and a pair of tight skimpy briefs.

The visual caught Bede so off guard that, his hands in fists, all he could do was roar in response. "What are *you* doing out here?"

Who the fuck walked around half-naked in the middle of the night, in the middle of nowhere? Weren't there bears or some shit like that, roaming around, looking for snacks?

It didn't matter. The worst person in the world had caught him doing one of the most intimate things. Bede could jack off in front of the chief of police if they'd wanted him to, but he would never have cried. Would never have felt as vulnerable as he did now, tears drying on his cheeks. More exposed than even Galen in his state of half-undress.

Galen would blab or consult one of the other team leads or whatever. Didn't matter. Bede was going to leave the valley first chance he got, so he would never have to live through this moment again.

"I went for a swim," said Galen, his voice as calm as if he'd just come across Bede waiting for the local bus. And while somewhat astonished, as the bus didn't run through the valley, he seemed completely unperturbed by Bede's presence, or his emotional state.

"In the middle of the night?" Bede didn't even bother to lower his voice, and heard the echo of his quiet rage across the surface of the lake, bouncing back from the gray ridge beyond. "The fucking *middle?*"

If there'd been moonlight, maybe Galen would have seen the tracks of tears on his face, but since the moon was only a silver fingernail brushing across the trees, that part would remain known to him alone.

Or maybe Galen had seen Bede's face in the light of the flashlight. Plus, his voice was thick, he could hear his own sorrow ringing in his ears. Embarrassment flurried hot around the back of his neck, along his cheeks.

Galen stepped forward. Instinct kicked in and Bede shoved Galen in the middle of his chest, which sent Galen's clothes flying.

"Hey, back off!" Galen's voice was strident and as loud as Bede's had been. "What is your fucking problem?"

Keeping his balance, Galen was silver-shouldered and slender, in dark-colored skimpy briefs that looked like they'd be dry like the rest of Galen's body, at least the part that Bede had shoved with his palms. Galen'd brought a towel, now snagged in the grasses, and probably had dived into the water stark naked, because who would want to walk around in wet briefs? Nobody.

Naked. Galen had swum naked in the dark lake. Unconcerned equally about who might be watching, or what might lurk in the lake's depths, waiting to eat the next human who dared trespass its waters. Rubbing himself dry with a towel before donning those briefs again. Collecting his clothes so he could enjoy the cool night breezes.

Bede stepped back, but not away, and in an instant, they were grappling, like two junior high boys with the impulse to fight over something that wouldn't matter come lunchtime, and who didn't quite know how. Pushing and pulling, with grunts, up close, and while the fight was a decoy for Bede's own sorrow, he had no idea what Galen's deal was.

Anyone else would have backed the fuck down when Bede Deacon stepped up for a fight. *Anyone* else.

Up close, Galen's skin was scented with lake water, and was warm in the coolness of the night air, the damp ends of his hair sticking to his cheeks as he clutched at Bede's shoulders. Tearing his shirt. Growling, like *he* was the wild beast in the woods, and not bears.

In an effort to get away before his body betrayed him, Bede stepped back, which sent Galen tumbling to his ass, pale legs sprawling in a come hither manner, one boot flying, leaving his foot bare, and Bede just had to look away.

"*Seriously*," said Galen. "What is your *fucking* problem? I just came for a swim to be alone for one damn minute, and you're acting like I caught you jacking off or something. Man."

With a groan, Galen started to get up and, on impulse, Bede grabbed his forearm, curling his fingers around Galen's elbow, hauling him all the way to his feet.

His chest heaved, and he didn't even know how to ask himself what the fuck was going on, though there was a voice shouting in his head. It was making his head hurt, and he felt bad about what he'd just done to Galen. Galen would ache in the morning, and he didn't deserve that.

Galen was up close again, their arms still clasped, forearm to forearm in the dark. Galen's eyes tracked across Bede's face, and one eyebrow dipped. Then he pulled his arm free.

"Didn't your mama tell you it's rude to shove people?"

Bede'd never had a mama, though he'd had his Aunt Lorraine. She'd raised him as best she could, which still left him exposed to bad elements in the neighborhood, and allowed him easy access to drugs and crime and the lifestyle he'd enjoyed for many years.

Until he'd gotten arrested in that alleyway when he'd lost everything that meant anything to him. Leaving him with thoughts that jerked forward and back as he sank beneath waves and waves of jagged images, of Winston bleeding out, of the alley smelling of cordite, dying because of Bede's insistence that they could make so much money. Of the cop in the driver's seat, unconcerned that Bede's heart was breaking, saying *I've got the main drug dealer in custody, cuffs on.*

He let go of Galen and Galen stepped back to pick up his flashlight, and it was at that ordinary motion, so familiar, of a man collecting himself after a scuffle that tears spilled out of Bede's eyes again, rolling like hot mercury down his cheeks.

Horrified, Bede clapped his hand to his mouth to stop the gasp that followed, the hitched breath, a barking gasp, as he tried so hard to stop. And failed. And failed. And *failed.*

"Are you crying?" asked Galen, and then a second later, "Oh."

Galen moved closer, his fingers brushing Bede's hand, still clamped over his mouth, a gesture he'd probably not meant to make.

"Hey." He paused, blowing out a slow breath, then turned away, nonchalant, as if he'd not just caught the valley's most hardened criminal sobbing his eyes out like a little kid.

"You know." He grabbed for his jeans and pulled them on, zipping and buttoning up like it was just another day at the gym. "It's got to be hard coming out of prison after five years."

He tugged his snap-button shirt back into place, and fiddled with the snaps, looking down at his hands before lifting his chin to look at Bede again. "I don't think I could have lasted one minute behind bars. But you did. And now you're here. It's going to get better, I promise."

Galen slipped his boots on over his bare feet and slung his towel over his shoulder. As he picked up the flashlight from where it'd been shining a stream of white light across dried pine needles, he said, "I was in Torrington for two weeks for the training. They even took us on a tour of the place. You were probably there. In that yard with—everybody."

Bede knew how those prison tours went. Wanting to make the best impression, visitors were shown a fake version of the prison, all cleaned up, devoid of trash and smell, even prisoners. Meanwhile, everywhere else was crowded and dank and smelly and noisy.

The thought of white-bread Galen trotting around the shiny-floored halls of Wyoming Correctional, being shown the nicer parts of the prison, getting little glimpses of one-man cells, empty and tidy, ready for their next occupant, was almost surreal. Or the dining hall, clean and swept between meals. Even the yard, but only when it was empty—the thought just about made him bark a loud laugh.

Bede felt like he'd been behind bars forever and then some, and now, standing in the cool dark woods in a hidden valley in the wilds of Wyoming, it hit Bede with a sudden clarity that he did not want to go back there. Ever.

There was a risk that Galen would mention to one of his fellow team leads that he'd caught Big Bad Bede in the woods crying. But maybe he wouldn't say anything. Bede couldn't make Galen not talk, so he was just going to have to risk it. After all, he'd taken bigger risks than this one. All that was at stake was his pride, not his life.

"Maybe I was there," said Bede, answering the specific question rather than respond to Galen's sympathy. He wiped his upper lip with the heel of his thumb. "They herded us around when there were tours, you know. Keeping us out of sight."

"Oh, I figured as much." Galen tilted his head back, as if appraising Bede. "You going to be okay?"

Bede couldn't take it anymore. The kindness, the concern. Galen had seen him at his most vulnerable, and he needed to get away before Galen was even nicer to him, because that would surely break him.

He turned on his heel and strode down the dark path like he had done it every day of his life, and knew where every bump and knot of grass was. He didn't and stumbled in the dark, and kept on going. Anything to get away from Galen.

107

CHAPTER 13

GALEN

Galen must have ground his teeth together in the night because in the morning his jaw ached as well as his back, and he had to sit up slowly. With his head in his hands, and the faint chirp of birds on the other side of the canvas roof of the tent, he waited for his head to stop pounding, but it never did.

Then he remembered the tussle between him and Bede the night before, and how he'd slipped and fallen. Not when Bede had pushed him, or even when they'd stood close in an almost-embrace, so close he could catch Bede's scent, and feel the muscles along Bede's arms beneath his grasp. No. Galen had slipped when Bede had stepped away.

Then Bede had hauled him to his feet, and that's when Galen figured out what Bede had been doing in the middle of the woods.

Bede had been crying all by himself. In the dark. Sobbing even, affected by something so deep inside of him that he'd been unable to stop even when Galen had come close to him.

The sound had made Galen's heart hurt in sympathy. And though he didn't quite know what Bede was upset about, Galen knew what it was like to have your soul ripped open by loss and grief.

The green canvas above his head glowed in the early morning

sunshine, warming slowly, scenting the air inside the tent, and he knew he needed to get going. He had a job to do and a team to lead, and a tiny headache couldn't keep him in bed.

The thing to do was get moving, so he got up, dressed, and went to take a shower, and shave, and get ready for his day.

On the way back from the showers, he stopped at the first aid hut to grab some Tylenol and took two of those. By the time he made it to the mess tent, he knew he wasn't going to mention his encounter with Bede the night before.

And certainly he wasn't going to mention that Bede had been crying. A man had a right to his feelings, his privacy, no matter who he'd been before he'd come to the valley.

All of this whirled in his head as he climbed the steps to the wooden platform in front of the mess tent. Gabe was standing there, chatting with Royce, something about wild mustangs and a one hundred day training challenge.

"I couldn't do it," said Royce, sounding amazed. "But those young ladies certainly know how to make it happen." Then he saw Galen there and smiled. "Oh, my, you look stiff."

"I stumbled and fell on the path when coming back from my swim last night," said Galen. He'd not realized he showed any signs of his tussle with Bede, but it was too late now. The lie was out.

"You might use some arnica cream," said Royce.

"What?" asked Galen, blinking, looking over Royce's shoulder to the interior of the mess tent, telling himself he was not looking for Bede. "The what now?"

"Like arnica cream," said Royce. "It contains *Arnica montana*, which is very good for dulling pain."

"The first aid hut has some of that," said Gabe, looking at Galen with some consideration. "But it's in the drawer, not in the cupboard."

"I'll be sure to grab some."

Galen stepped to the side, and saw that yes, Bede was sitting at the long table nearest the side of the tent. He had a cup of coffee in his hands, like pretty much everyone else, but he was by himself, eyes on his cupped hands.

The memory of Bede crying, the aching vulnerability in the sound, as if his sorrow had come up from the center of his soul, made Bede seem more like an ordinary guy. One who had not committed atrocious crimes and who was not afraid to show his softer side.

And suddenly Galen felt a surge of desperation that he should get to Bede before anyone else did. So he could reassure Bede that he, Galen, was not going to tell anyone about the night before.

"How'd it happen?" asked Gabe, as Galen turned to shoulder past Gabe and Royce.

"Like I said," said Galen. "I wasn't holding my flashlight quite right and tripped over a root. Or something."

He shrugged at Gabe's raised eyebrows of surprise, and added, "Just clumsy, I guess."

The suspicion on Gabe's face raised Galen's level of worry that someone would find out about their encounter on the path and come down hard on Bede about it. By the time he was able to grab some breakfast and slide into the seat across from Bede, who looked at him with wary, dark eyes, Galen felt almost desperate to assure Bede.

Bede's hands were around a white china mug that was only half filled with very black coffee, which also looked like it had gone cold, from sitting there and being mostly undrunk. His eyes looked like he'd rubbed them raw, with half-rings of faded purple beneath.

"Hey," said Galen as he lifted a fork to dive into his stack of pancakes, a food soft enough to be chewed with a sore head. "You look like you ran into a bear in the woods last night. And lost."

"A what?" His hands tightened around the mug, his expression bleak as he looked at Galen.

Reassuring Bede wasn't going to be easy because it looked like Bede didn't want to talk about it.

At any other time, Galen would have picked up his tray and gone to sit elsewhere.

But Bede winced as he looked down, his hands flexing around the mug, and Galen knew there was a whole lot more going on than them having taken jabs at each other the night before. With purple scoops of shadows beneath his eyes, Bede looked like he'd not slept at all.

So Galen leaned forward, resting on his elbows on either side of his plate, and said, "As far as I'm concerned, I didn't meet anyone on my way back to my tent last night."

Bede blinked at him, and a moment later, Owen and Toby sauntered by them, trays in hand as they bussed their places, and the moment was taken by silent hands.

"Guess we better get to work," said Galen, shoving his pancakes into his mouth with large forkfuls.

"Okay," said Bede. Then he paused, took a sip of his coffee, and shrugged. A shrug that was so slight, it was hard to discern the *I-don't-give-a-shit* from the *Sure-I-don't-mind-I'm-up-for-whatever*.

But before Galen could respond to that, Bede got up from the table and stormed out, almost throwing his coffee mug in the bussing tub. Leaving Galen on his own, running behind his team when he was supposed to be out front, leading it.

The task that day was to follow the yellow flags they'd placed and dig up the knapweed. Which was simple enough and left Galen hoping that the day would go well, without any problems or fights.

They grabbed shovels and pickaxes from the shed by the paddock and started digging up knapweed along the road on the other side of the team leads' tents. But, in spite of the fact that they all wore their matching straw hats and *looked* like a team, it didn't go smoothly. Partly because Toby and Owen started off the day by competing to see who could dig the slowest and complain the loudest, as each clump of knapweed was trenched out of the ground.

Galen went over to them, shovel in hand, and opened his mouth to either encourage them, or enforce a more effective work ethic, when Bede stepped around him. Stepped in *front* of him, like he was the boss of everything.

"Get to work, you losers," Bede said, a low growl beneath each word. Which made Toby and Owen shut up and start digging.

Bede had stepped in, probably trying to help, but it made Galen feel inadequate as a team lead.

Galen opened his mouth, not sure whether he wanted to thank Bede or tell him to step back because he, Galen, was in charge of this particular team. A huge chunk of his earlier sympathy for Bede vanished beneath the hot sun, though he made himself shake it off, made himself focus on the work.

Because it was so hot, one of the cooks brought out a cooler full of ice and bottled iced tea and water. Galen knew he should have thought of this.

Feeling like the worst team lead ever, he made a point of keeping an eye on the time, encouraging breaks once an hour or so. He was feeling pretty good when he picked up the cooler, along with his shovel, and led the team along the path around the lake to another long stretch where they'd flagged knapweed.

This area was a little way out from where the path went into the deep woods, where the temperature felt around five degrees cooler. It was also quite near the spot where Galen had encountered Bede the night before, when Galen had been dressed in only his briefs, and the unsnapped shirt, which had danced about and not covered very much.

Making himself concentrate, Galen decided they would work on the exposed part of the path and then move into the shaded area when it got really hot, and get a good bit of work done before lunch.

Toby and Owen must have had other plans as they charged past him into the shade.

Galen was just about to open his mouth and say something about it, when Bede reached out and grabbed both of them, dropping his shovel in the process, and drew them back into the bright sunshine.

"There's plenty here to dig out here, assholes," he said, baring his teeth at them.

Galen had no idea why Bede was stepping into the team lead role yet again, but he didn't relish the idea that Gabe or anyone would find out that Galen sucked at it.

"Knock it off, Bede," he said. "This is the second time you've done this. I've had enough. It's not your job to tell them what to do, it's mine."

"Then why don't you *do* it then," said Bede, stepping close, chest out. "You can't let these knuckleheads slack, or they'll just keep slacking."

"If you'll let me do my job, I *will*," said Galen, loudly, very nearly giving in to shaking his finger in Bede's face.

"If you would do your job, I wouldn't have to."

"I *am* doing it," said Galen, unable to keep his cool and totally confused as to why. "And if you would back off, I can keep on doing it."

Standing just about in the shade, their new, matching straw cowboy hats tipped back on their heads in identical ways, Toby and Owen looked like they were about to place bets on who would come out on top and be the winner in an argument that was pretty much unwinnable.

Sweat gleamed along Bede's forehead beneath the brim of his straw hat. His teeth were bared, intense, as though he was stepping back into his role as a drug lord, a kingpin directing his minions to run faster, collect more money, sell more drugs.

Up close, Bede's skin was warm, dark hair sticking to his temples as his hat flew off. In the bright sunlight, his eyes were dark, fury stirring them even darker.

Up close, the scent of his sweat swirled around Galen, alive, touching him everywhere, soaking into his lungs.

"Just stop," he said, giving in and poking Bede in the center of his very broad chest. "And don't do it again."

"Or what?" snarled Bede, spreading his arms wide as if to make himself look bigger.

Or what? Galen couldn't back up his threat, and both of them knew it. Of course he could blab about Bede crying in the darkness, though he would never do that, but the instant he thought it, he could see that Bede *saw* him think it—

"Go ahead," said Bede. "Why don't you try and lead your team the way they should be led."

He stepped back, lifting his arm to wave at the pair, Toby and Owen, skulking beneath the shade of the trees.

"Go ahead," said Bede again, and when Galen tried to step back, thinking to extricate himself that way, Bede's elbow caught him across the face with a hard clip, and blood spurted from his nose, a hot red spray in the sunlight.

"Shit." That was all Bede said, as if he hadn't meant for that to happen. Funny thing was, Galen knew that.

"Oh, for fuck's sake."

Galen cupped his hand around his nose, tasting the bitter copper taste in the back of his mouth, on his lips.

Toby and Owen hooted with laughter as they clapped each other on the back. Galen's hat fell off as he tipped his head back and tried to stop the bleeding that way.

Blood was leaking down his neck, even with his head back, and he couldn't hold that position for very long or go blind looking up at the sun.

"Fan-fucking-tastic."

"Hang on," he heard Bede's voice say. "Toby, get me water and ice from that chest, and Owen, see if you can't find some paper towels. I think I saw a roll in the tool shed."

Bede's hands were on Galen's shoulders, steadying him, walking him into the shade so he could tip his head back and not go blind. Strong fingers brushed his hair from his face.

"Why don't you sit down."

"Okay, yeah." Galen sat down, hiding his wince from his fall the night before, and blinked up at the pine boughs above his head. Caught a glimpse of Bede's calm expression as he reached to take something from Toby, who had rushed up and screeched to a panting halt.

"Got both, Bede," Toby said.

"Thanks."

Then Owen came up and handed something to Bede.

"No paper towels," he said. "Just this cloth. It looks pretty clean."

"Okay," said Bede. "You guys put the tools away. Clean up and get some lunch."

With mumbled acknowledgments, and clangs of metal shovels and pickaxes, Toby and Owen rushed off.

Now, in the cool shade, Bede's focus was on Galen, and they were alone.

"Rinse your mouth with this."

Galen tipped his head forward and felt Bede's fingers, full of ice, on the back of his neck. In front of him was a plastic bottle of water, already opened, and Bede was holding it to his mouth.

Taking a large mouthful of water, Galen swished it around, glad to be rid of the hot copper taste of blood in the back of his throat.

"Now spit."

With raised eyebrows at Bede's bossy but friendly tone, Galen leaned away from Bede and spit out his mouthful of water, then gladly gulped water down when Bede held the water bottle to his mouth again.

When Bede handed him a handful of ice and guided Galen's hand to the back of his own neck, Galen sighed at the coolness, and felt his shoulders relax. Then, when Bede poured some water on the mostly clean cloth and wiped Galen's face in long, gentle strokes, Galen shivered all over.

"I didn't mean to do that, you know," said Bede. He hunkered close, one booted toe in the dirt, one hard, curved knee pressing against Galen's upper arm.

"I know." Galen took a long drink of water to give himself a moment to figure out what else he needed to say. And whether he wanted Bede to back off, or whether he wanted another strong hand full of ice pressed to the back of his neck.

He wanted the latter, so he just up and said it.

"More ice, please."

Without a word, Bede reached into the cooler and brought out a fistful of ice. Water dripped from his fingers as he placed the ice on the back of Galen's neck.

Galen closed his eyes and savored the feeling. That of not having to move for a good minute or two. That of Bede's hand on his neck, spreading out warmth from his skin as the ice melted. That of Bede's presence looming and protective.

"You got to be firm with those guys," said Bede, breaking the spell, however unknowingly.

"I know," said Galen again. He reached to wipe the back of his neck, and Bede's fingers dropped away. Then he took another huge swallow of water and wiped his mouth with the back of his hand. "I keep expecting they'll step up and do some real work, only they never do."

"They will in time," said Bede. He stood up, grabbed more ice, and made an ice ball in the white cloth with it. This he handed to Galen, who placed it on the bridge of his nose. "I've worked with guys like this. They want to be told what to do. It makes them feel safe."

"Safe?"

He watched Bede grab the last bottle of water from the chest, open it, and lift his cowboy hat to pour it on his head. Then he put the hat back on while small beads of water ran down the sides of his face and onto his neck.

"Gives 'em structure," Bede said with a wide smile. "Believe it or not, they love it. It tells them their place in the world, and that makes them feel safe. And when they feel safe, they'll more easily do what you ask them to do."

Galen knew that Bede had led many men in his life. He would have had to, in order to grow his drug empire. Only now, he was using that knowledge to help Galen using words and a tone of voice that Gabe or Leland might have used.

"Thanks," he said.

Maybe he'd turned a corner and maybe his days as team lead weren't destined to fail. And maybe making friends with a guy who he wouldn't have wanted anything to do with only a few weeks before wasn't a bad thing. No, not a bad thing at all.

"I'm going to change into a clean shirt," he said as he watched a bead of water trace its way across the plane of Bede's tanned cheek. "Meet you at the mess tent?"

"Sure thing, boss," said Bede. He bent to grab the small ice chest, hefting it quickly, then winked at Galen. "See you."

"See you," said Galen faintly as he watched Bede stride along the path to the main part of the compound. And mused to himself that this was not how he'd expected this morning to have gone.

CHAPTER 14

GALEN

Galen made his way to his own tent, and took off his shirt to look at it. There was a bit of blood along the collar, but nowhere else. A spray of stain remover and a good soak in cold water and the shirt would be good as new.

He put on a clean shirt before heading to the mess tent. As he stood in line at the buffet, he got a few astonished looks from Toby and Owen, and anyone who had caught sight of his red and swollen nose.

Bede was at the far end of the table where Toby and Owen sat, eating his lunch, not looking like he was enjoying it very much.

Gabe came in, Blaze on his heels, and stood in the buffet line behind Galen.

"What happened this time?" Gabe asked.

With a quick glance in Bede's direction, and a fierce desire to shield Bede from anyone's ire, Galen grabbed a tray and plate and cutlery and began helping himself to the lasagna and salad.

Clearing his voice to draw attention to himself, he said, "Damn shovel popped back and whacked me good." He even pointed to his face with a *What the fuck gesture*, making the moment a comical one and not one where he was out and out lying. "I lost my grip, I think."

"I see," said Gabe, with a lift to his chin and a sidelong glance in Bede's direction. "Did you ice it?" he asked. "Do you need time off?"

"No, I'm good." Galen nodded to show how good he was, though it made his head throb. His face hurt from his hairline to his mouth, but he'd be damned if he was going to complain about it. "I'll be fine."

He was planning to eat lunch with Gabe and Blaze, because it seemed the better way to distract him from his accident with Bede's elbow. But then he sat across from Bede, just the same.

"Thanks," said Bede, almost muttering it as he concentrated on the contents of his plate. Then he looked up, as if he knew Galen was on the verge of asking him why he would say thanks. "For not saying anything."

"It was an accident," Galen said. He wasn't a tattletale, never had been.

Bede's response was a slight flush on his cheeks, like it mattered to him that Galen had lied to Gabe. That it mattered to him that Galen understood that, yes, it had been an accident.

After lunch, they picked up another small chest of bottles of water and iced tea, and grabbed picks and shovels from the tool shed.

As they worked in the shade along the path in the woods, things seemed to calm down, with the members of his team following his lead and simply getting down to work.

He made sure the team took breaks every hour, kept the pace steady but not too fast, and privately he longed for the days when he took instructions rather than having to be responsible for what everyone else was doing.

"Hey," said Toby, just as Galen dug his shovel quite deep beneath a narrow patch of knapweed.

Galen lifted his head, expecting some kind of shenanigans.

"What do you need, Toby?" asked Galen, pausing.

Owen and Bede paused as well, leaning on their shovels. The pair of them, Galen had to admit, looked a little cute in their matching poses, elbows on shovels, one hip cocked, and their matching shirts and straw cowboy hats.

"What're we going to do with all this knapweed we dug up, boss?" asked Toby.

After a moment, Galen said, "That's a good question, Toby."

He already knew the answer. After Gabe assigned him and his team the task of getting rid of all the knapweed, he'd done some research. He'd already ordered plastic jugs of vinegar and Castile soap, and knew exactly how many sprayers were waiting for them in the ranch's supply shed on the other side of the hill.

And while it might be just as easy to explain this to his team, in a flash of *What would Gabe do?* and encouraged by Toby's curiosity, he decided to turn the question back to Toby. Back to all of his team.

"We can stop work early today and use my laptop to look it up. How does that sound?"

Toby straightened up as though Galen had pinned a merit badge on his chest for asking good questions. Owen gave him an elbow, like he was trying to keep Toby from getting uppity, but seemed pleased for Toby just the same. As for Bede, he cast a long gaze at Galen, before picking up his pickaxe and digging the point at the dry dirt, focused on his task.

Around late afternoon, Galen announced that it was quitting time, led the way storing tools in the shed, and after only a little apprehension, led his team to his own tent, where his laptop was.

As Galen went into his tent to get it, Toby and Owen scrambled onto the wooden platform to peer inside of his tent, jostling for a good view of how the boss man lived.

But not Bede. He merely waited at the bottom of the step as if getting to use a computer with pretty good Wi-Fi didn't impress him at all.

Except it did. That was plain to see for anyone who was looking. Bede's eyes went to the laptop that Galen carried beneath his arm, fingers curled at his sides as if to keep himself from reaching out for it. Which only made sense, as Galen had seen the inside of Wyoming Correctional's computer lab, with its five wheezing on-their-last-legs desktops and one battered Chromebook, and knew, or felt he knew, how much Bede had been missing technology.

Once in the mess tent, with pre-dinner soda and pretzels and nuts arrayed before them, it was Bede who reached out, volunteering to be lead man on research.

They all stood behind him as he sat at one of the long tables and opened the laptop. He opened up a web browser, Google Chrome, Galen was pleased to see, and entered the search terms: *knapweed, destroy, dispose.*

They could all read, of course, but Bede gravely gave the summary.

"We should dig it up, like we're already doing. Dispose of like regular trash, in trash bags to be taken to the dump. Spray the ground with vinegar and soap solution." Bede looked up at Galen, in a way that somehow got to him, though he couldn't explain why. "What kind of sprayer? Like a hand-held spray bottle? That'd take forever."

"Yeah," said Toby. "Forever."

"They've got hand-pump garden sprayers up at the ranch," said Galen, slowly, as if the thought was just occurring to him. "We could borrow those. Take a break from digging tomorrow, and spray instead. Then we'll get some black garbage bags from the supply hut and maybe take a trip to the dump on Friday, so those bags aren't just sitting around." He looked at his team, but they were already smiling. "How does that sound?"

Toby was practically jumping up and down, giddy with the idea of using an ordinary garden sprayer, and Galen had a moment of giddiness himself. *This is working. I can do this!* But then Toby bumped into Owen, and the two of them started grappling, pushing against the table, and sending pretzels flying.

He pulled Toby one direction, and thankfully Bede pulled Owen the other direction.

"You guys need to stop fighting," said Galen, as he eased his laptop away from the edge of the table.

"You and Bede fight," said Toby.

"Yeah, like all the time," Owen chimed in. "Just today, in fact."

"Well, we shouldn't have been," said Galen, just at the same time that Bede said, "We kissed and made up, so it's all good."

The laugh escaped him, and though it jarred his nose, it felt good, and his smile at Bede came without notice, and the returning smile from Bede was warm and genuine.

Distracting himself, Galen tucked his laptop under his arm like a fussy librarian with a precious book.

"I'm going to put this away," he said. "You guys are at leisure until dinner."

Quickly walking away before they could stop him, Galen practically trotted to his tent.

There, he dug for his small travel bottle of Tylenol and socked back three with a swallow of water, the last of it, from his water bottle. Maybe he should get some of that arnica-whatever-it-was, like Royce had suggested, because his forehead felt sore, like the Tylenol couldn't touch it.

Right before dinner, he scurried to the first aid hut and dug in the drawer for the tube of arnica.

After squinting at the tiny print on the label, he carefully spread some along his forehead and the bridge of his nose, and told himself he wasn't imagining the almost immediate effects. Sure, his forehead still hurt, but when he touched it, it wasn't quite as sore.

In line for the buffet in the mess tent for dinner, he scooted right up to stand behind Bede. Who, he realized, this close up and facing away, was a half a head taller than Galen and, beneath his shirt, was muscled all up and down. Not that Galen was staring.

"Hey," he said, tugging on Bede's sleeve.

Bede whirled around as though Galen was an unknown threat, but when he saw it was Galen, his stance relaxed.

"Got to be careful doing that," said Bede. At Galen's confused expression, he added, "I got all these reflexes."

"From prison or before?" asked Galen, unable to stop himself.

"My whole life," said Bede with a sigh.

"I didn't mean to be rude," Galen said.

"You weren't," said Bede. "Don't worry about it."

Dinner was a quiet affair, as the heat seemed to be getting to everybody, and there wasn't a campfire, either.

It wasn't any cooler on Thursday, as the sun was blazing through the trees with no clouds in sight and no wind to stir the air. Galen could finally say that he knew what being in an oven felt like. At least his team had hats to shade them, and they had the ice chest of water close at hand.

Galen made sure his team was wearing gloves, himself included, to pack up the pulled knapweed into black garbage bags. It made a nice break to do that instead of dig in the dirt, even if the edges of knapweed prickled on his skin when the sleeve of his shirt pulled up. And it was even fun to toss the bags into the back of one of the silver trucks, and to pile in.

As Galen drove up the switchbacks, doing his best to ignore the solid masculine form of Bede in the passenger seat, with the window open and his arm resting there, shirtsleeve rolled up, Toby leaned forward from the back seat.

"Do we get to stop at Starbucks?" he asked loudly in Galen's ear.

"I believe I have enough money for pup cups," he said.

He tried to hide his grin, but after Bede threw back his head and laughed out loud, blue eyes sparkling as he glanced at Galen, Galen didn't bother to hide it.

Maybe there was a way to balance being a nice guy with being a boss who kept his team on target. It did seem he was going in the right direction, but perhaps he should pull Gabe aside and have a quick chat about it, get some advice.

On the other side of the Ranchette's Stop 'n Go was where the county landfill was located.

Galen parked, and was barely out of the driver's seat before his team was up and at it, pulling black plastic bags out of the truck bed and tossing them on the pile with the other black plastic bags. With some glee, Toby and Owen sometimes threw the bags at each other, and Bede snorted with a low laugh as he picked up the fallen bags and shoved them on the pile.

Loose knapweed flew, prickly and dusty, but they made short work of the task, and were soon sweating beneath the blazing sun. And it did blaze, coming down as though ejected from a flaming torch.

There were no trees near the landfill, and again, no breeze, but his team smiled as they piled into the truck, wiping sweat manfully from their foreheads with the backs of their arms before placing their hats on their heads again. Almost in unison, as if they'd practiced for hours.

And then Toby leaned forward, grabbing Galen's headrest to pull himself up with, and in the rearview mirror, Galen could see the hopeful look in his eyes.

"And now coffee," he said, grinning as a whoop of joy bounced off the inside of the truck's cab.

Galen grinned in response, a grin he turned to share with Bede, and in that moment it felt so natural, he didn't even question it. Bede grinned back at the prospect of special coffee, or maybe at the joy of the moment, shared between the two of them.

There wasn't a Starbucks anywhere near where they were, but there was a Caribou Coffee at the Ranchette's, so, after paying the fee in the metal slot in the paybox at the landfill, which was right before the cattle guard that served as a gate, that was where Galen headed.

"We're on our best manners inside, right?" asked Galen as he parked the car and turned off the engine.

As they got out of the truck, he realized that they were all a bit grubby, and who knew whether or when a fight might break out.

But, somehow, while his team huddled in front of the glass case full of baked goods, looking up at the menu board, giggling like school kids on an impromptu outing, nothing bad happened.

And, after various mochas and one honey lavender espresso shaker were ordered, the latter by Bede, they all hurried to take sips of their drinks before sitting down at a round table in the corner of the very lovely and air-conditioned coffee shop.

Bede groaned, his hands cupped around his tall glass, almost shuddering as he swallowed.

Galen stifled the urge to ask Bede how long it had been, a not very good sexual innuendo. Besides, he knew how long it had been.

He'd read all of their files, and knew how long they'd been behind bars, and how long it'd been since any of them had done anything like what they were doing, sitting in a coffee shop to drink their over-priced, fancy, and very good coffees. Just like regular folks.

This, then, was part of the normalization process the training in Torrington had gone on about. *Do normal things with them and they will become normalized to the outside world.*

At the time, Galen hadn't quite understood what the trainer had been getting at. But, now, seeing the evidence in front of him, how the shoulders of all three of his men relaxed, he finally understood. And felt quite pleased to see the predicted changes taking place right before his very eyes.

"It's so fuckin' hot out there," said Toby, but when Galen gestured over his shoulder at the small table with a mom and her two young kids, his eyes widened. "Oh, sorry. It's really hot out there."

With a nod of approval at Toby, Galen drank his own white choco-late mocha, which was almost too sweet, but made a nice treat.

Across from him, Bede looked like he was about to make love to his espresso.

Galen stifled the urge to say something about it because, really, he needed to drag his mind away from the images that conjured up. Bede on his cot in his tent, making love to a nameless someone. With kisses slow and sweet, those dark eyes half-lidded.

"You sure do love those," said Galen.

"Coffee in prison is shit," said Bede, looking up. He took a long sip of his coffee and seemed to sigh, as if the caffeine had just hit his bloodstream like a bullet. "Some guys had privileges. They had coffee makers in their cells. I was not one of those people, so every time I drank that coffee in the dining hall, a little bit of me died inside."

He smiled, as if to show he was joking, even if Galen could see the truth of it in his eyes.

"This is actually too sweet for me," said Galen, lifting his paper cup, brushing his thumb through a smear of dried whipped cream. "I like—"

He paused, realizing that not only Bede was listening quite intently, but Toby and Owen were, as well. All three of his team were leaning forward, as if what he was about to say was more interesting than anything they'd heard in days. Perhaps even years.

Which was when he remembered from his training that sharing bits of your life, your experiences, with your team, was just as important as listening to your team. So he soldiered on, even though it felt a bit strange to be the center of attention.

"I like coffee served in a diner mug. You know, those thick white china mugs?" All three of them nodded, their eyes going wide. "Somehow, when you stir in sugar from those glass canisters and stir in the half-n-half from those little plastic cups, the coffee tastes perfect. It tastes even better when someone comes around and gives you a warm up."

With a smile and a half-defensive laugh, Galen took a slug of the overly sweet white chocolate mocha, and added, "Back when I lived on the family farm, my dad and I tried to get a couple of those mugs but short of ordering them by the case—"

"Or stealing," added Toby helpfully.

"Yes, or stealing them," said Galen, laughing again. "Yeah, we never could find any online. Maybe I'll hit up the diner in Chugwater some day and ask them to sell me a set of four."

There was no-one in the coffee shop who came around to offer Galen a warmup, but he finished his white mocha just the same, then gathered his team, and led them to the truck.

"Are we going to pick up those hand pumps next?" asked Owen as they all piled in, which was a surprise, as usually Toby seemed to be the mouthpiece of the pair.

"Yes, we are," said Galen. "Then we can break for lunch and spray this afternoon. And it's movie night tonight. Does that sound good?"

He did not have to ask for their permission or approval, but just as he'd been able to involve them in the research about what to do with the dug-up knapweed, he realized that getting their feedback engaged their attention and energy. And already the general spirit of the team seemed to be on the rise.

They drove to the ranch in the ever-growing heat, jacked up on caffeine, and laughing as they found bits of knapweed gnarled into the cotton of their shirts, the hems of their blue jeans.

At the ranch, they picked up the pumps from the supply shed, and it was a spray-fest that afternoon in the valley, as his team took turns spraying the ground and each other. They would all need showers before dinner, but what would it hurt, as the spray was only vinegar, water, and liquid Castile soap.

It was toward the end of the afternoon, when he was just about to call a halt to work, that Galen's phone buzzed in his pocket.

He pulled it out to view a text message from Maddy that his books from Amazon were due to arrive later that day, and did he want to pick them up or did he want someone to bring them down to the valley?

Galen hadn't recalled clicking the box for overnight shipping, but maybe he had. Didn't matter. The main question that popped up in his mind, given his recent trend of involving members of his team, was whether he should put the books away himself, or ask Bede to do it. After all, the books had been selected by Bede.

He texted her back, saying he'd pick them up before dinner, and if she needed to close up early to just leave them on the front porch of her office.

Putting his phone back in his pocket, he told himself he wasn't making a special effort just so he could see the pleased surprise on Bede's face, except that was a bald faced lie. He couldn't wait for Bede to get the books.

CHAPTER 15

BEDE

Maybe Bede should not have taken over corralling Toby and Owen, even if Galen had seemed a little in over his head. But, if there was anything Bede knew how to do, it was control a pack of unruly criminals, ready to shoot first and not give a fuck after.

And even if that pack consisted of only two somewhat lame and not very effective thieves, at least it gave him something to do. Something to think about other than his own woes, though maybe he'd strong-armed them too hard, harder than he should have.

He'd already been thinking about not ordering Toby and Owen around anymore when Galen had stepped up to him and jabbed him in the chest with a stern finger and told him to back off. Like he wasn't afraid of Bede *at all*.

The quarrel had continued to get out of hand when Bede had accidentally clipped Galen in the nose.

He'd fully expected that would get him kicked out of the program, and he would regret that, because he was starting to fall in love with the valley and all of its moods.

Except Galen had just said, *Oh, for fuck's sake,* just as his nose began to bleed in earnest. Tipping his head back, clamping his nose with his hand as he squinted up at the sun, was just about more than Bede could resist.

Sure, with one of his own men, he had always been stern. *Walk it off. Bleed somewhere else.*

But with Galen, Bede had gathered ice and clasped it to the back of Galen's neck, almost without thought. Made him rinse and spit. Wiped his face with the cloth that Owen had raced to get, after dampening it first.

Then, hunkered down at Galen's side, Bede had dispensed sage wisdom, when all the while he wanted to run and fetch a pillow so Galen could lie in the shade and just rest. Wait till his nosebleed had stopped.

Galen would have a hell of a headache come morning, but when Bede had explained he'd not meant to do it, Galen had understood.

I know, he'd said. And then he'd told Bede he was going to put on a clean shirt and that he'd meet Bede in the mess tent.

Once there, Galen had not only failed to mention their tussle from the night before, but when Gabe asked Galen about his nose, Galen out and out lied. He said that he'd lost his grip and that a shovel had whacked him in the face.

Then, in the afternoon, Galen had surpassed himself because instead of telling Toby and Owen what to do, making them feel safe the way Bede would have done, Galen had turned it around.

It happened when Toby raised the question about what they were going to do with the knapweed. Galen had said, *That's a good question, Toby,* when surely, surely, he already knew the answer.

Then he'd offered up his own laptop so they could research the best answer.

Back in the day, Bede had owned a top of the line MacBook Pro, and had created dozens of spreadsheets to help him keep track of shipments and the weights of cocaine bundles, and the rent on the meth house in a dodgy part of Denver, and utility payments that must never go unpaid, lest drugs stored in a warehouse might be spoiled by heat or cold.

It was a pleasure for Bede to use Galen's fairly fast Dell, and to search for basic things like *knapweed* and *dispose of*.

Bede had to hand it to Galen for being so clever, because everything seemed to shift, and the tone of the team changed right then and there. And Bede felt his own spirits being lifted up, just like Toby's and Owen's seemed to be.

From there, the afternoon leaped from good to great, because not only had Bede been able to use a super-fast laptop, they'd also gone for coffee.

Sure, he'd thought for certain that when Toby had demanded they go get coffee, Galen would say no. But Galen had said yes, looking adorable as he joked about being able to afford pup cups, seemingly pleased that Toby had suggested it.

Going into the air-conditioned coffee shop, with its round marble-topped tables, and glass case full of baked treats, was a little like Bede imagined arriving in heaven would be like. The place smelled like good coffee and baked sugar, and of the scent of good coffee beans being roasted in the back rising in the air.

Sitting across from Galen as he savored his lavender espresso buoyed Bede up more than he thought it could.

He saw Galen watching him as he sighed into his frothy drink and smiled from behind the foam of his own white chocolate mocha. It was as if the two of them shared a secret that Toby and Owen simply couldn't understand.

The conversation turned, naturally, to coffee. Bede had complained about prison coffee, and from there, Galen had told them all about his love for the kind of coffee mugs that a diner might use. That, along with a brief mention about the family farm, the pang in Galen's voice quite clear, at least to Bede, gave Bede more insight than he had only moments before.

But what was he supposed to do with how that made him feel, kind of jumpy and interested at the same time? And how was he supposed to stop staring at Galen's pretty face, flushed pink with the rush of overly sweet caffeine? Stop staring at those gray eyes that sparkled with laughter?

Bede loved to laugh. He and Winston used to laugh all the time. In prison, there had been no laughter, and no reason to smile. Sure, he'd laughed and smiled, but it had all been faked, just to keep up appearances.

Now, though? He'd laughed more than he had in five years. Plus, at the end of his first week in the valley, it was starting to feel different. *He* was starting to feel different. And what was he supposed to do with that?

After the coffees, they piled back in the truck and Galen drove them to the ranch, trundling up the dirt road that went through the middle of the ranch, them with their elbows hanging out the truck's windows as they went past a line of ranch guests with binoculars over their shoulders, guests who waved at them, and they waved back. Just like they were regular guys. Just as though nobody in the place had any idea that any man in that truck had spent time behind bars.

It made everything feel new and possible and just fucking different from Bede's old world, where everywhere he went he was known and recognized as a highly regarded lynchpin in the drug world. There was no way he could go back to that, not with a feeling like this sinking into his bones. Making him feel good all over.

Another surprise came when Bede was in his tent after dinner, alone, his blood-dark boots in his hand.

He debated whether he would put them on and go to movie night with everybody else. Outside the tent, in the woods, warmth was fading from the day, slow, low sounds and high, quick sounds, and small chirr-chirr sounds. He had no idea what was making any of it.

He took a pair of new white socks and his cowboy boots, and sat on the bottom step of the wooden platform, the boots on the step, his feet in the dust.

Somewhere he'd read that the earth was electric, and that it got recharged from above whenever lightning hit it. That electricity could be soaked in through bare skin. Which was probably all bullshit, but he did feel a sense of calm wash over him when he sat like this, with the low purple cloak of dusk settling all around.

"Barefoot, eh?" asked a voice.

Bede looked up. Galen was coming up the path with an armful of Amazon box.

For a second, he just blinked as Galen plopped the box down on the ground at Bede's bare feet, and sat on the bottom step next to Bede as he waved a hand over the box, which sat between them like newlywed bundling.

"What's that?" asked Bede. It was all so very surreal, having Galen there, noticing his bare feet, acting like them sitting there in the middle of the woods in a purple dusk was actually quite ordinary, when it was anything but.

"It's your books, from the list you wrote down," said Galen. "I figured I'd let you take your pick of what you wanted to keep with you, then put you in charge of putting the rest on the bookshelf in the mess tent."

When Bede had been with Winston, and even before that time, he'd never considered a book anything he'd want to spend time with. Even in school, he'd done his best to avoid actually cracking a book open unless he had to.

But once in prison, books had become his lifeline. The prison library had an odd selection of both fiction and non-fiction, everything from how to build a fire to the history of football.

The books had been old, worn at the edges, frankly unloved. He'd read everything he could get his hands on, just the same, to keep his mind occupied, to keep thoughts of Winston from creeping in like stray shards.

The books in the Amazon box would be brand new. And, being from his own list, however haphazard, they'd be something he'd actually *want* to read.

He'd want to keep all the books, but he didn't mind sharing them.

"Here." Galen stood up, reached into his pocket, and pulled out a small jackknife. He opened the blade and, with one smooth motion, cut open the Amazon box. "There you go. Have at it, and we'll see you at movie night."

Evidently Bede's absence had not gone unnoticed. Probably Kell had said something about it.

"Didn't realize it was required attendance," he said, making it a joke.

As Galen walked away, back into the woods toward the main compound, Bede thought he saw a hitch in Galen's shoulders, as if he'd snorted laughter at the odd comment.

Turning his attention to the box, Bede pulled out book after book. The titles were all the ones from his list and included a whole bunch of books he'd not asked for. Which meant that Galen had thought about it, too, and ordered anything he thought might be enjoyable to read.

Bede reached in and pulled out *The Road, The Water is Wide, The Shining,* and *Demon Copperhead,* and took those to his shelf in the tent. Coming back out, he pulled on his socks and the blood-red boots and, packing the remaining books back in the box, he made his way to the mess tent, the books getting heavier with every step.

The lights were on when he got there, with everyone milling around the crock-pot of nacho cheese and laughing at someone's antics in taking too much, waiting for the movie to be set up.

Ducking down, Bede quickly put the books on the shelf, rearranging them to suit himself, rather than anyone else, and left the box for someone else to dispose of.

By the time he'd put the books away, he stood up and realized that nobody was paying him any mind and that all the good seats in front were full.

So he sat in the back row, enjoying the press of the inside of his new boots against his toes and realized he could see Galen's profile.

Galen was smiling as he was talking to someone, Gabe, probably. And he was lovely to look at. So pretty.

Bede shifted in his seat, and rocked his booted feet, taking a long slow draw of breath.

Knowing that he didn't want to watch a movie, not all stirred up like he was, he slipped away. Trotting down the steps, he thought he smelled something dark and rich in the air. It sure wasn't the odor of woodsmoke from the sanctioned campfire, that Bede knew for certain. No, it was pot, and the good stuff too. Freshly flown in.

He followed the scent all the way to the first aid hut and then went around it.

There, an autolight on the side of the roof illuminated a young man with sloppy dark hair, and a five o'clock shadow that looked too perfect not to be carefully groomed. Around his wrist he wore a bracelet that looked like it was made of thin strips of braided leather.

He was slouched against the wall, one booted foot propping him up as he spun a spiral of smoke from his mouth. He pulled the joint away from his pursed mouth, looked at Bede, and winked at him.

"Is that pot?" asked Bede. He'd never gotten high a lot, his business had required him to be too much on the ball for that, but it'd been ages since he'd had any, and he needed something to relax him, just now.

At the young man's nod, Bed asked, "Can I get some?"

Wordlessly, the young man handed over the joint, the moisture from his mouth still on the tip as Bede pulled in a long, slow draw.

Yes, the stuff was fresh, the smoke smooth around the edges. It was as good as Bede would have sold, back in the day, before he'd gotten into dealing cocaine. And the effect, rather than feeling like a clap upside the head, like cocaine tended to give him, the few times he'd taken it, was a gentle ease into relaxation, the aftertaste holding only the slightest trace of bitterness.

"Thank you," said Bede, holding the joint out.

"Take another," said the young man. "I got plenty." He pulled out a battered Sucrets box, held it up, and pulled out a stubby white joint.

Bede bent and touched the smoking end of the joint he held and waited till the joint in the young man's hand caught and began to smoke.

As the young man drew in a lungful, the smoke swirled above their heads, limned by the auto light as it blended with the spicy pine scent all around them, both of them looked up to watch the moths dance in the autolight.

"Share your troubles, man," said the young man.

"There's this guy," said Bede.

"There's always a guy," the young man said with a low laugh that sounded rueful.

"I've been here a week." Bede paused, taking a draw from his joint, pausing to lick his lips as his sense of relaxation deepened. "Never thought I'd make it even this far. But this guy."

Bede paused, not quite sure what to do with all the feelings let loose inside of him.

"This guy," prompted the young man.

"He's so annoying." Bede let out the smoke, swirling it on his tongue as he turned this thought over. "But kind of sweet, too. And so fucking pretty."

Maybe his attention shouldn't be turned by a pretty face. Maybe he should still be mourning Winston, clamping back his sorrow. Not moving on. Being faithful. Maybe he should. But it'd been five years. How long was long enough?

"How pretty?" asked the young man.

Bede glanced at him as he inhaled another lungful of smoke. Then he looked away and imagined that as the blue twilight came fully down, he could see stars poking through the darkness above the tops of the pine trees.

"Really pretty, but it's not just his face, which is, you know, sculpted." Bede made a gesture, drawing his fingers in the air in front of his face. "Or his long legs. Or his hair, always in his face. He's just one of those people."

"Those people," said the young man.

"You look at them, and you just know—" Bede paused to exhale, licking his lips again. "He's a real person. There's nothing fake there. The lights are on in those gray eyes and everybody, and I mean *everybody*, is home."

"You like 'em smart, then."

"I don't know." Bede inhaled a lungful of clear, pine-scented air, an apéritif to his next draw of pot, and let it out slowly. "Maybe I do."

Winston had been smart, with a brain for numbers and a knack for sniffing out undercover cops, or drug dealers who would welsh on you as soon as they'd walked out of the alley.

Maybe smart wasn't the word to describe Galen, and pretty didn't seem enough. And maybe it'd taken Bede a whole week in a strange place and several tokes of the good stuff to realize it. That Galen was nothing like Winston.

Yet something inside of Bede stirred at the thought of how he sure as hell hadn't laughed as much as he did when he was around Galen. Never enjoyed delivering dry zingers just for the pleasure of hearing Galen laugh.

It was as if, when he'd gotten out of the white prison van, he'd stepped into a whole different dimension.

"I like 'em smart *and* annoying."

Just as Bede was about to take another draw, footsteps came from around the corner, and Galen was there. There were sparks in his lovely gray eyes as he scraped the hair back from his face, as if he simply could not believe what he was seeing. Looking even prettier than in Bede's mind's eye.

"Are you smoking *pot*, Bede?" Galen asked, loud and angry. "And you, Beck. What are you doing? Smoking is not allowed in the valley, you *know* that."

With a laugh, Beck took a draw, held in the smoke, and blew it out slowly, like he was the toughest kid on the playground and simply unafraid, or at least unworried, about getting a whole lot of detention. He pinched out the orange-embered end of the joint with his thumb and forefinger, then drew out his Sucrets box to tuck the joint away.

"Just don't tell Royce, okay?" Beck said with a jaunty smile.

"Honestly, what the hell are you playing at?"

Galen directed this fully at Bede.

"It's been so hot," continued Galen. "The woods are dry as a bone. It's a fire hazard. You could start a forest fire."

"Not playing," said Bede, casually, slowly, enjoying the pleasant eyeful of Galen, hopping mad, flushed. He drew himself up straight, his back pressed to the side of the first aid hut, and couldn't hide his slow smile. "I'm just smoking. And looking." His eyes swept Galen up and down, slowly, a warmth spreading through him. "Enjoying the view, as well."

At Galen's rough sound of astonishment, Bede chuckled as he snubbed out his joint between his thumb and forefinger and handed it to Beck. Who added it to his Sucrets box, which he placed in the pocket of his blue jeans as he picked up an army green duffle bag that had been waiting patiently at his feet.

"That the guy?" Beck asked, pausing at the corner of the first aid hut, one hand spread across the wood.

"How could you tell?" asked Bede, turning to look at Beck.

"Sparks are flying, man," said Beck, and then he was gone, disappearing around the corner of the building like so much pot smoke.

In his relaxed state, his first truly relaxed state in over five years, Bede did not care that Galen was right there, witnessing this particular conversation.

Who knew what conclusions Galen might draw from such a confession as Bede had just made, but he was a free man, wasn't he? Free to think whatever thoughts came to him. Free to feel whatever he felt, including a hot streak of desire for a man that he wouldn't have even noticed five years earlier. A man that, according to every convention he could think of, he simply could not have.

Well, he could look. So he did.

"What is going on with you?" demanded Galen, taking a step closer. "How much did you smoke?"

Bede shifted up from the wall of the first aid hut and also took a step closer to Galen. Now they were less than a foot apart, standing in the smoke-laced glare of the auto light.

Bede's impulse was to answer the call shifting inside of him, from his belly, along his thighs. The relaxation brought about by the pot shifted into desire, released on a cloud of inhibition long gone.

As Bede well knew, the lights were on in those gray eyes and everybody was home, and he saw exactly the nanosecond that Galen figured out what Bede's intentions were. Or what they would have been, had Galen not flat-palmed Bede against the wall and taken a step back.

"You're high," Galen said, his voice low, accusatory.

"That's an understatement," replied Bede, equally low. "But just sos you know, I don't do it that often."

He could move forward or he could stay where he was and draw Galen to him, but again, Galen surprised him.

"This is bullshit," he said, and turned on his heel. "I'm going back to the movie. You can do what you want, but if you do join, change your shirt because now you smell like pot."

Now Galen was gone and Bede was all alone. The high of pot, an elusive mistress, was fading by traces in his system, but the smile remained on his face.

Maybe in the morning, when he was fully sober, he might think differently, but as for right now, he knew he was right. He liked 'em feisty and smart and high-minded. The sharp gray eyes didn't hurt at all, not one bit. Or those long legs. That hair.

He'd confessed this to Beck. More importantly, he'd all but confessed it to Galen.

There was no taking it back. He didn't want to.

He had no idea how any of this would look come the morning, but in that moment, he was glad about the pot, so he could say what he thought.

He knew that Winston would have approved of Bede speaking his mind.

Winston was a moment-to-moment kind of guy, always striding into the future. He would have been disappointed in Bede if he let himself be held back by a memory of what was.

Yes, he could keep Winston in his heart as long as the memories lingered, but maybe it was time for a future of his own.

CHAPTER 16

GALEN

S till smelling the reek of pot all around him, Galen made his way to the mess tent, but the movie was over, the night had gotten a little cooler, and everyone was headed to the campfire.

There, Blaze quickly built a fire, and nobody paid Galen much mind as he sat on one of the hay bales where he could see the reflection of dancing flames on the almost smooth, barely ruffled surface of the lake. There was no moon, so the stars were out, blinking overhead as they danced in the solar breeze.

Royce held court, sitting on a large hay bale near the fire. He read one of the ghost stories from a Foxfire book out loud, his voice dipping or rising, depending on how intense the story was.

Galen didn't believe in ghosts and thought the idea of reading aloud to a gathering of grown men, half of whom were criminals, was perhaps a waste of time.

Still, being still, sitting there as the evening grew darker, allowed him to gather his thoughts. Or at least to attempt to gather them, as they were scattering like little bits of dust, refusing to come together.

On top of all of them, however, formed the image of Bede's face, his eyes intense. As he'd moved closer to Galen in that area behind the first aid hut, his intention had been quite clear, though it was a bit of a muddle now. Had Bede been on the verge of kissing him?

Where on earth had Bede gotten the idea that Galen would ever, in a million years, want to hook up with him? To accept advances from an ex-con? There was no way. Simply no way.

He was shocked. But he was not made of stone, and something inside of his chest had responded when Bede had stepped closer, just about bursting through layers of muscle and bone.

He'd almost choked keeping it inside. It was as if that part of him, part of his heart, had taken on a life of its own.

And now, sitting by the campfire, he wanted nothing more than to be miles away so he wouldn't have to deal with any of this. While his team-leading skills seemed to be getting better, he was wary. It might be a fluke.

Certainly after Bede had been bold enough to make a pass at his boss, whether or not Galen responded, it would probably go back downhill. Fast. Zipline fast.

Realizing he was slumped forward, like a drunk yet to come off a bender, Galen straightened up. He pretended he was very invested in the ghost story Royce was currently telling, something about a woman trapped in a well who died and pioneers who stayed in a haunted log cabin.

Galen felt Gabe's attention on him and knew that he might have to fess up in their very first team meeting on Saturday about the fact that Bede had made a pass at him.

The ghost story ended, and a low, friendly discussion sprang up about whether or not ghosts existed. Galen used that time to make a hasty exit, without saying goodnight or anything.

He needed to be off by himself, so he took the path along the edge of the lake toward the dock.

He didn't have his swimsuit with him, so maybe he would just take off all his clothes and use the dock as a jumping off point. Use the dark still waters of the lake, speckled by starlight, to wash himself clean and start anew.

Then he could get rid of the intrusive thoughts pushing into him, all of which were tagged by images of Bede. Bede smiling. Laughing. The side eye glance he'd given Galen when he'd suggested they could get pup cups at Starbucks.

These were not thoughts he should be having.

But when he got to the dock, he saw someone was already there. It was Bede, hunkered down in the grass, his very fancy boots in the grass beside him. He was barefooted, and wearing only a t-shirt and jeans. Still stoned, obviously. Coming down from his high.

"What are you doing out here?" Galen asked, keeping his voice low, in case—in case what? Everyone else was at the campfire, and it was just the two of them.

"What?" Bede stood up, clasping the tops of the boots between the fingers of one hand. "Oh, this. I'm throwin' my boots in the lake," he said, the words soft and slow. "They remind me of Winston."

"You're going to *what*?" Galen knew he'd not misheard. In fact, the back-and-forth motion of Bede's arm was indicative of someone who was gearing up to throw whatever he had in his hands as far as he could.

"You heard me."

"I sure did," said Galen, sputtering. "But why would you do that to such nice boots?"

"What's it to you?" asked Bede, in that same, almost sleepy voice.

"I'll tell you what's it to me."

Bede was high and all kinds of vulnerable from the pot, so Galen took a deep breath and took a mental step back from what he'd been about to say. Stuff about how much the boots cost, how much it might cost to replace them. None of which was important in the face of what Bede was going through as he came down from his high.

And though, had anyone told him even weeks ago that he'd be handling someone like Bede with kid gloves, he might have laughed, yes. In their face. But he wasn't laughing now.

"Whatever is going on with you, throwing those boots in the water is not the answer," said Galen, thinking he might take the boots from Bede before he did toss them in the water. In the ranch's store, he'd seen with his very eyes the moment Bede had fallen in love with those boots, and in spite of everything, he didn't deserve to lose them.

Galen took a step forward.

"You going to turn me in?" asked Bede, clutching the boots to his chest.

"You going to smoke pot again?" Galen shot back.

Then Bede laughed, letting go of the boots so they crumpled to the grass.

"Are you laughing at me?" Galen's jaw dropped with astonishment.

"Yeah, I'm laughing at you," said Bede, his smile wide, still sleepy, still-pot induced. "You're not afraid of *anything*, are you." And in a whisper, he added, "Not even me."

"What the hell are you talking about?" Galen's question was loud enough, sharp enough, to echo across the lake, and come back with a slap.

"You just wade in and damn the consequences," said Bede with a wide, evocative wave of his hands. "In a prison yard, you'd be dead inside of a heartbeat. That or you'd be running the place."

"In case you haven't noticed," said Galen, totally confused, focusing on the only part of that he actually understood. "This isn't a prison yard."

He knew he was shouting, but he'd never been more confused in his life. Both by Bede's behavior and the shooting-up-from-the-depths-of-his-soul sparks that he could not control.

But Bede didn't move closer, didn't have the same expression on his face that he'd had behind the first aid hut. Instead, he looked tired, shoulders slumped. The aftereffects of the pot wearing off, perhaps. Or something else.

"Yeah, I noticed." The tone in Bede's voice was one of misery. As if being out of prison was far worse than being in it.

"You need to take those boots back to your tent," said Galen, making himself sound more stern than he felt.

"Sure thing, boss," said Bede, a little bit of humor seeming to return to him as he bent to scoop up the boots, clasping them to his chest with one arm.

"Put those on. Don't walk in the woods barefoot."

"Yes, boss." Bede put his boots on over his bare feet, one at a time, then straightened, looking at Galen with as much derision as he might eye someone in airport security. "That better?"

"Yes." Galen laughed low, in spite of himself. "Jesus, Bede."

Bede smiled at him, and even winked before turning to walk along the path by the lake, slipping into the dark trees like a ghost returning whence it had come.

Leaving Galen with his heart beating hard, not only that he'd imagined Bede might kiss him, but that he might welcome it.

In the morning, he'd have to deal with the fallout of their encounter.

But later. For now, he strode to the end of the dock, stripped down to his skin, and dove in.

The dark waters of the lake covered him with cool, silken layers, delicious and silent, and he swam underwater for a good long way before he surfaced through the glassy surface.

Keeping himself afloat by the barest movement of his arms and legs, he looked up at the stars in all their stillness. And let his mind go still.

Air and liquid pooled together in a sweet embrace for a good long while, slowing his heartbeat, cooling the flush from his cheeks. Then he shivered. Maybe it was time to get out.

Slow strokes brought him to the ladder on the floating end of the dock, and he hauled himself up, dripping. He had no towel, but his cotton shirt served the same purpose, and when he was dressed, he slipped on his socks and laced up his boots and slowly made his way through the darkness to his tent, and made a mental list of what he needed to do.

First, he needed to snag a meeting with Gabe and get some advice on how to better handle his team. Sure, at the end of his first week, things were improving, but he wanted to stay on track with that and not falter at his job of being team lead.

Second, he needed to figure out a way to keep the relationship between him and Bede strictly platonic. To find a way to pretend that nothing was happening between the two of them. Brush it off as an odd flicker of interest.

Third, he needed to pretend to hell and back that he simply did not care to know Bede better. That the laughter shared between them and long moments of friendly camaraderie were just that. Moments in passing. Not worth paying more attention to.

In his tent, he traded his lake-dampened clothes for clean boxers and a t-shirt, then brought out the stack of folders from the low shelf, found Bede's and thumbed through it.

His attention slid across the prison intake photos showing Bede in all his bad-assery-ness next to the text. Galen had scanned most of it before, but now read more slowly.

Raised by an aunt in a bad neighborhood, Bede had fallen into crime by circumstances not of his own making. But then he'd risen to the top of his game, shipping and selling drugs. Until the shootout.

Galen knew all of this. So what was he looking for? There it was. Winston Ludlow, the member of Bede's team who had died in that shootout.

Galen already knew this, but now he also knew that Winston was important enough to Bede that Bede's impulse had been to throw away a pair of much loved boots because they reminded him of Winston.

Slapping the folder shut, Galen put it back on the shelf. Then he sat on the edge of his cot, forearms propped on his thighs, hands dangling.

He knew he needed to get some sleep. The night was still warm, making him glad that he'd taken a dip in the cool lake. Unless it rained, which didn't seem likely, the following day would be hot as well.

And in the morning he found out he was right. The sun rose over the trees like liquid gold, and after breakfast, Galen took his team all the way to the bridge to start hacking away at the knapweed.

Right away, everyone was dragging their heels, large patches of sweat appearing along their backs and beneath their arms inside of ten minutes.

Even Bede was dragging, probably due to the aftereffects of smoking pot, but also because, even in the shade, it was too hot.

Bede was not only dragging, he looked ragged, as though he tossed and turned all night.

They worked for a while, but Galen knew what the guidelines were for the weather. In winter, if it was below freezing, you didn't work your team. In summer, if was above a certain temperature with a certain dew point, you pulled your team off the job.

Galen didn't have his phone with him to check the exact measurements, but he was just about to call a halt to work when Gabe stepped into the clearing beside the path. He was wearing his cowboy hat, and beneath that, a short-sleeved t-shirt, and probably the thinnest blue jeans known to man.

"What's up, Gabe?" Galen asked, going over to him. "I'm just about to call a halt."

"Good," said Gabe. "That was what I was coming to say. Early lunch. We've got fans and misters in the mess tent. This afternoon should cool off, but be sure to add extra breaks."

"Can do," said Galen.

He wasn't surprised to hear the groans of gratitude and the pleased expressions on the faces of his team. He led the way in propping their tools against the supply shed, and then to the mess tent. There, as he stepped into the coolness of the misters and tall fans, he breathed a sigh of relief.

Maybe, now that he wasn't so hot, he could figure out what he needed to do. To make a plan and to stick to the plan. Full speed ahead. That was the ticket, right? *Right?*

But, really, he had no idea. Hearts were fickle, including his own.

CHAPTER 17
BEDE

Sweating like he was trapped in hell's fiery inferno, Bede leaned on the end of his shovel and watched Gabe and Galen converse in boss-speak.

Were they talking about him? He didn't know. He was close enough to see their expressions, but too far away to hear what they were saying.

Maybe Galen was complaining that Bede had been smoking pot and had been relaxed enough to almost kiss his boss. Which was true.

And, standing behind the mess tent in that haze-induced state, it had seemed to Bede as if Galen almost welcomed it, because he'd risen up on his toes, an expectant expression in his lovely gray eyes.

Bede had no idea who the hell Beck was or how he fit into the valley, or even how he'd snuck an illegal substance into the valley.

Other than a sound scolding that would have done a governess proud, however, Galen didn't seem to bother himself much about it. And when Beck went off, duffle in hand, saying *Sparks flew, man*, Galen had blushed hard, then turned his attention on Bede, feathers flying as he explained the dangers of smoking and forest fires.

Galen's ire only made him prettier. Just about irresistible, but when Galen had departed to go back to movie night, all of the air seemed to leave Bede's body.

He had no right to even dream of getting together with someone like that. Couldn't imagine that Galen wouldn't tell someone what he knew about Bede. All his secrets.

Later, in the dark, in his pot-hazed state, looking down at his boots once more, he had felt the ghost of Winston all around him.

He'd really wanted to get rid of those boots, and he'd attempted to do so. Had gone down to the lake, and taken off the boots.

Sitting on his ass, feet in the grass, absorbing the earth's energy, he stared at the lake and imagined those depths and let the marijuana rocket through him, fading, then intensifying with every heartbeat.

He must have sat there for ages, because just as it was getting dark, Galen came up to him and demanded to know what the hell was going on.

Bede would have risen to the challenge, but as he got to his feet, Galen didn't back down, and it was either cry or laugh himself sick, but he was too tired for either.

When Galen had learned what Bede meant to do with the boots, he given Bede a piece of his mind. Coming right up to Bede, chest thrust out, his eyes blazing.

In fact, Galen was less afraid of Bede than anyone he'd ever met.

His cronies had always quivered in fear that they'd piss him off. The prison guards had, for the most part, not messed with him.

Even Kell had been leery, at least at the beginning.

But Galen? He looked ready to come at Bede with everything he had, and if that didn't make Bede fall for him all the more, he didn't know what would.

In the end, he'd done what Galen told him to do, which was to put his boots back on and go back to his tent.

Once there, as Kell watched, he'd silently wiped them down, and now those boots would be ready for the next time he wanted to wear them. After a quick shower, he'd flopped on top of his cot and basically passed out.

Now, the next morning, it was hot, but to his surprise, Galen dismissed them early, and led the way to an early lunch.

In the mess tent, both the misters and fans were going, making the mess tent a blissful oasis from the heat.

Standing in the line for the buffet, Bede was pleased, if a little surprised, to see Beck already sitting at one of the long tables.

He was digging into his cheeseburger and fries, and Bede grabbed his food and made a beeline to sit across from Beck. Galen sat next to him, with Toby and Owen bringing up the edges.

After a silent minute as they all began to eat, Bede wiped his mouth with his napkin, and said, "I'm sorry, Beck, but I don't know who you are. You're not a team lead and you're not one of the parolees, so—"

"I'm neither," said Beck, nonchalant, as he dipped a fry in the puddle of ketchup on his plate. "I'm Jonah's best friend and we made an arrangement for me to come up on the weekends. Which I do. Most weekends."

"Where do you stay?" asked Bede. Bede knew that Jonah was one of the parolees, but he'd not interacted with him much.

"Tent number ten." Beck made a gesture with his hand, shaping it like a pistol, shot it, and then blew away a cloud of imaginary smoke. "Closest to the facilities."

"But if you're Jonah's friend," asked Toby. "Where is he?"

They all looked around, but Jonah was absent.

"He and Royce are so fucking lovey dovey this weekend, I can't get a word in edge-wise." Beck made a broad gesture in the air as if to signal how done he was with Jonah's absence.

"Sorry. Lovey dovey?" asked Bede. Galen's eyebrows rose as he looked at Bede, the same question plain on his face. "Are they *together?*"

"Are they together?" Beck rolled his eyes. "They're fucking attached at the *hip*. But then, so are most of these guys."

"What are you *talking* about?" Galen's voice rose in a way that drew attention to him, so he hunkered down. "Am I blind? I never even noticed them together."

"Who's attached at the hip now?" asked Toby.

"Everybody."

"Is everybody fucking?" Bede asked out loud, guffawing.

Galen spit out his iced tea and had to dry his face off with his napkin.

Bede found himself staring hard at Beck, as if this would get Beck to spill all of his secrets. A little silence fell among the group, and nobody was eating. Four pairs of eyes drilled into Beck until he finally he broke.

"Okay," he said. "You wanna know? Here's the rundown. Gabe is fucking Blaze. Loudly. Every night." He gestured in the couple's direction. "Royce and Jonah are going through so much lube, from the sounds of it, that they ought to buy stock. They're probably off buying it now. And as for Marston and Kell—"

"I don't want to know," said Bede. "No details, please." He had no wish to find out something so intimate about Kell, let alone Marston.

"They are the cutest couple you have ever laid eyes on," said Beck primly, leaving the rest of the details to their imaginations.

"They are pretty cute," said Galen with a nod to affirm this fact.

"As for the rest of the parolees," said Beck, taking a look around the mess tent like he was keeping an eye out for enemy fire. "They might be fucking, but who's to say. They're a little more secretive about it, maybe."

The only thing on Bede's mind was not that this was going on, because guys in prison tended to hook up all the time.

Here, in the valley, it seemed like fraternization was allowed. Or maybe it wasn't *disallowed*, but nobody seemed bothered. If they had been, then all of this would have been called to a halt.

He couldn't stop himself from casting a glance in Galen's direction. Galen was studiously eating, keeping his eyes down. As if the whole conversation, Beck's big reveal, hadn't happened at all.

"Who are *you* fucking?" Toby asked Beck, because he had no filter whatsoever.

"He's not a parolee, dummy," said Owen, giving Toby a good jab with his elbow.

"Hey, I just want to know." Toby spread his hands wide to show his good intentions.

"Well, me and Gordy hook up sometimes," said Beck with a grin. "But I don't think he's in love with my tattoos."

As Toby and Owen began to grill Beck about his tattoos, a small silence fell between Bede and Galen. Galen was now looking at Bede cautiously, as if from around a corner, his eyes a little dark.

If what seemed to be growing between them was not forbidden, at least not by the rules of the valley, then what was holding them back was more personal than that.

As for himself, Bede didn't figure Galen would be the least bit interested. But then, if that was so, why did Galen keep looking and looking, like he was assaying the risk of reaching for a forbidden treat?

Bede wanted to find out. He very much wanted to find out, but he wasn't sure how.

In prison, he'd held himself back, so it'd been five long years without the touch of another human hand. Discounting the guards' casually rough treatment, that is.

The surge of want inside of him felt strange, foreign. A clawed, winged animal with nowhere to land.

He wanted to land, he very much did. But as he watched Galen looking away, he wasn't sure he'd get the chance.

CHAPTER 18

GALEN

During lunch, Clay, a ranch hand up at Farthingdale Ranch, had brought down a bag of mail that had been misdirected and hadn't been delivered to the valley.

As he handed the letters out, it felt a little like mail call at camp, with everybody waiting till letters could be arranged so Clay could hand them out smoothly.

Galen, chomping on a potato chip, looked at the letter Clay placed next to his plate and, dismayed, saw the red stamp and the return address from the IRS.

Heart pounding, he opened the envelope and saw the warning about a late payment, the amount due, and the amount of the penalty if not paid by the end of July. Which wasn't that far away. He needed to get on this before it blew up in his face and he ended up losing the farm.

The other letter was from the hospital in Cheyenne, with a statement about how much he owed, with a lot of extra fees added on that he'd not known about.

He couldn't possibly pay both the IRS and the hospital, but it would make more sense to reach out to the IRS first, so he didn't get the farm taken away from him. The hospital, which kept finding new ways to charge him, could charge him interest, and he could manage that. But his heart was racing, just the same.

This was the first year he'd done taxes on his own, without Earl doing the most of it, and himself hanging around the edges of the process.

The question was, when was he supposed to call the IRS? First chance he got.

Mulling this over, he finished his lunch and then pulled his team together, leading them out to the path just across the river, where a stray crop of knapweed had sprung up seemingly overnight.

Crossing the simple wooden bridge to the other side, the river willows curved over the path gave them all a respite from the sun. It was still humid, and it was still rough going as they hacked at the dry earth with their hoes, and used the vinegar and soap in hand sprayers to douse the roots.

"How did it get up this far?" asked Toby, not bothering to hide his tone.

"On people's feet," said Galen.

It didn't look like the knapweed had gotten very far out this way, but far enough, so when Toby, Owen, and Bede moved along the trail, Galen stepped back and pulled out his phone, the desperation that he'd kept tucked down until he could get a private moment rose in his throat.

Pulling the letter out of his pocket, he dialed the number for the IRS, and was instantly put on hold. Within five minutes, to his surprise, he got someone named Larry, who gave his ID number and asked what the issue was.

Galen recited the information from the letter, then asked, "What am I supposed to do? I can't pay all of this."

"You have to pay by the end of the current month," said Larry in tones that indicated he simply did not care. "Otherwise you'll receive a penalty and interest will be incurred."

"I'm willing to pay, I just need extra time," said Galen, shock rolling through him as he pressed the cellphone to his ear, as if that would convey to Larry the urgency of the situation. "Isn't there something I can do?"

"Let me put you on hold while I talk to my supervisor," said Larry. And then the line went dead.

Hands shaking, Galen went through the process again, and got hold of a woman named Susan.

She didn't give her ID number, but when she heard what Galen wanted, she told him that she needed to get a supervisor. Galen was again put on hold, and again the line went dead.

Now, pacing beneath the arch of a line of river willows, the shade dappled and spicy smelling, Galen took a breath and gripped his phone, almost tight enough to make the plastic squeak. Hot sweat streaked down the back of his neck.

"Why don't you just ask your accountant to help you with that?" asked a voice from behind him.

Galen whirled to see Bede standing there, a bottle of water from the small ice chest they'd brought with them in one hand, a dusty hoe in the other.

"What?" asked Galen, blinking the sweat from his eyes as he reeled, not just from the dire situation over money owed, money that he simply did not have, but from Bede's presence. All rugged and manly, sweating beneath his arms, his smile bright and sudden, as if he knew that Galen was drooling over him and couldn't help himself.

"Get your accountant to help you," said Bede, seemingly patient, though there was a smirk around his mouth. "Or your bank manager."

"What am I, moneybags?" spat Galen, wishing he too had thought to grab one of the waters from the ice chest. "I don't have an accountant. I'm my accountant." He spread his fingers across his chest, irritation rising.

"What you need," said Bede, casually, leaning on the handle of the hoe as if he were a farmer of renowned repute who knew everything there was to know about any crop you might care to mention. "And no offense, but what you need is a woman over fifty. She might have a raspy voice from smoking too much and a hairdo that is twenty years out of date, but she knows everything—and I mean *everything*—there is to know about every form the IRS has ever come up with. Her name is probably Susan or Betty. Get her on the line. She can help you."

"I just spoke with a Susan," said Galen, waving that idea away with a little laugh that he couldn't quite help. "It's not her. Wait, were you *listening* to my call?"

"Yes," said Bede. "There's a solution to this, I assure you."

Galen almost sagged with a sense of relief. Bede knew his troubles and wanted to help. Maybe this was Bede's way of saying thank you for not turning him in for smoking pot in the valley.

Bede chuckled and reached out his hand.

"What?" asked Galen again.

"Give me your phone," he said.

"No, I will not." Galen clasped the phone to his chest. He really shouldn't be taking care of personal business on company time, but this was urgent, though not urgent enough to give Bede access to his phone.

"Property tax, right?" asked Bede.

When Galen nodded, Bede held out his hand and said, "There's a form for that. I'll find Susan or Betty for you. The *right* Susan or Betty. She'll know just what that form is, but you have to press the correct buttons first. Go ahead, dial the number, and then give it to me."

From the sounds of it, up ahead on the trail, Toby and Owen were goofing around. Galen probably needed to get on top of that situation before it exploded.

More importantly, really needed to get his money problem figured out and fast, so he could stop worrying about it and focus on his job.

So, with a sigh, he re-dialed the number and handed the phone to Bede, who took the phone as though it was his own.

At each prompt from the IRS's bot answering service, he pressed a number, quite a different sequence of numbers than what Galen had entered, and pretty soon, Bede had the phone to his ear.

"Yes, this is Galen—" Reaching out, Bede took the IRS letter and scanned it. "Galen Parnell. Who is this? Yvette? Thank you, Yvette. I'm looking for an extension for this tax payment. I've got other bills and am just trying to get them in order. Can you help me?"

Bede's voice was soft and flirty, but not, it seemed, entirely disingenuous. With the melty tone in each word, the softness around the masculine, he sounded like he really meant what he was saying, that he, personally, was in dire tax straits.

"So it's not you? Who does that? Oh, Clara? Can you connect me? Thank you."

"It's Clara, not Susan or Yvette," said Bede, pulling the phone away from his ear as he gave Galen a wink. "My mistake." He paused, and then, focused on the call, said, "Is this Clara? Thank goodness. I think you can help me. What's the form for an extension when the payment for property taxes is late? Or a payment plan, if there's no extension?"

Bede listened for a good two minutes straight, flicking his gaze up to meet Galen's, his eyebrows curved in what Galen could only interpret as a hopeful expression.

Then Bede read her some of the information from the letter, then said to her, "You can? Sure! Yes, just send the confirmation number to the email on file. That'd be great. Awesome. Yes, you too, have a fabulous day."

Bede ended the call with his thumb, then handed the phone back to Galen.

"You've got a three-month extension, boss," he said. "She just filled out the form for you."

"How the *hell* did you do that?" asked Galen, his jaw dropping, struggling to wrap his mind around how unbelievably grateful he was for Bede's help.

"She had the raspiest voice I ever did hear." Bede shrugged, his grin widening. "Must smoke two packs of unfiltered Camels a day."

"But how did you *know* you could do that?" asked Galen. "You talked to her like you already knew there was a way—"

"I guess being a criminal comes in handy," said Bede with a laugh as he folded the letter from the IRS and handed it to Galen. "I worked with a lot of accountants, so I know a few loopholes, legal and otherwise. This one's totally legit. But really, people at the IRS are just people. They just want to file their papers, take all your money, and then go home." He shrugged again and then hefted the hoe in his hands, tapping the heel of it on the ground. "Let me know if you don't get that confirmation, okay?"

Open-mouthed, Galen watched Bede go up the trail and disappear around the bend, the leaves of the river willow folding dappled sunlight across his broad shoulders.

Galen's phone dinged, and he held it up, thumbing his email open and there, like a bright shiny star, was the email from the IRS.

He opened and scanned the email, seeing the confirmation number and the date, three months out, for the full payment. He could manage that. He had time. He could figure out his life.

By October, he'd have the bonus from the valley job and several months' payment from the tenants at the farm. There'd also be honey to harvest, which would bring in some ready cash. As for what would happen to the farm, that was future Galen's problem.

His only problem, at that moment, was catching up to his team and making sure Toby and Owen didn't bash each other's heads in as they fought over who got to go back to the compound to bring out more vinegar. And to keep his eyes on the task, and not on Bede's strength as he dug more knapweed than Toby and Owen combined. Not to mention how eye-catching he was, those shirt sleeves rolled up, the dark-eyed glances he sent Galen's way from beneath the brim of his straw cowboy hat.

The afternoon went by quickly, and right before dinner, while his team was busy getting into the buffet line in the mess tent, Galen paused at the bottom of the wooden steps, and dialed the number from the hospital bill.

Thinking hard about what Bede might say, how he might say it, Galen used his softest, most upbeat voice and explained what he needed from them.

"I can pay it," he said. "I sure want to pay it, but I need to break it up into smaller payments." He lowered his voice even more, making himself sound a little helpless and overwhelmed. "I just can't figure out how to make that happen."

The woman on the other end of the line, who might have been named Julie, sighed. He heard keys clicking and then she said, "Okay, you're all set. Your first payment is due end of August, and then every month for eleven more months after that."

"Will there be a late fee?" he asked, trying to mask his disbelief at how easily this was happening.

"No, you're all set up. I'll send you an email to confirm. Is there anything else I can help you with, sir?"

"No, thank you," he said, and when she hung up, he hung up, and then stood there, grasping his phone and holding it out as if for someone to examine.

He climbed the wooden steps to the mess tent, stepping out of the conversation and into the bustle of the meal. He looked up to see Bede standing with a tray in his hands, fully loaded with what smelled like baked spaghetti with tons of cheese.

Bede grinned at him and then turned away, as if he was full of himself because he knew more about the ins and outs of the IRS as a criminal than Galen ever would as a law-abiding citizen, which was, quite simply, the icing on the cake.

He owed Bede a thank you, a hearty thank you. He should have said it at the moment when they'd been standing beneath the arched willow branches, and not waited till now. But he needed to say it now, even if he had an audience. It was the right thing to do.

Standing in line for his meal took only a moment or two, then he planted himself across from Bede like he'd been drawn there by some invisible magnet. How nice it was to have someone's support. How nice it was that, against all odds, Bede was his dashing rescuer.

Galen clattered his silverware to draw Bede's attention, as he seemed focused on his plate. But when Bede looked up, that smirk firmly in place, Galen knew that Bede had been aware of him all along.

"Everything all right?" asked Bede, casually eating, laughter in his eyes because now, as both of them knew, Galen owed him one.

"Yes," said Galen, quite clearly. "Thank you for your help earlier. Using your technique, I called the hospital too, and I've got an extension and a payment plan, so I'm all set."

"There's always a Susan or Betty at anyplace you might want to do business," said Bede, nodding like the wisest of sages. "Just be sweet and respectful and she will help you."

Galen should not be drawn into that smile, should not feel the gears in his mind shifting, as the idea that all criminals were idiots faded away to be replaced with the idea that some criminals were smart. And kind. And helpful.

Should he be so grateful? Could he have found Susan or Betty on his own? Maybe, but it would have taken ages and instead of eating his dinner, he could be standing in the woods, doing his best to find some shade while he waited on an endless hold with the worst music imaginable.

He let himself look at Bede for one more minute, at the way a lock of dark hair tumbled across Bede's forehead, the way his jaw firmed as he smiled. The way he always wore the sleeves of his snap button shirt rolled up, sweat gleaming along his neck, buttons open as far as possible without actually undoing his shirt all the way.

Then Galen looked away.

Smart guys always drew him in. Strong forearms were always a treat for his eyes.

Galen made himself focus on his meal, and made mental notes about how he still wanted to talk to Gabe about how he might better manage his team. Maybe along the way he'd figure out how to ignore that pull, that steady, steady pull, of Bede's brilliant smile and dark blue eyes.

CHAPTER 19

BEDE

By the time Saturday rolled around, Bede figured he had a good handle on things, better able to navigate a Winston-less future. But naturally, that was when Galen reminded him at lunchtime that there was a mandatory counseling session right after lunch for all parolees.

At Wyoming Correction, counseling had been an on-again, off-again event that nobody had kept track of. He'd stayed away from those meetings as much as he could.

While he didn't want to complain about having to go, as that always drew more attention than was wanted, luckily Toby expressed what probably all of them were thinking.

"Do we have to?" asked Toby in a voice that grated on Bede's ears.

"You do," said Galen, even prettier when he was relaxed and smiling than when he was all riled up and pissed off.

"And what'll you be doing?" asked Bede, fully expecting to be told it was none of his business.

Of course Galen surprised him, but then, maybe Bede's help about that IRS bill had softened him up.

"We have a team meeting during that time," Galen said, standing up with his tray. "After that, we'll have some light maintenance work. And then Sunday you have the whole day off."

Bede hadn't had a day off in years. Not in the five years he'd been in prison, where he always had to be on and ready for anything. And not before that, as the drug trade went on twenty-four-seven.

Hustling to bus his tray, he stood behind Galen and, over his shoulder, quietly said, "Explain what you mean by day off."

"It's exactly what it sounds like," said Galen, not looking at Bede, but turning his head slightly in Bede's direction, creating an intimate circle of two. "Meals are at the usual time, but you don't have to be at any specific place or do anything. Some people have visitors, which is allowed between the hours of ten and five. You can nap. Swim. Read one of your books. Whatever you like."

Hands now empty, Galen turned and looked fully at Bede, giving Bede the idea that Galen was considering the fact that men behind bars never experienced a simple and honest day off. Of what it might mean.

"Ask in the counseling session if the idea of a day off continues to be confusing for you," said Galen, the corner of his mouth twitching as he teased.

Bede's mouth twitched in response, and for a moment it felt as though they were two young boys in the back pew of a solemn church trying not to laugh. And he'd not laughed in five years behind bars. Not since Winston died.

"I'll be there," said Bede.

He could not let himself believe that a new location, a new environment, could make so much difference in how he felt. Calm, reasonably happy. And especially that someone who, by his very existence, should not be Bede's friend, could make him laugh.

A parole officer was generally thought of as the enemy. You couldn't laugh with the enemy, could you?

Because of the heat, Bede grabbed a shower before the counseling session, and put on a clean t-shirt before striding back to the mess tent.

His small excitement at the idea of having an hour to just sit around, basically napping in the back row, was squashed by the circle of metal folding chairs that had replaced the long tables.

The rest of the parolees were already seated, and a very young man, looking out of place with his bright cheery smile, waved Bede to come on in, using his clipboard like a baton.

Out of the corner of his eye, Bede saw Galen going into along the path that would wind in front of the team leads' tents. Galen turned to look at Bede over his shoulder in a way that was probably not meant to be flirty but was. Those gray eyes scanned Bede up and down, then he looked away and disappeared into the woods.

Which meant that Bede had to focus on the counseling session, and pretend he was totally interested when in fact he was not. He took a seat, crossed his arms over his chest, and didn't bother to contain a low glare aimed at the counselor.

Who was not just young, as many of the counselors at the prison had been, but youthful. Hopeful. Eager to be of use.

All of this was demonstrated by his slightly nervous introduction —*Hi, I'm Micah*—and the way he began a little speech about how proud he was of the Farthingdale Valley Fresh Start program, and what a great man Leland Tate was.

The way he sat on the edge of his folding chair. The way he asked their names, taking such care to pronounce them right, then marking something on his clipboard, that smile always in place. Bede nearly sprained his eyeballs in an attempt not to roll them every other minute.

He manfully soldiered through the forty-five minutes of group counseling, responding to questions aimed at him, pretending to pay attention to everyone else's responses. He was about to run screaming out of the tent, when Micah handed out a packet of papers to each parolee, along with a brand new pen, and made the offer of a clipboard from the box beside him.

"Your assignment for this week is to fill out this job application and self-evaluation questionnaire. The Fresh Start program isn't over yet, but it's never too soon to start looking at what your next steps will be. I've written my cell number at the bottom of each application so you can text me with any questions you might have." With a laugh, Micah added, "In the real world, of course, you'd fill this form out online, but the paper and pen will give you time to think. To make notes to yourself."

Now Bede did let his eyes roll as he took his packet and his pen and hell, why not, a clipboard as well. At least the meeting was over, as Micah was standing up, telling everyone what a good job they'd done and that he looked forward to reading over their responses when they scanned and emailed them to him.

Micah was an idiot, opening himself up to all kinds of trouble. None of them had phones they could use to text him. But there was the old-fashioned landline in the mess tent, so Bede supposed that some of the parolees might think it funny to call Micah in the middle of the night.

That wasn't Bede's problem, though. The information on the application was the problem, and he glared at it as he stomped out of the tent and stood at the bottom of the steps while the parolees passed him in a swirl of energy.

He watched as Jonah thumped down the steps and flew into Beck's arms, Beck who had been leaning insouciantly against a pine tree, half a smirk sent Bede's way.

Bede watched them as they walked off and saw when Beck pulled his Sucrets box out of the pocket of his blue jean as he and Jonah walked off. Just two bad boys going to have a smoke in the woods.

Shaking his head, now all alone, Bede realized how hot it was standing there at the bottom of the steps. It had been hot all day, and didn't look to be letting up any time soon.

Just what were rich folks supposed to do the following summer when their tents got so hot, the air so still and unable to filter out the weird sounds coming from the woods all around? He couldn't imagine that they would put in air conditioning, as that would ruin the expensive, back to nature vibe.

In the meantime, he had to fill out this dumb form. It would be cooler by the lake, so he went there and plopped himself at a picnic table.

He took off his work boots and socks, and sighed as the coolness of the earth soaked up through the bottoms of his feet. Lifting his head, a bit of a breeze caught up with him, swirling from the almost-flat surface of the lake. A hillside of pine trees rose from the lake all the way up to the gray streak of Guipago Ridge, distinct and sharp against the blue sky.

With a clonk, Bede put the clipboard down on the picnic table and flipped through the job application, glaring at the blank spaces he was supposed to fill out. Which would be easy enough if he'd had an ordinary life, but he hadn't.

He'd been raised in a neighborhood where everybody knew everybody. When he'd been young and needed some quick cash, he'd just go to the corner bodega and help out for an afternoon. Or he could rent himself as a mule, and carry mysterious rolled-up paper bags sealed with duct tape, dropping them off at the local garage or one of the run-down motels on Colfax.

After high school, his first real job had been counting dollar bills in somebody's basement. From there, he moved on to weighing cocaine to be placed in rolled up paper bags.

He'd advanced through the years, and never had to apply for anything, so the empty boxes and spaces on the paper in front of him loomed like angry eyes.

Bede had hardly listened when Micah had droned on about coming to a crossroads in your life and how to take steps to make good decisions. Break down the issue. Talk it over with your friends. Weigh the consequences.

That last had been, Bede was sure, an unspoken warning about making bad decisions, the kind that would land your ass back in jail.

Bede had done his five years, and he sure didn't want to end up behind bars again. But what else was there for him? A return to the neighborhood in Denver, somehow get his own place back, the one he'd shared with Winston? Except Winston wouldn't be there.

Going back to Denver without Winston seemed surreal, meaningless. While he knew everybody there, they would be looking at him with sympathetic eyes, and not one of them, not *one*, would understand what he'd gone through. The scream that tore his heart out as he watched, handcuffed, unable to help, as Winston died in front of him.

Bede was sure that to the cops it hadn't mattered that a drug dealer was bleeding out, just like they didn't care when a whore got messed up in a back alley when she'd gone there to hook up with another john so she could make her monthly rent.

Well, was the unspoken opinion, *she was just a whore, after all.*

Likewise, Winston had just been another drug dealer.

In his three-piece suit, he had risen through the ranks till he only dealt with high-level suppliers, the ones who could afford to rent out entire floors at the Oxford Hotel in Denver. Who had contacts on the coast or on the border and could ship in cocaine by the truckload.

For Bede, the lowlifes in his world had been those junkies who would do anything for their next fix. This had nothing to do with Bede, of course. When Bede happened to see a junkie on the street, he might briefly wonder if he'd been involved in the sale of whatever made the junkie's teeth fall out, their bones rattle beneath their skin. But he never slowed down.

He'd never really understood what it felt like to be like one of those whores or junkies on the other end of that kind of derisive opinion. That is until he'd been arrested and incarcerated, treated like he was less than dirt beneath a guard's boots.

But now, sitting in a beautiful glade, at a picnic bench that still smelled of new paint, looking at the view of a glass-surfaced lake reflecting the long, imposing beauty of the ridge behind the pine trees, maybe it was time to turn over a new leaf. Become a guy who raked leaves from his lawn in the fall and shoveled snow from his front side-walk in the winter.

He'd never cared about any of that before, and now the application was showing him how hopeless it all was to become a regular guy because how was he supposed to fill out this dumb form? It was an assignment like back in school, and he had not studied.

Even if he did fill out one of the blanks with where he worked: 319 Adams Street (sometimes), or how long he'd worked there: two years, or who he'd worked for: Ralph the Mouth—there was no way Ralph would be willing to validate that, yes, Bede had been his best delivery boy for those two years.

If Bede put any of that on the form and Ralph found out? Ralph would kill him, and then the cops would have another dead body on their hands.

Even if Ralph didn't find out and kill him, Bede was a convicted felon.

He might—*might*—be able to get a job at a car wash in Cheyenne, or one of those dingy breakfast diners that seemed to spring up like dandelions only to go under inside of six months because too many people were getting food poisoning.

It was that or go back to Denver and wade through all the crap only to end up in a Winston-less world, all alone, and with most of his regular contacts and customers being suspicious that he was wearing a wire.

It would take years to build up enough trust to be able to get his old reputation back. Years before, he could afford the kind of three-piece suits he'd so loved to wear. He didn't really know any other kind of life, but what choice did he have?

It was a fucking crossroads, wasn't it. The fucking counselor had said it was, like he knew what Bede was up against, and it made him want to slap Micah good and hard.

Bede had skills, just nothing anybody in the real world would want.

He tossed the clipboard across the surface of the picnic table where it caught on something and teetered at the edge, threatening to fling itself to the grass.

"Something I can help with?" asked Galen's voice from behind him.

Bede turned, and if a fresh breeze sprang up all around the second he clapped eyes on Galen, it must have been a fluke. But no. The surface of the lake ruffled in response, and the air smelled like warm pine needles.

"No," said Bede, reaching for the clipboard, ignoring, or trying to, the soothing calm that Galen brought with him that surrounded him like a cloak.

Of course, the answer was no. No, he didn't need help. No, he didn't need *Galen* helping him. No, he didn't want to create a new life for himself.

His answer had to be no, because otherwise it'd be yes. Yes, he wanted help—needed it—but no, he did not want Galen to see him at his lowest point, where he'd so painfully come to the realization that if he wanted to move on, he'd have to make some hard decisions, and figure out how to go back to square one without totally demeaning himself.

"Seriously, no," said Bede as Galen slid along the bench on the other side of the picnic table.

So now that pretty face with its flushed cheeks and on-the-edge of laughter gray eyes, that mess of hair suddenly Bede could see himself sliding his fingers through—all of this was framed beautifully by the pine trees, the gray ridge, and the bowl of blue sky.

For a second, a full pound of his heart, Bede found himself wanting what he simply could not have: a new, law-abiding life with this guy. A lawn raking, show shoveling, grocery buying, bill paying kind of life. Full of the laughter that teased him now from Galen's gray eyes.

Yes, Bede had come to a crossroads in his life. He was willing to admit it, but at the same time, he had no idea whatsoever which direction he should take. But if taking the straight road made him feel the way that looking at Galen made him feel, then maybe he would say yes.

CHAPTER 20
GALEN

The first week of any job was always tough, and sitting in Royce's tent, even with all its graceful touches, from the Keurig coffee maker and dozens of pods to choose from, to the little swamp cooler that made Royce's tent an oasis of comfort, Galen felt a little wiped out. There was no escaping the fact that this summer was coming down warm, warmer than any summer Galen could remember.

Granted, they were all sitting a little close, their knees brushing. Two men sat on the cot and two men sat on small, wooden folding chairs that Royce had acquired from somewhere.

"I've got ice cold lemonade here in this cooler," said Royce, gesturing to it. Gratefully, Galen reached out his hand.

"Thank you," he said, and looked down at the printed agenda in his lap. Royce's idea, no doubt, because while Gabe was the head team lead, Royce seemed to be the main organizer of meetings. He took a sip of the freezing cold citrus drink and winced with pleasure.

"Jonah went all the way to Chugwater to get them," said Royce, pleased.

"Shall we get started?" asked Gabe, eager, it seemed, to get down to business.

Galen cast a sidelong look at Marston, who was eyeing the drinks, but hadn't taken one when Royce had offered. "You got another of these frozen drinks?" Galen asked.

"Raspberry," said Royce, handing it to him, puzzled that Galen would take two. But Galen handed the drink to Marston, who took it, a small pleased smile on his face as he unscrewed the top.

"Thanks."

"Welcome."

Settling back in his seat, Galen paid attention to Gabe, and then to Royce, whoever was speaking, as they went over their concerns. The main issue seemed to be that they were discontinuing the token system for the showers.

"What token system?" asked Galen.

"It had been a way to get an estimate for water and propane usage, but we've already pretty much discontinued it." With a smile, Gabe added, "Turns out, Gordy takes the longest showers at forty-five minutes a pop, but far be it from me to ask him what he's doing in there."

Galen laughed under his breath, found himself relaxing, and followed along as the conversation shifted to the next topic, which was riding lessons and horse care.

"I realize you've been busy with the knapweed, Galen," said Gabe, and suddenly Galen felt all three pairs of eyes on him. "But will you be able to pick up the riding lessons and horse care this coming week? It's an important part of the program."

"I just figured—" began Galen, straightening up, thinking he'd somehow misunderstood what he was supposed to have been doing all week. "That the knapweed job was kind of critical?"

"It was and is," said Gabe. "And you've been doing a good job with it, too. It's just that I was on the phone with Leland and he was asking. Figured you could split the days between the knapweed and the horses. You might have to start carting hay out to the pasture along the river, since it's been so dry."

"Will do," said Galen, letting out a small sigh of relief that's all

Gabe was worried about. Though he might be worried about more, if he knew what had been going on in Galen's head since day one.

That, though the team was coming together pretty well, he still sometimes felt out of control when attempting to get his team to focus on the work.

As for Bede, Galen didn't think there was any way to ask Gabe what to do with Galen's feelings for Bede that seemed to have taken on a life of their own. He'd seen Bede cry in the dark. He'd seen Bede, under the influence of pot, flirty and smooth. At the time, he'd not thought to wonder whether Bede would be as flirty when sober, but there wasn't a really good way to ask that. Nor a good time.

Bede had done him a huge favor with the IRS. So huge that Galen's troubles with them had all but vanished into smoke.

As for the unexpected hospital bills, they, too, were firmly under control. All due to Bede's knowledge of the system. He owed Bede, frankly, but had no idea how to repay that debt.

The meeting trundled on, focused on low-level issues such as littering by the parolees, and an old joint that had been found behind the first aid hut.

Galen had seen Beck tuck a used joint carefully away in his Sucrets box, but maybe one had fallen by accident. He wouldn't mention it then, keeping Bede and Beck's secret safe.

Lastly, they discussed the heat, and what would happen in the following summers when actual guests had paid to stay in all the tents.

Royce suggested his little swamp cooler for each of the tents, and Gabe agreed that was a good idea, and they could always raise the nightly fee to something closer to five hundred dollars. At which point Galen had to stop himself from scoffing out loud at the amount of money some people had.

Then Gabe said they were good for now, but maybe they needed a bigger place to hold team lead meetings starting the following Saturday. Even if Royce pouted at this, he had to agree, since they were all pretty much sitting in each other's laps.

As they filed out, Galen rushed to catch up with Gabe.

"Yeah, what's up?" asked Gabe, in his equable way.

"Got a question for you."

"Sure," said Gabe. He jerked his thumb in the direction of his tent, and said, "I'm headed to my tent, so if you don't mind watching me roll my socks, I've got some time."

Galen followed Gabe to his tent, which was as neat as Royce's tent, only less busy with decorations and extra appliances. There were also no dust bunnies beneath the cot, no stray toothbrush, no haphazardly made bed.

"Have a seat," said Gabe, gesturing to the other cot as he pulled a laundry bag from the shelf between the cots and dumped the contents on top of the cot.

Galen questioned himself as to whether he should share his personal confusion about Bede. Except those feelings, whatever he wanted to call them—affection, the strong pull of unnameable urges—were currently in his own head, in his own chest, and needed to stay there until he could sift through them.

Instead, Galen explained the struggles he'd been going through, then finished up by saying, "I thought they were getting a free ride, which made me irritated. I thought they weren't working hard enough. Then the day we took the knapweed to the dump, everything seemed to click into place. Sure, it's good now, and they work hard. Only I'm worried about losing control because I don't understand why anyone would become a criminal in the first place."

"Think about it this way," said Gabe as he carefully folded folding a mountain of identical white socks. "I have read the folders of all the men in the valley, but let's just focus on your guys, since that is your main task. Right?"

Galen nodded.

"Why are they here?" asked Gabe, but it was a rhetorical question, so Galen kept his mouth shut. "They committed a crime. Smart or foolish, they got caught. They also paid their time. Spent their days and nights trapped in a very small space with other men, some of them violent, most of whom they did not know. And then they came here. Why? Surely they could have gone home, back to their old ways.

With the rate of recidivism in this country, over forty and sometimes as high as fifty percent, it would have been the easier, most expected option. But they did not go home. Again, why?"

Thinking that this wasn't rhetorical, Galen took a breath. "I honestly don't know, and maybe that's part of my problem. Why are they here if not to do easy work, get free food, and have a comfortable place to sleep?"

The issue felt old and worn, as if he'd been tearing at it a while and just needed to let it go.

"Very good point," said Gabe, stacking his rolled-up socks in neat piles. "You've got to look at this on a case-by-case basis. Take Toby. You think he'd sign up for a summer like this on his own?"

Slowly, Galen shook his head. It was easy to see, when Gabe pointed it out like he had, that Toby wouldn't make a move without Owen.

"Owen led him here," Galen said.

"Exactly right. Which begs the next question."

"Why did Owen come here?" Galen suggested.

"Right. And why *did* Owen come here?"

"Because he thought it would be easier than going back to breaking into houses or picking locks," said Galen, the realization of it flickering into focus. "He's a low-level criminal. Always takes the easy path. The valley seemed easier, and now that he's here, it's easier to stay than to leave."

"Right again," said Gabe. "The benefit of this program will come to them in spite of themselves." Gabe looked at Galen exactly like a teacher might at a prize pupil. "And what about Bede? Why did he sign up?"

Galen shook his head. "I have no idea."

"Sometimes," said Gabe slowly, his gaze drifting to the opening of the tent where the heat shimmered in the trees. "We know the answer. We just don't think that we do. What's the first thing you thought when I asked you why Bede was here?"

"Kell," said Galen, promptly. "He came because of Kell."

"Why?"

"Why?" asked Galen, but he realized he knew the answer to that, too. "He once said Kell was like a brother to him, so of course he'd follow Kell to the valley."

"Just because someone has committed a crime, many crimes," said Gabe. "Doesn't mean every part of their life is a crime. Bede's got feelings. He cares for Kell. I reckon he came just to shut Kell up—" Gabe paused to laugh under his breath. "In the mess tent, I overheard Kell on the phone almost every other day, just begging Bede to fill out the form. Could you have resisted that sunshiny kid? I don't think I could have and obviously Bede couldn't. Even if he meant to leave the second he got here, and I could see it in his eyes that's what he was thinking he was going to do, he stayed."

The idea of Bede's presence in the valley became awash with a kind of warmth. First Galen had seen Bede as a hard worker, and then a vulnerable one, when he'd witnessed his tears in the dark of the woods. Then had come the help with Galen's bills. And now this. Bede staying because he'd changed his mind, something Galen would have bet money would never happen. And if that change could happen, what else was possible?

Kell was smarter about people than his young years might suggest, having seen beneath the granite surface of Marston's unsmiling face to find a wealth of affection and devotion. He obviously held Bede in high regard, in spite of, again, superficial indicators that would suggest Kell stay far, far away from him. Instead, he was overjoyed to have Bede as a tent mate.

"He stayed because—" Galen paused, then shook his head. "I don't know why he stayed. I have no idea."

"Well, he might not know why either, but he's glad he stayed," said Gabe, his voice lowering to seriousness. "Keep your eyes open. Make your mind a blank slate. Consider what it might be like to be released after five years in prison, and why on earth you would not go back to what you had before. Bede was making a shit ton of money, and he had a lot of power and influence. He could have that again inside of a heartbeat. But he's still here. Walking around barefoot every chance he gets."

"Yeah, go figure," said Galen, a tornado of thoughts whirling in his head. "I told him it wasn't safe, but—"

"You might ask yourself why he does that, as well."

"I will," said Galen.

This was an assignment on a whole 'nother level, but a flicker of brightness inside of him told him that he was glad he'd get to find out.

Every man on his team had made decisions, good and bad. Now that they were in the valley, they had opportunities being placed in front of them. It was Galen's job to aid and assist them.

Most importantly, he wanted to find out why Bede stayed.

Thanking Gabe, Galen stepped out of the tent and stood on the wooden platform, letting the faint breeze brush across his skin. He felt a new confidence that he could do the job that he'd agreed to do.

In the meantime, he needed to gather his team together so they could put in a good afternoon's work attacking the knapweed. At the end of the day, they'd put away their tools and clean up, and then everybody would get a whole Sunday off. Well worth looking forward to.

But first, where was his team? Surely they were done with the counseling session by now.

He marched along the path to the mess tent, where he found a few parolees lounging at tables as they glared at their clipboards. Of note, Toby and Owen were having a clipboard battle, giggling like mad when the clipboard missed, and howling when it didn't.

"Guys?" asked Galen, then he raised his voice. "Guys. Stop a minute."

"Yes, boss?" Owen asked, and Toby echoed him.

"How's it going with the applications?" Galen asked. "You guys know what to do?"

"Sure do, boss," said Owen, and Toby nodded.

"Great." Galen paused as if the thought had just occurred to him to ask where Bede was, though that had been his main objective. "Where's Bede? I need to check on him as well."

"Down by the lake," said Owen.

"Yeah, the loser," added Toby, making the shape of an L on his forehead with his thumb and forefinger, all with a complete lack of fear or respect.

With a nod and a wave of thanks, Galen turned and tramped through the woods, following the push of cool air that came from Half Moon Lake.

CHAPTER 21
GALEN

From between the trees he could see glints of crystal blue water, and the stark blue of the sky over the ridge. And there, sitting at one of the picnic tables, was Bede.

There was no mistaking that broad back, those strong arms, the white t-shirt that Bede was wearing when surely a long-sleeved cotton shirt would be better protection from the sun. He was hatless, too, bent over the picnic table.

When Galen came closer, he could see Bede was scowling.

Circling around, he saw that Bede was scowling at a stack of papers clamped on a clipboard. He had a pen in his hand, but it looked like he'd rather bore a hole through the paper than write on it.

It looked as though the counselor's job search assignment was going over just about as well as a ton of lead.

"Something I can help with?" he asked, because that was his job. And also, Bede had done him a favor. Maybe he could return it.

"No," said Bede, scowling hard enough to make him look like he was debating getting up and walking right out of the valley. "Seriously, no," he growled.

Galen sat across from him at the picnic table, just the same. His view was not the lake and the trees and the ridge. His view was Bede's angry face, strong lines deepened by what Galen could interpret as frustration, for the application in front of Bede was completely blank.

"Barefoot again, I see," said Galen with a small smile.

"Yeah." Bede shook his head and rolled his shoulders back, as if to relax them. "It's hot as hell, and this helps me stay cool."

It was hot, though it seemed pointless to point out to Bede that he'd be cooler in the shade and that, paradoxically, he'd be cooler in a long-sleeved shirt and wearing his cowboy hat. But then that would have covered up the dark black tattoos that curved and angled along one side of his neck and along his left arm. Would have obscured the definition of muscle where it crossed over bone. The trickle of sweat that made Bede's dark hair curl behind his ears and stick to his forehead.

So much of Bede's strength was often hidden behind attire appropriate for manual labor. So much of Bede now, as he absorbed the energy of the sun, was on display—muscles, tan skin, dark blue eyes—and so incredibly eye-catching that Galen forced himself to look down at the clipboard.

"So, what's the problem here?" asked Galen.

It might be that he was making a mistake in offering his help, that Bede would get pissed and turn him down. That Bede wouldn't even trust him that much.

He found that he very much hoped that Bede would not turn him down. That Bede would let him help. That Bede would trust him.

"Applications are a pain, no matter who you are," Galen said, then he asked, "What are you good at?"

"Being a team lead," said Bede with a small laugh and a wink at Galen, so cute and sweet that Galen had to smile.

"No, seriously. That's how you start the process, by thinking about your skill-set."

Bede looked at him for a long, silent moment, as if weighing his options. Then, with a small nod, he said, "Okay. Here's the problem." He tapped the top sheet of paper with his pen. "I never filled out one of these in my life. And even if I had, most people I worked with don't want their names on *any* application. You follow? They'd be arrested, and I'd be dead."

"Yeah, I follow," said Galen, and he actually did. Mack the Knife or whoever Bede had worked with would probably prefer that his name be kept out of any and all conversations.

"I'm not stupid," said Bede. "I *get* the point of the exercise. But even if I fill this out with fake-but-realistic information? My crime is a level two felony. I spent five years behind bars. Should have been eight, but Kell busted me out by nagging the parole board to death. I paid almost three-quarters of a million dollars in fines and not enough, obviously, on legal counsel. Not any of that matters because nobody is going to want to hire me."

"You could get a job at a car wash or something like that," said Galen, but even as he said it, he was not surprised by the fact that Bede banged at the edge of the picnic table like he meant to push it over.

"Yeah, right," said Bede. "That's not enough to keep me in Grapenuts." Then he laughed, and Gabe chuckled under his breath at the image of the very handsome Bede sitting at the breakfast table, hunched over a bowl of the world's worst-tasting cereal. "You get what I mean," Bede said, and then leaned forward, his elbows on the table. "There's no way this is going to work for me. I got nothing to go back to and there's nothing to move forward to."

"I've filled out a few applications in my time," said Galen, speaking slowly to get his thoughts in order. "But mostly, I got hired because of who I knew. Worked at the dairy in Chugwater during high school because my dad sold goat milk to them. Worked the baseball games because even though I wasn't eighteen, my dad knew a guy. So probably—and I'm not making promises—you could expect that your team lead would put in a good word for you. And that Leland would, too, on my say-so."

"So I have to stay in your good graces to get anywhere?" Bede shook his head and pushed the clipboard away. "Well, I'm used to that. In my old life, it was all who you knew. Drug deals are done on handshakes, and if you fucked a guy over, you were history. Criminals are honest, believe it or not."

"Except for the *committing a crime* part." Galen couldn't help but laugh out loud at Bede's pretend shocked expression, enjoying the sparks of pleasure at the way Bede's mind worked. And he loved that Bede laughed in response, a low chuckle as he shook his head, as if he was pretending to think that Galen was out of line.

"I know honor among thieves is a thing," Galen said. "But you still ended up here. Maybe it's time for something else?"

"Maybe." Bede's eyes were serious and level as he looked at Gabe. "I just don't know what that would be."

"Well," said Galen, considering this. "You could get a job with a landscaper. There are several in the area, and again, you'd get two recommendations, Leland's and mine. Or think about this. This next week, I'll be teaching you how to ride, how to look after a horse. You could get a job at a ranch. Maybe not a guest ranch," said Galen, flicking his eyes to the top of the trees which covered the northern hillside of the valley, beyond which lay Farthingdale Guest Ranch. "But a working ranch, and there's lots of them in this area. Maybe even the BLM, the Bureau of Land Management. They always need guys to do stuff up in the hills."

"Whoa, whoa," said Bede, putting his hands up as a barrier. "I am a city boy and that is taking it too far." He might have sounded irritated, but he was grinning and Galen grinned in return at the thought of Bede in his three-piece suit and tassel trimmed loafers trying to make his way in the wilderness on the lookout for lost cattle.

"Yeah, well," Galen paused. The connection between them was good, and he didn't want to mess it up. "At least it's got you thinking. That's all this is." He waved his hand over the clipboard and all the blank pages, their edges flapping gently in a sudden, slight breeze. "A place to start. You can fill in that application with fake information to satisfy the assignment, but the real point is to start thinking about your options. What your skills are. The end of the summer is still a ways away, and between now and then, you can change your mind every five minutes. How does that sound?"

"Yeah, yeah," said Bede. "The counselor said something like that, but I guess I tuned him out."

Galen had a profound sense of satisfaction when Bede took a deep breath, his shoulders relaxing, the lines in his strong neck sleek with sweat. Galen imagined that Bede was curling and uncurling his bare toes in the dust as he thought about what Galen had just said. What it meant. And what he was going to do with it.

Was it enough to believe that Bede might opt in, take his place as a regular working Joe? Pick up his paycheck, and find a safe place at the end of the day to sip at a cool beer and dig his toes in the dirt.

And what if Bede *had* been a regular guy? What if Galen had met Bede at some other time, outside the confines of the valley program? What if he'd bumped into Bede at a ball game or a bar or the grocery store and he'd not known that Bede was a drug dealer?

He didn't even have to think about it. He would have fallen *hard*.

"Well, I better get to it," said Galen, rather than anything else he wanted to say or ask or think.

The warm summer day was having an effect on the barriers in his mind. That wanting to know about Bede in order to help him, was not the same as wanting to know about Bede in order to get to know him in very un-team-leadership ways.

It'd been a long time since he'd felt a connection like this, and Zeke didn't count. Zeke had been a distraction, a handsome-eyed, steel-jawed distraction who had summarily and politely sent Galen packing. And anyway, Zeke had been straight and Bede was—not.

Anyway, he shouldn't be thinking like this. He had a responsibility to all the men on his team, Bede included. Which precluded mooning after Bede's silky tan skin, the curl of his bright smile. The sweet way a bit of hair was now stuck to Bede's forehead, a tumbled plaster of hair that Galen's fingers itched to push back. To make Bede more comfortable. To get Bede to smile at him.

Nope. He needed to move away, and fast.

"I'll see how Toby and Owen are getting along with their applications," said Galen, standing, pressing his palms to the surface of the picnic table, untangling his legs from the attached bench seat.

"They're probably goofing off in the mess tent," said Bede.

"Yeah," said Galen. "Well, I'll see you at the equipment shed in about half an hour. Yes?"

"Sure thing, boss," said Bede. The look he gave Galen seemed to contain a whole lot of *What if* questions. Then Bede tilted his head back, eyebrows rising. "And I can just make all this stuff up?"

"Yes, you can," said Galen. "It's just an exercise to get you thinking. Not a real application."

With a nod, Bede's attention turned to the clipboard, and now Galen's eyes focused on the back of Bede's neck. The rough edge of his hairline, as though Bede had cut it himself, doing a blind trim, because there was no one to ask for help. No one he dared ask.

Galen swallowed the sudden tightness in his throat, undone by the rush of empathy. Not something he would have felt at the beginning of the week, but something he was sure feeling now. What he did with that feeling was totally under his control. Wasn't it?

CHAPTER 22
GALEN

On Sunday morning, a frantic call had come from Mr. and Mrs. Conners, the tenants on the farm, who said the pump on the well wasn't working, and they couldn't do their laundry.

They didn't know, or perhaps wouldn't have cared, had they known, that Sunday was Galen's day off. He'd wanted to sleep in, get in a swim, a nap, and catch a movie in the mess tent that night. And maybe get some time to process his feelings for Bede.

Privately, since the couple and their little girl were so keen to live green, Galen thought they might have taken their clothes to the crick and pounded them clean with a rock, right?

The farm was up Highway 211, just at the bend where Threemile Creek intersected with Horse Creek. Which meant he could go, take care of business, and get back to the valley before lunch.

When he got there, he could see that the door to the pump house had been left wide open.

The small shed around the pump was there to keep the wind and rain and sun out so the mechanism wouldn't rust, and so the wires wouldn't get damaged. It'd worked for years when his dad was alive.

"Gosh," said Mr. Conner when Galen explained it to him. "We saw that it was open, but we didn't think it would matter."

Ignoring his own flare of irritation, Galen discovered the trouble was that the power cord to the irrigation pump had shorted out, so maybe a rodent had nibbled on it.

It took him only twenty minutes to fix, but he'd spent an hour and a half driving to and from the hardware store in Chugwater, where he grabbed some lunch.

When he got back to the valley, later that afternoon, it was with a rush of gratitude as he carefully made his way down the switchbacks, in among the shadows between the tall pine trees, the air smelling brightly of the lake. Granted, they could have used some rain, but it was a beautiful day, just the same.

As he made his way to the mess tent, much of the valley was already there, taking advantage of the two standing fans that blew the air around in a casual way. The tables were set up for dinner and the amazing smells drifting out from the kitchen made Galen's belly sit up and take notice.

His eyes were drawn to Bede, who was sitting at the long table on the left side of the tent, closest to the buffet tables. Beside him, Kell, his mouth wide with a smile, was chatting a mile a minute. Marston was on Kell's other side, keeping a watchful eye, but for once, he seemed content just to be there.

At one of the other tables, Jonah and Beck, his green Army duffle bag close at hand, as if for an imminent departure right after dinner, were talking loudly. Beck's eyes were glassy. But then he'd probably been smoking pot all weekend.

Stepping into the mess tent to join the vigil before dinner, Galen did his best to make up his mind whether or not he should sit next to Bede.

Of course he could sit anywhere, but if it was near Bede, across from him, say, then they could take up their conversation from the day before. And Galen could find out how the application had gone, and did Bede have any questions? Did he need any help?

And yes, if he asked Bede that question, he should ask Toby and

Owen if they needed help also—but that's not what he wanted to do. Any conversation with those two would be stodgy and dull. Except he was their team lead and shouldn't be making these kinds of judgements. Right? Yes, exactly.

Except what he wanted to do was sit with Bede.

"Hey Galen, got a minute?"

Turning to see Gabe there, Galen nodded yes and tried to focus.

"Sure, what do you need?"

Galen had to fight to keep his attention focused on what Gabe was saying, something about the riding lessons in the morning, that the three horses he'd need had been selected and would be haltered and tied in the paddock, and that if Galen needed help with the lessons, one of the team leads could step up to make sure things didn't get out of hand—

"Or we could call Zeke down here," said Gabe, startling Galen out of his attempt to see around Gabe's shoulders at what Bede was doing.

"What?" Galen asked.

It turned out that Zeke, *the* Zeke, was on tap to become a team lead in the coming weeks. Which would have bothered Galen a whole lot more if his whole being wasn't zeroed in on Bede. Who, evidently, had won the raffle to be the person to select the first movie of the evening. Gordy won the raffle to select the second movie, but all Galen could do was wonder which movie Bede would pick.

Previous movie nights had produced very prison-centric movies that had been more grim than Galen cared for. All the parolees had enjoyed them, however, and would hardly be interested in Galen's taste.

Both Bede and Gordy came over, DVDs in hand, to give them to Gabe to hold until after dinner.

"Oh, *The Sting*," said Gabe. "That's a good one, Bede. And yes, Gordy, *Rocketman* is a good choice, too. I'll keep them safe."

Before Bede went to get in line for the buffet, he shared a wink with Galen as if to say, *I picked it out because I thought you'd like it.* Which was funny and strange at the same time because, while he'd been sick, Galen's dad had often mentioned *The Sting* and that he and Galen should watch it together sometime.

Earl Parnell had passed away too quickly for that to happen, and now Bede unwittingly had brought all kinds of emotions to bear on Galen's heart. What would Bede say if Galen told him about that part of his past?

"I can manage," said Galen, his voice coming out faint as he watched Gabe stack the two DVDs on the table by the tent's opening. "I don't think we need Zeke, but I'll let you know if we do."

He did not want Zeke there for all kinds of reasons, not least of which was Galen's tragic, semi-desperate, and totally failed flirtation with Zeke.

It wasn't even that Zeke, the far better horseman no matter how you looked at it, would do a better job than Galen and show him up. No, it was because something had changed for him this week.

Before, it might not have mattered, but now he felt a sense of anticipation about how his team would respond to the lessons.

He knew them as individuals now, and had a better handle on things, and wouldn't be making assumptions. Plus, he really wanted to see what Bede would look like on horseback.

He did, he really did want to see that, but he shouldn't be thinking this way. In spite of the fact that, as Beck had described, many in the valley were hooking up, surely it wasn't ethical.

Feeling a bit desperate, Galen grabbed some dinner and sat next to Royce and Jonah and Beck. The lemon-herb trout, Tuscan beans, and garlic bread were amazing. The only thing missing was a nice cool beer to go with it.

Even better, when the tables were assembled for the movie, and Galen sat down at the long table in the second row, the tables now parallel to the screen, Bede suddenly plopped—there was no other word for it—right down next to him.

So. It wasn't Galen's fault that something warm and exciting arced between the two of them. Not his imagination, either, not when it was so bright and fizzing he could almost see it in the air.

Right before the movie started, just as the popcorn bowls were being passed around, Bede flashed him a bright-eyed smile and looked carefully away.

It was as if he knew how Galen's heart was racing and how he was thinking about the past. About what he and his dad had shared, and all the future laid before him that he would never get to share with his dad. And even though the screen flickered with the golden handsomeness of Robert Redford, while he watched the scene of the first con job being pulled off without a hitch, Galen's throat ached with tightness, and his eyes grew hot.

Now he was a mess, and though only the darkness knew, and the crunch of popcorn and general sounds of amusement covered the hitch in his breath, he kept still, ever so still, so Bede wouldn't know that the tears began streaking down his cheeks.

It didn't matter that he'd witnessed Bede crying out in the woods at midnight. Or that since Galen hadn't told, and never would, Bede never would, either.

It was too much. Yet to get up and leave would draw more attention than he needed just then, so he kept still and let the sadness ripple through the laughter, because maybe life was just like that. A lesson he'd started learning when his dad had first become sick, and which he was continuing to learn, a long painful lesson that would probably go on forever.

He'd not realized he was half-standing until he felt a warm grip on his forearm.

He looked down to see Bede, his eyes shining in the light from the screen.

"All right?" asked Bede.

His grip was light. Galen could have gotten free, jerked free, even, to express his anger at being touched. But it was the warmth, the weight of those fingers, that stayed him. Allowed him to take a deep breath and sit back down again.

"Chocolate," Bede said now. "Peanut M&M's and popcorn go brilliantly together. Here."

Bede quietly pulled the bowl of chocolate closer and made sure the popcorn was right there.

A bit mindlessly, Galen tried the combination. His lips tasted of salt and sweet together, and it was amazing and distracting in just the right way, a surge of sugar in his veins, with enough salt to satisfy his tongue.

"Better?" asked Bede, though it was obvious he didn't really need an answer. Too many people might hear and it would disturb those around them.

The answer was too long and too convoluted for Galen to figure it out anyhow, so he nodded, and crunched away on the popcorn, his hand cupped to his mouth, using pure will to keep his eyes focused on the projection screen.

The Sting was followed by *Rocketman*, and while the music was raucous rock-n-roll compared to the softness of the ragtime in *The Sting*, it was soothing to sink below the sound and the movement and the story, and he was able to collect himself.

When the movie was over, Galen got up to help with putting everything away, and found he was violently thirsty and that his face was tacky with salt. The lights came on, moths dancing about as if they'd been waiting all night for that moment, the hum of the standing fans mixing with the low chatter as the long tables were returned to their usual places.

"Here," said Bede.

Galen turned to find Bede there, holding out a cool bottle of water.

"You drink that," said Bede, pushing the bottle in Galen's direction.

Bede wasn't smiling. Those eyes watched him, as if waiting for Galen to take a drink. Which he did, wiping his mouth on the back of his shirt sleeve.

"Thanks," he said, wondering how it had come to this, Bede helping him, and not for the first time.

Bede was turning out to be vastly different than Galen had expected. And it wasn't just his dark, good looks, but also how his confidence mixed with vulnerability, and the way he could make Galen laugh at any moment.

When was the last time he'd laughed? And when was the last time he'd felt this way, that if he reached out he would be met with the same from Bede?

It had to be a monstrous joke that life was hurling at him. And yet —Bede's expression, focused on Galen as he handed him a bottle of water, was kind. And patient. Still. A waiting gentleness that washed over Galen like a blanket.

Well. He needed to get the hell out of the mess tent. Bede was being nice, was all. A repayment of Galen's kindness to him.

So, with a nod and a general good night, he left the cleaning up to everyone else. Going back to his own tent, he gathered his things for a shower and, along with Gordy, who was the only other person in the structure, took a long hot shower, and imagined the water was washing away all of his troubles.

CHAPTER 23

GALEN

By the time Monday morning rolled around, he was ready for breakfast. Afterward, he gathered his team and took them to the paddock.

There, three horses waited patiently, halters on, chewing on hay nets that had been left for them. They flicked their ears in Galen's direction as he led his team right up to them.

"Horsemanship starts with this moment," he said, pausing at the gate in the wooden fence. "Did you know that a horse can hear your heartbeat from four feet away? They can, and if you are calm, and keep your heartbeat steady and slow, they will feel safe. If you're not calm, if your heart is racing, then they will think something is wrong, that they are in danger. It's your responsibility to make sure your horse feels safe at all times."

He looked at his team as they watched him, like they were waiting to see which way he would jump.

They stood in a row, properly dressed for a riding lesson. Cowboy hats. Cowboy boots. Long-sleeved snap button shirts. Blue jeans. Even Bede was keeping his sleeves rolled down, at least for now. Which was good, because it meant that Galen could concentrate on the lesson, rather than anything else.

"We'll start by grooming the horses, and learn the different parts of the horse," said Galen, feeling confident about his ability to teach good horsemanship skills from the ground up. "And then we'll saddle them—"

"When're we going to ride?" asked Toby, his voice loud, disrupting the morning. Two of the horses jerked their heads up, their ears going flat.

"It's a progression," said Galen, keeping his voice even, reaching out to pat the neck of the nearest horse. "And did you notice the horses' reaction to the loudness of your voice?" he asked. "You should keep your voice calm and even around horses. Around any livestock. Understand?"

Toby nodded with wide eyes, his shoulders tight as if preparing for a hard smack along with the gentle scolding.

"I didn't mean to scare 'em," he said.

"I know you didn't," said Galen. "Let me assign you your horse, and then I'll show you how to act around them. Toby, you're on Penny. She's the one with the long eyelashes. Owen, you're on Diamond, so named because of that white diamond in the middle of his forehead. And, and Bede, you're on Ripley. I think he's named that after the movie, *The Talented Mr. Ripley*. Maybe because he looks like Matt Damon?"

All three horses were ordinary chestnut horses, Penny being the only mare, the other two, geldings. The horses might not have been purebred, but they looked at Galen with steady brown eyes, as if they knew he was the one in charge, their ears flicking forward and back as Galen explained the various part of the horse, demonstrated how to untie the lead, and how to hold the lead when walking a horse around the paddock.

After a smooth twenty or so minutes of this, Galen sent Toby into the shed to bring back a small handful of horse cookies, and showed his team how to keep their hand flat to feed a horse a treat. Then he reached into the bucket with the grooming tools and instructed his team on how to use the body brush.

"Slow and easy," he said. "Front to back, always with the horse's coat. If the horse moves, move with it. Always be present, in the moment."

He handed each one a brush and told them to go stand by their assigned horses. Naturally, they all stood in the wrong place, near the horse's haunches and too far away to do much good, even Bede. Gently, Galen guided them closer to the horse's head, at least to start with. Then he used Toby's body brush to demonstrate what he meant and urged them to try again.

Soon, the wariness of his team settled into something more like attentiveness, with each of them looking at Galen every now and then as if to make sure they were doing it right. Then he showed them how to clean the horses' hooves, and how to comb through their manes and tails.

"Ease the comb through, don't tug," he said as he walked around each horse, keeping a close eye out. They would do this task before and after each riding lesson so they would become more familiar with not just being around a horse, but also how to take care of it.

When finally it came time to saddle and bridle the horses, he could sense their excitement rising. He used Penny, Toby's horse, to demonstrate how to throw a saddle blanket on, and how to tug the blanket in the direction of the horsehair, not against it. How to land a saddle gently on a horse's back. How to tighten the cinch. How to loop the stirrups over the saddle and adjust their length.

He heard Bede muttering "What now?" so he went around Ripley's backside, smiling at Bede's frown of frustration.

"This is going to ruin my manicure," said Bede, pretending to complain, which only made Galen laugh out loud. "I don't know what length the stirrup should be."

"You could guess," said Galen, gently, as that was what he imagined Bede had been attempting to do. "But here. Put your fist under the leather flap and lay the stirrup on your arm. The edge of the stirrup should hit the bone of your shoulder. If it doesn't, it's either too short or too long. Here."

Up close, he could smell the scent of horse on Bede's skin. See the gleam of his eyes from beneath the brim of his straw hat. Which made it really hard to focus.

Galen did his best, demonstrating how to measure the length of the stirrup with his arm, keeping his eyes on Bede the entire time to make sure he understood. Then he had Bede repeat the motion, and when Bede nodded that he thought the stirrup was the right length, Galen nodded in return.

"I'm such a city boy," said Bede, a bit plaintively, as if he wanted to be let go from the entire lesson.

"That you are," said Galen, and it didn't sound like an insult at all. Rather, it felt flirty and sweet, as if watching a city boy struggle to turn into a country boy was one of his dearest-held fantasies.

No. He needed to focus on the lesson for his whole team, and fast. So he went back over to Toby's horse, Penny, and demonstrated how to mount, how to sit in the saddle, and how to dismount. When his team were all on their horses, he looked at them with a bit of pride.

"Well, you look like cowboys at any rate," he told them, smiling, turning his gaze away when Bede, in the style of all the best cowboys in any western movie ever made, tapped the brim of his cowboy hat and winked at Galen.

Bede sat thick-thighed in the saddle, the reins looped around the saddle-horn as he, yes, rolled up his shirtsleeves in big square folds, as if he knew his forearms were like poetry to Galen's eyes.

Yanking his attention back to the lesson yet again, Galen led them through how to neck rein, and how to urge the horse into movement.

Once they were all walking their horses around the interior of the paddock, all in a row, he reassured them it was okay that they were going slowly because that was the way to start.

After two times around the paddock, he sensed his team getting a bit bored, so he urged them to trot. Which they did, the horses' hooves scuffing up dust in little clouds just above the ground, tails flicking, heads shaking, making the bridles jingle.

Then Toby kicked Penny and, startled, her head high, she burst into a canter and tumbled into Ripley, who reared up and sent Bede flying into the fence with a loud bang.

Galen's heart stopped, anger pulsing that Toby had been rough with his horse, and terrified that Bede was badly hurt.

Rushing over, Galen thought to settle Penny, and then Ripley, but he hadn't accounted for Owen, who dismounted and simply let Diamond go racing around the paddock, reins and stirrups flying. Toby, still astride Penny, was pulling on her reins, hard, and he needed to stop.

"Toby, dismount," Galen said, reaching out for Diamond, grabbing the tail ends of her reins. "Owen, hold your horse. *Bede.*"

This seemed most important, that Bede was utterly still beneath the lowest wood railing, as if, in another second, he might roll out of the paddock, just to get away from sharp hooves, and never return.

Bede was on his back, his hands hovering as if he was reaching for invisible reins, a grip, anything to steady himself. But he wasn't moving.

His face numb, fear jolting through his whole body, Galen went to his knees, but didn't allow himself to touch. He knew better than to move Bede, knew that he needed to determine whether Bede could move himself.

"Bede," he said, low, leaning close. "You okay? *Bede.*"

Desperation flourished in his gut, his throat, but then Bede blinked, and looked up at Galen, squinting.

Galen moved between Bede and the blazing sun, and touched Bede's face, the long scrape along his cheek from the fence, brushed the dust from his chin. Traced his hair back from his forehead with a few faint fingers.

"Can you move?" he asked, ignoring the flutter in his heart when Bede's eyes closed, and he went pale beneath his tan.

"Give me a minute," said Bede, low, husky, a wince passing over his features.

From behind him, Galen heard Owen say, "We tied the horses up," and Toby saying, over and over, "I'm sorry, I'm sorry."

Shaking off everything, the pounding of his heart, the worried hovering presence of Toby and Owen, and the worry that he would never be as good an instructor as Zeke, Galen leaned forward, his arm slipping around Bede's shoulders.

He hadn't meant to do it, but now their faces were close, Bede's warm breath on his cheek. Close where he could see the wince around Bede's eyes, the struggle in his body against the pain of his fall.

"Anything broken?" Galen asked, reaching to touch the curve of Bede's cheek, then drawing his hand back. "Bent? Sprained?"

Bede opened his eyes, a flash of dark blue, and laughed under his breath. "If I say yes, that I'm hurt very badly, can I have the rest of the day off?"

"Yes," said Galen, smiling, taking a deep breath, his whole body sighing with relief.

If Bede could make jokes, then he was okay. But the lesson was a disaster. Galen doubted if anyone on his team had learned anything, but he needed to draw the lesson to a close in a professional way, so that his team would be willing to try again.

Galen gently helped Bede to his feet. He pressed Bede's hand on the top fence railing so he could steady himself, and looked him over.

Bede nodded as if to say that he was really okay. Galen was tempted to take Bede to the nearest emergency clinic to make sure he was okay, but then Bede took a step and another, and pushed his shoulders back.

"I'm okay," he said. "Stop fussing."

With a small snort of laughter, Galen took another breath and gestured Toby and Owen close. "Let's do everything in reverse. Let's take off their tack and put it away. We'll groom them, give them a treat, wipe down the tack, and then it'll be time for lunch. Okay?"

He got nods from all three, then watched closely as they unsaddled and groomed their horses, walking around each horse and man, reaching out to guide as needed.

The work seemed to settle his team and, in turn, that settled the horses. Their ears went forward and their heads were down, relaxed, tails switching the flies in a mild way.

"Good, Toby," he said, coming alongside Penny. "Slow pets to the neck is good. It's not just that you're grooming your horse, you are connecting with her. And next time, don't kick like that. It's cruel and unnecessary."

Likewise, Galen made sure to praise Owen as he drew the body brush slowly across Diamond's chestnut rump. "That's right, Owen. Keep your body close as you groom. That'll let Diamond know where you are at all times."

As for Bede, he looked a little stiff as he carried his saddle and blanket into the shed, but he wasn't limping.

The look he threw Galen as he came out of the shade of the shed indicated in no uncertain terms that Bede did not want Galen fussing over him. So even though he wanted to, Galen didn't fuss, but he did stay close until his team had finished the task, fed the horses their treat, and released the three chestnuts into the field.

The trio promptly went close to the herd, dropped their heads, and began nibbling on the short, summer-brown grasses.

"Lunchtime, guys," said Galen, waving them close. "You did good today. And while accidents happen—" Galen paused to let the idea of this sink in, giving Bede another once-over, "—they can be avoided by paying attention at all times. These horses are domesticated, but that doesn't mean you can stop paying attention. Okay?"

"Okay, boss," they all said in unison.

"This afternoon, we'll go back to treating those knapweed holes, and tomorrow, after breakfast, we'll have another lesson with the horses."

He sent them off to lunch. Bede followed the others, then turned, pausing as if to wait for Galen, but Galen waved him away.

He walked down to the lake along the path and stood in the shade of the few willows that grew there. The lake was flat and still and, with the sun overhead, a dusty blue, like the color of an abstract painting.

He needed a moment to himself.

Had he not gone slowly enough, explained enough? Toby hadn't been acting up, it had all just gotten out of hand. He wouldn't blame them if they asked for a different instructor in the morning. Someone like Zeke, for example.

With a sigh, he doffed his cowboy hat, ran his fingers through his hair, then put his hat back on. The afternoon would go better for sure. Tackling the knapweed wouldn't be so rough, if they were only doing it half days.

He would keep an eye on Bede and make sure he was okay. Then he would pull one of the other team leads aside and ask for advice. He could only do his best. That's what his dad had always said. He believed it before, he could believe it again.

CHAPTER 24
BEDE

At first Bede only noticed a twinge along the left side of his neck, a mild ache that he dismissed Monday afternoon as the team attacked a string of knapweed that straggled up the first part of the path that led along Guipago Ridge. He was able to keep up with Toby, Owen, and Galen, no problem, and even volunteered to go to the supply shed to get more vinegar for the hand-held pumps because it would give him a chance to stretch his legs.

But on the way back, lugging the five gallon drums, one in each hand, the whole length of the left side of his back started to object, as if he'd just gotten done lifting more than his usual weight in the gym.

A day's rest might cure that, but he didn't have a day. Plus, he could not be outshone by the pair of housebreakers, so he needed to keep up. And, especially, he did not want to whine. Whining was for quitters.

So he kept his mouth shut, all through the afternoon, and through dinner. After which, bowing out of movie night, which they were having because it was too hot for a campfire, he grabbed his stuff and took an early shower.

The facilities were empty, with only a faint breeze through the upper screened-in transoms, and the faint flicker of moth wings against the lightbulbs. Even Gordy was not there, so it was a luxury, as it gave Bede a rare moment alone.

He undressed, laying his clothes on the bench inside the last shower stall and, naked, did his best to turn and see his shoulder and back in the mirror. He sucked in a breath. His shoulder was black and blue. There were bruises down his left leg, as well, from where he'd hit the fence and then the ground.

The horse Toby'd been on, Penny, had been startled, coming too fast, and his own horse, Ripley, had freaked out. Maybe had he been a better horseman, as skilled on horseback as he was in trading cocaine for cash, he could have stayed on better. Not gone down, sprawled on his ass like a fool.

Dazed from the fall, Bede had looked up at Galen, those eyes full of concern, hands reaching for him, touching his face. Asking questions, pulling Bede out of his confusion. And then Galen's arm had come around his shoulder, cradling him as though he were fragile, made out of bone china.

Bede almost came apart then, succumbed to the tenderness that seemed to surround him, soaked through him. It'd been a long, long time since he'd experienced such a rush of sweetness. Gentleness, those gray eyes so watchful and caring, and all the while his head had been pounding.

Galen's concern shook him to his core. His fear of being weak raced all over the place, so he'd gotten to his feet, taken care of his horse, and held his head high. Took care of what needed to be done.

When Galen had sent them off to the mess tent for lunch, Bede had looked at Galen, who waved him away like he wanted to be alone. So Bede left him, though he very much wanted to stay, and he wasn't sure what he was supposed to do with feeling like that.

When the three of them arrived at the mess tent, Gabe said, "You guys are sure dusty."

Toby had opened his mouth, on the verge of blabbing about what happened, when Galen had shown up.

"It's really dusty in the paddock," Galen said, spreading the cloak of protection over all of them. "I do hope we get rain soon."

Galen had not paid any special attention to Bede, or sat next to him during lunch. And in the afternoon, he almost never looked at Bede, not if he didn't have to.

It was as if the moment of tenderness between them had brought down some sort of shield, a shield that didn't permit any looks or touches or laughter between them.

In the shower, Bede let his muscles soak in the warmth of the water a good long while, and felt better for it, even as his mind swirled around the memory of Galen's arm around his shoulder, that moment of closeness, Galen's mouth close enough to kiss.

Then Gordy stomped in for one of his famously long showers. The spell was broken, so Bede turned off the water, dried off and got dressed, feeling a bit better. Heading back to his tent, he found Marston and Kell on the top step, holding hands the way young lovers did and, giving them both a smile, went inside the tent and crawled into his cot.

It was only in the morning that he remembered that he could have gone to the first aid hut and gotten some pain meds. That is, he could have done, but it didn't feel safe to soften, and he didn't want to be seen going there.

He made himself forget about the pain, though he felt stiff from head to toe while taking another riding lesson and grooming horses. All the while Galen seemed to be ignoring him except for business-like comments such as *Good job, Bede*, and *Always keep your hands light on the reins*.

In the afternoon, beneath the blazing sun, they attacked the knap-weed again and, looking up the hillside as he rested on his hoe, elbows akimbo, Bede ached. His shoulder was stiff, and his left leg was seizing up so badly, he wanted to throw it in and say *I quit*.

Horseback riding was too dangerous and digging up weeds was too menial, especially for a drug kingpin who used to rule over his domain, dictating who could sell and who could buy. It was a whole other world from the valley and, more importantly, very different from Galen's world. Where you did the work, and paid your bills, and kept your nose clean.

It wasn't until Wednesday afternoon the pain was so bad that Bede was just about crying. But he didn't want Galen to see him crying again—too much vulnerability for him, too much exposure. And while Galen had shown his own tender side, he was hardly likely to have much sympathy.

What? Your shoulder and back feel broken in three places? Walk it off, loser.

Maybe Galen wouldn't think that. He probably wouldn't, but Bede didn't want to whine. So he walked it off until he couldn't anymore, and could barely take a breath without flinching.

He figured he managed to hide it long enough, before he broke down during dinner on Wednesday, slipped out of the mess tent, and went to the first aid hut.

It was unlocked, as Galen, during the introductory tour, had said it would be. The cabinets were unlocked, the drawers, too. As Bede flipped through everything, he could see there wasn't anything hard. No oxycodone, and certainly no cocaine, which was to be expected.

There was arnica cream and several hefty tubes of Voltaren. He swallowed three heavy duty Tylenol, dry, and stood there with both tubes in his hands, wondering whether arthritis cream would be better than regular pain cream, which one would be more potent.

Unsnapping the buttons on his shirt, he figured he would use both. But as he lay his shirt on the metal table in the middle of the room, he heard a sound behind him, turned too fast, and winced as he saw Galen standing there.

"You left the mess tent so quickly," Galen said. "It's cool enough for a campfire—shit, *Bede*. Why didn't you tell me you were hurt so badly?"

It would have been so easy to simply cave, collapsing into a puddle so Galen could put him back together again, like he wanted to.

But it would be hard, too hard. After five years of holding himself to himself, Bede didn't think he could let himself be weak. Couldn't let himself open up his chest and show Galen his pain.

But Galen had tracked him down, in spite of Bede's efforts to hide. And not only that, he came into the first aid hut, his silent strides bringing him to Bede's side, his hands cool on Bede's hot skin, his touch tender.

"These bruises go all the way across your shoulder," Galen said, his gray eyes concerned. "They look awful. You banged into that fence pretty hard. Why didn't you say?"

As Galen took the tubes from Bede's hands, Bede could only look at him through half-lowered lashes, biting back a hiss as the first stroke of cream touched the back of his neck.

"I was going to use both tubes," said Bede, struggling for normalcy, a facade that cracked when his voice did. "Layer them."

He wanted normalcy, but he was not going to get it, not when he was about to melt beneath the onslaught of Galen's kindness.

"Then I'll use both."

Galen guided Bede to sit on the rolling stool, hands stroking down both of Bede's shoulders from behind. The left one hurt like someone had slammed it with a hammer. The right one didn't hurt as much. And all of him shivered beneath that touch.

"You should have told me," said Galen, muttering as he eased the cream along Bede's shoulder, the back of his neck, gently down his ribs. "You should have."

Unspoken was the question: *Why didn't you?*

Maybe Galen didn't ask it because he already knew the answer, that Bede didn't want to be seen as weak.

Galen applied the cream along Bede's shoulder and part of his back, first from one tube and then the next.

Then he did it all again, easing the healing cream into Bede with his fingers. The swirl of his palm was warm as he worked his way down Bede's back, not stinting on the cream, going wide with his strokes, fingers curling along the ribs on Bede's left side.

He even worked the cream into Bede's left arm, going all the way down to the elbow, as if he knew how far those stabbing pains had reached.

"I want you to rest and relax," said Galen, sternly, as he put the caps back on the tubes. As Bede stood up, mouth open, ready to protest, Galen shook his finger at him. "No, I mean it. Work will have to go on without you. We're nearly finished with the knapweed, anyway."

The knapweed wasn't the issue. It was the idea, sudden and sharp, that the summer would end, and Bede would take his certificate and leave the valley. After all, he wouldn't be allowed to stay, and Galen would go back to his regularly scheduled life.

The future loomed like a vast, empty landscape that threatened to swallow him. At the end of summer, there would be nothing holding him in place.

"You should go to bed," said Galen. "Can you manage?"

Bede didn't turn around, and before he could say yes or no, Galen had placed the shirt on Bede's shoulders, gently, like a feather.

The Tylenol still hadn't kicked in, and it felt like it never would, but Bede could feel a certain warmth left by the creams, as though they were doing their best to get blood flowing beneath the surface of his skin.

Galen came around to the front of him and reached as if to help do up the snap buttons on Bede's shirt. Bede half heartedly batted those hands away and, snapping his shirt closed, stood up, at once dizzy and mesmerized by Galen's closeness.

"Are you going to be all right?" asked Galen. "Maybe I should take you to the urgent clinic in Farthing, just to get you checked out."

"No."

Galen moved a step closer.

Bede could feel the reaction his body had when somebody cared. Sure, he was a big, bad drug dealer, the scourge of Denver, feared by all. But Winston, having known him for so long, had often treated him with such concern, so it was crazy that he was having the same reaction to Galen now.

"You did take some Tylenol or something, right?"

"Three," said Bede. "Guess I should have taken them days ago."

He shrugged, not willing to admit that he wished he had something stronger. That he knew a single line of cocaine and several repeated doses afterwards would have wiped all of his troubles away for a good several hours, even if he never took cocaine. Not that

Galen would have liked to hear any of that, so he kept his mouth shut.

"Bed. Got it?"

Bede waved Galen away, waved away Galen and the response his body was having, loopy from the mix of creams, the tenacity of the pain in his shoulder and neck, all of it.

"See you in the morning," Bede said and then left the first aid hut as fast as he could.

He did not shower, as that would remove the pain cream. He was too wiped out, anyway, stiff against the pain, his heart dodging bullets of care.

Once in his tent, empty because Kell was with Marston at the campfire, no doubt, he tore off his work boots and socks, stripped off his jeans and, wearing only cotton boxers, lay on the top of the cotton blanket and sheet, the tail ends of his shirt trailing on his bare thighs. But at least he was cooler now.

Galen hadn't been kidding about the fact that temperatures were going down in the valley. He could feel the breeze shift across his skin, as he covered his eyes with his forearm and simply willed the Tylenol to work.

If he wanted to, he could call any number of dealers in Wyoming and they would, forthwith, bring him what he needed. Sneaking through the dark woods with packets of cocaine.

He wasn't going to do that. He wasn't an addict, he was just in pain.

It was good to lie still, to simply breathe in and out and imagine the pain drifting away, even though it would pound to the surface of his skin, sinking down with some effort. Rising again.

There was no getting away from it. He should sleep, but it wasn't coming, and within an hour he heard footsteps on the wooden platform.

Thinking it was Kell, he attempted to use his elbow to prop himself up, but it was Galen.

He came directly to Bede's bedside, a bottle of water in one hand and a small, slender, amber colored prescription bottle in the other.

"What?" asked Bede, the word more a grunt as he sat up. Part of him wanted to draw the cotton sheet up to his waist. The other part of him wondered if Galen liked what he saw. The cotton boxers were summer weight, and the cloth felt like kisses on his skin.

"I brought you something," said Galen. "Scoot over."

Obediently, Bede moved to the tent side of the cot and watched as Galen sat down in the curve of Bede's waist. Galen held out the bottle of water, and also the prescription bottle, but Bede had to sit up to take them both. He moved his legs to slither beside Galen's legs.

"There's, like, seven in there," said Galen. "They should help."

Bede blinked to focus on the prescription bottle.

"This is *codeine*." Bede shook the prescription bottle at Galen. "And who is this? Lance Greenway? Is this a stolen prescription? Are you dealing in *drugs* now?"

"That's Maddy's husband," said Galen with a little laugh. He grabbed Bede's hand around the bottle, gripped it lightly, and shook the bottle right back at him.

"She's the admin at the guest ranch. Lance had knee surgery a few months back, and doesn't like pills. I remembered. Drove up there and asked if I could have them for you. She said, yes, and that I should take you to be looked at, and I said I'd keep an eye on you. Figured you could take one now and work your way through the others as needed." With another low laugh, Galen grinned at him. "You might have been a cocaine dealer, but there's nothing in your record that says you were an addict."

"It's really shady you giving me someone else's drugs, you realize," said Bede. He wasn't really bothered by it, but the comment made Galen smile.

Bede looked at the pills. Within twenty minutes of taking one, the pain would be gone. Just like that. Which was, he knew, the reaction that addicts had upon buying even an ounce of cocaine. Flat out fastest escape from life known to man.

"Take one," said Galen. "I'll wait and watch and make sure of you."

Doing as he was told, perhaps for the first time in his life, at least outside of Wyoming Correctional, Bede tapped out the tiny white pill, placed it on his tongue, and took a nice swig of water.

He watched Galen watching him. Swallowed slowly, unsure about the rush of pleasure as he watched Galen's eyes widen.

The flirtation, however small, made something twist in his heart.

Their two lives were not the same. It could never happen between them and, besides, the end of summer loomed.

"Thank you," he said.

"Drink the rest of it," said Galen, a bit bossily. "You need to stay hydrated."

"Yes, sir."

It was a term Bede had used often when he responded to prison guards over the last five years, sometimes sarcastic, sometimes in jest, sometimes to fly below the radar by seeming to be the most obedient prisoner who ever existed.

But to Galen, it was with pleasure that he said it. Galen was right. Galen had come to him with fast medicine to take away his pain. The last time that had happened had been years ago. Before prison. Before Winston had died.

As to whether Galen was just a nice guy or something more, well, that was a mystery Bede didn't think he was going to be able to resolve.

"If you don't feel better by morning, I am taking you in whether you like it or not." Galen's expression was stern, but there was a softness behind the words.

"Okay," said Bede as he wiped his damp chin with the back of his hand.

In the stillness that settled between them, Bede could hear the pine trees rustling outside the tent. Hear the night sounds growing.

The hoot of an owl, at least he could identify that. The *chrrr-chrrr* of something else. Before they had been loud and a distraction, but now they seemed a perfect accompaniment to the warm summer night.

"What is that sound?" he asked, his body slumping into relaxation as the pill kicked in. "Like a click and a whir."

"Cicada," said Galen. "And maybe also bats."

Galen's body was warm alongside his own. Bede's bare leg brushed Galen's blue-jean encased thigh, his shirt sleeve rumpling up from his forearm where it brushed against Galen's snap button shirt sleeve.

He could sense the rise and fall of Galen's chest as he breathed and wondered what Galen would look like dressed only in cotton boxers, wondered what was beneath those clothes.

"Take off your shirt. Lie down and let me rub some more arnica on you," said Galen. "Then you can go right to sleep."

"Sure."

Letting out a breath, Bede tore off his shirt and stretched out face down on the cot, his feet half beneath the sheets, the cool air from the lake a blissful caress across his naked back and thighs. He heard Galen's small gasp and knew his bruises looked pretty horrible.

More importantly, back home, except for Winston, he'd never turned his back on anyone. He'd certainly never done that in prison. But here, it felt natural to do so. To hold back the flinch as Galen's cool hands touched him. Stroked his skin. Eased the cream in with a slowness like molasses in winter. As if Galen had all the time in the world and the jovial camaraderie of the campfire held no charms for him whatsoever.

"Better?" asked Galen.

"It's kicking in," said Bede, his words muffled by his pillow, his arms folded beneath it.

"What?" Galen leaned forward. So far forward and so close that Bede felt the stirrings of Galen's longish hair on the back of his neck. The whisper of breath in his ear.

"It's kicking in," said Bede again. He'd turned so his mouth was clear of the pillow, and there Galen was, there Galen's mouth was, his hands on Bede's neck, resting so simply, like a blissful wish that Bede was free of pain.

Bede was a sucker for all of this, so long forgotten and now remembered all in a rush. "I'm good," he said, rather than anything else he wanted to say.

"Okay."

Galen leaned back where he sat on the cot and pulled up the cotton sheet, laying it along Bede's body, like another whisper.

"Remember," said Galen as he stood up. "You have tomorrow off, so rest and heal. Got it?"

"Got it, boss," said Bede, smiling into his pillow as Galen just about tiptoed out of the tent.

As the pain went away, Bede wallowed in the ghost whispers of Galen's touch until Kell returned from the campfire.

Bede was almost asleep and Kell might have been doing his best to keep quiet, but Bede was awake now, and turned to look at Kell as he got undressed beneath the light of the single bulb.

"Galen was looking for you," said Kell, whispering like they were in church. "Did he find you?"

"Yes," said Bede. "He's all bossy about me resting."

Kell made a sound that was acknowledgement and *Good night* all in one.

Bede debated telling Kell the truth. That Galen had come looking for him, and his treatment of Bede's bruises hadn't felt entirely professional.

Bede was in love with the valley and he was a sucker for back rubs and for men who made him laugh and he was a sucker for everything that Galen was. He didn't want to leave the valley or Galen.

But he didn't say this, partly because Kell didn't need to carry the weight of Bede's confusion, and also because saying it out loud might make it more real than he could deal with right now.

Instead, he sank into sleep and in the morning, though he did his best, he did not stay in bed. He took half of a dose of codeine, the small pill snapped in two pieces between his fingernails, and saved the other half for bedtime.

Then, after a hot shower, and a good breakfast, he joined the team at the paddock for the riding lesson.

Galen raised an eyebrow at him and shook his head, muttering admonishments to take it easy, and this Bede did. He almost felt like a new man and pretended he had no idea why.

CHAPTER 25
GALEN

During the riding lesson, Galen kept his eye on Bede while doing his best to look like he wasn't turning into a mother hen and failing miserably. He noted that Bede seemed to be holding his left shoulder a little stiffly, but other than that, he seemed fine.

At least the air was a little cooler, with puffy clouds coming over Guipago Ridge, bringing along with them the promise of rain. The slight breeze mixed the scent of moisture with the dust from the paddock and the horses' coats as they curried and brushed.

"We're only walking today," Galen said as he helped his team saddle their horses and mount up. "Then we'll turn and walk the other way."

"But I want to trot," said Toby. The words were on the verge of a whine, but then Toby seemed to think better of it and pulled the whine back.

"We're not trotting yet, Toby," said Galen. "Perhaps tomorrow."

He was getting better at being stern, perhaps, because Toby might have been muttering under his breath, but he did as he was told and kept his horse to a walk. Behind him in line, Owen was laughing at Toby.

Behind Owen, obediently walking, Bede sat straight in his saddle, his legs long along the horse's sides, his wide grin sparkling at Galen beneath the shadow of the brim of his cowboy hat. Of course, he wasn't smiling just at Galen, surely. But Galen gave him smiles in return, and it was absurd, yet felt so perfect and right.

No. Galen couldn't think of that. He was going to focus on the lesson, and after lunch he'd take his team up the dusty path toward Guipago Ridge, where they would attack what seemed to be the last of the knapweed. They'd finish by Friday afternoon, hopefully, then they'd be off to the tavern for the celebration to mark their first two weeks in the valley.

Galen made a mental note to remind Leland about the phones, and to make reservations at the tavern, and felt well pleased with himself as he turned his attention back to his team.

"Rest those hands easy, Owen," he said. "You don't need to keep tugging on the reins unless you're giving a specific direction to Diamond. Walk on."

The horse lesson ended smoothly, which he was glad for, and though he could really have used a mid-day swim, his team insisted on sticking close as they went to lunch, and as he didn't want to invite *all* of them—

He wanted to invite Bede and *only* Bede for a swim, and promised himself the swim would happen the first chance he got.

The afternoon was simmering hot, the air very still. As they walked up the trail to the ridge, they were in a cloud of dust because somehow they were working in the exact spot, edged by sharp granite boulders, where no breeze could find its way.

At least the view over the valley, the shimmering round half circle of the lake, was amazing. And while Galen would rather be swimming, he did his best to keep his team engaged, rather than wilting in the heat.

"I think there's a bat hideout somewhere along here," Galen said as they took a rest break, drinking large gulps of cool water from plastic bottles.

He looked at his team. Even Bede seemed only mildly interested, and Galen didn't know enough about bats to draw them in.

"There are hawks up here, as well." That brought a little more interest, but not very much.

"Are there bears?" asked Bede.

Galen shook his head and wiped the sweat from the back of his neck with his red bandana. "Not this time of year. In the fall, yes, you'd have to keep an eye out, as they're foraging around, looking for food."

The heat didn't let up even as they finished work for the day and toted their tools, hoes and shovels and hand pumps, down the path to the supply shed. They were running behind, so there wasn't time for a shower before dinner, though Galen paused as they lined up for the buffet, tugging on Bede's shirt sleeve.

He'd been watching Bede all day, for stiffness, for any sign of discomfort, and now that they were standing so close, that was when he could see the strain along Bede's neck.

"You should take something," he said, telling himself that his heart's pace didn't pick up at Bede's nearness, at the idea of doing something so bold as to let his body enjoy that closeness. "Stay ahead of the pain."

"I'm all right." Bede rolled his shoulders in a slow and mesmerizing way. "I'll take it at bedtime. It'll help me sleep."

It wasn't until after dinner, when they were all seated around the campfire, listening to Royce read aloud about bats, that Galen felt a restlessness creep up on him.

The night was beautiful, and though the firelight flickered upwards in a graceful arc of white and orange and blue, he couldn't sit still. There was a fingernail moon slicing across the darkness of the lake, and beyond that, some mystery in the trees beckoned. Across from him, Gabe shifted restlessly, and Bede, sitting on the hay bale next to Galen, shifted likewise.

"I'm going for a swim," Galen announced, standing up. He couldn't quite bring himself to invite just Bede, but maybe it would be all right if he made a general invitation because maybe only Bede would say yes. "I'm going to get my swim trunks. Who's with me?"

"But it's dark," said Gabe, even as he went to grab the bucket of sand and dirt to throw over the fire.

"Don't be so pedantic," scolded Royce as he snapped his book shut, flicking his flashlight on and off, like some unknown morse code.

"Do we have swim trunks?" asked Bede. "Was that the red thing in the plastic bag at the bottom of my box?"

"Yes, that's it," said Gabe. "After the first couple of nude swims, Maddy thought it more civilized to order everyone a pair of swim trunks."

As everyone stood up, Galen realized that his swim would not be a solitary one. Certainly not one that he could share with only Bede.

What he should have done was pull Bede aside and offer a private invitation. Or maybe it was better this way. He was an idiot if he thought being alone with Bede in the dark, both of them half naked, was a very good idea.

He went to his tent to change into his swim trunks, grabbed a towel, his flashlight, pulled on a t-shirt, and slipped barefoot into his cowboy boots. He knew he looked ridiculous, but all of this would make it easy to dry off after his swim.

He took so much time that by the time he was going along the path through the thickest part of the trees along the lakeside, he heard the voices and the splashes up ahead, which meant everybody was already at the dock.

Hearing a footstep on the path behind him, he turned, the beam of his flashlight swinging around with him.

Bede was coming up to him along the path with quick strides. The starlight caught the sharpness of his eyes, the shoulders of his white t-shirt, and gleamed off his dark hair.

Bede came up close, not pausing. Then he took Galen by surprise, his hands clasping Galen's head, that breath warm against his mouth. A swift kiss, then a whispered curse, as if Bede had been drawn to this moment against his will.

Bede's fingers caressed him as he pulled back, sweeping Galen's hair behind one ear, and then the other. Then Bede paused and in the low light of the flashlight in Galen's hands, his eyes searched Galen's. Looking for an answer. Yes or no.

Galen took too long to respond, then Bede kissed him again, sweeping an arm around his waist, like he was some captured damsel who needed to be tamed. Another arm around his neck brought him into an embrace that absorbed him.

Though Galen raised his hands, dropping his flashlight, his towel, it wasn't to push back. No, not when this felt like his first kiss, *the* first kiss, in ever so long. The feel of Bede's mouth, the sweep of tongue, taking away everything else but that connection.

Then with a gasp, Bede pulled back, roughly, as though he pulled back from the heart of temptation itself.

Galen tongued the inside of his lower lip, tasting Bede.

He felt Bede's heartbeat through the thin cloth of his t-shirt. The swirl of Bede's scent all around in the clear, still air. Then he rose on his toes, his bare feet slipping inside his cowboy boots, and brushed his lips gently to Bede's.

He had no idea where or how this might continue, the energy between them wrapping around him like ribbons, but he wanted it to.

"They'll miss us if we don't show up," said Bede, whisper-soft. He ducked his head to search Galen's eyes, his face.

"True?" asked Galen, ready then and there to throw everything out. All he knew. Who he was. What he hoped for. All for another moment, for this moment, to go on and on. Forever.

"We don't care," said Bede, though there was a hopeful question in his voice that Galen knew was his to answer.

There was no one on the path behind them, so they might have slipped off together, but in this moment of quiet, the jagged beating of his heart slowed. It might be nice to let the moment grow again on its own, to build between them as they swam in the dark waters of the lake.

"A swim is nice," said Galen, in response.

"And we really shouldn't," said Bede. He paused to swallow, then said, "Do what we're doing."

He kissed Galen again, and in that second, with all of Bede's mastery of the situation, it was easy for Galen to see how Bede used to be. Polished. Sophisticated. Demanding. At nightclubs in Denver, with cocaine being bought and sold in the back, while hopeful attendees waited out front for the velvet rope to be lifted so they could join the throng of gaiety.

Bede had never had to wait in line. Probably never even stood in one. And here he was in the deep, dark woods with Galen, his hopeful eyes brightening as he stepped back and let Galen go, based on the promise of more, later.

Bending, Bede gathered his and Galen's things, then, with his hand on the small of Galen's back, escorted him to the dock, making Galen feel, once again, like the damsel, and Bede his handsome rescuer.

As they neared the dock, the cacophony of pleasure and activity and laughter filtered through the trees beneath the silver moonlight. Someone had brought out four or five kerosene lanterns and these were turned to their highest, creating a circle of light at the land's end of the dock.

The far end of the dock, though, floated into darkness, bouncing on small silver peaks that broke beneath the stars and the very narrow moon. Toby, perhaps, was going on about acquiring some blow-up floats to mess around on, and Gordy agreed.

Galen dropped all his stuff, stripped off his boots and t-shirt and, with a yell, raced to the end of the dock, then dove into the dark water. The heat of the day was cut off by the cool cloak of water swirl all around him, soothing him.

He burst to the surface with a laugh, and paddled closer to the dock, keeping himself afloat and still as he looked up at Bede. Who stood at the edge, lit from behind by the kerosene lamps, expression obscured.

"How come that doesn't freak you out?" asked Bede, his hands on his hips. The light of the kerosene lamps made shadows around his body, giving Galen glimmers of the stars on Bede's skin as he took off his t-shirt and boots.

"How come what doesn't?" asked Galen, taking one hand to wipe at his eyes, his nose, as he treaded water.

"What if there's something in the lake?" Bede waved an expressive hand over the surface of the dark water. "Some Stephen King thing?"

"This is not a Stephen King lake, I assure you." Galen swallowed some lake water as he laughed. "Those are all back east. This lake only has moss and fish and maybe some frogs?" He really had no idea, only that it was perfectly safe. "Grow some balls and dive in already, would you?"

"Yes, boss," said Bede with a laugh, and then he cannonballed into the water, sending shards of foam and water into the air, spraying Galen's face.

Maybe they were being watched as they dog paddled close to each other, gasping with laughter. Or maybe everyone was too busy to care.

"I keep feeling like something's going to eat my feet," said Bede, making a comical face that made him look like he was only twelve years old, on his first night at sleep-away camp. "Or that I'll feel mud between my toes."

Galen barked out a laugh and tossed his hair from his eyes. It was the best night ever. The most fun he'd had in years, and all because an ex-con had slipped through the woods and kissed him. Was swimming with him now, complaining about mud and dark water and scary things that might lurk in the depths.

He shoved off all doubts for future Galen to deal with. This was his now to enjoy. Where was the harm? There wasn't any. Just a delightful swirl of water and laughter as the two of them swam to the dock, climbed up, and attempted to dive off at the same time.

The end of the dock was quite bouncy, and Galen couldn't be sure that someone, Toby perhaps, hadn't come to jump up and down and make the dock rock quite hard, grunting with effort, just to see Galen and Bede tumble into the water rather than dive.

"It's supposed to be more solid than that," said Gabe as Galen surfaced, laughing and gasping at the same time. But then Galen saw that there were several next to Toby, using all their combined efforts to jostle the diving efforts of anyone who tried it. "Hmmmm."

They swam for an hour, both him and Bede being diligent to stay a little bit apart, at least some of the time. Never mind that Galen didn't ever like an audience, he didn't want anyone making assumptions about them. Not until—after. After the promise of Bede's kiss had turned into something more and he'd had time to process what it all meant.

He didn't know what to make of that kiss, but he'd enjoyed it with every part of his body and soul.

CHAPTER 26
GALEN

Friday morning was hot again, but Galen's team operated in tandem with each other, digging the last of the knapweed, stuffing the knapweed in black plastic bags, then spraying the area with soap and vinegar. All while taking breaks to drink cold water or iced tea from the cooler, then getting back to it. He couldn't be more proud.

It was after lunch, when Galen was going over the remaining work for the afternoon, and how fun it would be to tell them to quit work early so they could go to John Henton's Tavern for their two-week celebration, complete with new refurb phones, cold beer, and a arousing thank you from Leland Tate himself.

Except, just as they were about to head out to the path up to the ridge, Gabe caught up with them.

"Hey," he said. "You got a minute?"

"Sure," said Galen, gesturing to his team that they should stop and see what Gabe wanted. "What do you need?"

"What's up, boss?" asked Toby, then he elbowed Owen, as if to make sure Owen saw how funny he was.

"I've got good news and bad news," said Gabe, but he was smiling, so Galen knew that the bad news wasn't very bad.

"What's up?" asked Galen.

"Well, Leland can't make it to the tavern tonight," said Gabe. "Evidently it's a special occasion for him and Jamie, so he's busy. Says he can make it tomorrow, if that's okay with you and your team."

"Sure." Galen looked at Toby, Owen, and Bede, each in turn, and he could tell that they didn't quite remember that he'd told them about the outing, but then he'd told them on their first day in the valley, so it was understandable. "That okay with you guys? For our outing to be tomorrow?"

They nodded, so Galen turned his attention back to Gabe.

"Here's the fun part," said Gabe, tipping his cowboy hat to the back of his head with a smile. "There's a bunch of canoes in Cheyenne that need picking up,"said Galen. "And after you pick 'em up and bring 'em back here, I imagine they'd need testing. Who here knows how to operate a canoe?"

Oddly, Owen raised his hand, and then Galen raised his.

"We can take care of that for you, Gabe," said Galen, and the afternoon suddenly seemed a whole lot more fun.

"I'll text you the address and invoice," said Gabe. "And I'll let Leland know you're good for tomorrow."

As Gabe walked in the direction of the paddock, Galen turned to his team.

"I say we put our tools away and get going."

There was a race to see who could get to the tool shed first, and then a race to the truck.

"Shotgun," shouted Bede, running as fast as he could, looking like he was tempted to trip up Toby, who was close behind him. Owen, with his long legs, was right behind Toby, and last came Galen. Who didn't have to race to the truck because he already had a front seat.

"Starbucks again this time?" asked Toby, panting as he got into the back seat of the truck.

"Pup cups for everybody," said Galen, grinning as he started the engine.

Galen hummed as he drove, his hands loose on the truck's steering wheel as they headed down the blacktop road to the highway that took them into the small but still bustling metropolis of Cheyenne. And all the while, Bede smiled as he looked at Galen out of the corner of his eyes.

The sporting goods store was in the southeast part of Cheyenne, in a strip mall that had a Starbucks. So after they went into the store to get the four flat bottom hulled canoes, one blue, one yellow, one green, and one red, and strapped them into the back of the pickup truck, they traipsed over to the Starbucks. There to mill around considering the many options, getting in the way of regular customers, creating a little party all their own.

After a short absence, Toby came up with a little paper cup in his hand. In the cup was a pile of whipped cream. He proudly announced that he'd lied that he had a dog in the truck, and they'd given him an honest to God pup cup.

"Is it real whipped cream?" asked Galen. Toby grinned and swiped a taste, and announced proudly that it was.

Back in the valley, Galen pulled the silver truck into the shade of the pine trees that loomed over the gravel parking lot.

"I say we unload the canoes, grab our suits, and try them out. Sound good, team?"

Every man on his team gave a shout of affirmation, and happiness welled up inside of him. Everything was working, going his way, and it was a moment he wanted to mark, somehow, so he wouldn't forget how good it felt.

CHAPTER 27

GALEN

There used to be an old flatboat tied up to the dock at the pond on his dad's farm. It'd been old when Galen had paddled around in that pond and, just when Galen had gone off to college, it had finally fallen apart, never to be replaced.

Now, as Galen and his team ported the four canoes to the lake, his excitement was high because the idea of having a paddle on a body of water on a bright sunny summer's day would be a little like time traveling into the past.

They had plenty of help porting, as well, because as his team carried the first canoe past the mess tent and along the path to the floating dock, they drew the attention of every man in the valley. Which only made sense because the canoes were sleek and trim, brand new and brightly colored.

Once all the canoes were tied to the end of the floating dock, Toby and Owen ran back for the paddles and life vests. Then Gabe gave a little speech about safety and though he seemed like he was trying to be serious, it was easy to see he was excited, too.

"We have the rest of the day off," Gabe said, spreading his hands wide. "Go get your suits," he said, and as everybody ran off, he yelled, "And don't forget to bring sunscreen and towels!"

It had the feel of summer camp. Even though Galen had never been, he knew about it, had read the stories. Seen the film.

His tent was pretty close to the lake, so it didn't take him long to pull on the bright red swim shorts, grab his sunscreen and a towel, throw on flip-flops, which he'd found in the box and never thought he'd get to use, and race back to the lake.

Everybody was at the dock when he arrived and, from the shouts, it seemed like fights were about to break out over the canoes. There were only four canoes. Each could hold two men. There were currently thirteen men in the valley, which meant five men would have to wait for their turn.

Naturally, all the team leads stepped back to wait. That is, except for Marston, who was dragged by Kell to the red canoe, like a kid at a carnival who simply couldn't wait to get sick on the wildest ride right after eating lunch. Which meant the rest of the canoes were filled with parolees, none of whom were wearing life vests, and most of whom had no idea how to use a paddle.

In the midst of all this, the noise, and the laughter, water being splashed—on purpose—Galen took off his flip-flops, dropped his towel and sunscreen, ran as fast as he could along the dock, and dove into the depths of the cool, cool water.

A bright blue silence cut him off from the cacophony of everything in his life. His father dying. The bills. The stupid tires on his truck that really wouldn't last another winter.

Yet the cool silence was unable to keep away thoughts of Bede because something about Bede drew him and wouldn't let go. He wasn't sure he wanted it to.

Breaking the surface of the water for air, gasping, Galen caught a glimpse of Bede diving into the water, his body cutting the surface close to where Galen was, treading water.

When Bede came up for air, sunlight sparkled on his dark hair, shaggy like a dog's, and on his tan face, and on the droplets on his shoulders. As he tread water, he came a little closer, his blue eyes on Galen, as if he was testing the limits of how close he could get with a potential audience watching.

Close. Galen was letting Bede tread pretty close, and he didn't know whether or not he was worried about that.

Apparently, there weren't any rules against hooking up, but Galen wasn't a hookup kind of guy. But what kind of future would he have with a—yeah, an ex-con? Even a nice one, as Bede was turning out to be, wouldn't want to come back to the farm with Galen, or help him figure out what to do with it. And there was no way in hell Galen was trekking down to Denver to set up a new life there.

And yet—he was irresistibly drawn to that white-toothed smile, that strong, handsome face, the water sliding down Bede's temples. His strong shoulders keeping him afloat.

Then there was the way Bede had helped him with those bills, teaching him a new way to interact with the faceless bill collectors on the other end of the phone. He'd been appreciative of Galen's help with the fake job application, as well. The two of them had not just kissed, they'd shared a lot of laughter, and they'd connected in an amazingly deep way.

All of that was more than Galen was ready to resist, even though he knew he should.

"Good, huh?" Galen asked, shaking a bit of water out of his eyes. "How's that shoulder?"

"It's fine," said Bede, smiling. "Man, I missed the water."

"No swimming pools in prison, then," said Galen, thinking it was strange that this hadn't occurred to him before. But then, he was distracted by the way Bede's lips moved with lake water dripping across his mouth as he spoke.

Bede laughed out loud, his arms creating half arcs in the surface of the water, in a mesmerizing, steady cadence.

"Some ex-cons, you know, they miss the craziest things."

"Like what?" Galen felt something beneath the water and realized it was Bede's feet.

He didn't move away, letting their limbs mingle like human seaweed. Or in this case, lake weed, even though he knew the lake was very deep, and all the plantgrowth would be found along the shoreline.

"Coffee," said Bede. "I missed coffee."

Galen nodded. He already knew about that one.

"I missed really good beer," said Bede, now. "Like a Pilsner. Ice cold. Haven't had any in over five years."

"And?" Galen knew that the tavern they were going to on Saturday night had very good local beer, and he smiled as he anticipated watching Bede enjoy one.

"Water," said Bede. "Lots of water."

Bede's eyes scanned the horizon of green pine trees, the gray slash of what could be seen of Guipago Ridge above that, and then finally he looked straight up, where a bit of cloud was stretching across the sun. Then he looked at Galen again.

"Showers in prison are ten minutes at most. The water pressure sucks, isn't all that hot, and showering with a bunch of crooks who don't have any manners or restraint is about as gross as it gets."

"So you must love the showers here."

Galen felt the bleakness of that idea come at him fast.

"I'm not actually supposed to be here, but then you probably know that," said Bede, suddenly. He looked over his shoulder as if to check how close anyone was to them. "I wasn't going to apply for the program. It's not for the likes of me, you see. But Kell—"

Bede lifted his head, his eyes seeking, and Galen turned to look at what he was seeing. Kell and Marston were in the red canoe, the prow of the sleek boat slicing through the water as they made their way to the center of the lake.

"Kell talked the parole board into it. Seriously. And he hammered at me all the time to apply, so I applied." Bede's fingers broke through the surface of the water, silently. "This is all such a break for me. One I don't deserve, and I fully realize that. But it's making me think about my life in ways I never thought was possible when Winston was alive—"

"Winston," said Galen, wanting to encourage Bede to continue. "I read in your file he was one of your men. He was the one who got shot."

"Never mind," said Bede, his attention coming back to Galen. "The point is, we don't deserve this. None of us do. But we're here. It's pretty cool. And I, for one, am grateful."

With that, Bede slipped up through the water to float on his back. Hands spread wide to keep his balance, his eyes closed, water slipping down his cheeks like tears, while the sun blazed overhead. His legs came up to the surface, muscled, damp, his red swim shorts sticking to his upper thighs, the slight hair on his chest streaming down like arrows.

The tattoos were now fully on display, blocky patterns on his upper arms, both of them, and a sleek curved shape that arced across his neck.

With his body dipping below the surface of the water and rising above it moment to moment, Galen felt drawn to touch those tattoos, and he wanted to pull Bede aside to ask him what else he missed in prison. Maybe he should also ask Toby and Owen what they missed, and maybe do something about it.

Taking a deep breath, Galen dove back under the water, then let out the air from his lungs, but slowly.

He opened his eyes in the lake water, saw the darkness below and the bubbles from his lungs rising lazily to the surface. Saw the thrash of canoe paddles, and over-eager arms and legs that didn't quite know how to coordinate themselves.

When he broke the surface of the water again, Bede was on the dock, wrangling for his turn at the green canoe. Royce was at his side, making large, expressive gestures, and Galen realized Beck had joined them, wearing worn, camo-patterned swim shorts.

Eventually, Bede stood back and let Royce and Jonah take over the green canoe, with Beck slithering into the middle. The canoes were two-man canoes, and probably weren't meant for three, but as long as Beck kept still, they would be okay—which he did not, and the three of them were toppled into the water with shouts of laughter.

From the dock, Bede was laughing so hard that he was doubled over, and as Galen swam close, he felt that laughter, that sense of joy and amusement settle over him, buoying him up.

"I'll take a turn with you," he said as he climbed the ladder at the end of the dock.

"Sure," said Bede.

He grabbed the line of the empty blue canoe, which came floating toward them, seeing as how the occupants, Toby and Owen, had decided that rocking back and forth was the best fun, and they'd ended up tumbled into the water.

"I can paddle, I guess, but don't know how to steer."

"I can steer," said Galen, settling himself on the back seat in the canoe. He picked up the paddle and twirled it in his hands as he watched Bede gingerly get into the canoe and sit on the front bench seat. "Don't you worry your pretty head about that."

He smiled as Bede looked over his shoulder, that wide grin in place. Then Bede took up the paddle, and together, Galen doing his best to match Bede's strokes, they eased out into the lake, a large blue and gold circle of the sun on the water all around them.

The pleasant interlude on the water lasted all afternoon, and though there were clouds forming along the ridge, there was no threat of rain or lightning, so they could wear themselves out. Finally, Gabe announced that it was dinnertime, and they all swam or paddled back to the dock.

Galen took charge of dragging the canoes up to the bank and turning them upside down so they could dry. Beck and Bede stayed to help him, and quite soon Galen made his way to his tent. There he grabbed his shower things, eager to wash the lake water away, get dressed in dry clothes, and have a good hot meal.

He took a good long shower, using way more liquid soap than was probably necessary. When finally he rinsed off, every single bone in his body felt like it was melting.

Sure he could work twelve-hour days, but messing around and goofing off for an afternoon? Was exhausting. Fun, but exhausting.

As he was putting on his socks and tying up his boots, he realized he'd been slumped over on the bench, just sitting there for a good long while, and that he needed to get a move on. Hustling, he gathered his things and opened the curtain, swishing it back just as Bede was stepping in.

"Sorry—" Bede stopped, putting his hand to the frame of the shower to keep his balance, to keep from running over Galen. "I didn't hear anyone inside. Thought it was empty."

"It's empty now," said Galen, thinking Bede would move back so Galen could slip out and leave Bede to his shower.

But Bede didn't move and Galen didn't move, and it took Galen a full second to realize that Bede was still in his swim shorts, the bare skin of his shoulders and chest sun-warmed, with little drops of water silvering his hair. That his arm was raised, shower things tucked under his other arm, and that he simply wasn't moving.

"What do you need, Bede?" asked Galen, his voice coming out a croak.

Then Bede kissed him, one hand cupping his cheek, moving to curl his fingers around the back of Galen's neck.

Bede's lips were warm, a soft caress, rather than the hard aggression that Galen, quite simply, had been imagining pretty much from day one. This kiss was followed by a second, equally gentle, then Bede sighed and caressed Galen's cheek with his own.

Bede's skin was warm, and his breath was warm, his fingertips cool where they tangled in Galen's hair. He should get it cut so Bede wouldn't have to worry about it—

—he should pull away. Falling for kisses on a darkened path in the woods was one thing. This was another.

He should stop this. But he didn't.

The moment lingered, the two of them standing in the partly curtained doorway of the last shower stall in the row. The other four showers were occupied, the water flowing at full bore, steam billowing up to the ceiling.

Hot water and privacy in a shower. That's what Bede had been missing.

Galen should let him get at it. But he wasn't going to.

A bit urgently, he rose on his toes, lay his palm on Bede's cheek, and breathed into the next kiss, claiming it.

"Hey," he said, looking into Bede's eyes.

Unspoken was the idea that even though pretty much everybody in the valley was hooking up, according to Beck, he for, one, did not enjoy an audience, which they currently would have just as soon as the water was turned off in one of the other stalls.

As to where this might lead, he simply had no idea.

"Yeah," said Bede, low, breathy, urgent, his jawline trembling beneath Galen's touch. "Yeah?"

Galen's own fears were pushed behind by desire that raced through him. He had no idea what came next, but he wouldn't mind more of this sweet connection, the low shine in Bede's eyes.

He wanted to answer the question that lingered on Bede's mouth. A mouth that Galen now knew the taste of. Just as he knew the contours of Bede's face, the tenderness of his touch. The length of his bare legs. The array of tattoos on his skin.

"Yes?" he said, his voice rising, nerves echoing through the word.

He wasn't afraid, not exactly. But he'd always lived by a personal sense of right and wrong.

Thoughts clamored in his head. That, since he was a team lead, sleeping with one of his parolee was not a very bright idea.

Bede had said that the valley was a chance he never thought he'd get. A chance to start something new. Take his life in a new direction.

Maybe that direction was one that Galen also wanted to follow. He wouldn't know unless he tried, but he needed a minute, or maybe a lifetime, or maybe just a heartbeat.

Maybe it was in those dark blue eyes to make fun of Galen's reticence. Or maybe that sparkle, diamond-bright, was pleasure at Galen's agreement.

Either way, the soft smile that went with it emboldened Galen to lay a last kiss on that mouth, and then he hustled away, just as the shower in one of the stalls turned off and a soft humming ensued, along with the low hush-hush sounds of a damp body being toweled off.

Maybe he was crazy. Or maybe he was fearless.

All he knew was that this was the most alive he'd felt since his dad had passed away. Even his daydreams about Zeke Molloy hadn't come close to this. To this reality that felt better than any daydream.

CHAPTER 28
GALEN

At dinner, through the general chatter, exclamations over the amazing fish and chips, Galen kept his eyes on Bede, who sat catty-corner from him on the opposite side of the long table. This wasn't strange. They normally sat together. They were on the same team, after all.

While already feeling the lance of nerves in his gut, he could see that Bede was acting like this was any other day. That he'd not just kissed Galen as he'd come out of his shower. That there wasn't a very good—albeit tenuous—possibility that they were going to strip to the skin in front of each other and lay hands upon one another and—

"I'd forgotten how good it feels to go swimming," Bede was saying to Kell and Marston, who sat to Galen's left. "One of the things I missed on the inside. Being fully submerged. You know?"

Galen glanced at Kell, who was nodding sagely.

Marston, who'd never been in prison, looked a tad confused. But then he said, "I never thought about it like that before." He wiped his mouth with his napkin thoughtfully for a moment, then asked, "What else did you miss?"

There was no lascivious wink in Galen's direction, no come-hither tone in Bede's voice when he answered, "So many things. Like good food, quality food. In prison, I made myself eat whatever was on my tray just to stay strong."

"And some of it was pretty gross," said Kell with a shudder.

"I'm not talking down to maggot-infested level," said Bede, cutting low through the air with his hand held flat. "But, you know. The bread was old, the spinach was slimy. Like that."

The conversation continued on in a casual way, not like an interrogation, but as if Marston truly wanted to know. Which he might, seeing as how deeply Marston was in love with Kell.

"I missed fresh air that hadn't been filtered by a chain-link fence and razor wire," added Bede.

"I can imagine," said Marston in a friendly way, though it was quite obvious that he really had no idea.

Come to that, neither did Galen.

He'd lived a free man his whole life, and the only time he'd been locked in anything was the one time recently that the door to the men's toilet had jammed at Ranchette's Stop 'n Go. He'd managed to shove his way free, internally laughing at the escapade, and how his dad would laugh when he told him, and then he remembered his dad had passed away and that there was nobody to share the joke with.

"I also missed—" Bede looked down at his empty plate, shaking his head, a small grin lighting his features, as if he wasn't sure he should share what he'd been about to share. But then he looked up and said, "Standing in the grass in my bare feet. Or standing in the dirt, it doesn't matter."

"Bare feet?" asked Marston, and Galen leaned forward to hear the answer. He couldn't help himself.

"You can't go around barefoot in prison," said Bede. "It's not just the mold in the showers, and the floors are kept pretty clean, lots of mopping as punishment, you see." He smiled, shaking his head, as if the memory was good, rather than, actually, quite sad. "Another inmate sees you barefoot, they'll stomp on your toes. And just try stepping out in a prison yard without boots on. You'll step on a goat's head burr, many of them, inside of two minutes."

Sitting back, sympathy rising, Galen's misgivings churned inside of him right next to fraught nerves and a heightened sense of want.

Finishing his dinner, he made his way back to his tent. It wasn't even close to sunset, and the tent was set aglow by the sunlight coming through the pine trees, accompanied by the familiar scent of sun-warmed canvas, the bright smell of pine, and crushed pine needles.

What came next between him and Bede? He had no idea. Should he make his bed before he went to movie night? Should he change into clean boxers? Should he forget the whole thing?

Well, one thing was for certain, he wasn't going to lollygag in his own tent like some damsel who needed rescuing.

What he really needed to do was put the kibosh on this whole thing, nip it before it became unruly. Because, reasonably, in the real world, he would not be hooking up with an ex-con.

But the valley wasn't like the real world. It was a place of green swathes of trees, a cool blue lake, startlingly clear skies. A place apart where dreams might turn into reality.

Leaving the bed untouched, as it was made anyway, and not changing clothes, Galen stepped out of his tent and strode along the path between the trees in the direction of Kell and Bede's tent.

He should have encountered someone, but perhaps they were all at the mess tent in preparation for movie night. But there was nothing and no one at the moment. The woods were eerily silent as the sun streamed through the trees, slicing in yellow angles, creating long, slanted shadows.

He'd gone as far as the spot where the two main paths through the trees intersected and paused, planning to go left to Bede's tent, when he heard a rustle in the woods.

Turning, he saw Bede coming toward him.

Everything slowed down as his focus narrowed in on the way Bede had rolled up the sleeves of his blue chambray shirt. The fact that he was wearing his cowboy boots, which made his legs look ten miles long. How his shirt was unsnapped in a come-hither way. The tumble of dark hair across his forehead. The way his eyes widened, then narrowed as he saw Galen and began to walk faster.

Everything sped up.

Being caught in Bede's arms, strong bands of iron, Galen was shocked by his body's own response to a sudden and heated kiss, the lances of pleasure up his legs, the banding around his groin. The heat of pure desire that seemed to come out of nowhere and settle over him in pops of invisible glitter.

"Bede," he gasped, his palms pressing against Bede's chest because he needed some air. A moment to steady himself.

Bede circled warm fingers around the back of Galen's neck and drew him close. Not quite close enough for a kiss, but close enough for their noses to brush, and for Galen to imagine he could feel the whisper of air from Bede's eyelashes as he surveyed Galen's face.

"It can't hurt us," said Bede, almost whispering.

"What can't?" asked Galen, both confused by the statement and distracted by the idea of being hurt.

This would hurt. All of it. Getting together with Bede would be good, but any connection he was likely to make—was *sure* to make—was making—would be trampled at summer's end. Bede would go his way and Galen would be left with the tatters of his heart.

He never got in bed with any man until he had feelings for him, and here he was. His body plastered to Bede's, all up and down, a hot sear. Desire hot, his skin flushing, his reason a runaway herd of horses. Oh, yes, he had feelings for Bede. Confused ones. Good ones.

"Whatever this is." Bede paused, his gaze fully on Galen now, his eyes wide and open. "Whatever we are."

Before Galen could speak—though certainly no part of him, not *any*, was saying no—Bede's hand, withdrawn from his neck, leaving a cool space behind, was between Galen's thighs. Those fingers, pressing against denim, drew up in a slow, languorous trail.

Heat building in Galen's belly, his groin, his whole body sighed, muscles turning liquid, the parts of his brain that could still think sparking out until he could not think at all.

When was the last time he'd been touched like this, responded like this? Since before his dad had passed away, that was for sure.

The summer before, when he'd come on to Zeke Malloy, it had been in stops and starts, and had ended in a polite but firm rejection. And maybe he'd not been attracted to Zeke, but to the idea of him. Someone to lean on, someone strong, someone to enfold him in firm arms when the night got too dark, and the sense of loss and grief became an overwhelming tar-black puddle.

Bede didn't know about Galen's dad or what had happened, how sudden his passing had been, but he was acting as if he did. He caressed and kissed Galen's face, sweeping away astonished shock with that mouth of his, and with his hand, he cast spells that Galen had no idea, simply no idea, how to ward off.

And when Bede undid the snap and zipper of his jeans, sliding his hand inside, not stopping, his palm warm against the bare skin of Galen's belly, he knew he didn't want to stop any of it.

Pleasure rippled as Bede's fingers curled around his cock, warm inside his boxers, taut against his belly. There was no shyness in Bede's touch, only boldness in each caress, only an earthy, animal insistence on taking this happenstance meeting in the woods to an exact conclusion.

There were no holds barred, nothing hidden as Bede, with his touches, brushed his cheek against Galen's, sighed in his ear.

The gasp of that mouth against Galen's, the warmth of him, the tug of those fingers—all of this swept Galen up into a maelstrom he was unprepared for.

"Don't you—" began Galen, but the words and the question and any thoughts hidden behind them vanished as Bede's arm tightened around his waist.

Bede's hand, hot palm against silken flesh, bore down on him and pulled him up and up until Galen's head jerked back with a force sharp enough to nearly sever his spine.

There was simply not enough air in his lungs and he gasped, eyes wide open, dark sparks and bright ones circling around his vision as he collapsed in Bede's arms.

"What?" he asked. "Was *that?*"

"What you needed," said Bede with a sweet kiss to Galen's mouth. "What I wanted to give you. In case this was the only time I could."

What Bede had just given him was an encounter that should have taken place in a honeymoon boudoir, complete with a trail of rose petals leading up to the two-person bathtub in the middle of the room. Not a stand-up undefinable *something*, his blue jeans open to the air after a raw encounter between a parolee and his *boss*.

But while it had been raw, there'd also been sweetness. Gentleness. All of which was now stamped on Galen's very soul, and now what the hell was he supposed to do with *that?*

"You don't have to do anything," said Bede, and it took Galen a moment to realize he'd asked his question aloud and that Bede had answered it aloud, rather than the two of them communicating on a soul-deep level. "It's just to enjoy. Like life, I suppose."

He drew back, his arm still around Galen's waist and, one-handed, tucked Galen away in his boxers, and then zipped up the zipper and closed the brass button.

"What about you?" Galen asked as it seemed like, felt like, Bede was prepared to walk away into the woods without his fair share.

"Oh," said Bede with a laugh, shaking his head, his smile bright, his eyes sparkling. "I don't like doing it standing up."

"What the hell?" asked Galen, unable to stifle his own laugh even as it mixed with a sudden flare of irritation. "You don't get to just do that and walk away."

"Sure I do." Bede moved close for a second to tuck Galen's shirt tails into his blue jeans. Then he stepped away and waved for Galen to follow. "C'mon. We'll be late for the movie, which, according to Kell, is *Cool Hand Luke.*"

A classic prison movie. Of course. What else would they show in the mess tent with a bunch of ex-cons crowding around? Laughing at the funny parts, critiquing anything they didn't agree with, and of course they would know because they'd been there.

Maybe all of them hoped one day to be as cool as Paul Newman, but that idea didn't matter as much as the fact that Bede was, quite simply, walking away. As if nothing that had happened between them mattered. Did it?

Galen found himself bereft at the idea, and hurried to follow after Bede, close on his heels. Trotting. Panting. Awash with feelings, his whole body swirling with desire for more.

By the time they both reached the mess tent, Galen was sweating, damp beneath his arms, between his legs, and still short of air as his body attempted to settle into a semblance of normal. Whatever that meant, anyhow.

There was no going back from knowing what Bede tasted like, how soft that supple mouth was, how strong and decisive those hands were. What remained unknown beneath Bede's clothes was an undiscovered country that Galen knew he shouldn't want to discover. But he did. Oh, he did.

Everybody in the valley was in the mess tent, settled in folding chairs that faced the propped up screen on the rail along the buffet table.

Two standing fans had been set up to keep the mess tent cool and airy, in spite of the heat of the early evening. The smell of popcorn was in the air, the sound of excited jostlings, low comments. Bowls of fresh, salty popcorn were being placed on small tables at the edges of aisles, and the soda machine was going full bore.

As Bede went and grabbed two seats at the end of the second aisle, nobody remarked that the two of them had arrived together and that they weren't altogether tidy.

Nobody remarked that Galen was unusually flushed about the face and neck or that Bede's grin was wide enough to light up the dark. That his hair was sticking to his forehead, and that veins stood out on his forearms as he grabbed a bowl of popcorn and passed it to Galen.

"You want something to drink?" asked Bede, as nicely as a boy on his second or third date. Polite but casual, as if the relationship between them was well on its way to being firmly established. "Iced tea?"

Galen blinked. He favored iced tea over milk or soda, and Bede had noticed.

"Have you been watching me?" Galen just about hissed, but he was laughing, too.

Bede chuckled in response as he got up to go over to the iced tea dispenser. A second later, Galen bowed his head and looked at the overflowing bowl of popcorn in his lap, slathered with butter and sparkling with salt and something that might be white cheddar powder.

He was sure that what he was getting himself into was not feasible, no sir. But a large part of him saw the irony, a deep, dark humor, in his current situation. He'd gone and done what he'd never thought possible: he had feelings for Bede. It was not just that his body was still flush with pleasure. It was the fact that his heart was full, that he felt good for the first time in a long time. There was no way he wanted to let any of that go.

When Bede took his place in the chair next to Galen's, he reached casually across Galen to dig his fingers into the bowl. Shoving a fistful of powdery, salty popcorn into his mouth, he winked one blue eye at Galen, and then turned his attention to the screen.

"Watch the movie," Bede said, as if he knew how scattered Galen's thoughts were, how his body refused to settle. How his brain kept racing on and on to the future, and the future after that. To the edge of the horizon, all awash in confusion. Just what had he done? Had he fallen in love at long last?

He didn't know, but he wanted to find out.

CHAPTER 29

BEDE

Galen was nothing like Winston, but in a subtle parallel, he ate his popcorn the same way that Winston used to. With a cupped handful of popcorn held to his mouth, munching on the first kernel to encounter his tongue and teeth. Then he crunched away, a horse at its net, watching *Cool Hand Luke* with avid eyes.

Unlike Winston, however, he didn't laugh at the bits that were screamingly funny to criminals, like the egg-eating scene. Galen did seem to appreciate Cool Hand Luke's continual defiance, at least until the end, when Luke got killed, and then Bede realized that Galen didn't like the movie at *all*.

"I suppose we could ask for a Disney film next time," said Bede, leaning close so only Galen could hear. The response he got was a silver flash from those gray eyes, and a slight shrug.

"At least they don't have chain gangs anymore," said Galen, taking another scoop of popcorn, holding it to his mouth. One or two kernels fell to the floor, but he ignored them.

"Actually, they do," said Bede. He'd never been on a chain gang, or a work camp, as the younger inmates called them. "They're mostly in the south. Arizona, I think. Maybe Oklahoma. Alabama?" He didn't really know, except from the grapevine at Wyoming Correctional, and he hadn't cared to investigate further. "I heard the one in Arizona is pretty humane. I don't know about the others."

Galen shifted in his seat, not answering, and it was easy to see that the subject made him uncomfortable.

When the next movie started playing, the growing darkness outside the mess tent made it easier to see the grainy black and white images on the projector screen. This one was *The Defiant Ones,* an older movie about two convicts escaping from a chain gang while chained together.

Bede had heard about this movie, but never seen it. He wanted to stay and watch, but one look at Galen told him Galen did not want to see it, and that he'd really love to be somewhere else altogether.

"Shall we go?" Bede asked, leaning close, one hand on Galen's thigh to signal his intent. Not just go, as in leave the mess tent, but *go*, leave together, and end up in Galen's tent together.

It'd have to be Galen's tent, because the last thing Bede wanted was for Kell to walk in on them. After all, Bede's tent was half Kell's.

Galen drew his attention from the screen and focused on Bede. His dark eyebrows lowered as he thought.

"Where?" he asked, his voice a bit husky, as if he already knew the answer to that.

"Your tent, I think."

Those four simple words had an effect on Galen that Bede could hardly keep up with. Surprise. Then desire. Then doubt. All of this flickered across his sharp features inside of a heartbeat.

"C'mon, it'll be fun," said Bede. Fun had different meanings, of course, but he didn't think Galen misunderstood him.

"Fun as in arcade fun, or fun as in haunted house fun." This was not a question.

"Definitely the second one," said Bede with a grin and a small laugh. "C'mon."

He stood up, and while he didn't offer his hand to Galen, he felt as if he had. From behind, someone threw a handful of popcorn at both of them.

"Down in front!"

Bede led the way, slinking along the outside of the row of tables, almost tiptoeing down the wooden steps. There he waited for Galen, who was seconds behind. In the semi-darkness of deep twilight, Bede followed Galen along the path to his tent, fourth along in the row of tents designated for team leads.

They went up to the wooden platform. The light wasn't on, so Bede waited while Galen unzipped the tent and stepped inside, giving Galen one more chance to back out if he wanted to. But he didn't back out. He held the tent flap open like an ingénue on opening night.

"Come on in," he said, stepping back, the single overhead bulb casting a long shadow over the floor. "And we're going to do this my way."

"What do you mean, my way?" asked Bede, already laughing as he wrapped his arms around Galen's waist and pulled him close. "Like Frank Sinatra?"

Galen laughed, burying his face in Bede's neck, his breath warm, the laugh moving his body in a gentle way.

"He was arrested, you know," whispered Bede into Galen's hair.

"For what?" Galen didn't lift his head but instead brushed his nose and lips along the muscles of Bede's neck, making him shiver.

"For seduction," said Bede. "That's what I read in an article once."

He ducked his head to kiss Galen's temple, pulling his arms closer, making Galen's body arc a little way back.

"I told you we're doing this my way this time. In bed."

Galen rose up and pushed on Bede's arms, and for a quick second Bede imagined that Galen wanted him to let go. He was about to. Then Galen clasped his hands along Bede's forearms, stroking with his fingers.

When he began to tug Bede's shirt out from his jeans, Bede realized how this was going to go. Galen was no shy flower, no ingénue, but rather a man who wanted Bede. A combination that Bede was unable to resist.

Even if they were together for only for this time, a short span in the middle of a hot Wyoming summer, it might be enough. Or it could be too much.

Bede was feeling just a stab of trepidation when Galen gently leaned forward and kissed Bede lightly on the breastbone, letting Bede's shirt drop along his shoulders. Then he used his hands to tug the sleeves off all the way and smiled up at Bede at this slight accomplishment.

"You're all muscle," Galen said, his fingers tickling along the inner side of Bede's arms. "And these tattoos—I love them."

"Got 'em way before I was arrested," said Bede, chuckling low in his chest, standing as still as he could for Galen's inspection as he looked down at his own arm. "Getting tats in prison is just a way of getting an infection as fast as humanly possible. Wouldn't get one behind bars on a bet. These are from a tattoo artist in Denver. I told him what I wanted, and out of respect for the Maori people, they are stylized but not actually tribal tattoos. If you see what I mean."

"Maori?" asked Galen. "Why Maori?"

"I dunno." Bede shrugged slightly. He'd never really been able to explain, even to himself, why he felt drawn to the Maori culture, though his interest might have started after watching a rugby game where the All Blacks team performed their traditional haka before the start of the World Rugby cup match. "Just 'cause."

Galen traced the edges of the blocks and curves that went over his shoulder, and a little way down his left arm. The curve along his neck swooped to represent an ocean's wave. All black, dark as night.

"I'm not a tattoo guy," said Galen, under his breath as if to himself. "But these are nice."

"Nice," said Bede in mock anger, pulling Galen to him so they were hip to hip. "Hours and hours I spent in the chair and these are *nice*?"

"Very nice," said Galen, amending, punctuating the words with kisses along Bede's collarbone, which made him shiver. "Pretty damn nice."

"C'mon," said Bede, not wanting to wait any longer. "You said bed. Let's do bed."

"It's a cot really," said Galen with a snicker.

Bede wanted to swallow him whole. Instead, he used deft hands to strip Galen to the skin, all the while absorbing the pale angles of his body, the jut of his hips, the softness of his belly. The shiver that ran through Galen as Bede placed his full palm on Galen's thigh, squeezed a little, then let go.

"You are delicious," said Bede, his voice guttural and low as he pulled Galen's naked body against his clothed one.

"So are you," said Galen. "But you should be naked, too, so I'm not on my own here."

Gladly, Bede tore off his clothes, tossing them in a heap near where he'd piled Galen's clothes. Then he pulled Galen into his arms, and half-closed his eyes with a sigh at the delicious feeling of skin-on-skin.

Galen's cock was hard against Bede's belly, and his own cock had stood up and taken notice long before that. He was so ready he was weeping from the tip, and there was an insistent pull in his groin that told him to go fast, even though he wanted to go slow.

"Oh, shit." Galen's whole body jerked in his arms.

"What?"

"I don't have any stuff."

"Stuff for what?" asked Bede, getting a pleasant eyeful of the sweet blush that danced high on Galen's face. He knew what Galen meant, and playfully teased, "Stuff for Parcheesi?"

"No," said Galen, then his mouth opened, and he laughed and said, "I mean lube. You know that's what I meant."

"We don't need lube," said Bede, desperation rising in him that they should not stop. "We can get along this time. Order it later. We're sure to use some later. I just want to—"

It would take too long to explain, so Bede pushed Galen to sit on the bed, then went to his knees, spreading Galen's thighs with both hands.

"Jesus, Bede, here."

Bede looked up to see Galen holding out a pillow, then Galen leaned forward and urged Bede to use it for his knees. "The floor is too damn hard for that."

"Agreed," said Bede, using his fingers on Galen's knees to spread his legs again. "I just want to do this."

"Fine."

Bede felt Galen's fingers lifting his chin, found himself caught in the beautiful snare of those gray eyes.

"And then I'm going to do it, 'cause I don't want this to be one sided like the last time."

"Yes, boss," said Bede, then he laughed at Galen's face, the play of emotion there as he seemed to remember their daytime roles. Boss and worker. Parole officer and parolee. "Don't think about that now, okay? Just enjoy."

"Okay."

With satisfaction, Bede watched Galen lean back on his elbows, watched him spread his thighs further than Bede had asked him to. How Galen's eyes closed, his longish hair becoming ribbons on his shoulders.

Now Bede could get to work. Could lean close and take in Galen's warm scent. Could run his mouth over the hardness of Galen's cock, soft, dry except for the clear sheen of moisture on the top.

Bede licked that quickly, felt Galen jump a little, then licked again, more slowly this time. He drew his tongue down Galen's cock, once, twice, then leaned up to suck the entire of Galen's cock into his mouth.

Galen's cock was hard, the quiver of his whole body unstilled by the pressure of Bede's hands on his knees. Bede could sense each tremor that went through Galen with each suck of Bede's mouth on him.

And savored it, the quivers, the taste, the hum of delight that Galen made, as if he'd waited his whole life for Bede to come to him, for Bede to go to his knees and take Galen in his mouth all the way down. All new, every sensation rippling through him, as if nobody had ever done this to him before.

"Good?" asked Bede, pausing to ask, just to make sure.

"Uh," was the only sound Galen made, as if he was overwhelmed by pleasure and could not gather even a single thought in that beautiful head of his.

Bede had to stroke his own cock to quiet it, to tell it to be patient, even though he was on the verge of coming, just from that single sound.

He hurried his adoration of Galen's cock, sped up his sucking, a bit of stroking as he took his hand and caressed between Galen's spread thighs, cupping those tight balls, leaning to lick each one, patient and slow.

"Oh."

The small sweet sound Galen made told Bede that Galen was about to come, and though he wanted to linger and then linger some more, he knew he wouldn't last through another sound like that, so he rose up and sucked harder, stroking the length of Galen's cock, swirling his tongue, and savored very jolt of Galen's body as he came in Bede's mouth.

Swallowing, Bede leaned back, sweeping his hands along Galen's quivering thighs, slow, and warm, and quiet. And laughed as Galen struggled to push himself up from where he'd collapsed on the cot.

"Bede," he said, a smile in his gray eyes. "Now you, right? Now you."

"Now me," said Bede.

Though he could have tended to Galen's needs all night, he knew Galen had meant it when he'd said they were doing it his way. That they would not only be using the cot, they would share the pleasure, and not have it be only one way. Even if nothing else had made it clear that Galen was a good man, a very good man, this did.

Bede crawled on the cot, straddling Galen's hips with both his legs, and laughed when Galen tumbled him to his back in a haphazard sprawl. Galen leaned close, close enough for his hair to tickle Bede's face. Then Galen kissed him, giving him a taste of himself, such an intimate gesture that Bede's heart sped up.

"Do that again, I'm going to come in two seconds," he said.

"Can't have that," said Galen with a quick smile. "Be good for me now."

"Yes, sir," said Bede, going utterly still as Galen slithered to the floor and pulled Bede's legs where he wanted them, bent over the edge of the cot.

Bede stared at the ceiling of the tent, the pair of moths going in circles around the light, as if they were at a dance, and the lightbulb was the center of the dance floor. When he felt Galen's hands on his shins, he looked up, and yes, Galen was smiling at him from between Bede's knees, looking at Bede as though he'd discovered something wonderful in him.

Shoving every thought out of his head, past, present, future, Bede lay back, and flung his forearm over his eyes.

"Everything okay?" asked Galen, his hands sweeping up to Bede's knees, then going still.

"Yeah, just—" Bede stopped to catch his breath. To still the pang in his heart that it had been so long and the last person to touch him had left the earth over five years before.

But he didn't want to think of Winston. Not now. He had something special right before him, and that was what he wanted to treasure, to take with him in the dark when he fell asleep.

"Just hurry, cause I'm not going to last."

Galen obliged him, using his hands and his mouth, sweet and quick, to bring Bede to pleasure. His mouth was warm, and the sensation of sucking, the swirl of Galen's tongue, was enough to jolt Bede into coming before he could even take a breath.

He loved the feel of Galen licking him clean, the strokes to his quivering belly, but he didn't take his forearm from his eyes until he felt a last, soft kiss on the inside of his thigh. Then Galen sat up and moved over Bede, pressing his chest to Bede's chest, an embrace of body and heat that surrounded him with the beat of Galen's heart.

"Seriously, are you okay?" Galen asked with a soft kiss to Bede's shoulder. "Did I hurt you?"

"I'm good," said Bede. He pulled his forearm away and saw the concern in Galen's gray eyes. "Just some ghosts, is all."

"It's been a long time, yeah?"

This question was asked with warmth and kindness, and when tears prickled in Bede's eyes, he blinked them away as fast as he could.

"Longer than for you, probably," said Bede, putting a flip of impudence in his voice to distract Galen. Then, in spite of his earnest desire to stay awake so he and Galen could have a good cuddle, perhaps one that lasted until the end of time, he yawned hugely. "Man, that swim."

"Yeah," said Galen. "Me too." His yawn echoed Bede's and then he smiled, petting Bede's chest with long, slow, warm strokes.

"Get your laptop and order the stuff before we both fall asleep," said Bede, pretending to be gruff, as though Galen had been arguing with him about this the entire night.

"Yes, sir," said Galen and, with a laugh, he got up, pulled on his boxers, and tugged his laptop from the shelf. Then, while sitting on the edge of the cot, he opened it up and started typing. After a few clicks, he looked up at Bede.

"It'll be here tomorrow," he said.

"Can I stay?" asked Bede, and then hid a wince at Galen's expression, which told Bede that maybe all of this was too much, too fast, for Galen. "I'll go," he said.

"You can stay the next time," said Galen, folding the laptop closed, and replacing it on the shelf. "I just need to—" He paused to tuck his hair behind his ear.

"Get your head around it."

"Yeah."

Galen leaned to kiss the middle of Bede's chest, but he was too far away, and the kiss landed smack in the middle of Bede's stomach. And since he was very ticklish there, he curled up, burying his laugh of protest in Galen's pillow.

"Next time for sure," said Galen, and now his kiss landed in the middle of Bede's back, and it felt like a secret message that everything would turn out just fine, if only Bede had a little faith. In himself. In Galen. In the future.

CHAPTER 30
BEDE

S aturday was as hot as every other day of the week had been, though, in the afternoon, when they were putting away their knapweed tools, hopefully for the last time, a slip of a breeze kicked up and Bede watched Galen look sagely at Guipago Ridge, a gray line above the trees.

"It might rain," he said, tipping his cowboy hat back. He looked at them and shook his head. "Then again, it might not." With a smile, he took off his hat, scraped his hair back, then put it back on again. "Well?" he asked, looking at them as if shocked they were still standing there. "Aren't you going to go get ready?"

"Ready for what?" asked Bede, and Toby and Owen looked equally puzzled.

"Why, for your two-week anniversary, of course." Galen shook his head as if they were the biggest fools on earth. "We've got reservations at the tavern. John Henton's Tavern, in town. We're going to have beers and burgers. Plus, you get your refurb phones with six months of data on them."

Bede remembered being told about this, the promise. The carrot before the stick. At least that's what he'd thought two weeks ago. That this was all some big scam to get a whole lot of work out of them without putting much into them.

However, he'd been so deep inside the day-to-day activity of the valley that he'd forgotten to believe he was being taken advantage of. Plus, having a phone to call his own, even if it was a refurb phone with limited data, seemed like a genie's wish appearing out of nowhere. He hadn't had access to a cell phone in five years, so it was pretty exciting, even if there was no one to call—

"Do we have time to spruce up, boss?" he asked, even if he already knew the answer.

"I should certainly hope so." Galen smiled at them all, though it seemed his smile lingered in Bede's direction. "Shower. Shave. Clean shirt. Polish your boots. Everything. Make me proud, and meet me in the parking lot around five thirty."

While the rest of the valley was lining up in the mess tent, Bede hurried to his tent, rushed through his shower, shaved too fast, almost nicking himself three times, and was in the parking lot in plenty of time. Sweating, yes, most of his cologne burned off, but he was ready. He'd never been so ready, not just to go out, to go somewhere other than the valley, but to hang out in a bar with Galen.

Had someone told him that when he'd arrived in the valley, he would have laughed himself sick. Yet here he was, heart pounding with anticipation as he raced through the trees to the parking lot.

Galen was already there, twirling the key fob around one finger, his straw cowboy hat tipped back on his head, and he was whistling. Some nameless, nearly tuneless tune, but he seemed so happy that Bede had to stop and just listen. Absorb. Maybe this was enough, this now. Galen and him, sharing what they could.

When Galen saw him there, the smile that broke across his face made Bede feel like there were angels singing in the trees. Pure nonsense. Utter bullshit. But that didn't stop his heart from fluttering as Galen walked over to him.

But before they could even so much as reach out and touch hands, Toby and Owen were stomping through the woods in their direction. Galen's eyes whispered a promise before he turned to greet the housebreakers, and then there was the usual scramble as to who had shotgun.

Bede won, because he had years of practice staring down the worst drug dealers, so surely he could stare down two half-assed criminals who would rather take the second row of seats, just the same.

As Galen drove, Bede noticed a shaft of what looked like gray clouds coming toward the ground, and pointed at the distant horizon.

"Will it rain?" he asked.

"That's virga," said Galen. And when Bede mentally asked, *What's that?* Galen explained it. "It's moisture coming down that doesn't quite make it to the earth. I always feel sorry for it, trying so hard and not making it. But it's pretty, and it means you can smell rain coming."

Galen rolled down the windows and turned off the AC, and a waft of fresh, damp air swooped around the truck's cabin. They were all still inhaling it when they got to Farthing, and Galen pulled up and parked the truck a short block away.

"You didn't lock it," said Bede as they marched to the tavern's front door.

"Don't need to," said Galen. "It's Farthing."

And if that wasn't a painful reminder of just how far apart their worlds were, Bede didn't know what was. Still, he shoved that aside and trailed behind the others as they went into the tavern.

At the hostess stand, a young woman in a cheery red-and-white checked apron checked for their reservations. Which, in such a small town, Bede would consider completely unnecessary—except the tavern was *hopping*.

People were waiting on the benches in the small foyer, standing two deep at the bar, all waiting to be seated. The four of them, thanks to Galen's reservation, got seated right away, menus in hand, in a nice booth toward the back of the tavern.

The booth was polished pale wood with long red bench-seat cushions. On the walls were wagon wheels and braids of wheat, two rusted branding irons crossed over each other. A western motif on crack. There'd even been an old buffalo hide coat in the front of the tavern, though who would want to wear something that thick and heavy looking, Bede had no idea.

It made him smile and when he looked at Galen sitting across from him, Galen was smiling, too. It would have been nicer if Toby and Owen weren't also there, because then it would be more like a date. But then, if it was a date, he'd be wishing it was already over so he could be alone with Galen.

A smiling waitress came up, expertly rattled off the specials of the evening, and asked them if they were ready.

"We can have beer?" asked Toby, and Owen looked like he wanted to know the answer as well.

"Yes, you may," said Galen. "Limit two. Though maybe we could add in a shot of whiskey or something, seeing as how we've been working so hard in this damn heat."

They all ordered the same thing, deluxe double cheeseburgers, along with a variety of different kinds of beers, and Galen held up four fingers. "Four shots of your finest whiskey," he said.

"Sure thing, hon," she said. "I'll be right back."

Bede settled in his seat, his whole body sighing at the thought of having whiskey again, and not toilet bowl gin. Of having a cold beer. A phone.

While they waited for their order, Leland Tate came striding up to them, and it was easy to see why Leland got such deference, such praise from everyone who worked for him. He was tall, broad shoul-dered. Held his head high, like he owned the place and expected everybody to mind their manners.

"How's it going, Galen?" asked Leland, as Galen stood up to shake his hand. Leland shook all their hands, then held out the white plastic carrier bag in his other hand, as if to show he'd brought it with him.

"It's going good, sir," said Galen. "This is Bede, Toby, and Owen, whom you've already met online," he said, pointing to each one in turn. "Guys, this is Leland. My boss's boss."

"Nice to meet you fellows face to face," Leland said. "I want to say how proud I am of you all. I've been getting good reports of your hard work and attention to detail. I know digging up knapweed is not the most glamorous of jobs, but it's necessary since it's an invasive plant that sucks all the water out of the ground. The horses will appreciate it, because they can eat the grass that will grow. And next year's guests will appreciate it because they won't have to look at it."

Bede didn't want to think about the following summer, but he sure did appreciate it when the waitress came back with a round tray and handed out their shots. She even had one for Leland, who took it and held it up.

"Here's to the valley," he said. "And here's to you boys who are making it happen. We couldn't do it without you." He drank back his shot.

In echo, Bede drank, shuddering with appreciation at the smokey taste. It'd been a long, long time since he'd had anything as civilized as that whiskey.

Leland held the bag out. "I'll be off, but before I forget, here are your phones. Enjoy them in good health."

He handed the bag to Galen, tipped his finger to his forehead, then turned around, and as he walked out of the tavern, the crowd split before him like the waves before Moses.

Bede turned his attention to Galen and the sleek white carrier bag in his hands. One by one, he handed out sturdy phone-shaped boxes to each of them, and one by one they fell silent as they opened the boxes.

Bede's phone was black, which was fine by him, and though the phone was supposed to be refurb, it looked brand new. There was even a plastic sheet on the glass surface that needed to be peeled back, inch by erotic inch.

"Who're you going to call?" asked Galen. "Who's your first phone call to?"

For a second, Bede thought Galen was making a joke from the old Ray Parker Jr. song. *Who you gonna call? Ghost Busters!* But no. He was asking for who specifically.

Bede knew Winston's number by heart, though by this time, five years on, that number had surely been assigned to someone else. A

257

grandma in Utah, probably. He gripped the phone in his fingers and swallowed hard.

"What's the matter?" asked Galen. "Is your phone broken?"

Now Bede had three pairs of eyes, a fourth and fifth pair, if he wanted to count the waitress and her helper, who'd come up to the table just then with two circular trays full of food. He shook his head and leaned back and smiled, pretending everything was okay even though it wasn't.

He'd done that a lot in prison, especially in those first years, not wanting to give off any indication of the sweeping helplessness that would engulf him whenever he thought of Winston. As the years had gone by, the attitude of not giving a fuck had gotten easier, only now it was as if he'd forgotten how.

"No, it's fine," he said, forcing brightness into the words. "They're just a whole lot thinner than I remember."

"Yeah," said Toby and Owen just about in unison, and Toby added, "Lighter, too."

Bede put his phone aside and concentrated on his meal, the icy cool beer, bitter with hops, just the perfect distraction as he swallowed a mouthful and felt it slide down his throat. It tasted just like the beer he'd told Galen about when they'd gone swimming, and that moved him more than he'd expected it to.

He ticked the moments by in his heart until he felt a bit more normal, chomped through his cheese fries with appreciative sounds, and pretended that Galen's gaze on him wasn't protective and concerned.

Pretended extra hard that the idea of this didn't dance around strangely in his gut. This was what happened when you opened your heart, a realization he'd not even needed years behind bars to teach him.

Only Winston had been able to crack him open. Only Winston had loved him, and laughed with him, cared about him. And if it seemed Galen felt the same way about him, well, it was a fluke that would only last till the end of summer.

Smiling as he drank his second beer, wishing he could get a second shot of very good whiskey, he made it through the rest of the dinner, and, thankfully, his heart settled down by the time dessert came.

He wasn't much of a dessert guy but he ordered the carrot cake just to be sociable, and ended up passing most of it to Owen, who'd gotten the same, gobbled it down, and had been eying Bede's leftovers.

Galen drove them back to the valley in the heavy darkness with the faintest glow coming from along the top of the bulky foothills. That was soon doused as the truck trundled down the switchbacks into the valley.

Once in the parking lot, Owen and Toby took off like they'd been shot out of a cannon, their phones' faces aglow as they eagerly argued about who would call whom.

"Five bucks says they are both calling their fellow not-yet-arrested housebreakers," said Bede, because those two were just dumb enough to call and brag and get sucked into their old lives now that they had a way to connect to them.

"You okay, Bede?" asked Galen, coming close. He reached out to tug Bede close to him, looping his fingers in Bede's belt loops. "There's something about the phone. You've been quiet ever since you opened that box."

The last thing Bede wanted to do was burden Galen with his troubles.

"Not now," he said. "Maybe later."

He'd been thinking that once he figured out how he felt about it all, it being what was happening between him and Galen, he'd be able to talk about it out loud. But then Galen asked, "Later, for what? Do you mean this?"

Galen rose and clasped Bede's face in his hands, his fingers warm, the dark air swirling around Galen's face, pulling the angles and planes into focus. Then Galen kissed him, softly, as if it were their first kiss all over again.

Bede let himself be swept up, to be petted and loved on because it felt so good, he was unable to resist.

CHAPTER 31

BEDE

"Do you want to come to my tent?" asked Galen, and when Bede didn't respond, he felt another tug on his belt loop.

"Yes," said Bede, because of course, while Kell might be in Marston's tent, he very well might be in tent number eleven, reading a book, waiting to hear all about how Bede's night out had gone.

He let Galen lead him like a well-trained pup to the path that went along the front of the team leads' tents.

Of course they could have gone through the woods and not risked being seen, but Galen seemed eager. It was just as well, for by the time they reached Galen's tent and tiptoed up the wooden steps to the platform, Bede was more than ready to devour Galen, or be devoured by him.

Galen had just about pulled Bede's snap-button shirt out from the waist of his blue jeans, when Bede started doing the same to him. The dark evening air cooling on his skin made him shiver, then Bede soothed him, stroking his sides, his waist, with warm fingers, leaving Galen breathless.

"Did the stuff get here?" Bede asked, peppering a light kiss to Galen's mouth, to his neck, along his collar bone.

"It did," said Galen, boldly as he turned on a flashlight and placed it on the small shelf so the light spread itself on the ceiling of the canvas tent.

"Amazon to the rescue," said Bede with a smile.

Galen's answering smile and the sparkle in his eyes were as bright as if he'd been showered by moonlight. Only there was no moon, and no stars, just the quiet shadows of the green canvas tent as they undressed and tumbled into the clean-sheeted cot.

Galen let Bede lead the way, as though he was standing on the edge of something and might fall.

But Bede would not let him fall. Rather, Bede took the stuff that Galen pulled from the shelf, and opened the small plastic bottle of lube with one hand and dexterous fingers, not even looking down.

Then, hugging Galen close, their breaths mingling, the warmth between them rising, he prepped Galen from behind, lubed finger going in, then two. Gentle and sweet. Slowly, slowly, as though he might be anointing Galen for some holy ritual. As though only the most careful of touches was allowed, the lube cooling on his skin, the ease of his fingers inside of Galen, causing a low groan to build inside of him.

"Face to face," said Bede in a whisper. "It's better this way."

With a sweep of his hand, Bede trailed his lube-cool fingers across Galen's cock, sweeping along its hard length. More shivers, more slick-soft sounds as Bede slid the lube down his own hard cock. Then, when Bede reached for the small, foiled condom, Galen gasped out loud.

"Don't," he said. "Don't use that."

All of this went against Bede's normal protocols, but in that moment, he wanted skin-to-skin and nothing less. His body surged forward, demanding it. He felt his eyes blazing as he silently demanded it, looking right at Galen, into his dark eyes.

"Okay," said Bede, a little breathless himself as he hugged Galen close and then released the tension in his muscles, his hand going between his legs, guiding himself to Galen's anus. "Okay."

Bede felt the sweat drip from his forehead as he lifted himself above Galen and eased Galen back on the pillows.

The night air, sweet with coolness, swept across the side of his cheek as Bede eased himself inside of Galen's body. Eased and withdrew, eased and withdrew, the cadence mesmerizing, the rhythm slow. As if they had all the time in the world. As if Bede's patience was endless, but endless only for Galen in this moment between them.

He picked up that rhythm, feeling joyous, triumphant when Galen tossed his head on the pillow and arched his neck, his whole body seeming to beg for more, and then more.

"C'mon," said Galen, guttural, low, a sound meant only for Bede's ears. "Don't hold back."

Cupping Galen's hips in his hands, Bede moved even closer, shivering at the feel of Galen's warm thighs on his own, spreading for him, then clasping him. Which urged him to move faster, his hips snapping as he drove himself into Galen's body.

The moment when the world collapsed around him, his seed spilling inside of Galen's body, his heart was full. Full of the push of desire and the thick, soul-deep urge to hold Galen to him and never let go. Never let go of this feeling of connection, the sorrow of its imminent passing, the sorrow of the future tomorrow when he and Galen would be separated at summer's end.

Heat washed over him, taking with it those soft feelings, replacing them with his body's own urges, then he pulled out so he could curl his fingers around Galen's cock and worship it with his mouth, and feel and taste Galen's hot, sweet release.

As they settled in the cot, breathing hard, and then softer, twined together like warm ribbons, with only the soft cotton sheet pulled up, Bede felt himself relax for the first time in hours. They had something together, and this was now. Tomorrow could not be counted on, but then, it never could be. At least not in Bede's world.

He twirled Galen's hair around his fingers as Galen traced lazy swirls across his chest. Then Galen sighed, and Bede looked down.

The only light they had was a flashlight, which gave them light enough to see by, but left shadows to hide in, so he couldn't see Galen's expression, only feel his soft breaths across his skin.

"This was good," said Bede, drowsy in the dark, but focused on Galen at his side.

"You seemed stressed earlier," said Galen, then added, "But when I asked, you didn't say."

"Okay."

That was fair. Galen seemed like Winston in that way, that the sharing should happen in balanced measures. Tit for tat.

This made Bede's heart ache all over again so, braving his own internal warnings that he should just shut the fuck up, he told Galen about Winston. Not just about how much he missed him, but about all of it. The years they spent together.

"We'd known each other forever," Bede said. "Winston was always by my side. Always *on* my side. He made me laugh, like you do. And yes, he was a criminal, like me."

"And now he's gone." Galen's hand became still on Bede's chest, the palm warm, fingers spread out as if to catch Bede's heartbeat.

"He died," said Bede, short. "There was a shootout the day I got arrested. A bullet from the other gang got him and he bled out before the ambulance arrived."

Bede left out the part about the incompetent, unwilling cop, and that he blamed him and that the only reason that cop wasn't dead already was that a gang member had shot the gun that killed Winston. He held all of that back. There was too much rage in the idea of this to unleash it on the gentle-hearted Galen.

"His name was in your file. Winston Ludlow." Another soft breath as Galen lifted his chin to look up at Bede. "I knew he was on your team, but I didn't realize he was your partner. There was no mention of it." After a pause, Galen bent his head and kissed the soft curve of Bede's chest, an acknowledgement, a blessing that he knew would never be enough. "I'm so sorry."

"I've had five years to get over it," said Bede, attempting to shrug it off, only managing a half-hearted twitch of one shoulder. "Though I don't suppose I ever will."

"Sometimes you never do," said Galen, sounding wise. He reached up to loop his arm around Bede's neck to pull himself up so his head rested on the pillow next to Bede.

Bede turned on his side so he could look at Galen, and absorb the lines of his beautiful angular face. Those silvery gray eyes that seemed to search for answers to questions he didn't even know how to ask.

"I've not gotten over my dad dying. Don't suppose I ever will."

"When was that?" asked Bede, reveling in this new information.

"Last summer," said Galen with a hard, little swallow. "Spring and summer. Cancer took him fast, so it was mercifully quick, though I didn't think that at the time. Only that I wanted one minute more. Just another second. Anything. He died in hospice. They took good care of him and me, both. Now I've got the family farm, and have no idea what to do with it."

"Tell me." Bede, his heart speeding up a bit at the idea that he and Galen trusted each other not just to bare their skins, but their souls.

With a hard-drawn breath, Galen began to speak. He talked about the farm and the current tenants. About lavender and goats and bees. About how he'd sat at the kitchen table all of last winter and stared at the snow, overwhelmed by the decisions needing to be made. About everything, fast and urgent, as if he'd never talked to anybody about any of this up to that moment.

"I didn't want to do this program," said Galen, a bit rueful, his mouth curving into a smile. "As you probably guessed. But I owed Leland because he held my job for me while I took care of my dad. He offered me a loan, as well, to keep the farm going, but I turned that down because then I'd owe him even more. But he's a great guy. Seriously. If not for him, I'd still be up at the guest ranch, I guess. Shoveling shit. Taking care of guests."

"Is it better here?" asked Bede.

It didn't matter the answer. He just had a sense that, like Winston, Galen needed someone to flip the switch open so he could get it all out. Then, unburdened, he could better figure out what he needed to do. Bede was more than happy to be that guy.

"It is and it isn't." Galen rolled onto his back.

Bede rolled too, propping himself up on one elbow, his hand on the flat of Galen's belly, pushing the sheet down a little way, creating a curve like a white wave against his skin. And waited patiently while Galen seemed to prepare himself that Bede wouldn't like what he had to say.

"It's good money, and the work is interesting. You guys are interesting, that's for sure." Galen laughed, full throated, his eyes sparkling as he looked at Bede. "I will say this. Not all ex-cons are alike."

"Did you think we were?" asked Bede.

"I did."

"How?"

Galen seemed a little reluctant to answer, so Bede peppered his mouth with small kisses, then laid his head on the pillow next to Galen's, his arm looped over the top of Galen's head, fingers again in Galen's silky hair.

"That you were just dumb. All of you." Galen shook his head, then cozied himself into the curl of Bede's arm, his body. "Weak willed. And not very interesting. I've learned none of that is true, though I still don't get how someone could live a life of crime." With a shrug, he flailed his free hand as if to say, *There's nothing you can tell me that would change it.*

"Yeah." Bede let out a long-drawn breath. "I get that. Before I went into Wyoming Correctional, I thought there were two types of criminals. The ones you could trust and the ones you couldn't."

"And now you know."

"Yes, now I know. There's as many kinds of criminals as there are people." Bede laughed a low laugh, then kissed the plane of Galen's cheek. "Look at how much we've both learned! Gold stars all around."

Galen laughed in response, then shifted to turn into Bede's body, a curve of warmth to match Bede's own.

Bede's arms came down to circle around Galen's shoulders to draw him close. His blood raced at the added closeness, groin tightening, the back of his neck getting hot.

"Are you good for another round?" he asked, leaning in to nip at Galen's ear.

"Yes." The response came with no hesitation as Galen arched his neck, his hair spilling on the white pillow. "Yes," he said again, and his chin came down, his gaze on Bede's mouth. Flicking up to his eyes, his own eyes darkening to gray smoke. "Yes, please," he said. And then, again, "Yes."

CHAPTER 32
GALEN

The most glorious thing about Bede spending the night in his tent was that because it was Sunday, they could laze for a bit before getting up to go have breakfast. Sensibly, under the idea that the two of them could keep their relationship a secret, Bede got up to head back to his own tent.

Galen sensed a kiss on his cheek, that the sheet and light cotton blanket were drawn up over his shoulder. That the tent flaps were zipped shut. And then Galen could just drift back into sleep, sound and restful, the kind of sleep you might get when you knew there was nowhere for you to go or be. Or anything.

On Sunday, Galen tended to his laundry, and waved at Bede when he went to the mess tent for lunch.

They sat together. Of course they did.

Bede, who was glowing and flushed, had smiles for Galen and anyone he happened to talk to. But he was discrete. Didn't say anything about anything, not even when he ran up to the buffet line and brought back extra mayo for Galen's sandwich without being asked.

If Galen was being romanced with the purpose of getting back into his bed, er, cot, he was fine with that.

And then, that afternoon, they went to Galen's tent and fooled around like two teenagers and school had just gotten out for the summer. Heavy make out sessions. Handjobs. Blowjobs.

This lasted until they were worn out, which was right before dinner, when Bede crawled off to get a shower, and Galen slept until dinner, and the two of them grinned at each other like loons. Galen had never been demure, by any means, but this was more fun than he'd had in years.

On Monday, he woke up alone and sat up and swung his legs over the edge of the cot.

It was back to reality. Back to work, because he had stuff to do to earn his keep.

He needed to gather his team and start on the task of raking the paddock and the nearby field. Then he needed to check fence lines and make repairs as needed. Maybe Bede could help him with that.

They spent the morning in the paddock, and though Toby complained about raking horse manure by hand, it was only one time, and though Owen complained about having to haul the manure away in a wheelbarrow, they both pulled together and did the work he asked of them.

Meanwhile, Galen and Bede walked along the fence line, which was barbless cable strung between treated wood fence posts.

In the wintertime, the cable would draw tight in a freeze, and not need tightening. But in the summer, the metal warmed up enough to sag between the poles, and a hot day was the perfect time to tighten them.

Galen made a mental note of where the cable sagged, and how many tension hooks they'd need.

"We can work on this project this afternoon," he said to Bede, almost absentmindedly. He was so comfortable with Bede now, it was like working with a friend, and his orders were more like suggestions.

The sun was straight overhead by the time he figured they needed to head to the mess tent and get some lunch, but Bede stopped him, dragging him between the cables to the shade that was on the path right next to the lake.

He'd had enough of work, it seemed, and pulled Galen close and took his cowboy hat off to lie gently in the grass.

Bede's own hat fell off as he kissed Galen, unnoticed as he clasped Galen's head, twining his fingers through Galen's hair as if he meant to soak Galen in with every touch.

"Someone will see," said Galen, mumbling, his mouth moving against Bede's mouth.

"Who gives a fuck," said Bede, his voice as breathy as if he were reciting poetry.

The idea of Bede reciting poetry, let alone reading any, made the laughter bubble up inside of him, and when Bede asked, he shook his head and clasped Bede's hands in his own.

"I'm sure we'll finish early today," he said, and then turned his expression into puzzlement. "I wonder what might occupy my time when work is done today. I wonder, I wonder."

Bede kissed him again and scooped up the hats, carefully placing Galen's on his head, not forgetting to tip the brim in a jaunty way.

"I'm sure we'll think of something," he said as he put his own hat on, but in a foolish way, tipped to the back of his head in a way he might if he were a new greenhorn of a cowboy. Then, just for the flavor of it, he drawled, "Shucks, I have no idea!"

"You're a riot," said Galen, but his smile felt like it went all the way through him. "Let's break for lunch. And then after, we shall see what we shall see."

It was easy to gather his team as the day was stiflingly still, too hot to do much more. At lunch, Galen rehearsed in his mind how he would propose a short trip that did not include Toby and Owen, but would consist of him and Bede. And then scolded himself for excluding half his team.

Then the phone in his back pocket vibrated, and when he answered it, it was one of his tenants, Mr. Dana Conners, to be exact. His voice sounded strained, so Galen excused himself to take the call outside the mess tent.

"What can I help you with, Dana?" he asked, fully expecting the problem to be with the sump pump or the pigs that had escaped from the farm next door.

"Hey there, Galen," said Dana. "Look. We hate to do this, but we've gotten a spot at a dairy in Provence. They're providing accommodations and training and everything. We won't be staying in Wyoming. We'll pay through the end of July, but we leave for France almost immediately."

"Uh." Galen's jaw dropped. He felt cold all over.

He'd been counting on the rent from the Conners to help pay his tax and medical bills. They had a month-to-month rental agreement, with a hefty deposit, so they *could* leave. But without the August, September, and October rent, Galen would be so far behind there'd be no catching up.

Both the hospital and the IRS had already given him extensions. He didn't think they'd be willing to give him anything more.

"Is there any chance you'd change your mind?" he asked, pretending his voice wasn't on the verge of shaking.

"No, I'm afraid not. Carol is set on going to France. Little Connie can learn to speak French, too. So many wins there."

Galen didn't know anything about kids, so whether Little Connie could learn French, whether it would benefit her at all—complete unknowns.

"You'll lose your deposit," he said, flailing.

"Yes, we know," said Dana. "You keep it. We've really enjoyed your farm, but this is the best decision for us."

Galen said goodbye and ended the call with his thumb. Then, feeling numb all the way through, he went back to lunch. He wasn't going to mention anything, because nobody could help him, though Bede looked at him strangely.

"You okay?" asked Bede.

Of course, he would ask. Just a few moments before, Galen had been batting his eyelashes at Bede, and giving him flirtatious nudges with an elbow to Bede's ribs. Now he felt like stone, flat and cold.

"Yeah, sure."

Trying on a smile for size, Galen focused on finishing his meal, mumbled something about needing to check on supplies, and quickly took his tray and plates to the bussing tub.

In the back of his mind, he knew he should try to fake it just a bit better, perhaps even stay in the mess tent a moment or two to ask Bede about his job application form, and if he had any questions before he handed it in to the counselor.

Galen shouldn't have rented to the Conners in the first place, but any twinge of doubt had been overruled by the idea of having the farm being active for half a year because that would give him six months to figure out what to do next. Only he'd barely had three months of that kind of freedom. And now he was without any other solutions.

"Everything okay?" asked Bede, coming up to Galen as he stood in the middle of the path, unable to decide which direction he was headed.

Unsure what to do with the sweep of relief at Bede's arrival that seemed to obscure all of his worries, Galen let himself be caught up in Bede's energy.

Since the team leads and parolees were still piling out of the mess tent, Bede didn't kiss him or even touch him. Which was smart. Even if someone suspected what Galen and Bede were up to, it didn't mean that Galen wanted to put himself on full display, or answer any questions that he himself didn't know the answer to.

"Sort of," said Galen, scratching the back of his neck. "But I'll figure it out. Eventually."

Figuring it out on his own had been something he'd been doing since his dad got sick. Signing those hospice papers had been like taking the weight of the world on his shoulders, and the responsibility for the farm a stone around his neck. And now, once again, he felt it, that weight.

Which, somehow, when he was around Bede, now that he wasn't looking down his nose at him, had seemed to grow lighter. Less burdensome.

"No, talk to me. You don't look good."

"What?" Galen turned to focus on Bede, on his insistence that Galen talk to him, drawn in by that energy and care.

"You're all gray around the face." Bede made a gesture, drawing a circle around his own face. "You can tell me. Look, I don't know anything about anything, right? But I can listen."

Had anyone two weeks ago told Galen that he'd be grateful to unload his troubles by talking to an ex-con, he would have laughed in their face. But the Bede described in the folder Galen had in his tent, with a list of his crimes as long as a man's arm, didn't seem to be the same Bede standing before him now.

The image of Bede in that intake photo, dark, tattooed, and snarling, seemed a far cry from the flushed, tattooed, yes, and handsome man who reached out to tweak a curl of hair behind Galen's ear.

He was a sucker for that touch, the intent behind it. The way Bede's dark blue eyes tracked him, like a faithful beast simply waiting for its orders to attack Galen's enemy, regardless of from which direction they might come.

That Galen could think such things, all without proof. All based on his gut, and the way his body reacted, half-leaning in Bede's direction. Half-wishing it was night so they could go to Galen's tent and pound out their differences on that solid iron cot. And maybe get in a swim. Alone. Just the two of them.

None of that could happen until he got all of this sorted out. He reached to touch Bede, then after trailing a finger along Bede's strong jaw, he shook his head.

"I've got to go to the farm, take care of some business," he said.

"Did the cows get out?" asked Bede, the corner of his mouth lifting in a grin, as if to welcome the idea that any of this was a joke.

"Yeah, something like that," said Galen. "Look. You guys have the rest of the afternoon off. I'll be back by dinner. And then after? Maybe a swim, just the two of us?"

"Yes," said Bede. His eyebrows flew up, and that smile widened. "I'll keep an eye on those dimwits, no problem."

"Dimwits?" asked Galen, trying not to laugh at this.

"Lunkheads, then," said Bede. He spread his hands, like he was making a huge concession. "Definitely lunkheads."

Shaking his head, Galen had to force himself to go, had to march himself to the nearest silver truck and drive up Highway 211 to the farm, which was just above where Chugwater Creek and Threemile Creek met.

The Threemile gave the farm enough water to grow lavender and support goats and bees, creating a good place, a sturdy farm that had been enough for him and his dad. But none of it was enough for the Conners family, evidently.

CHAPTER 33
GALEN

Galen announced his arrival at the farm by beeping the horn in the truck as he rolled through the gate. Had there been goats, even secured behind good sturdy fences, they would have gotten out. Earl had always admonished his son to keep the gate closed unless it needed to be opened.

The Conners had been told this, though it didn't seem to occur to them that rules were there for a good reason.

As Galen parked, he could see the door to the shed was open, that the lavender, which should be coming into full bloom, was drooping in the heat. Which was because, as he could easily see, the irrigation pump was, yet again, not working.

The engine was whirring because the pump was trying to go, but couldn't.

Someone could easily make sure the system was turned off, take off the lid, and figure out why. Check the wires or the intake valve. Or call for the nearest handyman to fix it. But nobody had.

The Connors had been told how to keep the place running, but evidently Galen's trust in them had been misplaced.

Heat simmered in the air as Galen took all of this in, fury blazing behind his eyes, his chest pumping hard.

The door on the screened-in porch flapped open. The spring mechanism to control it must have been broken, for the door slammed shut as Mr. and Mrs. Conners, baby Connie in her arms, walked over to him in a pleasant, graceful way.

As if they imagined some Instagrammer was in the bushes filming their every move. As if they did not care in the least that Galen's world was falling apart around him.

"Thought I'd come out to see you folks," he said, setting his cowboy hat back a bit on his forehead, in case the shadow of the brim made it seem like he was glaring. "Do some repairs. Maybe to convince you to stay."

"That's not going to work for us," said Dana. "We've got papers for you to sign releasing us from further obligations."

"Like damage to my farm and crops?"

Galen's question came out clipped and hard and he didn't care. They'd gotten a lawyer involved when a good farewell handshake, and some understanding about the deposit, would have worked just as well. On the other hand, they were out good money that they didn't have to spend, and too bad for them.

"Come on in," said Dana, nonchalant, waving Galen close in a friendly way. Inviting Galen inside his own home. "Everything's ready for you to sign."

The porch was warm, but not overly so, but the inside of the house was cool, a blessing on such a hot summer day. It was the way the house had been built, decades before, a century, maybe. With thick stone foundations, and stone halfway up the first story. The windows were thick, keeping changes in temperature out, and the whole of it had been well maintained.

Now, though, the inside of the house had been decorated and set up as though there might be a troop of lookie-loos marching through at any moment, hoping to get a glimpse of how things worked. At the little cameras on tripods. There were circle lights, just about everywhere he looked. Lace draped over the side of the sofa in a useless way. Dried flowers, artistic and crumbling, were strung from the ceiling.

In the kitchen, the wooden farm table was covered with a flowered tablecloth. Which didn't look bad, just out of place.

On the table was a folder. As Dana spread the papers out and handed Galen a pen, it was easy to see, because Galen could read, that the form required Galen to release the Conners from any and all responsibility and damages, and that he would not impinge on future use of images, moving and still, that might show the farm as the Conners had used it—in perpetuity.

Galen knew he was in over his head. That when he rented the farm to the Connors, he should have had *them* sign a contract. Rather than trusting their smiles and pretty faces and earnest promises about their creative plans for the place.

Galen also knew that even if he had months of work to get the farm back to its former glory, he'd rather work his ass off than see the Conners on the property even one more day.

"You're required to vacate by tomorrow," he said.

"We don't have to do that," replied Dana. "We have till the end of the month. We agreed when we talked on the phone earlier."

"You've destroyed all the hard work my dad and I put into the farm," said Galen. "And now you're leaving earlier than we originally agreed, which alleviates you of any rights." He felt ice cold all over again. "I can have the sheriff here in ten minutes, and he'd drag you right off my property. And I'm keeping your deposit."

He was so angry, and he wasn't even breathing hard.

He could almost hear Bede whispering in his ear, saying, *Give 'em hell, Galen.* Because now he had someone in his corner. Not a dying father. Not a ranch foreman who followed all the rules. He had Bede, tough, experienced Bede, and Bede would want him to look out for himself.

He pulled out his cell phone and dialed the sheriff's number.

It was answered in two rings by Deputy Munroe. Galen would rather have spoken to the head guy, Sheriff Lamont, but this would do.

Galen explained the situation and how he wanted the Conners to vacate. He didn't bother to lower his voice so that the Conners heard every single word. Standing there all in a row, their eyes were wide with shock, as if they'd never been told no in their entire lives.

"They did *what* to the lavender?" asked Deputy Munroe, sounding as horrified as if the lavender had been growing in his own garden.

"They've not watered it. Not all summer. Or weeded. It's about to go brown and that's my whole crop ruined."

"You don't say," said Deputy Munroe, in a slow, cold way.

It was then that Galen remembered that even though Munroe wasn't from the area, being a transplant from Colorado, he was fiercely loyal to the citizens in his district. That, in fact, he might express more urgency about the matter than even the sheriff would.

"I'll be out there in ten," said Deputy Munroe.

"I've given them till tomorrow at five," said Galen, a little unsettled by the low growl that hunkered beneath Munroe's response.

"I'll be out there in ten," said Deputy Munroe again, and then he hung up the phone. "And they leave today."

"Better start packing," said Galen as he looked at the Instagram couple and their little girl. "He did not sound pleased."

Maybe the Conners didn't know how far the range of a sheriff's deputy went. Maybe they only knew county sheriffs from their movies and TV shows. Maybe they were hoping to record a story that would justify their next reel being entitled *Scary Sheriff Ran Us Out of Our Rental - We Are Shocked!*

Galen was sick of it. Sick of the whole thing. He didn't want to stick around for the deputy, but he'd call, and then he'd come back later that week, in the evening, to take stock of the place.

He might have to hire someone to make sure of the lavender and get a beekeeper out to make sure of the bees. Everything could wait, because now he needed to get back to the valley. Back to Bede.

Once in the truck, it took everything he had not to gun his engine and spray gravel all over the place. He even left the gate open, not stopping to shut it, because the Conners were, very likely, just going to leave it open again when they left, anyway.

It took too long to get back to the valley, in the heat that simmered over everything, making the grass shimmer and the gravel reflecting up hot silver.

When he got to the valley, he probably drove too fast down the switchbacks, and yes, he spun some gravel, but he was so grateful to arrive in the parking lot that after he turned off the engine, he sat there with his fingers clawed around the steering wheel, his whole body vibrating.

There was a light tap at his window. Bede. Standing in the long shadows of pine trees, waiting like a sentinel. Waiting for Galen.

Without preamble, Galen tumbled out of the truck and into Bede's arms, who held him tightly. There were soft whispers in his ear. The words he could not recognize, but the intention he could. Bede meant to soothe him.

He wanted to spill the whole sordid tale, but there wasn't anything Bede could do about it. So he described it as briefly as he could so Bede wouldn't worry.

"They were horrible tenants, but I got rid of them," said Galen. "I have to figure out how to pay those bills, but at least I kept their deposit, so that's something."

"We'll figure something out," Bede said, hooking his arm around Galen's neck. "Don't you worry. Now, let's get you something to eat."

The last thing Galen wanted to do was eat, but he knew he should, so he let Bede pull him to the mess tent. Let himself be guided to stand in the buffet line. Filled his plate with chicken and waffles, cornbread pudding, green beans and walnuts. It was one of his favorite meals, but he could barely stand to eat a bite. Only Bede's watchful gaze and the gentle push of Bede's thigh against his got him in motion.

As he ate, the general chatter rose up around him. It'd be movie night again, since it was so warm and still.

"We can duck out," said Bede, lowering his chin, giving Galen's shoulder a brush with his own. "Sound good?"

"Yes."

Of course, it sounded good. The best. He was all in, but as he looked over at Toby and Owen sitting by themselves, comparing phones as they shoveled food in their mouths, he knew he'd been neglecting his team. "Were you guys able to scan and send your applications to the counselor?" he asked Bede.

"Yeah," said Bede. "Micah ate it up." Bede gave Galen a grin, as if to remind him of what a bad boy he was, and how he didn't care about convention.

"And Toby and Owen?" Galen asked. He'd have to ask Toby and Owen personally, but it'd be nice to be prepared for the answer.

"Would you believe," said Bede, his eyebrows flying up. "Toby's got a background in woodwork. Carpentry. He's a natural, the real deal, even though he's only taken high school wood shop. And, turns out, Owen used to be a locksmith. Got into trouble over some gambling debts and went to the dark side."

"Oh, yeah, that's in the file," said Galen, his spirits going up. "Did Micah say anything back about it?"

"Yeah, he said he was thrilled. Said he had contacts and could hook them up with an interview when the summer's over."

The summer being over was now a black spot for Galen that didn't just threaten to grow larger and obscure everything else, it *promised* it. If he didn't get new tenants in to help him pay the bill, he was going to lose the farm.

"I'm done," he said, pushing his plate away from him.

"Me too," said Bede, though he made the statement turn into a question. Then he leaned forward so nobody could overhear them. "Let's go swimming. Just you and me."

"I just need a towel and my swimsuit," Galen said as he got up and cleared his place. Focusing on the small details rather than anything else.

"Why the swimsuit," said Bede, whispering wickedly in his ear. "Maybe the others might come to the dock, but not until the movies are over. You know? Besides," he added as they trotted down the wooden steps. "I'll keep watch."

Galen felt a laugh bubble up inside of him, and he gave Bede a shove. "Go on. I'll meet you there."

Once at his tent, Galen hurried into his swim trunks, grabbed a towel and a t-shirt to throw on afterwards, and slipped his cowboy boots onto his bare feet. This was perfect. Just Bede and him. He'd swim his troubles away, and then have Bede to snuggle up to afterward.

CHAPTER 34

BEDE

fter they came back from swimming and settled in Galen's tent. Bede had done his best to pull Galen out of what seemed like a very dark funk. Despite all of his touches, the open-mouthed kisses to Galen's neck, tender hands and mouth between Galen's spread thighs, which produced very satisfactory sounds of pleasure, Galen still felt like a block of wood in Bede's arms as they snuggled beneath the cotton sheet on Galen's cot.

"Talk to me," said Bede. "Please."

He waited a long moment while the noises outside the tent, crickets and owls, distant laughter from the floating dock. When Galen didn't speak, Bede leaned close and pressed his cheek to Galen's head, twirled that soft hair in his fingers.

"I know something happened today," he said. "Let me help."

He thought he would have to wait forever, but Galen took a deep breath.

"When I first left the farm to come to Farthingdale Guest Ranch," he said. "I was glad to leave it behind. You know. You leave home when it's time. Except then my dad got sick. His name was Earl."

Galen looked up at Bede, his gray eyes enormous, full of love for his dad. Bede hugged him close.

"Go on."

"When he died, he left me everything," said Galen. "The farmhouse, which was hand-built out of stone to keep the Wyoming winters out. There're acres and acres of fields, and the bend of Threemile Creek that kind of curves around all of it."

"I can picture it the way you talk about it," said Bede.

"There's lavender and bees and we used to have goats, and dad talked about growing pine trees for Christmas trees, except we never got that started—"

Galen broke off, turning his face into Bede's neck, and Bede held him even tighter than before, talking about the farm low and fast, as though he were reciting his prayers.

As Bede listened, he knew it wasn't just the financial troubles with the family farm, it was that the farm was a place that Galen loved very dearly, though he'd never talked about it like this before.

The feelings he had for the place glowed in his eyes, and the curve of his smile when he talked about his dad, or the lavender, or the time the baby goats got out and went over to the pond in mindless hops and left prints along the muddy bank with their tiny cloven hooves.

The farm was where Galen's heart was. To lose it would break Galen, that Bede knew with certainty.

It was already killing Galen to imagine getting further behind on the bills, or that he might have to rent it to some other asshat who would not and never could appreciate it the way Galen did.

There was no way Bede was going to let Galen lose what he held most dear, so, as Galen slept a troubled and tight sleep, Bede slipped out of bed, got dressed in utter silence, and laced up his work boots, as they would be most appropriate for this job.

He found Galen's flashlight and slipped out of the tent, leaving it half-zipped so that if Galen woke up, he might imagine that Bede had made a trip to the facilities and was taking his time coming back. Perhaps Galen wouldn't wake up till morning, which would be all right by Bede.

Arriving at the parking area, he took a deep breath, opened the door to the nearest truck, and clambered in. The key fob was on the driver's seat, right there in plain view, in case any thieves wanted to steal the truck.

Well, Bede wasn't a thief, no sir. He was only going to borrow the truck, and then he was going to bring it right back. And no, he didn't have a current driver's license, but what did that matter since he'd return to the valley before dawn?

Luckily, the tank was full of gas, though it would be empty by the time he brought it back. But he knew no one would remark upon it because no one in the valley, at least none of the team leads, would imagine that anything untoward had happened.

One of the silver trucks needs gas, one of them would say. To which another would respond, *I'll take care of it.*

All above board and honest. Such was the world Galen lived in.

And such was the world Bede had become accustomed to. At least he'd started to appreciate the open doors and unlocked drawers and the idea that you did not have to carry a gun or look over your shoulder every other minute. And the idea that the work you did was not illegal. A different world than the one Bede had come from.

There was still enough of that old world in Bede for the task that lay before him. He started the truck and drove quietly up the switchbacks and out of the valley. At the top of the treeless hill, a quarter moon sliced its way through a dark and starry sky.

He paused a minute to scan the area around him, and rolled down his window to check if he could hear an engine starting up, which would indicate that someone had discovered the missing truck and was in hot pursuit.

Maybe it was midnight. The world was certainly silent and almost still, with only a constant low breeze that swam through the truck, around Bede's neck and ears like a scarf of certainty. He was doing the right thing. What he was doing would save Galen's farm, and bring that sweet, curved smile back to Galen's face.

Bede drove along Highway 211, the ridge of hills to his right a dark blurry smudge, until he got to I-25. There he turned south, sank back in the seat and, with his hands firmly at the ten and two on the steering wheel, pressed down on the gas.

The speed limit was eighty. Bede went eighty-five all the way to the Wyoming border in dizzying darkness that zipped by his open windows.

At the border, he slowed to seventy-five, which was still pretty fast, passing only a few eighteen-wheelers and getting passed by a few more, which came up behind him and went around, chuffing their engines with impatience.

He saw no cops until he reached the outskirts of Thornton, where the highway curved and widened, and the green-lit clock in the dashboard told him it was just after two in the morning. He had maybe four hours before Galen woke up to discover Bede was not lying in the bed beside him.

Bede knew the way to his Aunt Lorraine's by heart, and it was easy, eerily so, to take the right exit from I-25 in North Denver, and scoot along the quiet streets to the area where she lived, on Vine Street just across from Russel Square Park.

Her place was a compact brick house that had been gloriously redone on the inside, where Aunt Lorraine sold drugs and conducted her affairs, and it was there in the alley behind the house, where Bede parked the truck. The wooden fence all around the property was tall to keep out any prying eyes, and the shed and detached garage were securely locked.

Aunt Lorraine liked things tidy for the most part, but the shed, where Aunt Lorraine kept ordinary things like clippers and a weed whacker and gardening gloves, was a space that only the hired gardener entered. He would have been instructed not to pry, so it was there, in a series of stacked plastic bins, that Bede had stowed some of his ill-gotten gains, anything liquid and untraceable, in the bins labeled, *Mom's Trip to Bermuda* on strips of masking tape written on with a big fat Sharpie. In plain sight.

Bede jimmied the lock on the shed, moved the German-made rotary mower to one side, and reached out to the top bin. Shining his flashlight, he could see there was a layer of dust and that no one had touched any of the bins, not in years. Five years, to be exact.

Aunt Lorraine had told him when he was grown that his business was his business and she didn't need to know. Didn't want to know in case the cops came by. Which, oddly, even knowing that his Aunt Lorraine had raised him, they never had.

Not stopping to make sure of the contents, Bede hauled all three plastic bins to the truck and threw them in. They were heavy enough that he didn't have to tie them down, and innocent looking, at least enough, so that they would raise no eyebrows from anyone who happened to look in the truck bed. All he had to do was get back to the valley, present the money to Galen, and the farm would be saved.

To make it look more innocent, he shifted stuff around in the shed and turned the lock shut so the gardener would not notice anything out of place.

If the bins were noticed to be missing, the gardener, hired for his circumspection, would not mention it to Aunt Lorraine unless she asked about it. Which she never would because surely she knew if the bins were gone, either Bede had taken them, or Bede would find the person who had taken them, follow them, and make them give the bins back, and *then* break both their legs.

But perhaps Galen wouldn't need to know that part. Instead, Galen should, Bede decided as he silently started the engine and trundled back to the highway, be prepared to be happy about the money and the fact that the farm would be safe and secure for the next few years.

Bede drove as fast as he could along I-25 to the Wyoming border, stepped on the gas harder, and almost missed the exit to Highway 211, which would take him back to the valley. It felt like he was coming home as he turned off on the small dirt road just outside the town of Farthing and took the smaller dirt road to the switchbacks that led down into the valley.

The sun was just coming up, so Bede parked and had to hustle to haul three bins, rather heavy from all the cans and plastic baggies of coins, into Galen's tent. When Bede tiptoed up the steps and placed the first bin on the wooden floor inside the tent, Galen was still asleep, curled up, his beautiful hair spread across the pillow.

He didn't even wake up by the time Bede had hauled in the other two bins. Then he raced back to the truck to put the key fob on the seat, and then dashed, panting the whole way, to sit on the floor of the tent, cross-legged, doing his best to slow his breathing so he wouldn't wake Galen up before he was ready to.

Bede didn't know exactly how much money was in those bins, but it should be enough, shouldn't it?

Legally the money should have been turned over as evidence when Bede had been arrested, but Bede had never told his lawyer about the money, and nobody, really, had ever asked him a specific enough question for him to have to, legally, talk about it.

There was still an issue, though. It wasn't like he'd stashed fifty bucks away from his illegal dealings. That much could be understood to be forgotten. It was more money than that. And as such, was subject to evidentiary proceedings. Or, that is, should have been subjected. But it hadn't been. And now it would save the farm. And, more importantly, save Galen's smiles. Save them for Bede.

He did this for love. If he was caught, or if Galen turned him in, Bede could go back to prison. But it would be worth it if Galen didn't lose the farm.

CHAPTER 35

GALEN

Tightly wound nightmares about buying an old house and simply throwing money at it, to no avail, had occupied Galen's entire night. He woke up restless with a headache, and when he reached out to the other side of the cot, not very far, really, he found it empty.

"Morning, sunshine," said Bede's deep voice from beyond a lump of pillow.

"Morning," said Galen in return, blinking as he pulled the pillow away and folded a length of sheet so he could figure out where Bede was in the dim, dawn-cool, green-tinged light of the canvas tent. "What are you doing down there?"

Bede was on the floor, sitting cross-legged, hands resting on his knees. He beamed a proud smile, eyes glittering with delight, and it was then that Galen noticed how dusty he was. That there were half circles of pale beige dust on his once-white t-shirt, and dark smears of something else on his blue jeans. Even his soft-looking yellow work boots were grimy with dust.

Next to him on the floor were three plastic bins, the ordinary kind you could get at Target or just about anywhere. There was a strip of masking tape on each one, and written on each strip of masking tape were the words, *Mom's Trip to Bermuda.*

Which was strange because Bede had never mentioned parents, much less a mother who had gone to Bermuda and who had asked her son, Bede, the drug dealer, to watch over three bins of whatever she'd brought back. Which, now that Galen thought about it as he sat up, very well could be drugs.

In spite of Bede and Beck's single dalliance with pot, drugs were not allowed in the valley, nor in Galen's tent, so what the hell was Bede up to? And why was he so dusty and grease-streaked?

Swinging his legs over the edge of the cot, the cotton sheet draping around his ankles like a friendly, soft snake, Galen rubbed at his eyes with the heel of his palm and did his best to bring his thoughts into order.

"What's going on?" asked Galen, his voice coming out morning rough.

"I've come to save the farm," said Bede quite brightly. "If this were a musical, I'd ask Judy and Mickey to sing about it, but since it's just me—" Bede laughed, low and sweet, the smile on his face a thing of beauty.

Galen laughed a little, having gotten the *Babes in Arms* reference, but he couldn't quite focus on the humor of it when the three plastic bins looked so out of place and Bede looked so unkempt.

"What are the bins?" he asked. "And what did your mom ask you to store that came from Bermuda?"

"Well, I don't actually have a mom," said Bede in a matter-of-fact way as he rose to his knees and started pulling open the lids to the bins. "But what I learned is if you wanted to launder money, you'd take it to an offshore bank account, such as you might find in Bermuda. Or anywhere in the Bahamas, really. Cayman Islands. British Virgin Islands."

"Launder money?" asked Galen with growing confusion, which soon turned to a kind of giddy horror as Bede pulled out plastic baggies that glittered with the coins inside, and old coffee cans that clunked when Bede put them on the wooden floor. And then came the dust clouds that surrounded the large plastic bag stored in each bin.

"Money?" asked Galen, his voice rising. "That's money."

"Yes, it's money, you smart thing, you," said Bede quite breezily as he reached into the nearest black plastic bag and pulled out a fold of bills and fanned it at Galen. "It's to pay the bills from the IRS and the hospital." Bede shrugged, suddenly looking at the money as he held it close to his chest and appeared to be counting it. "Of course, we'll put it in your account—or maybe we'll create a new account with a fake LLC—and then pay those bills, slowly, every month, following the payment plan. So as not to alert anyone that you've got more than enough."

"You—" Galen could hardly get enough air to ask the question. "You want me to put that money in my bank account? Wouldn't I be laundering it, then? Is that legal?"

The more important question was not whether the money was legal, because money stored in bags, cans, and even bigger plastic bags never could be. The question was not only where had the money come from, but how to get rid of it, only Galen couldn't get his brain around the right words to ask the question out loud.

"No," said Bede, looking up, his dark brows drawing together as though he was dismayed to find that Galen didn't already understand all of this. "But it's going to help you keep the farm. Otherwise, it'd still be in my Aunt Lorraine's garden shed."

Galen knew that Lorraine Deacon, according to the manilla folder with all of Wyoming Correctional's notes about Bede, was known to the police.

There'd never been anything to connect her to Bede's drug business, so she'd not been questioned or brought to court to testify on Bede's behalf when he'd been arrested. Yet, all this time, she'd been storing Bede's ill-gotten gains. Gains that Bede had earned buying and selling drugs. Right? That must have been where he'd gotten it all.

"Is this drug money?" The question came out very small because of an even smaller hope that the money was not drug related. An impossibility in this case, but Galen needed to know.

"Of course it is."

Bede shrugged, took out another fold of bills, and began fanning himself with it, one fold of bills in each hand. Perhaps this was done in an effort to be amusing, or to distract Galen from what was laid before him now. Three plastic bins of drug money that he was being told was for his own use. And the very handsome, dusty man whose eyes and smile were asking Galen to be pleased about it.

Galen stood up, swiped his hair back from his face, and swallowed just to get some spit in his mouth. There was a breeze from somewhere beyond the open tent flap, but it failed to soothe him.

"I can't take this money," he said, hoping his tone made it quite plain how impossible this all was. "It's drug money. It's *blood* money. I can't take it."

"What do you mean you can't?" Bede stood up as well and shook the bills in Galen's direction, like he thought seeing the money up close would persuade Galen to take it.

"It's *illegal* money." Galen's voice rose, becoming tight as he ground out each word.

"Well, what do you suggest I do with it, then?" asked Bede. He spread his hands wide in a what-the-hell-do-you-mean gesture, and meanwhile, several bills, twenty and tens, it looked like, fluttered to the wooden floor of the tent.

"I went all the way to Denver to get this so you wouldn't lose the farm," said Bede. "That's the important thing, right?" When Galen didn't respond, Bede repeated, "*Right?*"

Galen was on the verge of saying, *Take it back, take it right back,* so they could act like this never happened, even though he could never unsee it. Bags of money, drug money, *blood* money, in a circle on the floor of his tent, and Bede smiling like it was normal. When it was not and never could be. What had he been thinking to get mixed up with a drug dealer?

But before Galen could bend down and start shoving the money back in the plastic bin, a shout came from outside the tent. Galen went to pull back the tent flap and saw Marston standing there, looking sweaty and hassled, which was quite unlike him.

"Horses got out," said Marston. "The wire on the pasture was loose somehow, and now they're across the river. Get dressed and come help."

"You got it," said Galen, stepping back into the tent as Marston dashed off.

The interior of the tent looked all shadowy, with Bede only an outline, and the pile of money only a suggestion.

"What do you expect me to do?" asked Bede, his voice rising to a shout. "Turn it over? I'd be cited for breaking my parole. I'd need to hire an attorney with money I don't have, and it'd take months for an appeal. Either way, I'd be sent back to jail."

Galen briefly thought of Alice Marie Brenner, Leland Tate's attorney on retainer, but dismissed that as she wouldn't want to represent Bede. Or would she?

But that was beside the point. Bede was currently on one side of the law, and Galen was on the other. Their worlds were too different. Their hopes and dreams and futures were wide apart and could never meet. He'd been a fool to fall in love.

And he *had* fallen in love. Hard. With Bede's strong arms and steadiness, with the laughter they'd shared, dips in the lake. Oh, how quickly their minds had met and how quickly their hearts had entwined. And now he'd have to give it all up.

There were more sounds outside, heavy footsteps on the path to the paddock. They'd need to saddle up whatever horses hadn't gotten loose and cross through the river below where the rocks created natural low waterfalls.

"Get dressed," said Galen, shoving his legs into blue jeans. "I must have left some wire too slack."

"This isn't your fault," said Bede.

"Yes, it is," said Galen. His face felt numb. "All of it is."

"What are you going to do with the money?"

"It stays here," said Galen with a small snap, looking at Bede's blue eyes and the worry there. "You gave it to me, so it's mine. Help me shove it under the bed." He sighed as he tugged on a t-shirt and then grunted as he pushed the first bin neatly under his cot. "No sense making it worse than it is when someone comes by and sees all this."

Bede leaped to do his bidding, shoving the other two bins into hiding, then draping the sheet from the cot over the edge so everything looked tidy and neat. Innocent.

Galen felt the sweat on the back of his neck as he finished dressing, then grabbed his hat and stomped out of the tent. Bede was close behind him.

Bede wasn't wearing cowboy boots, so he would be one of the men helping to guide the horses back into the paddock, or making sure they didn't shoot off into the trees or, heaven forbid, follow the Yellow Wolf River all the way up the canyon to Aungaupi Valley. Then they'd never get the horses back.

The work of rounding up the horses would settle him, as work always did. But as he strode to the paddock and grabbed the first horse he saw, and saddled and bridled it, the back of his mind churned. Bede had meant well, but they were too different for the relationship between them to continue, and that was, quite simply, that.

Still, Bede had come into his life. Bede mattered to him, made him feel good, in all kinds of ways, in ways he'd not felt for a long, long time.

He had no idea what he was going to do, but he was going to do his best to keep Bede out of it.

CHAPTER 36

BEDE

Feeling as useless as tits on a snake, Bede hurried after Galen, who grabbed a horse from the paddock, saddled it, and flung himself astride like he was in an old-fashioned western movie and his Pa had just told him that the barn was on fire.

Bede couldn't quite feel the urgency until he was on the path along the lake, beyond where the docks and canoes were, and caught a glimpse of the shining backs of a band of horses galloping along the green and slanted hillside beyond the river. If they made it up the canyon, they'd be gone for good.

"Get back to the paddock," shouted Royce, as he pulled up his horse alongside Bede.

"What?" Bede knew he wasn't skilled enough to join the escaped horse roundup, but surely he'd be more useful here than back at the paddock.

"There's a gap in the trees that leads to the road," said Royce. His mouth was tight, as if he meant to hide his impatience. "If the horses get through there when we bring them back around, they might get hit by a passing vehicle."

The road Royce referred to wasn't a high traffic road, but Bede

297

supposed Royce meant to cover all the bases. The just-in-case scenarios that Bede himself had considered when dealing in cocaine.

"You got it," said Bede just as Royce whistled his horse into a gallop and was off like a chestnut streak through the trees.

Bede hustled back to the paddock, opened the gate wide, and took his post, along with Gordy, watching and waiting.

It didn't take overly long before he heard the galloping hooves coming in his direction, the horses racing in an impossibly thin and fast line around the lake, their tails like black and chestnut ribbons behind them, led by Gabe, and followed up by the other team leads.

It was kind of amazing to watch good riders, true cowboys, in action as they shouted and whistled and raised a lot of dust guiding the horses around the curve of the paddock and into it. No horse even came near him or Gordy, though a cloud of dust settled over them, and the heat shimmered in the air.

Once in the paddock, all the horses whinnied and shifted, looking for an exit, perhaps, or chasing the memory of running free. Or maybe they simply wanted a treat for being so easily guided back into captivity.

It made Bede sad to think of it. One moment they'd been running free, as they'd been born to, the next moment they were contained, reined in. The way they'd been trained to be.

They were like him. He'd been free once, and then contained, and now that Galen was pissed at him, it wasn't a sure thing that he wouldn't be back in prison by the time the sun went down.

Time would tell. In the meanwhile, Bede raced to secure the paddock with the horses inside of it, but was met by Galen, who dismounted in a hurry, grim and dusty, and sexy as hell.

Galen flapped Bede's hands away as he reached out for him, but he barely looked him in the eye as he did it.

"Can we talk about this?" asked Bede, low, as he gathered up the reins of Galen's horse, now riderless.

"No, we cannot," said Galen, equally low. "I need to figure out what to do."

"I'll just take it back," said Bede. "All of it."

He knew, deep in his heart, that the seemingly easy solution wasn't quite that simple. He could be spotted taking the money back, and anyway, Galen knew about it, which, evidently, made it something that had to be dealt with rather than sweeping it under the rug.

Trust him to fall for a do-gooder. A schedule follower. A hard-working man with the face of an angel, and hair to match, along with the principles of a knight worthy of King Arthur.

Oh, yes, he had fallen all right, and the hard glance of Galen's gaze as he took the horse's reins from Bede's hands so he could tie up and unsaddle and groom the horse made his heart ache. A deep ache that lanced at him. Totally unpredictable and unbelievably sharp.

It was like losing Winston all over again. Only this man, long legged and sweet, wouldn't be sad to leave Bede behind in his wake. He might even be glad to see Bede get his comeuppance and end up once more behind bars. Where he belonged.

He'd been an idiot to imagine that drug money could so easily be placed where it might do the most good. In Galen's hands. In his bank account. Used to pay off ridiculous bills to organizations that simply did not need the pittance they would scrape from Galen's hide.

He'd been an idiot, but he'd do it again if he had to. Do *anything* to fix this, though it didn't seem likely that Galen would give him another chance.

Galen had broadcast his doubts from the beginning, about the parole program, about parolees getting handouts and an easy chance at a new start. About Bede himself. And Bede had just proved him right, on all counts.

Bede helped where he could to get the recaptured horses settled with treats and fresh water, but he really only seemed in the way of more experienced hands. So with several tugs, he led Toby and Owen, who were also mostly in the way, to the mess tent for breakfast.

There, he put together a plate of eggs, bacon, and toast and sat down with that and a cup of black coffee. All of which he stared hard at for several minutes, his attention drawn to the open tent flaps of the mess tent. Waiting for Galen.

And when Galen showed up, dusty and grim, Bede waited for a

sign that Galen would sit next to him in a semblance of normalcy. So that they might pretend to get along, if nothing else. So that Bede could find the crack in Galen's armor and slip in to plead his case.

But Galen sat with the other team leads for breakfast, and participated in what looked like a very somber conversation, not so much about who was responsible for the escaped horses, but more how to prevent it happening in the future. It was as if the two of them had never met.

Bede made himself eat his breakfast and participate in, or at least listen to, whatever prattle Toby and Owen found amusing. He nearly sprained his eyeballs from rolling them so hard while at the same time watching Galen. His heart nearly jumped out of his chest when Galen suddenly got up, bussed his place, and marched over to where Bede, Toby, and Owen were sitting, and towered over them as they looked up.

"I need to run an errand," Galen said, his face grim, the words terse. "Can I trust you guys to groom the escaped horses today and then start raking the field?"

"Why only the horses that escaped?" asked Toby. "Why not any of the others?"

"Because." Galen took a breath, his eyes scanning the opening to the tent as if it was his dearest wish to escape the hellhole he currently found himself in, that of having to talk to ex-cons. "We need to let those horses know that this is a good place. That they'll be cared for here. That it's not a place to run away from. That staying will be worth their while."

"Sort of a horse's version of golden handcuffs, eh?" asked Bede with a small laugh, and found the echoing silence not to his liking.

Before, Galen would have joined in the joke, but now he did not. Instead, unsmiling, he stalked out of the mess tent, leaving the three members of his team somewhat leaderless.

"Guess we better get to it," said Bede, standing up, grabbing his tray. "Toby, can you get some bottled waters and put them in a small cooler, and Owen, you and I can grab and halter three horses and get started."

300

Of course, the two ex-housebreakers jumped to attention and did what Bede had asked of them. Of course they did, now that Galen was nowhere to be seen, and could not witness the skill with which Bede could lead men. Of *course*.

They were halfway through the morning when, while gently combing burrs out of the fifth horsetail that morning, it occurred to Bede that Galen might actually get it in his pretty head to take the *Mom's Trip to Bermuda* bins and turn them over to local law enforcement. Not realizing that in doing so, he'd be starting the engine that would eventually come and arrest Bede and send him back to prison.

Unable to stand it any longer, Bede made a vague noise about needing a break, and headed straight to Galen's tent. Standing on the wooden platform, half in, half out of the tent, he could see that the bins were gone. All three of them. It was as if they'd never even been there.

Heart jackhammering, Bede was about to turn around when he heard a gruff voice.

"What are you doing?"

When Bede turned, he saw it was Gabe, and that Gabe did not look happy.

"I was looking for Galen," said Bede, using his best *I'm-innocent* voice.

"Well, he's borrowed the truck and is on an errand," said Gabe. "And you shouldn't be in someone else's tent. Got it?"

With a nod, Bede stepped away from the tent flap, exhaling a long, slow breath as he considered his options.

Who knew where Galen had taken the bins and what he intended to do with them. The fact that the police hadn't already arrived was a good sign, though what the outcome of all this would be was another matter.

Should he stay or should he go? Should he remain to bravely face whatever firing squad was currently being gathered? Should he determine once and for all that however sweet the life that Galen had, it did not, would not, and should not include Bede?

Desperation continued to rise, a thick, choking mass in his throat that obstructed his focus and made his heart thump in his chest. He made it all the way till the afternoon, when he finally gave up and went to the parking lot and paced in the warm shade of the pine trees, kicking up dust with his work boots.

Nobody followed him or questioned why he wasn't working. Why he was lingering at the edge of a round circle of gravel, beads of sweat along his hairline like he'd been pounding rocks rather than gently grooming a handful of horses quietly munching on hay in the shade.

Nobody was asking because there was a high level of trust in the valley, which was, he only now realized, why the program worked. In spite of all of Bede's misgivings about it. That he knew.

What Galen didn't know, didn't have any reason to know, was that by turning all that money in, he himself would be on the list of interesting people the cops might want to talk to. Granted, a pile of ill-gotten loot worth less than seventy thousand dollars might not be on the top of their lists, but it might put Galen in the bullseye of attention he most assuredly would not want.

And Bede did not want that. He'd rather go to jail himself, for years and years, then put Galen through any interrogation, no matter how gentle.

Galen should never see the inside of a room such as an interrogation room, let alone a prison cell, and it made Bede's heart pound even harder at what he would do to prevent Galen from even being asked any questions about the money.

What wouldn't he do? How far would he go?

There was nothing he wouldn't do. And he would go to the ends of the earth for Galen because—

Because he loved him so hard it hurt.

He'd been caught in the snare of Galen's world to begin with. Soft and safe and sane. So different from the world he'd shared with Winston, whom he'd loved equally hard.

Now, in this place, almost tame by comparison, love for Galen had grown so much that his chest was tight, and given the chance would explode and enfold him, and he would never be the same. Making it so that he could never return to his old world.

He was fine with that. He didn't want to return to what once was. He only wanted Galen back safe and sound, in his arms, the money an old memory they could leave safely behind him.

The rumble of a well-tuned truck burbled through the pine trees, the slanting sun almost silver, dust motes dancing as Galen pulled into the parking lot and turned off the engine. A swirl of dust rose around the wheels, making the truck look like it was floating on a fine, light brown blanket.

It was with utter impatience that Bede waited for Galen to get out of the truck, and when he opened the truck's driver's door and just sat there, Bede couldn't wait a second longer. He went around the truck in quick strides and yanked Galen into his arms.

On his lips were tumbles of regret and apology, his muscles primed to hold Galen to him if he pulled back, and more sweet kisses, if Galen would only let him.

But Galen stayed still and did not pull away, a stillness to Bede's wired agitation.

"What did you do with them?" asked Bede, a quick glance in the truck's bed telling him the bins were not there. "You can't just *dump* them. Someone will find them and an investigation will start. Besides, your fingerprints are all over those bins and bags. The coffee cans take prints super well, you realize—"

Galen placed a hand on Bede's chest, a light touch amidst Bede's frantic ramblings that did almost nothing to calm him.

"I wiped them down. I wore gloves the whole time," Galen said in an unperturbed way, like Bede's anxiety had nothing to do with him. Like he carted off plastic bins of drug money every day. His eyes were serene as he looked up at Bede. "I took care of it."

"What?" asked Bede, his voice as loud as gunshot in the clearing. "What do you *mean,* you took care of it?"

"I distributed the money in a way I thought would do the most good," said Galen, his eyes steely gray.

Bede's eyebrows rose and his arms around Galen's waist tightened.

"One bin went to the LGBTQ safe house in Cheyenne," said Galen, as calmly as if he was describing ordinary everyday errands. "One bin

303

went to the food bank, also in Cheyenne, and one to the safe house for women in Cheyenne." Galen dipped his head, then looked up at Bede. "I cheated a little on that last one. As a man, I wouldn't typically have access to the address for such a place, but I overheard Maddy talking on the phone about donations, and just remembered it."

"All those places have cameras," said Bede, his heart beating hard.

"I wore my cowboy hat," said Galen, and now those eyes were gleaming with a small laugh. "And a red bandana kind of bundled up around my chin. Like a Wild West bandit, only in reverse."

"You're complicit in my crimes," said Bede, stern and astonished all at once. "It's a *crime* to launder money."

"Well, I wasn't going to *keep* it," said Galen, again as if this was simply a conversation about donating to good causes and not a conversation about laundering drug money. "It's in a better place and it's clean now. Besides." Galen took a breath, his gaze shifting as if he was looking for something to distract himself with as he delivered a painful blow. He looked up at Bede, an almost fearful light in his eyes. "I did it for you. I did it for us. I don't know exactly what we are or where we'll end up, but I did not want to be dragging a huge chain of guilt around with us everywhere we went."

"Chain of guilt?" asked Bede, suddenly picturing chains wrapped around those plastic bins and attached to them with ankle cuffs.

"You know." Galen made vague waving gestures, then put both his palms on Bede's chest. "Link by link, and yard by yard, I wear the chains I forged in life."

"Are you—" Bede took a hard breath, his fingers tightening around Galen's biceps. "You committed a crime for me and now you're quoting *A Christmas Carol* at me?"

"Yes." Another dubious look from Galen. This one said, *Of course, you idiot.* "I don't want that for us. Do you?"

For us. Galen had said the phrase more than once and the intention in those words indicated that Galen meant to keep Bede in his life. That he wanted Bede in it.

The tightness in Bede's chest still banged against his breastbone, but began lifting, floating up as if on soft, gray wings. And the idea that they were discussing a classic tale set in the dead of winter, almost arguing about it in the middle of a clearing on a rather hot Wyoming afternoon, made the laughter bubble up inside of him. And he couldn't help it.

"But you're a criminal now," said Bede, doing his best to keep a straight face even while the growing sense of joy made him feel breathless. "I just don't know if I can consort with a *criminal*." He ducked his chin, and let his hands fall to Galen's waist, his fingers curling light as a feather. "Are you sure nobody saw you? Saw what you were doing?"

"Nobody saw," said Galen, his eyes half closing when Bede gently brushed the dust from Galen's cheek with the edge of his pinkie. "Besides, if they ask, I'll say it wasn't me and you can say that I was with you all day."

"Lying to the cops already, my, my." Bede tipped close and swept a kiss across Galen's mouth, felt it curve into a smile, and smiled right back.

"I don't have a record," said Galen, stepping closer, wrapping his arms around Bede's waist. "They'll never think to ask." At Bede's astonished sound, he said, "I did a search on the internet about it. Very informative, the internet."

"Yes, that it is," said Bede, still astonished, still reeling, his heart fluttering just as hard as if he'd been on the verge of his first kiss.

He could hear sounds behind him, coming from the mess tent, and the smells of salt and grease as their dinner was being set out for them. "So, what'll we do now, boss?" he asked.

"We do what we were always going to do," said Galen as he lifted his hand from Bede's waist to sweep his hair from his face, putting it back right away. "We finish the summer. You pick up your certificate of completion, and I buy those new tires for my truck."

"What about the farm?" asked Bede and watched as Galen's expression turned serious.

"It is almost too late to rent to anyone else," said Galen, and Bede got the impression that the idea didn't bother Galen overly much. "Maybe Gabe'll let me take you guys up there to chop down weeds and fix the fence and take stock of the place. Give me some time to figure out what I want to do."

"I'd be up for that," said Bede. "And if more expensive coffee was offered, I know Toby and Owen would be up for it too."

"Yeah."

With a kiss, Bede smothered the single word that contained a sky full of doubt, and pulled Galen into his arms. Held him tight.

"We'll figure it out," he whispered into Galen's ear, a whisper in case the world might hear and disapprove. "And will you let me love you as we go along?"

The response was a tightening of Galen's arms around his waist, and a heartfelt sigh, some of the tension leaving Galen's shoulders.

Bede took that as a yes. The rest of it, they would figure out as the summer waned.

CHAPTER 37

GALEN

Galen could not have prepared himself for how it felt being a criminal. Not that he was, of course, but driving from the valley to Cheyenne with the plastic bins in the truck bed made him feel he was being watched with every passing mile.

He was an upstanding citizen doing a secretive deed.

Before he grabbed the keys to the nearest truck, he'd sat in his tent and researched the most likely places to drop off the money and have it be accepted. Some places didn't like anonymous donations, which his would most surely be. Other places had a more urgent need, perhaps, and would take anonymous donations, even if they were in cash and untraceable.

Then, after more research, he found out that he needed to buy microfiber cloths to wipe down the bins with, and he needed to wear plastic gloves—at all times—so his fingerprints wouldn't be left behind.

He'd seen enough *Forensic Files* and *Law & Order* to know how it worked. Or at least kind of. You couldn't leave traces of yourself behind. That's how they found you.

But since no one was actively watching him and seeing how

pleased the various charities would be to get the money, nobody would be.

Stopping at the WalMart, he purchased the cloths and the gloves and also a pad of paper, a pen, and a box of cheap letter-sized envelopes. A cheap cowboy hat. A thin red bandana.

Stopping at the Starbucks, conveniently located inside of the WalMart, he sat at one of the small tables and wrote three letters by hand, welcoming the charities to spend the money any way that they liked. He signed each letter with a single word: *Anonymous*. Then he made sure to remove the tape saying *Mom's Trip to Bermuda* from each bin.

The charities would not know the money was from the buying and selling of drugs. And since there would be no news announcements about missing money, they could accept it freely in the spirit in which it had been given.

It was in the middle of the day when he finally dropped the money off at the LGBTQ center, the food bank and, lastly, and most carefully, the women's shelter.

Women's shelter locations were highly guarded, and the address given out to only a trusted few, outside of the women seeing shelter there. He even went so far as to ring the unremarkable doorbell on an unremarkable and totally forgettable house in a cottonwood tree lined cul-de-sac on the edge of town.

A woman answered and stared at him with hard eyes. He gestured to the bin, gave her a slight wave, and stepped back, got into his truck, and drove away. He'd done that, rather than simply leaving it there because he wanted to make sure the shelter got the money.

For the LGBTQ center and the food bank, he'd been able to stroll into the lobby of each one and, hat tucked low, bandana pulled up, he made sure nobody was paying him any attention at all, and left the bins right there in plain sight. Then he made a casual, slow exit as if he'd ended up in the wrong place and was simply making his way out again.

He supposed, as he drove back to the valley, that he might keep an eye on the news to see if anyone reported remarkably mysterious plastic bins full of money showing up anywhere. Or maybe not. He'd done what he could. The money was no longer beneath the cot in his tent, and Bede's connection with the money was now an altogether invisible and insignificant thread that nobody, nobody, nobody would be able to follow.

Bede was as safe as Galen could make him.

When he came up to the Ranchette's Stop 'n Go exit, he paused the truck long enough to throw the gloves, cloths, and stationery away in a greasy-rimmed trash can next to the pump furthest from the red and white building. Then, feeling utterly terrified and pleased at the same time, he trundled back to the valley along Highway 211, slowly, watching the sun start its descent to the west, rolling down the windows of the truck to let the warm air dry the sweat from the back of his neck as he drove.

It wasn't until he'd arrived in the valley, pulling up in the parking lot and seeing Bede standing there, that he realized what he'd done. Committed a crime so that Bede wouldn't have to. Because he loved Bede and because Bede's expression when he'd explained how the money could get him sent back to jail had terrified him.

And suddenly Bede was there, tugging Galen out of the truck, wrapping him in strong arms. Kissing him gently, whispering words of apology that Galen simply didn't need.

Oh, he needed the kisses, light and sweet and peppered all over his face, but not the apology. Bede didn't need to handle everything on his own, not anymore. And without the drug money, they could begin anew.

Galen had explained what he'd done and why. And when Bede had asked, *And will you let me love you as we go along?* Galen had almost melted in his arms.

"Yes," said Galen, trying to be businesslike and failing, smiling up at Bede as the tension seemed to be lifting from his shoulders. "But first I need a shower. And then a hot meal. And from there, with my head clear, we can figure it out together."

Galen was able to grab a quick shower, with Bede impatiently waiting and not joining him because, for some reason, Gordy and

309

Owen *and* Toby all decided they needed before-lunch showers, too. And while their relationship might be something that was known, there was no sense blasting it all over the place, at least not yet.

They didn't have a moment alone. While they ate together, Toby and Owen told the tale of what happened during Galen's absence.

Toby and Owen had been on the near side of the river, far below the dam that was tucked at the narrow end of Half Moon Lake. Perhaps they had been goofing off, perhaps not, but they'd come across two horses who had managed to evade the earlier roundup.

The pair realized that the horses might be headed along the river, east, to Highway 211, where they would be at risk of getting run over by a truck or semi.

With quick thinking, both men had stepped in front of the cantering horses, water splashing as they came up the bank, and caught them by their halters. Toby had been dragged several feet, but the fact that two men and two horses were tromping along the river bank meant that those horses could be safely guided along the side of the lake to the paddock.

"Well done," said Galen, and he meant it. "That took guts."

"Guts and skill," said Owen with a wide, pleased smile.

After the meal, work resumed, fixing the wire along the pasture, raking up horse manure, jaunting off in one of the trucks, a flatbed trailer attached, to go pick up bales of freshly mown hay. After that, they of course stopped for coffee and pup cups at the Ranchette's Stop 'n Go, and returned in time for more showers before dinner.

It was only after dinner, and after the movie night that the two of them, just Galen and Bede, ducked out of, and when they were lying naked in each other's arms in the cot in Galen's tent, that Galen was able to settle the thoughts in his brain, which had been flying around like hungry bats at sunset.

"Well, that's done," he said with a sigh.

"Giving up your life of crime?" asked Bede with a low laugh as he stroked Galen's hair, making Galen feel like he wanted to purr.

"Maybe." That was a joke, of course. Galen wanted nothing more to do with any of that. "I've turned over a new leaf."

"Me too," said Bede, his breath whispering across Galen's forehead. But there seemed to be a question that Galen heard, so he looked up at Bede, and saw Bede's glance dance away, like he didn't want to answer any questions, but would if Galen asked it of him.

"Did you ever feel bad about selling drugs to kids?" Galen asked.

"Didn't sell 'em to kids," said Bede, his words a little stiff.

Galen planted a kiss along Bede's chest, tasting the salt, sensing the low thump of Bede's heart pick up a bit.

"I'll rephrase that," said Galen. "Did you ever feel bad about hurting people? Because those kinds of drugs hurt people."

"I never thought about it that way," said Bede with a low, almost motionless shrug. "Not till I met you. It was just a way of making money."

"A way of making money."

Galen felt the words on his tongue, the despair of it, the dead-end feel of it. Sure, you had to make money, to live, to pay bills, to eat. But to have that be the final destination? Made everything seem hopeless.

"But you have a different way now. If you want to help me on the farm at the end of summer."

He could hardly believe he'd brought it up. He'd meant to wait until the end of summer, to see how it felt, to his heart, to his soul, when Bede got his certificate and there were new tires on Galen's truck. Two simple tasks that needed to be completed.

The question he'd just posed to Bede had flung the gates of potential and possibility and future wide, wide open to an almost dizzying degree.

"I'll help you," said Bede, and his expression was earnest, making him look quite young. "But since we're dirt poor, I think you should ask Leland for that loan you mentioned he wanted to give you."

"I'll think about it."

Galen didn't want to think about it because the feel of that idea wasn't as nice as the feel of Bede's silky warm skin against his, the feel of Bede's muscles bunching as he shifted in the cot and turned so Galen was beneath him, and he on top, their bodies a connected sprawl of sinew and warmth beneath the light cotton sheet.

"What's that sound?" asked Bede, cocking an ear to the opening of the tent.

Galen listened and heard the faint crackle-crackle sound on the green canvas overhead as the shadows stretched long and a slight wind whisked the tent flaps about.

"That's rain," he said, tilting his head back so he could see into Bede's eyes. "First of the late summer. It's been so dry. This'll make everything smell nice."

"*You* smell nice," said Bede, whispering a kiss across Galen's mouth, lazy and slow.

"No, *you* do," said Galen with mock-fierceness. "You're the one who smells like water feels on my skin. In the lake. Deep, deep in the lake."

His mockery faded away as he realized the truth of it. That inhaling Bede's scent into his lungs felt just like diving headlong into Half Moon Lake, where the water swallowed him and the silence soothed him, and the cool depths lifted all of his troubles from his shoulders and cast them away.

"Hey." Bede, still on top, shifted down till he could cup Galen's cheek with his warm hand. "It's all going to work out. I promise you. You're not alone. You won't be. I'll be there. I'll work hard. It'll all be great. You'll see."

"You seem so willing."

Galen paused, because his surprise at Bede's willingness felt a little unkind. Sure he'd had his doubts about all the ex-cons, but that had been in the beginning. Since then, Bede had worked hard at learning the ways of the valley, just as Galen had worked hard at overcoming his own prejudices.

Still, if they were going to continue together, it was better to be honest up front.

"When I first read your file," said Galen slowly as he looked up at Bede. "You didn't seem like the kind of guy who would work hard at anything. And yet—"

"I've fallen in love with the valley," said Bede with a smile. He planted a kiss on the tip of Galen's nose. "With being a country boy.

Plus, you were so sexy on horseback this morning, if I wasn't already in love with you, I would have fallen at your feet right then and there."

"You make me want to dream again," said Galen, whisper-low. "Like it was years ago, before my dad got sick and died, and everything was easy."

"I'll do anything, even clean up goat shit," asked Bede, totally breaking the mood, making Galen laugh in spite of the serious twist in his chest. "Cause we're going to get goats and bunnies and chickies and kitty cats. Everything sweet. Everything."

"Oh my God." Galen pushed at Bede's chest pretending to be completely unamused, but all the while he could feel the blossom of hope and joy where for so long it had been a deep dark hole in his heart. Then he softened and curled his fingers around Bede's neck and brought him close for a long, slow kiss.

Maybe this would turn out okay. Better than okay. It would be wonderful because maybe in spite of everything he'd thought when he'd started, an ex-con was exactly the man he needed in his life.

EPILOGUE - BEDE

The snowfall was faint, a suggestion of white, but it limned the air with frost, and sketched a white ring around the sun, which was still shining even though it was snowing because that was Wyoming.

Wyoming in the middle of October was different than Wyoming in August or even September. In fact, the entire state was a fickle mistress who did what she wanted, when she wanted to.

You bowed to the weather and obeyed the seasons. And, as Bede hefted the axe over his shoulder, tightening his shoulders before bringing the axe down to split the round log he'd stood on its end, he knew he'd never been happier in his whole damn life.

At the end of summer, he'd gotten his certificate, a thick sheet of parchment paper tucked in a fancy envelope. He'd been presented the certificate at the closing ceremony in September, held in a white pavilion in the woods, elegantly arranged with bunting and colorful native flowers like cornflowers, and primrose, and wild bergamot.

Every parolee from each part of the program had sat in folding chairs, while all the team leads had stood in a row, a receiving committee of sorts.

Then there'd been a few speeches—Royce's had been way too long and had mostly been about flowers in bloom—then Micah, the counselor, had handed out the envelopes of certificates.

Along with the rest of the parolees, Bede had gone down the row of team leads and gotten a handshake from each and every one. They'd shaken Toby and Owen's hands, as well. It had felt like high school graduation, a ceremony that Bede didn't remember very well because he'd been drunk at the time.

Galen had been at the end of the line of team leads, and Bede had just about been blinded by the pride in that smile. And undone by the fact that Galen had risen on his toes, and added a quick kiss to Bede's cheek, right there in front of everybody.

Then there'd been beer to celebrate. Ice cold beer from a pony keg, served in red Solo cups, just like it ought to be.

In the clearing next to the pavilion, a buffet had been set up worthy of any football game or rugby match, complete with hot wings and celery strips with blue cheese dressing to dip them in. There was also mac and cheese, and Galen's favorite chocolate cake for dessert.

Gabe had brought out a very nice, very large bottle of Jameson 18, which he poured generously into those Solo cups, and that's when the ceremony had turned into a party.

Beck had brought his Sucrets box full of joints, and had passed them around like a proud father would at the birth of his first son.

Bede had looked at Galen.

Galen shrugged and said, "You are your own man."

So Bede had taken a joint, the smallest one he could see, lit it up from Beck's joint, and enjoyed the slow slide into total relaxation as he smoked.

The team leads had looked the other way, at first, then Royce, of all people, had given in and shared a joint with Jonah. Bede might have been drunk, might have imagined it, but Royce and Jonah had actually shotgunned that joint, which brought catcalls from Beck and put an expression on Gabe's face that said, *I think this is getting out of hand.*

But that was okay because it was the end of summer, and it was important to mark the occasion.

When Bede had finished his joint, he threw away the last stub of it, a fold of paper with a few ashes, and reached out to take Galen's hand.

"The future starts now," he said, feeling poetic vibes down to his soul.

They'd already packed their stuff into Galen's truck, which had been stored up at the guest ranch and which now sported a set of brand new and very sturdy truck tires. Then, with Galen in the driver's seat, and Bede riding shotgun, they'd driven to the farm.

The windows had been open and the music had blared, with the Black Crows singing about change in their pockets and about free milk and a cow. The sun had been shining, as it always did. Overhead, in that bright, brassy blue sky.

Once they settled in the farmhouse, there'd been a ton of chores to do on the farm. A shitton, in fact.

Because they owed money to Leland Tate, Bede threw himself into working from sunup to sundown. Every day of the week. Galen was at his side, every minute.

Together, they fixed the fence line. Bought goats. Weeded the lavender, prepping the beds for winter with bales of straw. They got a new door for the shed over the water pump. Put in a new screen door for the house.

Between all of this, they'd made love. Lots of love. Indoors, on the new mattress that Bede had insisted on. Outdoors, on a blanket on the grass. And after, they'd watched the stars come out.

Today, Galen was on an errand to Cheyenne, because if they were going to start raising goats for milk, they needed the best freezer to store the milk in.

Galen also wanted to buy enough wood to build a store that they would put near the main road. Galen's plan was to sell from the store come spring, which Bede thought was crazier than crazy.

"We can't stay out there all day and sell honey and shit," he said.

"We won't stay out there all day and sell honey and shit," Galen had said quite patiently. "Customers are going to take what they want and then they'll leave money in the box. Sure, Saturdays we can be out there, but most days, it'll be self-serve."

Bede did not explain that people were crooks because even if, in his old life, they were, in Galen's life, and in Bede's new life, they were not. At least not in this part of Wyoming. Maybe not even in the whole state.

His job, before Galen returned, was to chop wood, a cord of it, to be exact. He was just about halfway through it when the dark blue Amazon van showed up, trundling up the long driveway that curved from the main road.

"Hey, there," said Bede, gratefully putting his axe down, laying it carefully on top of the next log. He pulled off his gloves and went to meet the driver, a woman with short-cropped purple hair and an earring in one ear who was always on time and never messed up a delivery. "Is it here?"

"One box for Mr. Bede Deacon," she said, handing it to him as she stood next to the open door of her truck. "You sure do get a lot of deliveries, Mr. Deacon."

"I like new things," he said, which was true.

What was even truer was the fact that he'd been on a desperate hunt for the perfect china mug. Not just perfect, but the exact kind that someone might use when drinking coffee in a diner. White, sturdy, with a curved handle just the right size for your fingers.

He'd already ordered three sets, but those turned out to be fancy, or thin, just wanna-be-but-ain't kind of mugs. He'd sent those back and now he held in his hands another chance at getting it right.

"Thanks," he said, waving at her as she got in her van and drove off. Then, unable to wait, he took the brown box up to the house, making sure to wipe his boots on the mat before he stepped inside.

He placed the box on the kitchen table, which, draped with a red-and-white checked oilcloth, looked exactly as a farm table should. Cozy. Dependable. Big enough for a large and happy family to sit around while they ate supper.

There was no large family, but they were happy.

Bede loved living with Galen more than he'd even dreamed of, and shared meals at that table were quickly becoming a staple of their lives.

He'd been alone at lunch that day, having a sad bachelor meal of leftovers, but Galen was due back for dinner, so Bede opened the fridge and brought out two steaks to warm to room temperature.

Then he got a knife from the drawer and sliced open the tape on the Amazon box. First carefully, then quickly, then the inner box was in his hands. He squinted at the images of the four white china mugs.

Would he be fooled again by false advertising? Would he ever find the perfect mug for Galen?

Bede opened the inner box carefully, in case he was disappointed and had to send the mugs back. Again.

Pulling out the first mug, he almost didn't want to look, but there in his hand, was the perfect white china mug. His fingers fit around the curve of the handle. The lip was wide enough to be sturdy but not so wide as to make the coffee spill when he drank out of it. The white was a deep white, a satisfying white.

Galen was going to *love* the mugs.

Bede took them all out, disposed of the box (because they were a recycling kind of household), and washed each mug lovingly at the sink. He dried them with a fluffy kitchen towel, then placed them on another towel on the kitchen table. So Galen would see them when he came home.

Bede puttered around, putting salt and spices and oil on the two hunks of steak, and those he put on a plate, covered with a bowl, and went outside to chop the rest of the cord of wood. He worked hard enough that he didn't need a jacket, and was finished just as he heard the rumble of Galen's truck coming up the long drive.

Taking a moment, he posed with the axe. Stopped. Rolled up his sleeves, the way Galen liked them, and posed again. One gloved fist on his waist, the other gloved fist on top of the axe handle. His chin in the air the way he imagined Paul Bunyan might stand.

He didn't have a blue ox named Babe, but he did have Galen, driving fast up the drive, then screeching to a halt at the gate to the yard. Galen slammed the truck into park, turned off the engine, and before the engine could even start to ping as it cooled, he was through the gate and into Bede's arms.

"Gah," said Bede as Galen squeezed the air out of him. But he didn't really mind and squeezed Galen right back. "Did you get the strawberries?" he asked.

"There were none," said Galen. "But I got frozen strawberries so maybe you could make your coulis with that?"

"I could be persuaded," said Bede, but he had been on board since the moment Galen had suggested it to him. "Leave the groceries and come inside."

In the cool air, the groceries would keep, even the frozen strawberries. Bede laid the axe against the fence, opened it and pulled Galen behind him, tugging off his leather gloves at the same time. The screen door opened easily now that it had been repaired and swung quietly shut behind them.

Bede didn't even have to point to the mugs. Galen saw them and hurried to the kitchen table, picked up the first mug he came to, held it to his cheek, and crooned a sweet love song, both to it and to Bede.

"You found them," he said, his eyes half-lidded with love.

"I did, my sweet," said Bede. "I hope you got more pods for the Keurig, otherwise we'll be drinking hot water out of those things."

"I did," said Galen, nodding as he turned over each white china mug, one by one. "Hazelnut, vanilla, and regular."

"And?" prompted Bede.

"And lavender espresso, of course." With a smile, Galen put down the mug he held in his hands and sashayed over to Bede. There, to hug him close and whisper against his mouth, "Did you ever doubt me, my love?"

"It helps having it confirmed," said Bede with a mock growl. Then he wrapped Galen in his arms, and kissed him hard, and then soft, absorbing Galen's breath that felt like a whisper on his skin.

"The steak is coming to room temperature," he said. "Shall we go upstairs in the meantime?"

"What about the groceries?" asked Galen, drawing back, his arms on Bede's forearms, but it was easy for Bede to see that Galen was only pretending to be shocked that they would be so casual with their foodstuffs.

"Fuck the groceries," said Bede, almost roaring, but it was only for effect, because he planted more kisses on Galen's face, anywhere they might land, and hauled Galen under his arm and up the stairs to their room.

The steak could wait. The groceries could wait. Hell, the whole world could wait while he made love to the most amazing man in the world.

EPILOGUE - GALEN

Snow spat against the windowpanes and a high wind whistled outside. But it was warm inside as Galen sat at the kitchen table, a glass of red wine resting at his elbow. His eyes were on Bede, who stood at the gas stove, adding sliced mushrooms to the cast iron pan.

"Is that butter the right temperature?" he asked.

"Yes, my love," said Bede, almost absently as he plopped the mushrooms in the pan and used a wooden spoon to make sure they weren't crowded.

Galen hadn't doubted that Bede knew how to cook mushrooms. He just wanted Bede to know that he was watching him. And, dressed in a white t-shirt and blue jeans, a white apron tied at his waist, Bede was an eyeful. Worthy of being absorbed with ever fibre of Galen's being.

"You're cooking barefoot," Galen remarked.

Galen's dad, Earl, had always taught him to wear shoes while cooking, in case you dropped something that shattered on the floor, or if a spatter of grease happened to fly out of the pan you were using.

"Yes, my love," said Bede again, more on purpose this time, because

323

he knew he was being watched, and he knew Galen loved being called *my love.*

The mushrooms sizzled in the pan. Bede gave them a slight stir, waiting till they browned before he added any salt.

Galen knew this because Bede had taken the time to patiently explain it to him. *Wait till they're brown,* he said. *Wait till the water is cooked out, then add salt.*

After the first time Galen had tasted Bede's cooking, he would have done anything Bede told him to. In the kitchen, Bede was master.

The low light over the stove shone on Bede's dark hair, glinting on the moisture left from Bede's recent sip of red wine. Aproned and barefoot, he was the most beautiful sight Galen had ever seen, and that wasn't the wine talking. It was the truth.

"You should be like this always," said Galen. So, okay, maybe that was the wine talking.

"What do you mean?"

Bede took a sip of his red wine, wiped his bottom lip with his thumb, rested the wooden spoon on a small plate put by the stove for that purpose, and turned his full focus on Galen. Which always took Galen's breath away.

"Barefoot and pregnant," said Galen, laughing as Bede raised his eyebrows as though he was deeply shocked.

"You want to shackle me to this stove," Bede said, pretending to be hurt by this. "To this kitchen. To you—"

Bede's eyes darkened as Galen got up and moved close to Bede. He tugged him away from the stove, even as Bede turned down the gas beneath the mushrooms.

"Shackled, yes," said Galen, as he gathered Bede's warm body to him. "But to me, only to me."

Bede stuck out his chest, his arms going around Galen's waist. Now they were in an embrace, and Galen didn't care if the mushrooms burned.

"Are you proposing to me, Mr. Parole Officer, sir?" asked Bede.

His eyes were dark and hooded and Galen's breath left him all over again.

He wasn't afraid of Bede, even when Bede found humor in the dark things of the world. But he was a little afraid of the intensity with which he loved this man.

"You will marry me come spring," he said, pretending to be the fierce landlord, twirling his imaginary mustache while he demanded favors from the sweet young thing who was at his mercy.

Galen saw the laughter dancing in Bede's eyes, the desire for playfulness always in the center of Bede's being every waking moment. Behind that laughter, though, was a darkness, still waiting, as though Bede wanted Galen to propose to him for real.

He kissed Bede softly on the mouth and said, "Please marry me come spring. Please say you will."

Bede's eyes widened as though Galen had surprised him utterly. As though he was shaken to his core. His mouth opened as though he hardly knew what to say.

"I mean it," said Galen. He took Bede's wrists, and twisted them behind his waist so they were belly to belly in the warmth of the stovetop. "We can get married in the valley. In the white pavilion. We can get married before the valley opens to customers. Will you say yes?"

"Only if—" Bede paused, as if considering this with the utmost seriousness. "I will marry you, Galen Parnell," he said. "But only if Toby is my flower girl and Owen is my ring bearer."

With that remark, Bede tossed back his head, laughing deep from his belly as he pulled his wrists free, and cupped Galen's face and kissed him hard and then hard again.

"Anywhere you want," said Bede, his mouth moving against Galen's. "Anywhere you want it."

"I think Clay—he's a ranch hand up at the guest ranch—has a daughter," said Galen. "Maybe we can rent her for the afternoon?"

"Or maybe we can get a pair of donkeys to carry us up the aisle?" asked Bede in response, laughing low in his throat. "Those would make for great photos to send back home."

Back home for Bede was a neighborhood in Denver where you locked your doors at night and weren't surprised to see drugs being bought and sold on the corner. Galen knew Bede didn't want to go back to that or even send anyone there an invitation, let alone a photo of what was sure to be a glorious day.

"I'll see what I can do about the donkeys," said Galen, smiling against Bede's mouth. "But only if you say yes."

"Yes," said Bede. "Always, yes. Forever, yes. Yes, yes, yes."

This tumble of words was followed by more kisses, and soon the mushrooms went cold and the red wine warmed to room temperature. Except neither of them cared because the kitchen and all its domesticity would be waiting for them when they came back downstairs from the bedroom. Which was where they were headed.

DEAR READER—BEDE persisted about the donkeys, so Galen found a donkey from a rescue mission and gave it to Bede on Christmas Morning, complete with a soft pink and white halter. Her name was Trixie, and she had a bent ear from some accident that nobody knew the history of, and she had enormous brown eyes and a soft gray coat.

Bede would spend hours sitting on an upside-down bucket, brushing her coat and whispering into her bent ear, all the while feeding her bits of carrot and apple. Trixie, in turn, was totally devoted to Bede, and would often insert herself between Bede and Galen, out of jealousy.

For Valentine's Day, Bede found another rescue donkey and gave it to Galen. This donkey was a soft white, and his name was Casper.

When Galen would go out in the morning to begin feeding the chickens and the goats and the ducks, Casper would come trot-trot-trotting across the snow on his small, donkey hooves, bugling his love for Galen at the top of his lungs.

He was not jealous of Bede, and would take any treat that anybody would give him. Consequently, he was, in fact, quite round in the middle, and was very much loved.

And it was in this way, Dear Reader, that they lived happily ever after.

Thank you for reading!

If you enjoyed this book, please consider leaving a rating (without a review) or leaving a rating and a review!

Would you like to read more of my m/m cowboy romances? I've got a whole series you can binge on! Start with *The Foreman and the Drifter*, Book #1 in my Farthingdale Ranch series.

JACKIE'S NEWSLETTER

Would you like to sign up for my newsletter?

Subscribers are alway the first to hear about my new books. You'll get behind the scenes information, sales and cover reveal updates, and giveaways.

As my gift for signing up, you will receive two short stories, one sweet, and one steamy!

It's completely free to sign up and you will never be spammed by me; you can opt out easily at any time.

To sign up, visit the following URL:

https://www.subscribepage.com/JackieNorthNewsletter

facebook.com/jackienorthMM
pinterest.com/jackienorthauthor
bookbub.com/profile/jackie-north
amazon.com/author/jackienorth
goodreads.com/Jackie_North
instagram.com/jackienorth_author

AUTHOR'S NOTES ABOUT THE STORY

This story was told in sections, between bouts of real life and doubt and low energy and high energy.

I began writing *Dealer* in January of 2024, which was way too many months after the publication of *The Cowboy and the Outcast* in late September of 2023.

From January 2024 to the present (it is currently the end of July, 2024) is also a gap of months and months.

Add it all up and you get an eight month gap.

During that time I attempted to move to Arizona. I thought I had it all set up and that things would work out even though I'd not yet sold my house in Longmont.

But the place I thought I'd be staying during this transition time did not work out for various reasons.

Plus, I was terribly homesick and full of fear and quite quickly, simply drove back home, took my townhome off the market, unloaded my stuff and took to my bed for a good long while.

Have you ever been that exhausted and blank? I was, and I was also afraid that my writing mojo was gone forever.

On top of that, as the new year came, and I began plonking on *The Cowboy and the Dealer* (plonking is the only word I can use to describe how it felt), I realized that all the reasons for the move were still there. That coming "home" hadn't solved my problems, it had shoved them under a microscope.

Twenty years ago, my little townhome was on a corner, and the bus came four times an hour (two times in each direction, thus ever fifteen minutes), chuffing and growling. But I was at work all day, and none of that mattered.

Plus, once a month, I could see the full moon coming up from the horizon. I could see the mountains from my bedroom windows. I could see the storms roll in. It was a good place. A place where I felt safe and at peace.

Then the real estate growth began. All around me houses popped up. With more houses and condos, more traffic came. And more and more and *more*.

When I retired from my day job in 2019, I was at home all day and could see that the quiet little corner I had settled on became a raceway.

Letters to the traffic folks did nothing. The noise grew. Head-phones could not keep it out and the windows rattled with the rumbling engines.

I felt sick and shook and was irritated every other minute with the noise. My neighbors were fine. The neighborhood itself was nice. It was the noise and the rumble of engines.

Part of the problem was me, I suppose. I like to keep my windows open for a bit of fresh air, but that let in the noise.

Plus there were other issues: the townhome had begun to feel too big (over 2,000 square feet), and there were too many bathrooms (Four! But that's how they built 'em in 2004), and I couldn't keep up with the repairs. And the stairs! (Two flights!) And the Colorado winters had begun to feel more harsh.

It was while I had taken to my bed that I knew my original idea of moving to Arizona (and all the reasons for it) was the right one. It was going to feel like I was sawing off my own legs to move (and it *has* felt like that), but in the end, that it was time for a change, and that the change would be a good one.

But why Arizona?

Yes, why. I almost picked South or North Carolina as it is a quite beautiful area. But the horizons were limited by hills and I didn't really know anyone there.

I'd been to Arizona a dozen times, to visit friends, to visit the Grand Canyon. I've stayed at a lovely B&B near Mexican Hat, because I love it there.

Any chance I got, I drove down, or hopped on a plane to visit Arizona.

It is a desert, but there is so much loveliness here. Sure, it's a raw beauty, full of edges and dust. But there is no snow to shovel and the storms in monsoon season will knock you over.

I selected Arizona because it was warmer there. I had many friends there. The elevation was lower. I could afford to buy a nice house (with less square footage) that was on a single level, new and up to date.

No one told me about the summer heat! (Yes we did, say my chorus of friends. Yes, we DID.)

Truly the heat is to be expected, but I didn't think it would come on June 1st, topping over 100 degrees for days and days! I thought it would creep in, slowly so I could get used to it. Nope!

At any rate, amidst all of this, I kept plonking on *The Cowboy and the Dealer*, losing my place in the plot over and over because I had to hire a realtor.

While selling my house I had to sign a ton of paperwork, pack all my stuff, clean every corner, apply for a loan for the new house, and mourn the passing of the life I had been living. I said goodbye to everything, including my favorite hairdresser, my brilliant and patient dental hygienist, and my beloved coffee shop, The Brewing Market.

Plus, *Dealer* was giving me fits.

Sure, I could write about a guy who sold drugs to pay for his mother's chemo treatment (such as in *The Blacksmith and the Ex-Con*), but I struggled with Bede, who was practically born into the business and didn't have any qualms about making buckets o' moola on other people's misery.

I struggled with the shades of gray in his character, his love for Winston coming up against his feelings that he, Bede, had been given a raw deal with his five year sentence and a huge fine and a Class 2 Felony on his record that would never go away.

I struggled with Bede and Galen's relationship because who in their right might would fall for a drug lord? (Thanks to Angela, my fantastic beta, for walking me through ways to lever that relationship open.)

I did not, oddly, struggle with Galen's character. Galen, as you know, has had many setbacks, all of which distract him from the future he might have. He's got papers to sign, and bills to pay, and renters at the farm to deal with - all while grieving the loss of his dad.

All of which, as you might realize, are drawn from real life. Which made it nice in a way, as I could take notes about my own struggles and apply them to Galen's life to make it feel more real than it otherwise would have been.

Currently I am writing this in the house of an old friend, in the guest bedroom, one of two that have been set aside for my use.

There is plenty of ice and iced tea. The air conditioner is silent. There is no traffic in the streets, or very little. The coyotes yip at sunset and dawn, and the local owl hoots when it suits him.

I am living in limbo but I am a lucky author who gets to do what she loves for a living. And I'm going to keep on doing it.

Some time this week, I will go down to Tucson to visit Casa Cielo de Azul (House of the Blue Sky) to do a pre-drywall walkthrough. Then I will have lunch with a friend.

Then I will come back and take a soak in the small but lush pool that sits in the back yard of the house where I am staying and watch as the sky blossoms at sunset into colors of gold, blood red, and dusty orange limned with dark purple.

All of this helps my mojo to feel that it is returning to me. And gives me the inspiration and the energy to complete the final two books in the Farthingdale Valley series. And to turn my face to the future, where hope resides.

A LETTER FROM JACKIE

Hello, Reader!

Thank you for reading *The Cowboy and the Dealer,* the fourth book in my Farthingdale Valley series.

If you enjoyed the book, I would love it if you would let your friends know so they can experience the romance between Galen and Bede.

If you leave a review, I'd love to read it! You can send the URL to: Jackienorthauthor@gmail.com

Best Regards,

Jackie

facebook.com/jackienorthMM
instagram.com/jackienorth_author
pinterest.com/jackienorthauthor
bookbub.com/profile/jackie-north
amazon.com/author/jackienorth
goodreads.com/Jackie_North

About the Author

Jackie North has written since grade school and spent years absorbing mainstream romances. Her dream was to write full time and put her English degree to good use.

As fate would have it, she discovered m/m romance and decided that men falling in love with other men was exactly what she wanted to write about.

Her characters are a bit flawed and broken. Some find themselves on the edge of society, and others are lost. All of them deserve a happily ever after, and she makes sure they get it!

She likes long walks on the beach, the smell of lavender and rainstorms, and enjoys sleeping in on snowy mornings.

In her heart, there is peace to be found everywhere, but since in the real world this isn't always true, Jackie writes for love.

Connect with Jackie:

https://www.jackienorth.com/
jackie@jackienorth.com

facebook.com/jackienorthMM
x.com/JackieNorthMM
pinterest.com/jackienorthauthor
bookbub.com/profile/jackie-north
amazon.com/author/jackienorth
goodreads.com/Jackie_North
instagram.com/jackienorth_author

Printed in Great Britain
by Amazon

62643503R00204